The Shamans at the End of Time

Florian Armas

Copyright © 2019 Florian Armas

All rights reserved. No part of this publication may be reproduced, stored, distributed, or transmitted in any form or by any means, without written permission of the author.

Cover design by Fictive Covers

This novel is a work of fiction. Names, characters, places and incidents are the product of the author's imagination or are used fictitiously. Any resemblance to actual persons, living or dead, events or locales is entirely coincidental.

Table of Contents

Chapter 1 – Vlad	1
Chapter 2 – Vlad	27
Chapter 3	40
Chapter 4 – Vlad	50
Chapter 5	61
Chapter 6 – Vlad	78
Chapter 7 – Vlad	85
Chapter 8	103
Chapter 9	111
Chapter 10	131
Chapter 11 – Vlad	147
Chapter 12	156

Chapter 13	168
Chapter 14	178
Chapter 15	192
Chapter 16	206
Chapter 17	219
Chapter 18	233
Chapter 19	246
Chapter 20	254
Chapter 21	263
Chapter 22	269
Chapter 23 – Vlad	283
Chapter 24 – Vlad	293
Chapter 25	302
Chapter 26	313
Chapter 27	324
Chapter 28	343

Chapter 1 – Vlad

Technically, I've been a soldier from the day my conscription orders arrived seven months ago, on the day I graduated from university. The bright future in front of me is no longer bright. I am not a fighter. This is true. I never wanted to fight and, for all my training, I'm still not able to hit a moving target. The cold black rifle in my arm is a soldier's best friend, but still a strange object to me. I am better with a bow, or a sword, but modern wars are not fought with antiques. While this is not my first mission, there's been nothing like this before, and I wonder how my poor skills will cope when they attack us. Or my mind. Our enemies are of course moving targets. There is a strange irony in my being in the Special Forces. It's not for my shooting skills. Having two black belts in martial art helps in close combat, though. Two years ago, I was the European champion at judo. This year I should have been the Olympic champion, everybody was

2

expecting that, me included. It will not happen. Cosmin or Andrei can shoot a fly, at three hundred paces, with their rifles. *I have to watch their backs, but who will watch mine?*

Morning comes slowly, an opening eyelid over a giant black eye morphing into dark blue. With the binoculars attached to the top of my helmet, I can see the enemy soldiers around the hill we occupy. My device can track five targets simultaneously – the most dangerous ones – and feed them directly into my goggles. There are only seven of us, not even a platoon. On my arm, the tactical display records the movement of our enemies on the map: red spots sliding slowly across the screen. They are still far away and, hopefully, unaware of our presence. Down in the valley, the morning mist is sneaking along the river. Perhaps so is our death. There must be some iron ore in the entrails of the surrounding hills; the lazily flowing water has a reddish hue. The cursed color forces me to look away.

"When we get back, I will have someone Court Martialled," Dan growls, the fingers of his left arm dancing gently in the air to control the movements of his binoculars, his right hand gripping the rifle tightly. He never lets AI control his binoculars.

If we get back. As if he hears my thoughts, he turns toward me, and I struggle to avoid his stare.

There was no need to say what everybody already knows: we are surrounded. Dan is our lieutenant, in charge of our lives as well as his. His frowning eyes betray some inner search for a miraculous escape plan. We trust him, but what is coming now is something that none of us have encountered before, not even him. We can't even communicate with our base; our transmission would be intercepted instantly, and a missile would pay us a courtesy visit.

My eyes move again from the enemy soldiers swarming on my screen to Dan's face. Impassive, it reveals no feelings – as if his growl was just an illusion. He is a good lieutenant, or at least he has half a year more fighting experience than us, plus time at the military academy. I understand his apprehension. We are on this hilltop because the wrong coordinates were sent by a lazy soldier who did not take time to check the encrypted order he sent to us. Maybe he was dreaming of his girlfriend, or maybe his brother was killed in action. Or maybe it wasn't anything like that, just plain negligence. One wrong digit in the coordinates Dan received sent us into this hell. I can't say we were totally unlucky. Passing unobserved through the first enemy line during the night was a lucky shot, especially when we knew nothing about it. We even hummed a tune, walking through the forest to replace our comrades in an observation post that was supposed to be safe, at our edge of no-man's land. Instead we found ourselves on this bloody hill.

"This place is magical," Cosmin whispers, a few paces in front of me. His left hand makes an ample gesture, to include the whole hilltop in that magical spot. The hill resembles a half-bald man's head, thick hair on his nape, and a full beard. There is an old oak forest on the lower parts, some trees so large they could hide a car. The bald area is partly covered by old ruins that we had no idea about until today, no more than a few decayed stones arranged in a small circle between larger natural rocks. Propelled by some strange curiosity, we tried to find them on the maps, but there was nothing. "I can feel the energy surrounding us."Fingers spread wide, his left hand is now rigid and stretched in front of him, trying to feel what he calls the 'energy'. The quiet excitement in his voice transfers into my mind too, I don't know why.

Cosmin is a math teacher. I've known him since childhood. The same quarter of the city, the same school, the same dreams. Almost. One year older, he finished university the year before me. His dream was already taking shape: for one year, he taught children the beauty of math. "Life is like a math equation," he used to say. "It's up to you to find the most beautiful solution."

What solution did our marvelous politicians find? The last economic crisis went on for almost a decade, and they decided that war was the best way to end it. At least no nukes have been used yet.

What are my chances of getting out of here alive, returning home and fulfilling my own dream? My dream is to build planes, or even better, space planes ready to fly to Mars. Last year, I applied for several jobs, before graduating. By the time they answered, I was already in uniform. My parents informed them, and they promised to hire me when I got back from the front. With two permanent bases established on Mars and monthly shuttles to the Moon, there is a definite shortage of specialized engineers.

Cosmin is not just a math teacher. Some years ago, he found, in his grandfather's cellar, a box filled with strange books about spirituality and hidden mysteries from the past, and his life changed. He loves legends about energetic portals linking unknown places and time lines. I have heard them all. I don't believe in such things, but

5

Cosmin is a colorful storyteller, recounting lost civilizations that may never have existed and esoteric mysteries. No one can prove that Atlantis or Lemuria were real, but Cosmin is my friend. Why should I upset him? And he sees things that others cannot. I will believe that when I have proof, but I never contradict him. He takes my silent behavior as an endorsement of his peculiar beliefs.

"The main vortex is right there," Cosmin points at the stone resting my back and, involuntarily, I touch the stone. It's cold.

A cold vortex, I almost laugh, and bite my lip, unwilling to upset him. Convinced that there is nothing to see, I don't turn around.

"It goes a hundred feet into the sky. These ruins..." he continues, scratching his beard, his face thoughtful. "They must have been a temple a long time ago. What a pity to fight here."

What a pity to fight, period.

"Shut up, Cosmin," Toma growls. In normal circumstances, he would choose to ignore the story, and Toma is not the only feeling annoyed one right now.

"Let him speak," I say – better listening to Cosmin's fairytales than thinking about a hundred ways to die. There are so many ways to vanish in a war. I had no idea about most of them in my previous life. There is more for the imagination in a real war than in a hundred movies. All morbid. "Your vortex must go underground too," I tease Cosmin.

"Yes," he says quickly, unable to feel my friendly dig; it's so easy to get him to talk about the hidden things that no one but he is able to see. "It's like a hidden fire. Fire, walk with me," he casts something resembling a spell from his old books, his eyes tense and searching.

"Will this do it?" Andrei flicks his lighter and laughter fills the hill; the enemy is too far away to hear us.

"I'm afraid that your vortex won't help. What about a flying saucer? Can you summon one?" Dan jokes in his most serious tone, and that provokes more laughter. Even Toma joins in, a bit later, like an afterthought.

"Only a flying can," Cosmin replies, still laughing. "Make your choice. I have chicken or chicken." Our usual meal for more than six months already. Swiftly, he opens the backpack, and tosses a can out. Then he does it again, and again, his repetitive movements resembling a peculiar metronome, counting the seconds of our lives.

How I'd like to eat something cooked by Mother. My mind slips back to a past that has nothing to do with war and destruction and killing people like us. A past of love and happiness. A present of attrition and despair. Even the most regular meal with the family, a thing you used to ignore and take for granted, is now just a pleasant, distant dream you crave for.

"They are coming," Dan warns, watching the tactical com attached to his arm, and in sudden silence, we take up firing positions between the stones.

The first projectile hits the ground just sixty feet in front of our position. Alerted by the whizzing sound, Andrei and I withdraw a few seconds before the explosion, our backs pressed to the old stone protecting us, its coldness passing slowly through our uniforms. It's calming. We stare at each other and our nervous laughter fills the silence before the next explosion. We escaped. In the corner of my eye, I catch Cosmin squeezing the trigger

7

of his rifle, which has a silencer, and I know that one enemy is down. One of many. Another explosion shatters the earth to the left of our hell-hole. It seems distant, and I am not bothered by it. Unexpectedly, a lone shard of shrapnel hisses through the air in front of us. With a muffled sound, it hits a stone covered with dried moss, on our right, and recoils, leaving behind multi-colored sparks. Andrei bends in pain and grunts loudly. I hear gurgling, and his head rolls. My mind registers its fall with an unwanted level of detail. It seems impossible, but Andrei's head rolls down from his shoulders and falls into my lap. His body bends, then slips aside, away from me. In a few moments, the grass below changes from green to red, my camouflage trousers too. I can't move; I can't react in any way. I can still breathe. Logically, I realize that I am in a shock, not only because I am paralyzed, but because my mind has shed its self-preservation mechanism. Andrei's eyes are serene, like he is resting, like he is still alive. I have the foolish hope that he will wink at me and smile, telling me that it's all just a joke. *All war is a bad joke*.

My breath comes out in spurts, one in and out each second, and I feel as if I'm breathing like a dog trying to cool itself down. My pulse goes up; I am hyperventilating; the oxygen in my blood is 100 percent, my pulse 187 heartbeats per minute, and the monitoring Lifeband around my head sends messages to my tactical com, warning me. It's useless, my pulse still goes up. I feel an electric shock from the Lifeband, and I realize that I passed out for a while. The com shows me that I was unconscious for 5.7651 seconds. I don't understand the need for so many decimals, and I blink rapidly. Andrei's head is still sitting quietly in my lap, his blind eyes staring at me. *Death is like sleeping.* I look into his glassy eyes. All I can think now is to calculate the probability of that shrapnel hitting him and not me – a useless, yet somehow calming exercise, or at least numbing.

"Our planes!" Dan shouts with sudden joy, pointing up at the sky. He taps frantically on his tactical console, and I assume he's risking contacting our headquarters. "Nothing," he growls. "They are jamming us."

Andrei's head is still in my lap. I stare back with numb detachment at our front lines from where the planes were supposed to come; Dan is right. The moment I turn, a batch of missiles leave their places under the wings, and I follow them with the desperation of the dying man looking for his salvation: silvery fishes swarming the sky. Small at first, they grow with each second, approaching the hill, and spread out in a fan-like shape I saw in a medieval movie, some time ago, before the war. They look so beautiful in the sky. As I watch them, I'm still calculating the bloody probability that killed Andrei and not me.

"Nooo!" Dan shouts.

I don't realize what's happening until one of the missiles alters its course, coming straight toward us. "The probability," I laugh like a mad man, embracing Andrei's head. "The probability is so small..."

Explosion. A red column of dust and hot air covers our hell-hill. My nostrils are burning.

"I didn't expect you," an unfamiliar voice whispers in my mind.

That's the last thing I remember.

9

My eyes open again to reflections of a dazzling sun shining from patches of snow on the high peaks, and to a sky deep and radiantly blue, in a place that is not the hell-hill. It's not a hospital either. I am lying in the grass, in the middle of a meadow with coniferous trees here and there, surrounded by high mountains, similar to the ones around my grandparents' village, yet unknown. It's a calm spring landscape as lovely as a dream. There is no long tunnel and light at the end of my vision, no angels, no trumpets, yet it looks like the afterlife. *I had the vague impression of some kind of tunnel. A hot and dark one. If this is death...* I can't complain, at least not right now. Flying high, a predatory bird reminds me of the hell I've escaped from and that bloody plane. Explosions still reverberate in my mind, and I have a brief impulse to check if I am wounded. My laughter fills the silent place; you no longer care about wounds when you are dead. *Can I walk? Can I fly?* The bird is calling to me, and I jump up easily, unable to avoid a surge of dark images of the many wounds I saw during the war – other people's wounds. It was impossible to escape unwounded from that explosion. That much I know. And for sure, you can't die if you are not badly wounded. When I half-turn, I see Dan. He is dead too, and he is definitely wounded. The lower half of his body is missing, from the navel down. *Why is he like that*? I stare at my lower parts, fearing that they might vanish in a blink. Everything is in the right place, even Andrei's blood staining my trousers, small and almost dry rivulets running from thighs to ankles. *Where is his head?* Irritated by my own thought, I make no attempt to find it. With annoying pedantry, I observe more blood on my left leg. My fingers touch the canvas:

the blood is still viscous, and I have to fight a sudden impulse to smell and taste it. To avoid my macabre urge, I check the tactical com. It's dead. *Who needs such things in the afterlife?*

"Vlad," someone shouts, and I turn further. It is Cosmin, walking straight toward me. He is wounded too: a thin stream of blood runs down the left side of his face.

That's when I finally understand that I am dreaming, and I worry that, safe inside my dream, I have been badly wounded in real life. I shiver, and my teeth clack with a noise that sounds half comic. For a moment, I want to wake up. *Why? Enjoy the dream*. Or maybe I am too scared to return to a reality that might look like Dan. Or Andrei. Any moment I fear that his head will materialize in my dream, flying around me like the Cheshire Cat, all eyes and fangs. With unwanted precision, the memory of the explosion, which I am trying so hard to ignore, finds another way to resurface: the missile, whooshing as it falls on us, the blast, the hot dust in the air. Just a few seconds of a dark movie, repeated, over and over.

It's my dream, and I don't care to share my knowledge with Cosmin, not even when he embraces me tightly.

"We escaped," he cries, his tears running down my face together with his blood.

"Yes, we escaped." I pat his back. *At least, I escaped*... There is no way to tell him that he may already be dead. Before the explosion, Cosmin was twenty paces in front of me, and Dan was a few paces in front of him. *It makes sense*, I glance at Dan's half body. *Where is Andrei's head?* I fight against my impulse to look for it.

My dream has a strange clarity. Dan's open belly is a grim lesson in anatomy, and his blood soils the grass.

11

Closer to my eyes, Cosmin's blood looks so real, and the spots on my pants too. Again I fight the urge to taste it. Disengaging, I glance around, still patting Cosmin's shoulder. I can see many trees, and even see small branches and leaves. Rocks, a large river gleaming in the sun, delicate shrouds of cloud in the sky. The predatory bird is still flying above us, and my eyes follow it. My dream is strange not only in its content, but in the level of detail too. *We have to bury Dan...* I don't know what significance that might have in a dream, but I feel the need to do it. With a sigh, I turn my eyes back to the landscape.

"Don't worry," Cosmin tries to soothe me, his right arm still around my shoulders. "We will survive."

"Yes, we will survive," I parrot his words, mechanically, with no intention of mocking him – a voice void of feeling.

The burial is easy – we find a small crevasse in the ground with boulders around it. The hard part is carrying the corpse;, not because of its weight, after all it's only half of the real Dan, but because we want to avoid losing some more of him as we drag hid body along. Sobbing, Cosmin prays, then mumbles something that I can't grasp about Dan's energy going back to Mother Earth.

In silence, we return to the place where I woke up and find our heavy backpacks, but no rifles. *At least it's a peaceful dream.* I shrug.

"What should we do now?" I ask Cosmin. It should be me driving my own dream, but I decide to take things easy and be lazy. Such a wonderful feeling to be in control of your laziness during a war. There will be enough things to worry about when I wake up. *If I wake up...*

12

"We need to figure out where we are," Cosmin says after a while. "And we need help." He taps some commands on his tactical display. "It's dead," he mumbles, and I do the same with the same result. Even inside the dream, our tools have been jammed by the enemy. Silent, he looks around, then up at the sky, still blue, with some ragged tatters of clouds streaming far to the south. "I don't like that," he points to the predatory bird. "It reminds me of that plane." He doesn't need to say which plane. Neither do I. "This place is strange, like a different world. I feel it."

Any dream is strange. It takes me a bit of effort to stop a smile surfacing on my lips. *Why upset him?* Then I laugh at myself. Even in a dream, I don't want to contradict his strange beliefs.

"The energy vortex saved us," he says, thoughtfully.

"Of course. Let's move. That direction." I point down the meadow.

"Good idea. To find people we need to climb down. I am sure there is no war here."

For the moment...

We walk in silence, and from time to time, we glance up at the sky, quietly, in search of that bloody predatory bird. Its presence rakes my mind. Our paths seem strangely intertwined. It's still there, and I try to imagine its aerial perception from that high place. Eagles' eyes see things in two particular ways. The middle of the eye acts like a magnifying glass, looking for details, which means for prey. The outer side covers a larger area looking, of course, for prey too. *I can't be prey for an eagle*, I think, annoyed. *I'm too big*. Yet, in a corner of my mind, associating it with that plane, I fear that in a dream, an eagle is able to hunt me, and I may end up looking like Dan.

"I wonder where we are," Cosmin says after a while, his voice now calm.

In a dream.

"How far we are from the front line? They may think we're deserters if we don't return quickly."

"What makes you think that we will return?" Deliberately, my question is ambiguous, letting him decide between 'we can't' and 'we don't want to'. *Can I trick my own dream?* Unable to stop a sudden smile, I turn my head, pretending to be busy with the surroundings.

"You know," he says, worried, "even if we return, it will be hard to make them understand that we did not run away."

"Your vortex," I say without turning, a bit more maliciously than I intended.

"Vlad, do you really think I believe you when you agree with me on this subject? And if you don't believe me, who will? The Court Martial?"

I jerk my head back to him, just in time to catch his laughter, and I wonder if the real Cosmin is aware that I only pretend to believe his stories. "But do you agree with you?" I ask, curious and ashamed at the same time.

"Yes, Vlad. There are many strange things in our world. Some of them are hidden, and some we are afraid to learn about. Portals exist. In the past we were able to use their power. Maybe some are still active today, but we have lost our knowledge of them. Maybe. I feel odd energy sometimes. I can't explain why or how. I just feel it. It's real. And on that hill, it was quite strong."

"Any vortex here?" I gesture around. "Do you feel anything?"

"Nothing," he says.

My dream has outplayed me, and that has made everything more interesting. I don't know how other people dream, but for me it's like playing with a friend, waiting for a surprise that always comes. It makes sense, in the end; my dream counterpart is that part of my mind to which I don't have conscious access. And my mind knows that I only pretend to believe Cosmin. Once, I discussed the mysteries of the mind with him, late on a cold early spring night, around the fire, vapors and words leaving our mouths like pagan mysteries. That night, he was the watcher of our platoon, and after a pause, he told me that I had a strong unconscious mind, touching Mother Earth – whatever that could mean.

"Well," I go back to the game again, "if we are far enough from the front line to prove that no normal transport could take us here in such short time..." I leave my phrase unfinished, to allow Cosmin enough space to surprise me again.

"Do you really think a Court Martial will absolve us on such grounds?" Cosmin says jokingly, and for a moment I am tempted to tell him that we are in a dream. "Military judges are not famous for their logic." He scratches his beard, like he's trying to find a solution."Run!" he growls.

Sprinting after him, I turn my head in the direction he was looking, a moment earlier. Unconditional reaction is the product of camaraderie, trust and military conditioning. It has saved my life twice in the past. From the forest, on the left, a bunch of men bursts out, in the way that hunters chase their prey, spreading like the missiles from that bloody plane, trying to cut us off. They herd us down, toward the meadow's end, and we have no choice but to obey their order. The predatory bird resurfaces in my mind like a frightening shadow. I have no time to check if it's still in the sky. Maybe the eagle has metamorphosed into the savages hunting us. And savages they are, dressed in skins, hunting us with bows and spears.

The long mound, ten to fifteen feet high, resembling a sand dune, slows us; then from its top, we scramble fast and slide down on the grass. For a while we are safe. Two arrows hiss over the mound, hitting the ground a few feet in front of us. *They want to slow us down*. I am slightly faster, and I hear Cosmin's panting progress behind me. I adjust my pace until he catches me up. "Faster," I breathe, and Cosmin nods, unable to speak. Feverishly, I calculate that the archers must be more than two hundred and fifty feet behind us. *They are good*, I think, knowing what I know about archery. *The best archers a dream can provide*, I laugh inside. Gasping for air, we sprint faster, and my backpack becomes a burden, yet I don't think to throw it. Neither does Cosmin.

We skid to a halt just before we fall over a cliff that has appeared abruptly in front of us. Braking hard, our boots stir the gravel, and distant clicks, of small rocks falling, echo below our feet: clack, clack, for a few seconds. A moment of respite; my breath comes dry, cold and gasping in my throat. A hundred feet below, a wide river flows, at great speed, between massive rocks. I glance back; the savages are coming at a speed that puzzles me – they could beat any sprinter in an Olympic final.

16

"We have to jump," I say casually. *It's just a dream.* Cosmin is not convinced; for him everything is real, so I grab his hand.

"There could be rocks under the water," he says, hesitantly.

"Could be… There are arrows behind us." I point back to that certainty. "Now!" We jump together yet, in flight, our hands separate, each of us aloft with his fear. At first, arrows fly swiftly past us, whispering softly in intermittent cadences, leaving behind the mundane sensation of a surround sound theater.

Falling like a stone, I remember movies with people jumping over a cliff, moving their legs like they're walking in the air. I always found that ridiculous and don't try to imitate them, embarrassed to try. I don't know why I should feel embarrassed in a dream, but that feeling follows me all the way down. The other feeling I have is not fear, but utter disappointment – I was expecting to fly.

I hit the water with a splash. *It's cold…* I shiver. Cosmin makes the same splashing noise a second later. For no particular reason, I note that my body was two feet in the water by the time he hit. In dreams, gravity can vary. I have had some dreams in the past, taking place in strange worlds, where I could fly without wings. Going deep underwater, inside a cloud of gurgling, white bubbles, disappoints me even more– it would have been much easier to fly to the opposite shore. And dry. The cold creeps under my skin, and I don't try to move. From diving training at a seaside resort, a long time ago, I remember that the water will push me up. My thoughts linger for a while, recollecting the warm tropical sea and the multi-colored fishes swimming through the reef. With a tinge of fear, I hope that the 'push me up' rule applies to this dream too. It takes a bit longer than I was expecting to reach the surface, and I fight for fresh air, panting, my mouth wide open. Cold air hisses like a snake through my throat. *It was the backpack;* I realize the cause of the delay. *Quite realistic, this dream.* When I can see again, my first reaction is to look for the savages. They appear on the cliff-edge a few seconds later, shouting unknown words that get lost in the wind, gesticulating with their spears and shooting more arrows at us; but we are now more than two hundred feet away from the place we fell, plus the difference in height between our positions. *The water is faster than I thought, and we're slaloming. To distract the archers,* I realize. Somewhere to the side, more arrows hit the water with a short burp, before disappearing under the small waves. Their meteoric passage is short-lived, but I notice stone arrowheads. Soon, the shore bends to the left, and we are out of the savages' sight. I swim slowly, turning around to find Cosmin. He is some twenty feet away, floating face up, flowing calmly with the water.

"We have to get to the shore," I say. He does not answer, his right hand just makes a small gesture of acknowledgement through the water. Glancing at the shore, I understand his indifference; there is no way to 'get to the shore' – for as far I can see, the shoreline is nothing more than a hundred-foot-tall wall of stone.

Drifting looks easy at first, an occasional movement, the water carrying you effortlessly but, after a few minutes, I start to feel tired. And cold. The backpack is heavy, but I think it may have a role to play in my dream- I rarely have simple dreams, and sometimes they flow like a quest that I have to solve. For no reason, an old dream, in which I carried a heavy lyre with me for several hours through a desert, comes back to me. At the end of a long passage, I had to sing to a sentry so I could enter the oasis he was guarding. Behind me, Cosmin is as calm as before, and that unnerves me. It's my dream, and I should be the composed one. Still looking back at him, I hit a log, two foot in diameter, which is partly hidden in the water. A third of the log is visible, and I would have seen it, if I wasn't looking back at Cosmin. I gasp from the pain my ribs, and I curse my dream, the savages, the war and whatever else comes to mind. My left hand clings to the log, and at a snail's pace I climb up, until my belly is resting on the rough bark. It's an old oak. Still immersed, my legs act as an anchor; the log is slowing down, and Cosmin is getting closer.

"Come," I stretch my hand toward him, still irritated by his calmness. When his hand touches mine, I grab him. "You lazy man," I growl, pulling him toward me and the log. My position is uncomfortable; I am overstretching, but slowly I pull him until his head hits the wood. "You deserved that." I grin, though he can't see my face; his head is somewhere under my right arm. I turn my head awkwardly, just to let him see the merriment on my lips. When my spine starts to complain, I stop turning, my eyes fixed on the arrow tip sticking out of Cosmin's neck, right under his chin. "Well, it's my dream, Cosmin," I say, annoyed that my dream is already too long and too bloody. Usually, I don't have this kind of sick dream, and I blame everything on the bloody war still raging in the real world. *I must be wounded.* The Cheshire Cat's head that

19

looks like Andrei starts to fly around me, a dark reminder of what I should expect when the dream is over, and I stop complaining. I gesture savagely at the flying head, and it vanishes. *Enjoy the dream*...

Slow, like a well-trained horse, the log continues to drift, with me riding it on my belly, my right hand still holding Cosmin's. He follows us like a steer and, after a while, I finally grasp the rules of the dream: I have to use his body to force the log toward the shore, onto a sand bank sandwiched between the ridge and the water; the savages are now far behind us. When we hit the bank, the log shudders, and then aligns itself to the shore. My feet hit the bottom, and I am able to stand again in the shallow water, which goes now up to my chest. I pass Cosmin around the head of the log and pull him onto the sand until he is half out of the water. I don't have enough strength to pull him any further. Unhurried, I take off my backpack and lie down on the sand, not worried that I am wet and shivering. I no longer care.

After a while, the cold becomes too much, and I curse the dream again. My watch shows I've already spent thirty-seven minutes inside my dream. Quite a long time, and the watch could have misled me, yet somehow I have the feeling that those long minutes have really passed. I take off my clothes, and lean back. The spring sun is not strong, but the sand has a dark blue color and it's warm. After a while, I no longer shiver.

I must have fallen asleep. That is my impression when I am startled by a crow's cawing, coming from a tree not far from me. The sound is hoarse and lugubrious, like bad luck. And it goes on and on. *It's a male*, I recognize after opening my eyes. His head is moving back and forth, thirty feet away from me, working hard to emit those sounds just to irritate me. I stare at him, but he is not impressed. Neither am I. Just annoyed. I stare until my eyes hurt, then I close them. The sound doesn't stop. *Awful dream*. I grab a stone half hidden in the sand, but the crow flies off before I can throw my projectile. Stirred by the flapping wings, a curious effervescence swirls inside my mind, an unwanted revelation, taking me by surprise like a sudden storm.

"It's not a dream," I whisper, astonished not only by the abnormal event itself, but also by how quickly and easily I have accepted an unnatural turn of events that I would normally scoff at. My mind is unexpectedly calm, maybe because of Cosmin's weird stories, or maybe because I am a soldier, primed to see weird things, yet I can't think clearly. I don't shout, don't curse, don't jump to my feet; I just cross my arms under my head, feeling the warmth of the sand on my skin, silent, eyes tightly shut. The sun is just above me, and two warm spheres of light glow through my eyelids. *It's not a dream. It could be worse*... My mind is now more than calm, it's numb, void of feeling, unable to think, to question what has happened until I remember Cosmin, and tears flow down my face, washing away everything I have lost. When my tears have run their course, I find myself staring at the river without seeing it. My watch shows that one more hour has passed, and, however I try, I am unable to remember a single string of thought during that time. *I was not asleep*, I protest, and slowly stand up.

I have to bury Cosmin. The thought of burial passes through my mind for the second time in one day. *Not even a full day. First Dan, now*... Lacking the courage to

21

look at Cosmin, I check my surroundings: it seems to be a safe place, at least for a while. On my left, the large river glinting in the sun; on my right, a steep wall of stones, rising from the sand. *Who will bury me?* I shake my head with the awful thought that the savages may be cannibals, and I may find my final refuge inside someone's belly. I need to choose Cosmin's last resting place: but there is only sand. It takes me a while to dig the grave, close to the stones, at the highest point, where the water cannot reach it easily. After taking off his backpack, and breaking the shaft of the arrow, I drag Cosmin slowly, without looking at him through my tears. After a while, I stumble, unable to go further, and I freeze until I find enough courage to turn. *The bayonet.* Trapped by an old root, it acts as a brake. I untie Cosmin's belt, jerkily, still not looking at his face. An old image comes to me: stealing cherries from a neighbor's tree – a fourteen-year-old Cosmin smiling at me. I fill in the grave, still not looking at him – I want to remember that young face smiling at me. *Who will bury me?* I ask again. *Does it matter?*

"You are back in Mother Earth, Cosmin." I repeat his words after I finish my prayer. *If such a Mother exists.* I fall onto my knees, sobbing like a child.

Night comes fast, dark and uneasy, filled with many frightening sounds, and I am too frightened to light a fire or to eat. Inside the sleeping bag, I grip my bayonet until, finally, too tired to take note of every noise, I fall asleep. I don't remember my dreams in the morning. Awake, for a moment or two, I hope that I am back, among my comrades in arms, and Cosmin is still alive. I blink, then I blink again: the river is there and the blue sky. In the bushes above, a bird welcomes the rising sun. My watch shows seven AM. I believe it.

I'm hungry. Even at the worst times, your body keeps functioning. Absently, I open a can of military rations – it tastes better than ever before. Mechanically, I go through the self-preservation routine, learned during the war; I dig in the sand to hide the empty can. When I've finished, it looks like a small grave and, growling, I kick out at it. Leaving a trail of sand behind it, the can falls in the water with a splash. It reverberates in my mind, and I freeze, listening to the slightest noise. Unconcerned, the bird is still singing.

Free to worry again, I am still afraid to ask questions about my whereabouts and how we arrived here. It doesn't help that I have no one to ask. *Maybe I can ask Mother Earth*. The thought makes me smile madly until I laugh out loud. That releases some tension. *I can't stay here forever*. My military training and months of surviving at the front take over, and my eyes flick back and forth, river to mountains, avoiding Cosmin's grave. Without that grave, I can still think about some kind of normality, like stumbling over a cast of actors shooting a movie about the Stone Age or whatever mundane explanation I can find. But the grave is there, and the tip of the arrow is now in my hand: grey stone painted with blood, attached with resin to a small piece of wood. Arms wrapped around my knees, eyes closed, I let my mind drift home, where my parents were waiting for me to return from the front. Andrei's head appears in front of me, floating at the same level as my head. We stare at each other, eye to eye. Unconsciously, I try to push the head away. It performs a graceful curve around my hand and comes back to the same position, staring at me again.

"What do you want?" I ask, annoyed, and the only answer I get is the big grin on its lips. It looks so large that it almost surrounds the head. "I feel like Hamlet," I say, laughing, and that strange reaction brings some sanity into my mind. The head vanishes, and I have the impression that there was a touch of sadness in Andrei's eyes. "I need to think," I whisper after a while and take a stick from the ground.

Slowly, I write in the fine sand, which is mixed with dark blue clay:

1) I am a soldier.

2) There was a battle on the hell–hill.

3) There was an explosion.

4) I woke up here.

I glance at my body, as seeing it for the first time.

5) I still have my uniform.

"So where is here?" I finally ask the first useful question. "How did I arrive here? Who can answer my questions?" From everything around me – pines, willows, birches – I can assume the place is on Earth. *An Earth peopled by savages.* And the air is fit to breathe. "What if the grave is empty?" A sudden urge to open it makes me step forward, until I stumble over Cosmin's backpack. *It's not empty.*

I move back and write again in the sand.

SURVIVE

Maybe not all the people here are savages, I think, staring at my writing.

It looks like a childish game, but there is nothing else I can think of to keep my mind occupied with something that, at least in appearance, is constructive thinking. I don't want to calculate probabilities about Andrei's severed head again. I gaze at the river, inhaling slowly, and sense the soft, sharp, sweet smell of wood violet wafting down the ridge. *Spring. Like in the forest behind my grandparents' house. Like in my war.* Movement catches my attention – to my right and down on the riverbank curving away beneath my feet. I stare through some small bushes into a wedged slab of sand disturbed by a tiny motion. *Otter!* I smile at my own fear. The elusive animal disappears as fast as it came. *Was it really an otter?*

Recovering, I take some things from Cosmin's backpack: medical kit, blanket, compass, sewing kit, and a pullover –we're the same size, so we often borrowed clothes from each other. Then his bayonet and some cans of tasteless military rations. *Seven*, I count them. *Just a few days. I must hunt.* The small flint point of the arrow that killed Cosmin is weighing in my hand, and I know, via lessons from my uncle, who is a historian and archeologist, how to recognize a microlith point from the end of the Mesolithic period. *I know how to make a bow. A bow and one arrow.* I know from past experience, in summer archeological camps, that it's not easy to make such points; our savage ancestors were skilled tool makers. *Better than nothing. I can also fish.* A fishing spear is easier to make; one long thin pole, split into three or in four at one end. You slide a small piece of wood between the sharpened spikes, to keep them apart, and tie it well. *Good luck with fishing*.

My backpack is now too large and heavy, and my hands move inside it, trying to find whatever I can leave behind. The only thing not needed for survival is my *nai*, a curved pan flute made of twenty bamboo pipes– a gift from my parents that made our soldiers' evenings more enjoyable. I weigh it in my hand for a while, before putting it back in with a sigh. I recall my mother's delicate fingers, as she gave me the nai at my last birthday, before the war. An awful, sweet memory – it passes as fast as it came.

There are many holes in the rocky wall, and Cosmin's backpack fits into one of them. I cover the entry with clay and small stones – I may return later for things that might help to keep me alive. Stepping back, I check my work: it's not hard to guess that something is hidden there. *Once the clay is dry... I can't wait.* I have a strong urge to leave the place quickly.

Before I leave, I stop beside the grave. "Farewell, Cosmin. Rest in peace." I fight hard against a new wave of sobbing, and I can't find anything else to say. Only a few words for a friend I knew for so many years. Andrei's head appears in front of me again; it always seems to find the best spot to stare into my eyes. "Stay away from me," I growl. The head blinks, surprised, and vanishes. Surprised too, I turn away from Cosmin and walk slowly through the shallow water, along the bank, careful not to leave any trace that could bring the savages close to the grave. Cosmin deserves to rest in peace. In a few minutes, I arrive at a small tributary, and from there, I am able to leave the shore and climb for half an hour, before looking back again.

Chapter 2 – Vlad

Down in the valley, the nine-hundred-foot wide river flows between rocks larger than a house, stirring white whirlpools; geometrically imperfect, they spread in a network that has no rules, or no rules that I can understand. *Why this need to understand and dissect splendor or harmony?* It's like Cosmin's mathematical mind has found a fertile place in my own thoughts. There is no way to find order where there is none. I know that I should be alert and watch the path for danger, yet my attention is fixed on the landscape that attracts me like a magnet. *I am still in shock.* I try to absolve myself, as if that really counts when death is searching for you. Step by step, the rocky path leads into the mountains, along the small stream, and slowly the large river disappears from sight. With a last glance back, I tell myself that from now on it will be easier to stay alert. Well, as easy as it could be for someone accustomed to hiking through mountains without wandering hordes of savages ready to kill you. The stream's course is almost straight and slightly uphill, and the going is easy. Unconsciously, I am humming a tuneless monotone of a song whose words I don't remember.

A gust of wind carries the odor of a predator, and my song ends abruptly. The sensation in my nostrils is strong, suggesting proximity, but I have no way of knowing what kind of animal is following me through the bushes, only that its scent resembles one you usually find in a zoo close to enclosures holding wolves, foxes or polecats. An experienced hunter might be able to discern what animal it belongs to, but not me. With the bayonet gripped tight in my hand, I lean against a large rock and, eyes half closed, try to filter through the noise around me. *Outside winter, wolves are not dangerous;* I try to calm myself. Bears have a different scent, so wolves were the biggest danger I could think of. The environment is so familiar that I begin to think I am in Earth's past, or an alternate version, while in a corner of my mind a game of probabilities takes place. A game that I can't win. The moment I start to calm down, the image of the savages who killed Cosmin returns. *They don't smell like this.* I shake my head, yet the feeling, that there must be some importance in that image, doesn't leave me, even when I am walking again. I fix on a point up along the stream, just to force the savages to vanish from my mind. It takes me a while, but I win the fight with the unwanted invasion, and the awful image fades, replaced by something else. At first, I can't understand the new thing that comes into my mind, and I ignore it. The image is a blur, like in an ill-formed dream, but it looks like a cat, and I wonder what kind of message my unconscious mind is trying to convey. *Cats are not dangerous*. I shrug, relieved, and walk on, ignoring the image, which clings stubbornly to my mind. A few more steps, and the cat in my mind morphs into a saber-toothed tiger. Without thinking, I start to run. Andrei's head materializes on my left and follows me. I run faster. I can't outrun it. He flies in large circles around me, singing Stairway to Heaven. I feel mindless or even worse, headless. It's like my mind left me and moved into that stupid flying head. I still run. My left foot slips, and I slide down on the gravel. My knee hurts from hitting a boulder, but I go further on all fours until I can stand and run again. The head accompanies me. I stop when I run out of breath, and I collapse on the grass, panting heavily. *I'm acting like an idiot*. I am ashamed of my brainless reaction to a day dream, and I try to focus my mind in a more useful direction. I can't find one; I am too tired to think.

"What are you afraid of?" Andrei asks. "The saber-toothed tiger or me?"

"You can't speak, and there was no tiger." *Only my own fear. It could have been a weasel or a fox, or at worse a lynx, nothing large moved in the bushes.*

"Then who are you talking to? Is it so hard to answer my question?"

"How do you know about the tiger?"

"Do you really think that I am floating in the air around you?"

I am going mad. I close and rub my eyes, open them abruptly.

"Can you rub your brain too?" Andrei is now smiling, condescendingly. "It may hurt. The brain is a sensitive thing. You ran well. Good training for what is waiting for you."

I ignore his taunt, and try to calm myself with a Yoga breathing exercise. It takes me a while, but I finally recover, and Andrei's head disappears. Again I have the impression of sadness in his vanishing eyes. I don't smell the carnivore scent anymore, and I start to walk again.

After ten or more minutes, around a tight curve, I perceive a meadow, and I try to figure out how the open space will affect my survival chances. You can see further. You become visible. My mind is functioning in a similar way to when I calculated probabilities, while Andrei's severed head was resting quietly in my lap. That shock is still with me. A few more steps, and I am in the open meadow. The blue sky is now large and vivid, and I rejoice at the view. There are no more clouds, and the wind in my face carries a breath of familiar Spring fragrances.

On the left, there is a small forest of young pines, their trunks, as thick as a sixteen-year-old child's thigh, growing between the remnants of some green and mushy old logs that fell to the ground a long time ago. *The storms must be strong here.* Moving on, I see the bear. It's not like his large body materialized from nowhere; it was there all the time while I was checking out the meadow and the small forest. Standing on his back legs, the bear grunts and pushes, with his forelegs, against a pine that looks a little older than the others around it. Three children are sitting on the thin branches like strange overgrown fruits: a girl and two boys. Just to enhance the disturbed state of my mind I calculate the distance between me and the animal. *Sixty paces*, just sixty paces between life and death. The bear grunts and pushes again, and the tree shakes like a

31

toy. The human fruits are shaking too. Unable to move, I stare at the bear, and blink, hoping to make it vanish. It doesn't. A loud crack breaks the silence, and the tree leans slightly. Then it stops. Some small roots emerge from the ground, twisted like hardened snakes, on the bear's side. With its feet planted firmly in the ground, the bear lets out a long, frustrated growl, its claws leaving long parallel marks on the bark. A gust of wind carries animal scent and a pleasant odor of resin. I am lucky at least that, blowing toward me, the wind is my ally.

For no particular reason, at that moment, I catch the girl's blue eyes. She is staring at me, and I am staring at her, and her eyes hold a prayer. She can't tell that I am paralyzed by fear, and there is hope in her gaze. I try to take my eyes from her. Their pull is insistent, and I find myself unable to look away. It's like she has trapped me. Almost absently, I realize that she is pretty. A pretty savage, she is dressed like the people who killed Cosmin. Strangely, it doesn't bother me that she is a savage. The bear pushes again. She is still staring at me, hoping in vain that I can save her. The tree bends until its branches hit the next pine in the line. One boy cries, a thin crystalline voice of fear. Her eyes leave me, and I am able to move again. Desperate, I try to think of a way to retreat and vanish behind the rocks, away from the bear, away from her. I take off my backpack and, against my will, I step forward. Once, twice. Her large blue eyes are following me, and I am attracted by them in a way that I can't understand. The bear stands vertically, almost like a man. I don't know why I am so sure that it is a male, maybe because of his huge size. I've never seen a bear so close up. With surprising speed for his size, the bear let his body fall against the tree. One boy is knocked off by the shock and he is now hanging, his small hands gripping a branch, his skinny legs dancing in the air, over the bear's head. The older one helps him to climb back on the branch.

I am now ten paces behind the huge bear. Suddenly, the girl howls and throws cones and small pieces of wood onto the animal's head. Surprised, or just amused, the bear raises his head toward her. The size of an old French cheese wheel, his head stays immobile at a level almost two feet higher than me, while she keeps howling. I can see her looking straight at the animal and there is no fear in her eyes. My bayonet strikes the beast on its left side. It's the first time I've used it in combat; until now it was only good for opening cans filled with tasteless military meals. True to my training, I take care to fit the blade in parallel with the animal's ribs, which are slightly visible through the skin. Bears don't have much fat in spring, but they are hungry and fast. A small shock reverberates into my bones, and the steel plunges further in, scratching a bone. *This is not a training exercise.* My blade is now ten inches deep in the bear's body, and again I have the feeling of being in a dream that will end soon.

The bear grunts in a different way than before, almost humanly, and for some moments, he doesn't move at all. The dream-like feeling vanishes, and I pull my bayonet out of his flesh. It is harder than I expected. Slowly, the bear turns and falls onto four legs. I jump behind him, then on his back, gripping his ear with one hand. My bayonet strikes again, this time piercing his neck. Again, and again. I feel no desire to fight in the wounded bear. Uneasily, he tries to leave, carrying me on his back. I've never ridden a bear before, and a surge of pride overtakes me. With a groan, he falters, then his huge body crashes down, and I jump just in time to avoid being caught under several hundred kilos of dead meat. My arms are spread wide, red with blood, bayonet in my right hand, pointing up. Looking down, I still can't believe I've killed the beast with just a large knife. I feel nothing until his pungent scent fills my nostrils. The girl resurfaces in my mind, and I turn. Spread on different branches, the three children are still in the tree, staring at me in silence. All I can see are her eyes again. I approach the tree, and signal to them to climb down. The youngest boy, maybe twelve years old, comes first and I catch him in my arms from the lowest branch. The last one to come down is the girl. I put her down, in front of me, and we stare at each other from a proximity that expands her large eyes even more. I can't speak, but how would she understand me anyway? Lacking anthropological knowledge about living savages, I estimate her age to be around sixteen. My estimation would be more accurate if I could take a look at her skeleton. My uncle taught me how to do this when he took me to archeology camps, but I can't see her bones. And her body is much prettier than most prehistoric relics. She is slender, straight-limbed, fair-haired, in no way different to a modern human. Slowly, her right hand touches my neck, under my ear, sliding down to my chin, leaving behind the impression of a small electric shock that spreads quickly into my skull. Then she embraces me, speaking gently in a strange language. She stirs me in a way that has never happened before. There is almost nothing sexual in my feelings or in her embrace; just a strange, pleasant sensation that passes through me and I can't understand — an irrational urge that I must stay close and get to know her better. Anyway, that is neither the first nor the most important thing I've failed to understand in the last two days.

From the path that brought me here, shouting and waving long spears, a band of savages erupts into the meadow. There is no way to tell if it's the same band that killed Cosmin. I disengage from the girl, and unsheathe my bayonet again.

"Run!" I growl at the children, and I turn to face the biped animals attacking us. Half crouched and ready to fight, I know that I will die, but at least that will put an end to my insanity to grow more. And maybe the children will have a chance to escape. *They will become savages too*, I can't stop thinking. *They are still innocent children.*

The brutes stop abruptly, twenty feet in front of me, their eyes moving from me to the dead bear on my left, and back. Staring at me intently, they seem to be calculating the easiest way to slaughter me. Somehow, the fact that I killed a bear with just a knife makes them prudent. Prehistoric men were prudent hunters. I have nothing to say, so I just stare back at them, my legs suddenly weak, hoping that I don't collapse. The most unsettling thing about them is not their physical perfection. It is a feral combination of strength, agility, and that human-like intelligence, discernible in the eyes fixed on me, which are trying to dissect me in the way a predator dissects its prey. I try to quell the urge to run away from them, screaming. There is no chance of escaping that way, and I will end up like Cosmin. I breathe deeply, swelling my chest, trying, like any other cornered animal, to look larger and more menacing.

The girl shouts something I can't understand, and moves in front of me. With surprising speed, the smallest boy runs toward the savages.

"You stupid girl," I growl, and try to push her away. "You should have been gone by now. I've given up my life for nothing." She resists my push, and I realize that, while she is thin, she is strong.

A woman comes out from the group of men and the boy jumps into her arms. That makes me feel relieved and foolish at the same time. Then the girl moves too, and she embraces a young man. His left hand goes around her waist, while his right keeps hold of a long spear with a blade made of stone. A surge of bad feelings assaults me from two opposite directions. Something close to fear because he saw her in my arms a few moments before, and something that I could call jealousy, even though I am not sure if it's true, and why it could be true — I've just met the girl.

The man who seems to be the leader steps forward, feline and cautious, and stops five paces in front of me, staring silently. With the exception of a brief glance at the dead bear, his eyes have not left mine. I steel myself not to be the first to look away, but I sheath my bayonet and wait for his next move. His eyes are still measuring me, and somehow he seems displeased by something I can't understand — I haven't often met such people before, and the last experience was unpleasant. Maybe my military clothes are out of fashion. The silence grows, and I decide to make a show of civilization having a peaceful encounter with a lesser tribe.

"Vlad," I point to my chest, and move forward until I am just two paces away from him. I see his muscles tensing as the girl comes closer, speaking to him. In his sleeveless hide tunic, he looks taller and thinner than I was expecting, his muscles like knotted whipcords. *He maneuvers that heavy spear easily with only one hand.* I remember his entry into the meadow. *He was leading the savages.* Mechanically, my mind compares him to Cosmin's killers: those savages looked shorter and sturdier. And they were black-haired. The people in front of me are tall and blond. *Maybe I am lucky.* For want of a better idea, I extend my right arm for a friendly handshake. My gesture has no effect on him. *Shaking hands is not normal here.* I almost sigh.

"Malva." The girl reacts, her left hand pointing at her; abruptly she extends her right hand too, the tip of her middle finger touching mine. I slide my hand until our palms are parallel, and smiling at her, I teach them how to do a proper handshake. Smiling back, she responds enthusiastically, her hand pumping up and down, harder than I was expecting, shaking me.

Not bad. I go on smiling, and slowly disengage from her grip, which again gives me the impression of greater than expected strength. I half turn again toward the man, still keeping my hand extended.

"Darin," he says, his left hand beating his chest with a muffled sound, a minor variation of my introductory move, and then he clasps my hand too, and I have the impression of holding a stone. His strong shake is almost enough to unbalance me.

One by one, the other seven savages – two women and five men – test my hand's resilience; somehow the novelty of the ritual pleases them, and they are very enthusiastic about shaking me and my hand around. I can't say the same about their opinion of me; their eyes are still fixing me intently, with varying degrees of hostility, making me feel like I might be their next meal. There's such a strange contrast between their hands and eyes. The sixth in the line is the young man that I assume is Malva's boyfriend or whatever equivalent they have. My hand advances with some reticence, but he grabs it just like the others. His eyes are no different from the others either, the same suppressed hostility. Then comes the last one, a girl with green eyes, Selma, and I have the same stupid reaction as when I first met Malva – I am strongly attracted to this unknown girl. *Something is wrong with me*. Trying to absolve myself, for a moment, I allow myself to pretend this is a strange, long dream. *It's not a dream*. I shake my head, and force a smile to appease the girl, without realizing that our hands are still clasped. From the corner of my eye, I see one of the others going back to the entrance to the meadow, guarding the path winding down to the river. *The other savages?*

A strong pat on my shoulder wakes me up. It's Darin, pointing at the bear, mumbling something I can't understand. One word repeats several times: "orsa", and I guess that it means bear.

"Take it," I say, generously, thinking I have understood his question. Even in mid-spring, a large bear provides a lot of meat, and that lowers my chances of being the savages' next meal. This one is around five hundred kilos, at least, in my poor estimation.

Surprised, Darin mumbles something else.

"Yes, yes, take it," I repeat, like we are players in a pantomime.

Seeming to understand, Darin snaps some orders, and they quickly surround the bear. In five minutes, the animal is completely eviscerated. Then an argument breaks between them, about how to prepare the carcass, to make it easy to carry everything. I don't understand their words, but they are accompanied by many expressive gestures. Or so I think, and for half a minute I make good use of my math skills to calculate some possibilities. They have two ropes, but they look fragile. I have one that can handle two thousand kilos but, for the moment, I want to keep it hidden. One of them is working on the bear's back legs, trying to make some holes through the thick skin, and I think I understand what he wants to do.

Let me do it," I say in my most pleasant voice. I press my hand to my chest, then gesture that they should make space for me. "My bayonet is a better tool to pierce the skin." I wave it in front of them, and point at the bear, to make them understand that I am not trying to threaten them. Reluctantly, they move away from the carcass, their eyes fixed on me. With my bayonet, I make two holes in the front limbs, between ulna and radius bones, and repeat the process for the back limbs, between tibia and fibula. "It's done," I say, smiling.

One of the women picks up her stone knife and slices through the skin around the neck, then one of the men uses his stone axe to chop the head off. Another man goes into the forest and cuts four small sticks, about ten inches long, and the diameter of a large thumb. They fit well through the holes I've made between the bears' bones, and their ropes are good enough to tie the forelegs, then the back legs, together with two sturdy spears.

Thinking that eight people will struggle to carry the beast, I am ready to offer my services and replace one of the girls. Before I can speak, four men grip the spears and lift the bear like it was just a lamb. I probably don't look very smart; the girls are suppressing laughter as they look at me.

Chapter 3

On the top of the small hill towering over the long valley that led to their village, Siman was alone and bored. He would have preferred to play with his friends instead of sitting all day on the edge of the hill, watching the valley. It was important to keep the village safe, he knew, but still boring. Once in a while, something might happen, and the watcher would alert the village in a hurry. He would become a hero, briefly, but no boy had had the chance to be a hero this year. Apart from the young, restless watchers, everybody else was content with the situation; heroes usually appear in troubled times. There were three lookout posts around the village; two guarding the paths from the Great River, from where the Kalachs might attack. Kalach was their name for the Kala people across the Great River. The 'ch' suffix meant bad in the Vlahin language. One more lookout post lay to the north, higher in the mountains. The enemy could be deceptive and come from there too. Or friends from another Vlahin clan. The village needed to know in advance, in either case. Five times in the past, the Kalachs had tried to destroy their village and steal women. Siman was too young to remember the last two battles, and not even born the first time the Kalachs invaded their lands, but he was old enough to fear what had happened in the last one: eleven people of the clan had died in the battle, and twenty-three Kalachs, but who cares about dead enemies? The short, dark-haired Kalachs were too fond of the tall, blonde Vlahin women, and they liked to steal too. *The Vlahins never steal*, Siman thought with a tinge of pride, but there was a subtle countercurrent in his mind, telling him that sometimes it is easier to steal than to work.

"In half a year, I will be sixteen, have the ceremony and become an apprentice hunter," Siman said to no one, and his own words excited him. "We will dance through the night; the Chief will mark me, and from then on, I will go with the men. After I pass the rite," he sighed. "I will not fail." Nervously, he kicked a pebble that went clicking down the stones – it was not easy to pass the rite; most boys failed it in the first year. "That was not good," he told himself, watching the pebble recoiling noisily from one rock to another. A watcher should be silent. Ashamed and worried, he grabbed his knife, staring around for a minute or two, but no one was there to witness his blunder. Neither friend nor foe. The cold of the knife's sharp stone relieved him as, unconsciously, his thumb slid up and down on it, in the heavy silence.

Two minutes later, his thumb was still sliding along the edge of the knife, a small spot of blood coloring the stone. *Nothing happened, but I still failed*, Siman thought bitterly. *It will not happen again, and I will not tell anyone.* He sheathed the knife, and for the first time felt the wound on his thumb. Just a scratch, but he moistened it with saliva to hasten the healing, as the Shamane of the clan taught them. She was a wise woman. A moment later, he perceived movement down the valley, and his eyes expanded in expectation. In profile, with his thumb still resting in his mouth, he looked like an overgrown baby. Fighting his desire to run and alert the village, he crouched and slid down, hiding behind a rock, registering everything.

The incoming group was split in two, one man walking faster, two hundred meters in front of the rest. "Rand," he recognized the one in front. His brother. "Our men," Siman whispered, disappointed; he would not be a hero today. Despite the disappointment, this time he did as he had been taught by the elder hunters. He waited silently, hidden behind the stone, until he could count everybody in the approaching group. He knew all the groups that left the village through the south path, their leaders and how many people were in each. "Why was Rand apart from the others?" With a small surge of excitement, he waited until Rand reached the foot of the hill, then imitated a falcon's cry. In acknowledgment, Rand gripped the spear in both his hands, raising it over his head – the signal that all was well. It took Siman a few moments to climb down the hill. "What happened?"

"You are fast, little brother," Rand smiled, embracing him; then he disengaged, and his gaze hardened. "We found a band of Kalachs," he said, then waited on purpose, letting Siman's eyes grow larger. "They ran, but..." He stopped again, playing with his younger brother. "We've captured one of them. Close your mouth," he laughed, and his hand moved to push Siman's chin up. A clack of teeth followed, to Rand's amusement.

"Did you fight?" Siman asked, with the eagerness of a young boy dreaming being an adult, ready to conquer the whole world. Then fear came to him, and swiftly, he searched Rand's body for any trace of wounds. There was none.

"It was an easy thing," Rand bragged. "Sometimes, I wish to be a warrior, not a hunter."

"But that means war. It's a Kalach thing. War is bad," Siman interjected quickly; he was not without a certain capacity to think.

"Only if you lose, little brother. Only if you lose." There was something condescending in Rand's voice; he said the thing, but did not expect to be fully understood by a small boy – the irony of not realizing that he was only three years older. Siman remained silent, and only half convinced of that 'truth'. "Go and tell them, little brother," Rand gestured toward the north; the village was not visible from where they stood. "They are waiting for some good news." He laughed again, watching his brother sprint off, eager to carry his words. There was a malicious smile on Rand's face as he stared after at him.

"Kalach!" Siman shouted even before he entered the village, his thin voice almost strangled by the effort. Alerted, men and women grabbed their weapons and came out of their huts, running to the large open space in front of Shamane's house. "They've captured a Kalach," Siman shouted again, when he realized he'd seeded panic among his people.

"You stupid..." one man castigated him.

"Sorry," he gasped. "I ... I can't speak properly," Siman answered, ashamed, and continued running until he arrived in front of Moira, the Shamane of the village.

"Siman, you scared the whole village," Moira said, her voice calm.

"Sorry," he breathed. "They found a Kalach band, and drove it back over the river. Rand told me."

"Thank you, Siman. You need to rest now." She saw how consumed by the effort he was, and he nodded meekly before turning away – it was not his day.

"We need to greet him properly," one man shouted, waving his spear, and several other answered his call.

"No one is allowed to touch the Kalach." Moira raised her voice a notch. "You can frighten him, if that pleases you," she stared intently at the women and men in front of her, "but don't touch him."

There was a moment of inertia, then people moved in small groups, leisurely, toward the border of the village, and gathered in two long rows, between which the Kalach would have to pass. Excitement flooded their veins; four years had passed from their last fight against the southern savages. The Vlahins had won that fight, a thing that they would like to remind the prisoner in a proper way.

"When Siman arrived..." Moira said, staring absently at her people moving away. "For a moment, I thought that those two men the Mother promised would help us had arrived." Sighing, she questioned her elder sister, Elna, with a glance.

"They *will* come," Elna answered confidently. She believed it, but she also saw the hint of tension in Moira's shoulders. Another might have missed it, but like any shamane, Elna was trained in the art of observation. "We both had the same Trance Dream, three days ago, and entered the Mother's Web through the second River of Thought. Both of us have been shamanes for a long line. The future always comes through the dreams induced by the sacred smirna, and the smirna I prepared for me that night was stronger than usual. I used more Long Night Mushroom powder."

"That was my impression; you recovered slower the day after. Don't do it again. It will harm you."

"It may," Elna shrugged and stayed silent for a while. "I tried to reach the third River of Thought in the Web."

"That's dangerous, Elna," Moira said, worried. "You don't have enough Amber Stones to enter the third River. You could have died." The Vlahins were a stone tribe and stone occupied a high position in their beliefs. It was the Mother who created all the stones for them to use, and most of their tools and weapons were made of stone.

"I entered it once and survived. Now, we have to wait for the dream to take shape in the real world." *The Mother told me that we would win the next battle, but my mate would die, defending our people. I could not warn him. Why did she put that burden on me?* Elna breathed deeply, feeling as if her loss had happened only days ago. She had cried all that night – after making love for the last time with her mate – hidden in the forest, so no one could hear her.

"I hope you are right. I know ... a Trance Dream, is always right. Two dreams even more." A brief touch of resignation filled Moira's voice, but she recovered fast. "The Kalachs are growing in numbers. Each year, more of them are coming from south to settle on the Great River's south bank. Only the river has kept us from slavery until now."

"The river and our strength," Elna said in a bitter voice, remembering again that her mate died in the last fight, defending the village. He was the Chief of the village and she was Shamane at that time. While the men were shamans, the women were shamanes, but the one leading a clan was Shamane, her second name.

"And our strength," Moira agreed, and her palm briefly touched Elna's shoulder. "There were only a few Kalachs when the first group arrived south of the river, asking for a place to stay. More than fifty years ago, I was not even born in that time."

"Neither was I," Elna shrugged.

"What a mistake," Moira said, pain filling her voice. "Another group came, and another, until they became the masters of the southern mountains. It was not our clan they destroyed, I know, but still it was Vlahin land. There were eleven Vlahin clans south of the river. They are all gone."

"Moira," Elna said gently. *I know you are afraid*, she thought. *That fear was mine too before I lost my mate and passed the Shamane burden to you, but fear is not a good adviser.* "We are not our ancestors. We know the evil; we are prepared."

"Are we?" Moira asked. "They've stolen everything from us, even our language. They are using it now. Ah, I forgot. We've learned four words from their language too: war, warrior, steal and slave. And they are still coming, trying to cross the Great River. How many are there?" she asked, frustrated, her hand gesturing south.

"Many," Elna shrugged. "Their women can't lock their wombs, so they have more children than us, and they use both people and animals as slaves. They don't understand that people and earth must live in balance. We make our children with care, so we grow slowly. They don't care."

"Because of that hideous false god. How can anyone believe in a bull? A bull can't be a god. It's just an animal. There is only the Great Mother, and everything comes from her, that stupid bull included. How could they forget this?"

"They worshiped the Mother too. A long time ago."

"I know. What happened to them?"

"Who knows?" Elna shrugged. "Let's meet the Kalach. Our people are too eager to inflict some pain on him. Pay him back for past killings. I understand them..." She did not finish her phrase.

"I understand them too, but it's not our way, and I don't want trouble right now. At least not until the promised help comes. We have not fought for many hundreds of years. We were not used to killing people. We've fought three times in the last twenty years alone, to repel the Kalachs. Their bull likes to drink blood, and their previous Chieftain liked it too. They've killed; we've killed. Once it appears, it's not easy to dispel the idea of killing from people's minds, and we've lost many good people. I'm sorry," she added, after a brief silence.

"There is no need. Nothing can give my mate back, not even the Mother. We won each fight until now, but some of our men are looking at the Kalachs with hidden admiration Elna said, as if it had just come to her.

"I know. Darn, our Chief Hunter, is one of them. A few even have thought about that bull. Maduk, the second

Kalach Chief, is a good story teller, and knows many things. However much I want to, I can't stop him coming here."

"We have learned many things from him."

"Only what he wants us to hear. And some men feel empowered to want more. That bull again. Don't forget; he spreads knowledge on purpose. I agree," Moira stopped her with a nervous gesture, "they are more advanced, and some of the new things are useful, things that we've never discovered ourselves, but most of them are just to influence our people in the wrong way. I think I see them coming," Moira added quickly and walked faster.

"Rune has returned," Elna said, surprise filling her voice. Three men had entered the village from the northern path, one of them limping slightly.

"I did not expect him back until the evening." Moira stopped abruptly, waiting for her mate to join them. "The Mother made him come back early." There was relief in her voice.

"What happened?" Rune asked, his eyes wandering through the gathered people.

"The group led by Darin captured a Kalach. They were hunting in our lands," Moira said.

"He looks strange." Rune frowned, as if trying to see better, and both women turned.

"The prisoner is a mix," Moira whispered. "Perhaps his mother was a captured Vlahin." The man in front of them was taller and thinner than a Kalach, had light brown hair, a fair face and dark eyes. She entered the Mother's Web through the first River of Thought, stretched her mind to feel the intruder, and shook her head in frustration. An experienced shamane or shaman does not need psychedelic potions to navigate the First River, and all humans and some animals are unconsciously connected to it. A shamane or shaman can access it consciously and learn things. That's why they were never allowed to hunt. "I've never felt such a mind," she said to Elna. "It's so different."

"Concentrate," Elna whispered, even more surprised than her sister at what she found in the man's head, and she was a stronger shaman – she had five Amber Stones. Moira had only four stones and a half.

Eyes closed, Moira entered into the first River of Thought again, trying to learn more about the stranger's mind. "He has made two bonds," she breathed, and the abnormality of the situation silenced her. *It can't be.*

"I am not a shaman," Rune said, "but I never heard of a Kalach making bonds, and anyway it takes a month or two to make a bond. He just crossed the Great River today." Incredulous, he stared at the puzzled women, but got no answer from them. *With whom did the Kalach make the bonds?* He did not dare voice his question, realizing that something really strange was happening. He knew that the shamanes already had the answer – they could feel the bond between two people – and he braced himself for more surprises.

Chapter 4 – Vlad

The two girls, Malva and Selma flank me on the road I assume leads toward their camp. Having no alternatives, I agreed, with some reluctance, to join them, when they left the meadow. A brief memory of the other band that chased Cosmin and me played a role too. These people seemed to be more peaceful. I could be wrong, of course, but I preferred to think of them as different, to ease my fears. I needed to believe in my chances of survival. The invitation was made by Malva, and not by the man who seemed to lead the hunters, and I do not know how much influence she has on the leaders of their clan, or whatever form of organization they have. She is only sixteen years old after all. The young man who seems to be Malva's boyfriend is walking just behind me. Sometimes, I have the sensation of feeling his breath on the back of my neck. *It's just fear*. I force myself to ignore him, knowing that the more afraid I am the more chance that bloody head has to mess with my mind again. I fear my own insanity as much as my blood-soaked memories. They are related, after all. Even with my heavy backpack, I am moving faster than the four men carrying the huge bear. We walk in silence, none knowing what to say, in fact not knowing how to make ourselves understood. Before a steep curve, we stop to wait for the ones left some hundred paces behind, and I reach into my backpack for a notebook and a pen. The girls watch me intently, and the young man too, even though he feigns indifference. I can't resist the temptation to check their reactions and give the girls my notebook. They touch it delicately, then smell it, and I bite my lip to stop a smile. It doesn't matter; they are too absorbed by the new thing to observe me. I take it from Selma's hands and make a quick sketch, representing the head of a woman – just a few lines. If they were amazed by the paper, now they are in awe, even the man, who cranes his neck to catch a glimpse of my drawing. A wave of shame passes through my mind and, taking the notebook from Selma, I open it on the first unused page. *Let's try a more useful game.* Slowly, I set the thing on the stone in front of me. I see Malva pouting, disappointed, and her reaction is the same as any teenage girl. Slightly older, Selma is more composed, but she is no less disappointed.

"Finger," I say, lifting the forefinger of my left hand. "Finger," I say again, touching it with my right hand. Then I lift another finger and another one. "Finger." I touch them all.

"Dego," Selma says with a frown, raising the forefinger of her left hand too.

"Dego." I touch her finger while speaking. "Dego." I touched another of her fingers and she nods with a smile, while I take my time to write the word in my notebook.

"Hand." I raise my palm in front of them, fingers spread.

"Min," Malva says and her palm touches mine, covering it, her fingers spread too.

Involuntarily, I flex my fingers, gripping her palm, and she does the same, our hands now laced together. An undercurrent passes through my skin, and I have the same strange and pleasant feeling as I did when I saw her for the first time. Before I can react, Selma raises her hand too, and without thinking, I press my palm against hers and our fingers lace. The undercurrent and the pleasant feeling repeat themselves. *It must be shock from all that's happened in the past two days*. There is no other explanation for my strange, uncontrolled reactions. I am now hand in hand with two beautiful girls, and I don't know what to do. The new situation delights them; they smile, waiting for my next move in what they think of as a simple game. Our closeness delights me too, more than I like to acknowledge. Not that I don't want it, I just fear what might happen. I am stranger in a way that I never thought possible before. Gently, I disengage from them, and without trying to look at Malva's boyfriend, I write a new word on the page in front of me.

Ready to learn more, I press my forefinger to my lips, without thinking, staring alternatively at their lips. "Lip," I finally remember to say.

"Wiz," both girls say at the same time, touching their lips. Malva moves toward me and tries to imitate our previous game and press her lips to mine.

I react promptly and press my finger to her lips, keeping her at a safe distance. "Wiz," I breathe, watching Malva's boyfriend, who is standing just five paces from me, from the corner of my eye. His face is composed, but I know nothing about their ways.

Malva touches my lips and Selma does the same – one finger on my lips, another one on Malva's. A few moments later, we all burst into laughter, and I suddenly realize that they don't have the habit of kissing on the mouth. Fumbling through my memory, I remember that kissing first appeared in the Roman era. I am not sure how accurate my knowledge is, and I am not yet sure if this is Earth and whether historical associations are useful.

If this is Earth... I try to remember some of the things my uncle taught me during the summer archeological camps. From the physiognomy of the people around me, I could be in only three places: the Iron Gate of the Danube, the Tigris or the Euphrates, close to their exits from the Taurus Mountains. I have never seen the last two, but something tells me that they are smaller than the river I've left behind – their basins are not large enough to sustain such a great flow. And I saw the Iron Gate only after the dam was built, so it was difficult to compare. I force myself to stop pondering about the place until I can figure out if I really am on Earth. Learning new words is more useful.

After a while, the road curves to the left again, and I have the feeling that we are going toward the river. By the time we get close to their camp, I have written most of the words describing human anatomy, basic actions like walking, running or speaking, and the names of some animals, plants and features such as river, water, sky, sun.

I also know how to greet them, and I hope to do it properly when I encounter more of the Vlahin people, as they call themselves. Like anyone who has learned music from early childhood, I have a good memory, and I can remember most of the foreign words already, without reading them.

The camp appears suddenly, after another steep curve. It is built on a large terrace at the foot of a small mountain. From here, I can count seven huts, but there must be more on the part of the terrace I cannot see. I was expecting to find tents. Because of the permanent structures, it looks more like a village than a temporary camp. We climb a steep path, and I realize that this is the only way to reach the village from the direction we came. I glance up, but the sun is at its highest point. Still, I can see that we approached the village from the south. The path meanders through some large rocks, each of them a good place to surprise an enemy. At the entrance to the village, the first two people I meet stare at me like I am their next kill. I hesitate and slowdown. Malva grabs my arm and pulls me along, talking in a calm voice. I understand nothing. My mind is alert, and I feel like I'm back on that hell-hill, between the enemy lines, only here the distance between 'they', whatever that means, and me is much smaller and more dangerous.

"Kalach," one of them spits a word which seems full of bad meaning, glaring at me. Another spits the same word, and both come closer, their fingers closed in large fists ready to punch my face. My hand grips the hilt of the bayonet.

What the hell is kalach? Kill? I did not kill anyone. I saved them.

Malva shouts something I can't understand, and they stop, their eyes still angry. Her voice is surprising authoritative. I breathe out, emptying my lungs.

Are they cannibals? I swallow, trying hard to keep my composure, a cold fear gnawing at me. Even now I cannot say how I overcame it. Somehow, Andrei's severed head sitting so peacefully in my lap, and Cosmin's violent death, numbed my human feelings or my capacity to physically react to my own fear. *I saved some of their people...* I repeat this to calm and convince myself that I still am a human being.

As we advance, more people come from their huts, the same angry faces. Some of them have clubs or spears in their hands. Malva says something to me again and, this time, I feel a touch of panic in her voice, bringing back the memory of Cosmin's death. My grip on the bayonet becomes stronger and I half unsheathe it – a useless, or even dangerous, reaction with so many armed men swarming around. After a few more steps, Malva makes me stop; we are surrounded by some seventy people, women and men and a few children. We can't advance further without shoving people out of the way, and I am not willing to try. Behind them, an invisible man's voice shouts some angry words, and the crowd splits slowly in two. A man and two women are walking briskly toward us through a corridor flanked by angry people. There is a kind of austere dignity in their appearance; they look like the owners of the place. One woman exchanges a glance with Malva, and the frown on her young face vanishes.

Maybe they will not eat me...

I have no more than a few seconds of calm. On my left, a ten-year-old child grabs a stone from the ground. The size of a woman's fist, it barely fits into his palm. I slide my backpack's strap from my left shoulder until it hangs only on my right. Then I push it half in front of me. It touches Malva's upper arm lightly. She does not react, and I move slowly, half in front of Selma, who is on my left. My right hand goes for the small strap at the top. The trio that seems to rule the place is now just twenty paces away from us. One of the two incoming women sees the child too and shouts at him. Too late: the rock flies from his hand.

Instantly, I lift the backpack. At the same time, I grab Selma's shoulders, pulling her closer to me. Her head is between mine and the flying stone, which hits the backpack and falls to the ground in the silence of the people surrounding us. Even when he is limping slightly, the man in charge moves quickly to the boy and slaps him hard. His face crimson, the boy vanishes, moving fast, on all fours, between the legs of the elder people. There is no other reaction. Selma is still leaning against my body, half embracing me, yet I am not consciously aware of it, and none of us try to move. The people around slowly make more space and the three personages who seem to be their leaders come closer. I finally become aware of Selma's warm body, and I try to disengage gently, but she does not acknowledge my attempt, or she just ignores it, clinging to me. Malva turns and embraces both of us and, caught between fear and pleasant feelings, I have no idea what should I do. In that sudden silence, a strange thought comes to me: *They don't stink*. I bite my lip to stop a burst of laughter. *I am in danger, and all I can do is to worry about their hygiene. I hope my mind recovers soon.*

One of the two women in front of me speaks and signals something with her fingers and the girls step aside, leaving me alone to face three pairs of curios eyes. This I am at least able to figure: they don't look at me as if I am their next meal, yet I still prefer to look down, avoiding their eyes. In some cultures, locking eyes is considered impolite or even worse. It comes from our ancient past, when fixing your stare on someone was a prelude for an attack, or even more anciently, the interaction between predator and prey. The same women who spoke before comes closer, and her fingers touch my chin, lifting my head until our eyes meet. She has blue eyes, deeper than any I have ever seen. They bore through me, and I have the strange impression that the woman is trying to connect my appearance with something in her memory.

There was no way to see me before now, lady, I think, mildly amused. As my eyes sweep over her face, her own are on me. From so close, they seem like a morning sky, high in the mountain; she stares from under thin elegant eyebrows, one of them lifted in a delicate curve that suggests a question mark. Her face is striking – not exactly because of her beauty, which resembles a Greek statue, but from something transcendental that I don't understand. Her tanned deerskin dress is similar to what the others wear, but there are five concentric circles painted on her chest, a red color. The second woman has them too. Both Malva and Selma have five white circles. Looking discreetly around, I find that no one else has this ornament. It's intriguing, but I have no way of guessing what the circles and their color mean.

She speaks to me, but I just shake my head. After a while, she speaks again in what I realize is a different language. I shake my head again, and say something in my own language. It is her turn to shake her head.

We agree silently that, for the moment at least, we can't communicate except by signs, and she steps back, letting the second woman come closer. She repeats the same gestures, without speaking. The only difference is that, now, I am scrutinized by deep green eyes. She steps back too, and glances at her companion. There is a kind of tentative agreement between them. I suppose it's related to me, but I have no idea in what way. I hope it's not related to some appalling culinary issues.

The man is the next to come closer. His approach is different and his scrutiny takes longer. My bayonet is the first thing he acknowledges, then his eyes move step by step from my arms to my legs, assessing what kind of value I might have in combat, or so I think. My backpack follows and finally my clothes. He touches the canvas of my military jacket. I can read nothing on his face, but I am sure that he is slightly disconcerted by the unfamiliar texture.

He wonders what kind of animal produces such 'skin', I think, amused.

After a while, he points at my bayonet, and I bite my lip, not sure what to do. He is waiting calmly, his forefinger still pointing and, slowly, I unsheathe my blade and give it to him. The man takes it and weighs it in his hand. For the first time, his eyes react, contracting slightly. His thumb moves on the edge, and his eyes contract further. From his waist, he takes a flint blade and slides the tip of the bayonet across it. It leaves a white scratch behind. When he stares at me, his eyes are bland again, and he returns the bayonet to me. I sheathe it with disconcerted relief. For whatever reason, I felt almost naked without it, though there is no way I can defend myself against so many armed people surrounding me. Silent, the man steps back.

The three of them stare at me again, and I have the impression that the women are related; maybe they are sisters or cousins. I take some heart and press my right hand to my chest, and beat it twice as Malva and Selma taught me on the road. My chest answers with a muffled sound, and I realize that the sound is fainter than when they patted the skins covering their chests. Cotton is softer. "Vlad." Ending the Vlahin style presentation, I stretch my right arm out for a handshake.

Malva says something to them and the man steps forward, touching his chest. "Rune," he says, and he imitates my gesture. I grab his hand and shake it gently. He does the same, and for the first time I get an appropriate reaction, which doesn't shake my body together with my hand or crush the bones of my fingers. "Moira," he points to the woman who was the first to speak to me. "Elna," he points to the second one.

I see the man smiling for the first time and, at the same time, I feel a bead of perspiration running down my face. He is watching it.

Malva starts to speak to them again, gesticulating from time to time toward the dead bear, now lying in the dust. She raises her hands up, as if requesting attention, then she crouches down, looking far into distance, her hands shading her eyes. She startles and grunts like a bear, her face mimicking fear. She climbs a tree. Her body moves left and right, imitating the shaking tree, the child who almost fell, his fear, her fear, the way I approached the bear, step by step. So evocative is her pantomime that even my mind is absorbed. Their reaction is even stronger, and she plays skillfully on the emotions of the audience, elevating the drama. She points at my bayonet, then her hand plunges into an imaginary bear. The bear falls onto his four legs. She climbs him and stabs the bear in the neck. It looks like she is on a modern stage, in a play, and she feels at ease in the center of everybody's attention. Even without knowing the words, I am able to understand almost everything. Ecstatic, the eyes of the people around widen and narrow to the rhythm of her voice and gestures. After a while, there are no more angry stares directed at me. She ends the play by embracing me. Unable to add anything to the story, I stay silent, holding her in my arms. She leans her head back and smiles at me. Unconsciously, I smile back, the warmth of her body creeping inside me, and for the first time since my arrival in this strange world, I feel comforted, the way a child is comforted by his mother. Before I can react further, both girls grab my arms and pull me after them. From the path they have chosen, we are walking toward the largest hut in the village. Just in front of it, I turn and, half a mile away, the river glitters in the sun.

Chapter 5

"Vlad is not a Kalach!" Rune shouted, loud enough to be heard by everyone in front of him. "He killed a bear with just a knife and saved three of our children."

"It's a strange knife he carries," one man said.

"Strange it may be, but a knife alone can't kill a bear. Siman," Rune turned toward the boy, "why did you tell the village that a Kalach had been captured?"

Siman glanced at Rand, hoping that he would say something, but his older brother ignored him. *Rand knew about Vlad. Why did he lie to me?* Caught between the anger of being punished for something that was not his fault, and the thought that he might be called a traitor, Siman did not know what to say. Rune understood that there was more going on than he initially thought and did not interfere, allowing the boy to make up his own mind.

"Rand told me," Siman finally said, no longer looking at his brother.

"Vlad saved your other brother by killing a bear," Rune said to Rand.

"I thought he was a Kalach."

"Darin," Rune addressed the Chief of the Hunters, "you must discipline your oldest son. He will join the apprentice hunters for one month."

"Isn't that severe for a simple misunderstanding?" Darin asked, his voice venomous.

"Vlad saved your youngest son, and Rand acted like stupidly. The people in the village were worried, and Selma could have had her head smashed."

"Selma was not hurt."

"Not thanks to Rand. He will spend one month with the apprentices." Rune did not wait for an answer and turned, followed by Darin's angry eyes.

"Let's go, Rand," his father whispered. *I was shamed in front of the village*, Darin thought, his eyes fixed on Moira's back; his hate for her was greater than for Rune. *I am the strongest man in the clan and the Chief Hunter. I feed the clan, not that shrew and her cripple. She's already hoping that Vlad may be able to replace my son. Rand must break Vlad's bond with Malva. My son will be the Chief of the village, not a stranger. I will not allow it.*

Feeling Darin's stare with her shamane senses, Moira turned abruptly, and their eyes locked. Cursing inside, Darin was the first one to look away, and he walked quickly, vanishing behind a hut. *There's too much violence and resentment in Darin for him ever to make a good chief*, she thought. *My heart was right when I chose Rune as my mate, instead of Darin.* Seventeen years ago, Rune and Darin were her two bonds. It felt to her as if it was only yesterday. Today, her daughter, Malva, was bond to

Darin's son. She shook her head, and walked away too. The girls, Elna and Vlad were already at the large table on the covered terrace in front of her hut. Her path intersected with Rune's, and she took him by the arm.

"You are an idiot," Darin growled at his son, when they were alone, in front of their hut. "Next month, you were to have your first hunt and become a man. Now, I have to postpone it for half a year. Rune was so eager to punish you."

"Vlad made a bond with Malva," Rand said, nervously.

"And? Any girl or young man can have two bonds. That's the rule. You were her first. The bond between you two is almost half a year old, and he is a stranger. Act wisely, and Malva will be yours." *Rune wants to break Rand's bond with his daughter*, Darin thought, and a wave of rage passed through him. He did not display it, not wanting to worry his son even more.

"How did it happen so fast between them? It takes months to make a bond." Rand did not know about the other bond between Selma and Vlad. As any other Vlahin, he was able to know only his own bonds and the bonds his two girls had with another man. In time, he would learn about Vlad's other bond, as observation was also a tool for harvesting knowledge. Only the shamanes or the shamans knew a person's bonds by looking into their minds.

"Who knows? Maybe because he is a stranger. You think that the Mother may help him?" Darin suddenly understood his son's worries. "After Vlad honors the bond with Malva, you can challenge him. Win five challenges in a row, and his bond will shatter."

"He killed a bear with just a knife," Rand said, his voice oscillating between worry and bitterness. There was also a touch of fear, even though the challenges were not to the death. Weapons were not involved in the fights and Vlahins did not kill Vlahins. They were peaceful people.

"I don't know how Vlad killed that bear, but he is weak. I felt it when I shook his hand. He is not a real hunter, and you will win the challenges. I trust you." Darin patted his son on the shoulder. "You are only eighteen, but you are already one of our strongest fighters."

Rand looked, startled, at his father, in search of an explanation. The Vlahins named their men hunters, and ranked them based on their ability to provide for the clan. Young Vlahin men wrestled, but ranking them as fighters was a Kalach thing. The Kalach trained their best men as warriors or fighters, to invade other people's lands. They were trained to kill people, not animals.

"The Kalach have some things right," Darin said with a smile. "Men lead them, not some women who don't know how to hunt or fight for the clan. A day may come when men will be in charge here. We were born to lead, not those weak women. Did you see how subservient, and ready to please their mates, the Kalach women are? That's the right way."

Rand enjoyed some of his father's thoughts, but he also feared the power of the Shamane. She was in touch with the Mother. One day, almost four years ago, Moira warned him to stay away from water, for a while. With the bravado of a youngster who thought that the world belonged to him, he dismissed her warning, and went to swim, in the lake close to their village, with the other children of his age. A small landslide created a strong wave, and he was almost drowned. Undecided, he simply nodded at Darin, unwilling to speak about such a sensitive subject; yet he envied the Kalach men for leading their clan. "Did you meet the Kalachs, yesterday?" His father had been away for two days, and when they met in the morning, there was no way to speak to him about this with so many people around them. Apart from Darin's brother and Rand, no other Vlahin was aware of these meetings with the Kalachs.

"No," Darin said, his voice filled with displeasure. "They came to our side of the river. I saw them, and waited for them at the right place. They were heading there too then, all of a sudden, they started to run away."

"Chased by other Vlahins?"

"No, this is our land; no other Vlahins would come without asking for approval. The Kalachs were chasing something I could not see, but I don't know what could be so important."

"Maybe it was Vlad they wanted."

"Maybe. It doesn't matter. We will meet again in a few weeks. This time with Maduk. He is a man I trust, though I prefer the other one, Turgil. He seems stronger and more determined to help us, and he wants Selma as his mate."

"But it was Turgil who chased yesterday..."

"He is still young. Their Shaman favors Turgil too. One day, I will help Turgil kidnap Selma. If she is gone, Malva remains our only shamane apprentice, and her mate will become the Chief of the clan. Ready yourself for the challenges." Darin stared at his son and still saw some clouds behind his eyes. "If you fail to win the challenges, we will kill Vlad. He is a stranger, not one of us."

"He has the bond, what will people think? Or the Shamane?"

"Vlad is a stranger. Our laws don't apply to him. I don't care about that shrew of woman, and don't be stupid; we will not kill him in plain view. He will have an accident during a hunt. Don't worry, son, everything will be fine and, when the time comes, you will be the Chief of the clan. I will take care of that, and the Kalachs will help me." He patted Rand's shoulder. "Keep this from your mother and brothers; they may not understand it."

"Vlad saved my little brother," Rand said, to channel things away from killing. It was not the Vlahin way, and for all his father's evil influence, he was not yet fully corrupted.

"Son." Darin placed his hand on Rand's shoulder. "Sometimes you need to make tough decisions in life. I would prefer that you shatter the bond between Malva and Vlad, but if the need arises, I will not hesitate to kill him. Soon, we will move, with the Kalachs, against Moira. The bitch should be cast away from the village together with her cripple, and men of valor will lead our clan." *The bitch will be killed, but you are so soft, son. You are still young. In three or four years, I will make you a good Chief, and Malva will learn to obey you.*

"What's that?" Moira pointed at the strange object sitting on the table in front of Vlad.

"Notebook," Malva said. "It's used to store images and ... words."

Moira closed her eyes for a moment. "You can draw things on certain surfaces, but how can you store words?"

Without understanding their conversation, Vlad knew from the women's gestures that his notebook was its subject, and he opened it at the page were the head of a woman was drawn. Slowly, he pushed it in front of Moira, who was seated between Elna and Rune on the bench across the table. He was sandwiched between Malva and Selma. The adult Vlahins reacted the same way as their children did before: they admired the drawing, then gently touched the paper and smelled it. The scent of the paper and the glue used to stick the pages together was strong for their fine sense of smell, and unfamiliar too.

"What about storing the words?" Moira asked.

Malva stretched out her hand to take the notebook, and opened it at one of the pages where Vlad had written the mini dictionary of the Vlahin language. Not knowing how to explain what she wanted, she tapped over a word, then pushed the notes to him.

I understand what they want, but how can I explain it? Vlad thought, rubbing his chin. After a minute of silence, he reached into his pocket to extract the pencil. He opened the notebook at a blank page, near the end. MOIRA, he wrote in capital letters. "Moira," he said pointing at the woman. "Moira," he said again, tapping over the word with his pencil. "M." He tapped over the letter. "O" He tapped again and continued until he'd read out the name. "M. O. I. R. A. Five letters." He raised his left hand, fingers stretched, and counted them.

"I think that he associates a sign to each sound in your name," Elna said, looking at Moira.

"Then he must have a sign for each sound in our language. How many are there? I never thought about that."

"May I?" Elna asked, pointing at both notes and pencil, and Vlad nodded, though he did not understand the words. She struggled to handle the pencil, then wrote an 'M' which was distorted, but intelligible. 'A' followed, and then she pushed the notes to Vlad. "Malva," she said, pointing at the girl, who smiled shyly. "We need an 'L'. L," she repeated, and waited until Vlad wrote the letter. "V," she said again, and Vlad wrote again. She took the notebook and the pencil and wrote the last letter: A. "Malva," she said, and imitating Vlad, she tapped over the word with the pencil.

"Malva," Vlad said too, wondering how they understood such an abstract thing as writing so quickly. *They are not savages. Why are they so different from the ones who killed...? Or maybe they are not so different in how they think of other people's lives.*

Something resurfaced in his mind: a discussion with uncle Geo, in his other life. He tried to remember what had triggered that discussion, but the reason stayed hidden.

"We are less intelligent than our Stone Age ancestors," his uncle, who was a world class anthropologist, said. "Our intelligence level peaked around six thousand years ago. Society continued to evolve, and we discovered many things."

"IQ has risen continuously," Vlad countered.

"Our measurements are flawed. We analyze the acquired level of knowledge more than the level of intelligence. Take a savage who doesn't know how to read and write. He will fail any of our tests, obviously. But, what if instead of logical or geometrical associations we try to measure his intelligence by using a natural situation? Something like: there are five trees and a lion in the position marked with A. You are at B. Find a way to escape. This kind of problem requires more parameters to analyze than a comparison between two geometrical figures. Time means a different thing too, it becomes part of the solution. In nature, if you don't solve the problem in time, you will never encounter another one. The lion will not allow it. Now, if you fail an examination, you still have the chance to try again and again. Even our motivations are different. With agriculture, the survival of the fittest no longer played the same role as before, and we lost both physical and intellectual capacities. The food chain played a role too; grains and milk products introduced a new level of inflammation in our bodies and that influenced the brain too. Some new things and their noxious byproducts in the body were able to pass the blood-brain barrier. It's not that we became stupid, and the development of society compensated for our loss. We are still producing marvelous things and concepts." He stared at Vlad, who was not convinced. "Let me show you a movie." He searched in his computer, and started a movie with a chimpanzee who was able to memorize a sequence of nine numbers in the range from 0 to 9 – a human operator was pressing the buttons at normal speed in a certain order in front of the chimpanzee – to open a safe containing a banana. There were five tests, and the animal passed all of them, opening the safe. "I tried myself," Geo said with a smile. "I was never able to reproduce more than six numbers, and my best student was able to remember only seven correct numbers. And that level of performance did not happen in all our tests. The chimp's attention and memory are superior to ours, and that specimen was not even a wild animal, he was born in a lab. One more example: in nature, the chimps are good hunters too. They have a better ratio of success than lions, which are well-known predators. It's the chimp's mind and capacity for planning which makes the difference. Our ancestors were far superior to the chimps; if not, we would be the subjects in the lab, and they the researchers."

Vlad was still not fully convinced, but did not want to upset his uncle. *I have to try it myself*, he thought.

"Come tomorrow to university. I will enjoy using you as my special guinea pig." Geo smiled, understanding what was now in Vlad's mind. All his students had a hard time believing that a chimp was better at performing a task requiring memory and attention. It was about two aspects of intelligence, after all.

In his first test, Vlad was able to memorize only five numbers. On the seventh, he memorized eight. Driven by stubbornness, he tried again and again, but he never improved on eight numbers.

"Time to stop," Geo said, and patted his shoulder, after twenty tests. "You fared better than any of my students, but you learned music from when you were only six years old. You have a better memory. All musicians have. But you luck motivation," he laughed. "You don't like bananas as much as the chimp does."

Vlad's mind returned to the present, and he wracked his brain, trying to say something that could be understood. He failed. Around him, the Vlahins had the same issue, and a long moment of silence fell between them.

"Girls," Moira finally said. "His mind is different, but you are bonded to Vlad. You have already realized that. I don't know how it happened, and why it happened so fast, but one of you will become his mate. Only the Mother knows which one, and it may take a year or two until you will make the right decision. Take care of him; teach him our language and," she raised her forefinger, "learn from him. His tribe is more developed than us or the Kalachs, in ways that we may not even be able to understand. Knowledge is power, and it will help us survive these troubled times. In a few years, the Kalachs will again try to destroy our village and take our lands. And women." She glanced at the girls, followed by Vlad's anxious stare, and they both nodded. Moira did not tell them about the Trance Dream she and Elna had had just a few days ago. It was too early; they needed to wait for the second man to appear, the one who was more powerful than Vlad and ready to become a shaman. "Now, let's eat. I am hungry."

The Vlahins had two classes of people able to navigate through the five Rivers of Thought and contact the Mother: the women were shamanes, and the men were shamans. There were few differences in the powers they possessed. Unfortunately for their society, the last shaman had died more than fifty years ago, and their disappearance was a mystery for most of the Vlahins. Only the twenty shamanes from the Amber Stone Ring knew the reason of the shamans' disappearance, and of a prophecy given to the Grand Shamane, almost two hundred years ago.

Malva and Selma turned toward Vlad, and rubbed his belly. "Flam?" they asked in one voice, bursting into laughter.

"Flam." Vlad laughed too, then wrote the word for hungry in his dictionary.

The hut belonging to Moira and Rune was the largest in the village, and even had two small rooms for guests, attached to the sides of the main room, which was a rectangular construction having walls made of wattle and plastered with red loam. A long time ago, the Vlahins had learned from the local swallows how to use loam to make better plaster. The intelligent birds were using it to harden their nests. The guests rooms were wicker work, built of osier and reed, and were separate from the main hut. They were small, only eight feet long and five feet wide, and had their own entrances, but no doors. At dusk, Rune fixed a large skin in the upper frame with two small ropes. He pointed, satisfied, at his work, and said the word for door. Vlad memorized it, but for him, the skin, covering only two-thirds of the entrance, could hardly be called a door, but he thanked Rune, who seemed happy, hearing the right Vlahin word for such an occasion.

Before entering, Vlad glanced up: an almost full moon lit the world from above. He saw it without acknowledging its existence. The shadows were lengthening with the twilight, and they stretched inside his mind. He shivered without knowing why. It was not from the cold. Sensing his hesitation, the girls pushed Vlad inside the room, and they pointed toward the bed, also made of osier. His bed was already prepared; they had cut some dry grass from the mountain slope behind the village. The fur of a large bear was used as linen.

Did they use that fur on purpose? Vlad wanted to know if this was a sign, a reminder of his fight with the bear, something related to his social status, but there was no easy way to ask such questions. *I may be able to ask later, when I learn their language.*

"Sleep," Selma said in Vlahin, and she put her palms together, leaning her head on them. Malva pointed at the bed.

"That's obvious; a bed," Vlad said, knowing they could not understand him. He wanted to talk; he needed to talk. With the coming of the night, unwanted memories were sneaking into his mind. He was afraid of them. The night before, he had been too tired and numb to care. After a few moments, a burst of nervous laughter escaped him, unnatural and almost strident, yet it seemed to be contagious, and the girls laughed too. He enjoyed their reaction, not knowing that – with their shamane's senses – they felt his uneasiness, without understanding what could cause it. While the girls were not yet initiated, they came from a long line of powerful shamanes. "But I will not sleep on that fur." He opened his backpack and took out the sleeping bag. "I know you don't understand me, but I will sleep in this thing. Sleep," he pronounced the Vlahin word.

The girls grabbed the bag, and their fingers felt the softness of the material. They touched it with the gentleness of a mother caressing her infant.

"Let me show you," he said, and unrolled the bag on the bed. Then he unzipped it. "I will sleep inside." He pointed at the opening, then he mimicked undressing and lying inside the bag.

As if they had received a signal, Malva started to pull up her hide dress. Vlad froze, his puzzled eyes following her movements, which revealed her thighs, then a light brown triangle, a flat belly, and perfect breasts that swung slightly when the dress freed them. Like all the Vlahin women, she had only a tanned deer skin made into a sort of dress going down to her knees. It had short sleeves, almost touching her elbows, and intricate patterns of circular painting that intrigued Vlad. They represented the five Rivers of Thought, connecting the Vlahins with the Mother, but there was no way for him to understand their philosophy without learning their language first. Knowing how to say 'I am Vlad' and 'this is my hand' was not enough. Trying not to ogle, he turned his head away, while Malva slipped inside his sleeping bag. Turning, his eyes met Selma's who, without fully understanding the reason, recorded his unusual reactions and, a moment later, her dress followed the same path, freeing her body. She slipped inside the bag too, followed by his eyes.

"Come," Malva said, laughing and gesturing at him to join them.

For them this is natural, Vlad thought. *I need to adapt. This is something normal*. He sat quickly on the edge of the bed, trying to hide his arousal. "There is not enough place for all three," he said, knowing that they would not understand. *It's just an innocent game.*

Malva grabbed his hand and tried to pull him inside the bag. Understanding that it was just a childish game, without sexual connotations, he resisted playfully, and

Selma joined her cousin in the fight against him. His reactions were mainly motivated by his fear of being alone, and he fully engaged in a game that his normal self would have considered foolish. His childhood had ended a few years ago, and the war had matured and hardened him even more. All worries left him. He twisted away from their hands, immobilized Selma's legs inside the bag and moved to close it. She laughed, realizing that the bag was now half closed in a way she could not understand. Trying to escape, she moved slow and soft, giving him enough time to push her upper body fully inside the bag too. He moved again to close it, but this time Selma was faster, and contorting her body, she sneaked her left leg out of the bag, forcing him to push it back again. After two minutes of wrestling, both girls were now enclosed inside, only their heads still out. From time to time, a leg or a hand or just a finger pushed up through the canvas of the bag, which changed shape constantly, resembling a giant amoeba. With one hand, he kept the bag tight around their necks, so they could not escape. Not that they wanted to. From time to time, one of his fingers pushed into the bag, finding their ribs, and laughter filled the room.

Moira's head sneaked inside, and she entered, followed by Rune. "I thought that a horde of Kalachs had invaded the village."

"He is torturing us," Malva laughed. "Bad man," she finally said some words that Vlad could understand, pointing at him.

"Bad girls," Vlad retorted. He tried to add thieves, but the Vlahin word was still unknown to him. "My bag. Bad girls out." He tightened the bag around their necks and then released it, but he did not unzip it, testing their reactions.

Selma frowned for a few moments, then she realized that the small metallic thing, resembling a blade, was the key to opening the bag. Her wide eyes followed the sliding blade, opening the zipper. She moved it back and the zipper closed. Moira came closer, followed by Rune, both puzzled by the new thing. Six times, Selma's hand moved left and right, closing and opening the zipper. They understood the effect, but they couldn't work out the cause. After a while, she decided that there was nothing more to learn and slipped out of the bag, followed by Malva. Vlad eyed Rune, but he did not see any reaction on the man's face when the naked girls pushed him aside to recover their clothes from the floor. The zipper and the sleeping bag were more interesting.

They left the room, one by one, followed by his anxious eyes. Moira stared at him, her piercing eyes feeling his uneasiness, but she could not understand it. His mind was too strange for her, and she decided to allow things to follow their course. He wanted to say something, to ask them to stay longer, or even to stay with him overnight. He could not do it. Alone, Vlad tried to sleep, but sleep eluded him. A few flies and his own thoughts harassed him. After a few minutes of hunting, the room was free of its unwanted guests, and the physical activity seemed to keep his mind away from bad thoughts. For the first time, he looked at the walls, and found many holes in them, through which a mouse could sneak into the room. Moonlight filtered in too, patching the floor with faint spots of light. *This will wait for me each evening*; he shrugged. *I've slept in worse places during the war*; he shrugged again; the movement seeming to release some of his inner tension. He went back to his bag to sleep, but chasing his own thoughts away was a lot harder than swatting flies. *I am here and, barring some spectacular and improbable event, I will stay here. I have to learn to live here.* The repetition of 'here' annoyed him. He still wanted to be in a different 'here'. *I am here to stay*, he repeated, stubbornly. *They are Stone Age people, but not like the other ones who... I am at least that lucky. Cosmin wasn't.* His friend's face and fate resurfaced, and he curled inside his sleeping bag, biting his lip to stop a sob. *I can't change anything.* It took him a while to calm down and, strangely, he wanted to talk to Andrei's head, the only link to his lost world that now seemed so far away and unreachable.

"Andrei," he whispered. "I feel so lonely. I don't like to be alone. I am afraid."

He waited patiently, turning his head left and right, but the head stayed away. Instead of Andrei, the figures of his parents came to him – Vlad had an almost eidetic memory. Tears ran down his face. He cried silently, knowing that he probably would not see them again. It was late when he finally fell asleep and, in an unwanted turn, Andrei's head chased him through several nightmares during the night. It had two large and slightly curved teeth, seeming to belong to a saber-toothed tiger, and drops of blood dripped from them.

"A vampire tiger," Vlad moaned in his sleep. "What kind of world is this?"

Chapter 6 – Vlad

It is my third full day with the Vlahins and, despite my undeveloped senses, I feel some excitement filing the village. As usual, Malva and Selma come early in the morning to wake me up. They use the same method as on the days before, one of them tickling my face with her hair. I am a late bird, but there is no way to resist to such an insidious assault on my skin. It is Malva this time; yesterday, Selma woke me up, and the day before it was Malva again. This rotation still puzzles me, as I don't understand if there is a hidden meaning in it. Malva looks at me, and I know well what is in her mind; she likes the softness of my clothes. The Vlahins are good at tanning animal skins, but they can't compare with my cotton shirts. I play the game and pretend not to know what she wants. She shoves me with her shoulder, and I fall over the sleeping bag. Laughing, I take out a shirt from the place where I hid them, and lend it to her. She pulls the shirt over her head and dress. It's too big for her, and looks like a second, smaller dress. Her palms move over her waist, feeling the softness of the shirt. That only underlines her curves. Her movements are sensual, but not provocative. I doubt that they know the notion of being provocative. She is just playing for fun, and I have to cast aside almost everything I know about girls from my previous life.

"Come, eat," Malva says, using our short way of communication, as I am not yet able to speak or understand complex phrases. She pulls off my shirt and gives it to me, so I can dress.

"Language, first," I say, and ponder for a while how to learn about pronouns. "I," I finally say, pointing at me. "You," I point at Malva. "She," I point at Selma.

"Man, woman," Malva says, but I shake my head and repeat the pronouns, pointing again in the same specific way.

This time Malva does not hurry to answer, and both girls frown, then they speak to each other in low voices.

"I, you, she ...," Selma pronounces my words with a funny accent, making a long 'sh'. The following words don't mean anything to me, and she stops speaking, frustrated by my lack of knowledge. "I, you, she," Selma repeats. "Different words," she says after a brief pause. "I," she points to herself. "You," she points at me, and I nod. "Eo," she points at her. "Teo," she points at me. "Ea," she points at Malva. "En," she speaks to Malva, pointing at me. A threshold seems to be already passed and she puts her arm around Malva's shoulders. "Neo," she points at both of them, then she pushes Malva into my arms. "Veo," she points at us. She frowns, and I understand that she is struggling to find an example for 'they'. We need another person.

"Elna." I point at my backpack, thinking that if she understands what I mean, it will be confirmation that indeed she has taught me the pronouns and not something else.

The girls laugh, then Selma pushes Malva toward the backpack and she takes it in her arms. Their laugh is contagious, and takes me over too. "Ede," Selma points at Malva and the backpack, impersonating Elna. "Rune," Selma points again at the backpack still in Malva's arms, preparing for the masculine form of 'they'. "Edi," she says, gesturing at both girl and object.

She lifts her hands, and I understand that there are no more pronouns. It seems that, while they have gender, they don't have the neuter form for the third person singular or plural.

I repeat all the new words just to be sure and, when they nod, I write everything into my dictionary. For them, my accent seems to be as funny as is theirs when they speak a modern language.

After eating, we go to one of the meadows surrounding the village, as we did yesterday. This time, Rand is not joining us, and Malva stays close to me, while Selma keeps her distance. Yesterday, Selma stayed with me, and Malva was with Rand, only a few paces from us. We sit in the grass; Malva's shoulders are touching mine, and I feel the same expectation in her that I felt in Selma the day before, but I don't understand what they want from me. I wish to pass an arm around Malva's shoulders, but I know that she is Rand's girlfriend, and my position is too weak to challenge him on that. The strange thing is that I feel the same with Selma as I do with Malva. I hope that after a while the trouble in my mind will vanish, and I will start to act normally. It is not pleasant to understand that I am even more deranged than I acknowledged at first, but three days may be not such a long period of time. The mind has a tendency to heal slowly. Born from the bloody landing in this more than foreign place, my feelings are unnatural, and I want them to leave me, allowing something new with one of them, or with another girl. I am here to stay, to integrate, and that means having a family, at a certain point. For the moment, I feel as if my mind is conditioned by fear to search for human support, and the girls arrived when I was at my worst point, mourning and running from the savages who killed Cosmin. There is nothing normal in my feelings, and I wonder what would have happened if they were three or four girls instead of only two. *A harem*... I fight to stop a burst of laughter, just because I may upset Malva and Selma; they are too kind to deserve that. *I want to understand them better.*

I see Selma, rubbing her forehead in a meaningful way, as if she is trying to communicate something to me. Here yes lock with mine, but her gesture tells me nothing, though there is a clear expectation in her look. After a while, fed up with my lack of understanding, she turns to look at the valley. Less than a mile away, the Great River is glittering in the sun. For no particular reason, I am more and more convinced that it is the Danube, not the Tigris or Euphrates. *If this is Earth*... With a sudden thought, I open my notebook and count the words in my dictionary: there are more than three hundred already. If I am able to find some similarities with the Sanskrit or other Indo-

European languages, I may have the proof that I am on Earth and the Vlahins' land is north of the Danube. For all my efforts, I am able to remember only eleven Sanskrit words, not enough to make a statistical analysis.

Annoyed by my silence, Malva jumps up and leaves the meadow. With a reproachful look, Selma leaves me too. She signals loosely with her right hand, as if I should do something about Malva but, again, her gesture tells me nothing. I make a mental note that I must learn the meaning of the most common gestures too. In such hunter-gatherers communities a lot of everyday communication is done by hand or body signals. Alone, I repeat all the words in the dictionary twice, and I feel satisfied that I am able to remember each of them in a reasonable timeframe.

The sun is high now, and even though it's mid-spring, the warmth makes me feel lazy. *My last day on Earth was the fifteenth of April,* I can't stop thinking, but even if I am still on Earth why should I arrive here on the same calendar day? *Why not?* I shrug, and for the first time, I try to understand if there is a reason for my presence here, or if everything was just a kind of cosmic accident triggered by that missile hitting the top of the hill and the vortex in whose power I have started to believe. The word cosmic makes me laugh. *Why should I be so important for the universe?* My ruminations stir memories of Cosmin, and tears run down my face and, when my mind calms, I become annoyed for crying so often. I am a soldier after all, and I force myself to think of something else. I can't. At least, I am no longer sobbing, and Andrei doesn't come to bother me. I both fear and want that bloody head. It's the only 'person' from my previous life, and 'he' acts like someone from there, not from here. My desire is strange, as everything is in this new life. *I am sicker than I thought.* The new understanding passes through my mind like a burning arrow. It doesn't help.

Feeling movement in the corner of my eye, I realize that both girls are only a few paces from me. There is a touch of guilt in their stare, and they sit close to me, each of them taking one of my hands. I feel both relieved and ashamed, and again, I have no clue how to behave toward them. I choose to stay silent, and they don't speak either. After a while, the closeness becomes pleasant, and I am able to leave Cosmin's memory behind.

"Today, we have catamara," Malva finally speaks.

"Catamara?"

She starts to whistle, and it's clear that she is interpreting an unknown song. On my left, Selma is mimicking playing a flute, and she stands up and moves her hips in a rhythmic way. It looks like dancing.

"We offer the bear to the Mother, tonight. Your bear. River..."

I could not understand her last phrase, but her words stir some involuntary associations in my mind, and I start to sing Moon River. They are clearly delighted, and the moment I feel it, I can't remember the next verse, and stop abruptly. I still hum for a few moments. "Word?" I ask, and point at my mouth while I sing again.

"Cante," Malva says, and the name strikes me as being very close to the Latin languages.

I point at Selma and, without standing up, I move my legs as if I am dancing.

"Lune," Selma says their word for dancing, and does some more steps just to make me understand. This time, the word doesn't sound Latin at all. Her hand describes an arc over the sky, stopping at a certain angle. "Catamara starts ... sun..." She sees that I am unable to understand most of her words. "Starts... sun there," she says, pointing at some distance, in the sky, away from the highest peak, and I understand that the party will start in the afternoon. That makes me almost happy; my mind will have something to do other than going over awful memories or longing for so many lost people and things.

Chapter 7 – Vlad

It's too much for me: the infernal rhythm of their dances, the long sequence of dancing with no breaks between the pieces. My watch tells me I have been dancing for more than half an hour already. The others had been dancing for more than an hour, the girls included, and all of them look like they are just done with the warming up. The 'orchestra' consists of two women playing with a flute, and three men. Two of them have drums, the third one has both a flute and a large pouch of semi-rigid skin, which is filled with sand and small stones. When he is not playing the flute, he shakes the bag in time to the music. Both women and men have bracelets resembling castanets too. Exhausted, I barely manage to walk toward Moira's hut and then I collapse, leaning against the wall of my room. After ten minutes or so, Malva and Selma notice I've disappeared, and come after me.

It took them a long time to notice I'd vanished. I don't matter too much. No wonder, with my poor dancing skills.

"Dance," they say, standing in front of me, moving their hips in time to the music, their voices calm and smooth, as if they were not dancing like the devil only a few moments ago.

"Later."

"Now!" they shout, laughing and, grabbing my hands, trying to pull me up.

"Later," I repeat; nothing will persuade me to dance again, at least for a while.

The girls look disappointed but, in the end, they shrug and return to the mass of people still dancing in a frenzy that looks like madness to me. After another half an hour, both dancers and musicians finally take a break for some refreshments, yet it is clear, even to me, that the great feast featuring the bear meat will start later. The girls bring me something that looks like a burnt tuber. They show me how to peel it, and under that almost black crust appears something that looks edible, though I don't know what plant it is. I take a cautious first bite, but it tastes good, a little sweet, with a flavor that eludes me. They are eating the same thing, perhaps just to convince me that I will not be poisoned. *I may be poisoned by mistake*, I can't stop thinking. *Because my stomach may lack the right enzymes*. Usually, I am an optimistic guy, but this place and the way I arrived here always make me think the worst.

Selma points at the sun, on its path down behind the mountain. "Sun, one finger, mountain. Dance." She puts her finger in front of her eyes to make me understand how she measures time against the mountain.

Oh, no, I groan silently, calculating that I have less than half an hour before my next session of torture will start. *And I used to like dancing*.

"Dance," Malva says, her shoulder pushing against me. Her voice and gesture are both childish and amused, and she can't understand why I react like a tortured man.

If I don't dance, it's bad... If I dance, I may collapse and I will be the laughing stock of the whole clan. Maybe I can join the musicians. I remember that they liked it when I sang Moon River to them, in the morning, though my voice is not so good, but they don't know how Andy Williams sang the same song. I stand up, followed by their probing eyes. I enter and leave my room in silence, the thing I want to keep hidden resting in my left hand, behind me. "Close eyes." My right hand touches first Malva's then Selma's eyes. With broad smiles on their faces, they conform to my wish. To be sure that they can't see me, I stand in the doorway, while they sit on the floor, leaning against the wall. *How should I start? I know so many songs, and now my mind seems empty*. Nervously, I moisten my lips. Finally, I decide on Simon and Garfunkel's El Condor Pasa, and I purse my lips over the nai. Half of the first notes are wrong. *They can't know that*, I tell myself, but I take care to play quietly.

The girls jump to their feet and turn toward me. Their eyes are wide, and they are breathing fast, staring at me. I finally get into the song's rhythm, and the music flows through the village. Some heads appear from the hut nearby, and I stop playing. Malva takes the nai from my hand and press her lips to it. She knows how to play flute, but having twenty flutes in her hands is a different thing; still she manages to play some notes. Selma plays too but, instead of trying randomly, she takes one pipe after another, playing the whole range. She stops, with a pensive look, then tries again in reverse order, starting from the lowest note this time.

"Notebook stores words. This stores sounds," she says, still keeping the nai in her hand. Selma wants to say or to ask more, but she doesn't know how to cope with my limited vocabulary. Her fingers caress the wood of the nai gently.

"Name is nai," I say in my rudimentary language.

Malva sees Moira and Elna some distance away and hustles toward them. She speaks and gesticulates as if she is being attacked by a swarm of savage African bees. It is more than enough to convince the two shamanes that something special has happened. *I am done with the dancing*, I encourage myself.

Selma plays the scale again, starting from the lowest note, and the nai passes from her to Moira and to Elna. After a while, it returns to me.

"Play," both girls say in one voice, like they are twins.

I start The Sound of Silence again. There are no false notes this time, and finishing it properly makes me feel proud.

"Dance," Moira says, and I freeze, thinking that she wants me to dance again, but she points at the nai. "Nai ... dance."

Does she want me to play something faster? Reluctantly, I play a new song.

"Faster." Moira's hand gestures left and right, as if trying to give me the proper rhythm.

I offer several choices, but she discards all the pop or rock music samples. It takes her no more than ten to fifteen seconds to decide, and her hand makes a swift gesture that I interpret as being 'next'. Reconsidering their dances, I feel the need to slap myself. They resemble some folk dances I know, but I am not a real fan of that music and I know only a few tunes, almost all of them Romanian. Despite my worries, this time she selects two *hora* and *sarba* dances from the county where my grandparents live. The Old Man's Sarba and Sarba of the Fireman, are quite popular in their modern, but isolated, village in the middle of the mountains. I remember an Irish dance, and Moira chooses that too. The name of the dance eludes me. "Ireland," I say when she insists on knowing the name. My folk repertoire ends and, lost for choices, I try Hora Staccato. Moira says yes in less than five seconds. My next choice, Brahms, the Hungarian Dance no. 5. is accepted fast too, and this time she seems to think that there are enough dances for that evening. Her last two choices of classical music are puzzling me, but I don't complain, and actually classical composers were always trying to get the essence of music in their compositions. Moira might belong to the Stone Age, but I start to realize even more that, as a shamane, she must be an intelligent woman with a high capacity for abstraction. There must also be some degree of sophistication in their culture that I may be able to learn about later.

"River Dance...," Moira says, but I don't understand the words that follow.

Selma whistles El Condor Pasa, and I start to play it, though I don't understand the association Moira has made with the word 'river'. I see both Moira and Elna frowning, like they are not convinced by my music.

Pretentious audience... Mechanically, I switch to an ancient folk version I heard, some time ago, in the Aconcagua Valley, at a winery which provided both food and local music, part of their Musica des los Andes concert. For some strange reason, both the song and the taste of the Carmenere Wine are fresh in my mind, and I sigh, thinking that I will never taste wine again. The climate seems to be too cold to allow vines to grow, if such plants grow on this world which may or may not be Earth. I try to remember the name of the winery, but I fail. It's like my previous life is slipping away from me, and I play some false notes again. It doesn't matter, the new version of the song has convinced them and, anyway, they don't know that I made a mistake.

"River Dance...," Moira says, followed by the same unintelligible words as before. "Song name?" she asks, using a limited vocabulary this time.

"Condor." It makes no sense to use the whole name.

"What means condor?"

"Big bird." I make a sign on the ground, then I walk twenty feet and make another sign. I spread my arms like wings, then I point at the distance marked on the floor. Their eyes widen, but none of them comment.

"Good name, condor," Elna says, still wondering about the size of the bird they have never seen and never will. It seems that her inquisitive mind has found an association between the song and a bird she doesn't know. I want to know what she thinks, how she made that association, but how can I ask?

After making me play almost twenty melodies, Moira settles for Gabriel's Oboe song from The Mission movie, a piece written by Enyo Morricone, Zamfir's The Lonely

Shepherd and the overture of Enesco's Romanian Rhapsody No. 1 in A major. All of them work well on a nai.

"Condor, Gabriel, Shepherd, Rhapsody." Moira repeats, at the end, the names I gave to her. "Dance." She gestures at me, then at the place where the clan's singers have gathered again, properly refreshed. We walk together, and Moira speaks to the five musicians. I understand nothing. "One song," she gestures at the band of five. "One song," she gestures at me, her hand almost invisible against the yellow ball of fire looming over the horizon.

Yes, ma'am, I agree inside with a smile.

We start to sing, and people dance under a sun changing its colors to hues of orange, and then almost tangerine. When the dance session finally ends, one of the singers plays a long pattern on his drum. It comes in short and loud bursts of sounds, very similar to the medieval habit of using the drum before an important announcement is made, and the people gather around him.

Rune stands tall on a stone, so he can be seen by everybody. For a while, he remains silent, all eyes on him. He looks bored, and tension roses into the crowd. "Bear!" he finally shouts, pointing at me, and a cacophony of cheerful cries burst out. Rune gives a small speech, that is lost in the noise, and anyway I could not understand, but this I know at least: the steak is finally ready.

While the last sunshine is vanishing behind the mountain, the sky is fading to a radiant rose, but the mists that covers the waters of the Great River resemble a patch of quicksilver. Walking slowly, women and men gather again in a place that looks like a reversed Greek amphitheater. Elna comes and signals me to follow her. The girls come with us too, and we walk toward the top of the amphitheater. There is a bench, ten feet long, three feet wide, carved in the stone of the mountain, and Elna sits on it, inviting me to do the same. There are five concentric circle engraved in the middle of the bench, similar with the motif painted on their clothes. Their meaning still eludes me. The girls join us.

"Vlahins know you sing," Elna forces herself to use a limited vocabulary. "They trust ... you play." There is a word I don't understand, but everything is now clear: playing for the dancers was a step to gaining acceptance into the clan. I suppose that it's only a first step, but I keep the comment to myself.

Trust for what? I wonder. Even if I wanted to ask what for, I am sure that they would not understand my question or I would not understand their explanation or both. It's the end of the day, but I feel it like dawn and a new beginning. It comes to me that both twilight phenomena are, in fact, symmetric events on opposite sides of midnight, a cycle of endless creation and destruction, an Ouroboros.

"Now River Dance ...," Elna speaks again. I recognize the strange words following 'river' only because Moira said them twice before, but who knows what they mean? It must be something difficult to explain, as Elna doesn't even try. "River ... important ... Vlahins." She touches her forehead, but I have no idea what that means. Mechanically, I imitate her, but she ignores my gesture; it's clear that she doesn't expect me to understand, and the thought, that for them I am an ignorant savage, comes to me. I struggle to stifle the smile spreading on my lips; Elna seems to be really serious. "Order is important .... River Dance..." She stares at me, as if trying to imprint her words in my mind, the ones I understand, at least. "Gabriel," she looks again at me. "Shepherd, Rhapsody, Condor. Condor ... very important."

"Gabriel, Shepherd, Rhapsody, Condor," I repeat after her, just because of that seriousness in her voice, in her stare.

Moira and Rune join us too, while below, in the lower part of the amphitheater, people start to gather, forming four semicircular rows. The first row is only sixty paces from us. It's difficult to count, but there seem to be more than two hundred people down there, children included, and the children seem to be at least nine or ten years old. I don't see any toddlers, though I know that there are many in the village. Moira looks briefly at me, and under her studied calm, I feel a degree of anxiety. Then she glances at Elna, who nods slightly, as if she has more confidence in me.

What is so important? I wonder, then I remember from Eliade's History of Religions – a book my uncle forced me to read several times, as he thought that I had too much free time, though I never understood why he believed such a thing – that gatherings like this were used to make people feel closer to their gods. A spiritual communion. We could be wrong, of course; while some prehistoric cult objects have survived the vicissitudes of time, they came to us without a user manual. Deciphering what our ancestors thought or did in rituals is half science, half an exercise of wild imagination, and notoriously tricky. Once, some history students and I even tried to use mushroom powder to reenact a shamanic ritual we found in an old esoteric book. It was a Siberian ritual, and all we got was a bad headache, which felt far from spiritual. The pain was not enough to connect us with the magical world, and we did not try again. My uncle tried to make me study history at university, but I was a practical man, and all my childhood I had dreamed of flying. When I was still in secondary school, I enjoyed his summer camps in isolated and exotic places, and with my music skills, I received a fair share of the female students' attention, though I was two or three years younger. It was pleasant, but not enough to change my dreams. Flying filled people's mind long before we invented history and historians, even if I count Homer as being the first one.

Twenty paces in front of our bench, there are two, poles, nine feet tall, stuck into the ground inside a circle eight feet wide, which is marked with two circular rows of white and red stones, the size of a child's head. Two women come and set four fires around the circle, then put torches in sconces carved into the poles. Many details I observe only because someone involuntarily attracts my attention to them. From the geography of the place, the fires mark the four cardinal points, and the people are sitting south of us. The arrangement must have some esoteric importance to them, something like the axis mundi, but I have no way to be sure if they have such a notion. 'One of the worst mistake an anthropologist can make is to impose his own cultural habits when trying to understand another culture', my uncle used to say. Even if it is wrong, the association stirs my mind and, for the first time, I think that I should have chosen history as my field of study. While it's more interesting, knowing how to build rockets is not particularly useful now. Shamanism and mystery, not science, are flowing around me. *I should make some notes for my uncle.* Deep in my mind, a small part of me still has some trace of hope for a return to the civilized world. *I may even write a book and become famous. If I survive the war.* If I do return, the main issue is not to make notes, but to make my eventual readers believe me. For this kind of knowledge, according to my uncle, people do one of two things when they discover information that doesn't fit their interpretation of something that might or might not have happened many millennia ago. They ignore or even attack everything which doesn't fit into their beloved theories, or they become believers. The latter is less likely to happen. 'Science advances through funerals,' was one of my uncle's favorite quotes. The quote belongs to a famous physicist, I think, but it applies to any field of study, or so my uncle believed.

Silent and solemn, Moira steps inside the circle, and raises her arms. Her gesture is fluid, and there is a strange elegance in it that fully captures my attention. She resembles a prehistoric Pythia, keeping in balance the fate of the world. Her head is tilted toward the last vestiges of the sunset and the faintly glowing evening star. Like it's been cut by a knife, all the noise stops in the amphitheater. It's not yet fully dark, but this is the part of the day when the world falls asleep, and an almost unnatural silence settles around us. The air between the poles shimmers for a few seconds, like in a high voltage lamp, causing me to shiver involuntarily and raising the hairs on my arms. It must be just a figment of my imagination, but it brings to mind a scene from the movie

Metropolis, and I shake my head. *I am no longer there. I am here.* Selma slides her palm over mine, making even more hairs rise on my arm, for a different reason though, and I smile at her. It's an automatic gesture, perhaps more a grin than a genuine smile. She smiles back, and she is genuine. *Of course*, I complain inside. *Nothing is new to her. Nothing is as exciting to her as it is to me. Or strange.* The last thought tilts me in the right direction, and those unruly hairs calm down.

Elna knees behind me, and it's strange how well I feel that without seeing her moving. "Fear not," she says gently. Her hand sneaks under my shirt, along my spine, and a brief shiver passes through me. "Fear not," she repeats, and her warm palm settles at the base of my neck, bringing even more shivers.

What an irony, I think, *warmth makes me shiver*.

An undercurrent passes between her and my skin and, even stranger, I have the same sensation as when the doctor places a cupping glass on your skin to massage your back. Inside the circle, Moira still stands, arms aloft. She looks like an antique statue, and an invisible power seems to surge from her stance. "Sing now," Elna urges me, a slight tension surfacing in her voice.

The first notes of Gabriel's Oboe start to flow, going down the hill, and I almost have the physical sensation of feeling the sound waves moving through the air. Below, the people start to absorb the music and move slowly, left to right, like synchronized dancers. One row of people is leaning to the right, the next row to the left. They resemble the blades of a giant scissors. It looks so mystical, and I wonder; if this sensation passes through my mind, what kind of feelings are born in their minds, which are accustomed to living in a world of supernatural things? As if by its own will, the music flows further, silencing my thoughts, spreading over the valley. It engulfs me, and I am now alone with my nai. A peculiar sensation, that the night doesn't follow twilight as quickly as the previous day, floats around me, but I don't have the right mindset to search for an explanation; it's a perfect time to enjoy and wonder, not to think.

"Close your eyes," Elna whispers in my ear, and I obey, instantly. "Feel the First River of Thought coming to you."

I understand her words, though the true understanding will come to me only the next day. Something emanates from her palm and spreads into my skin, going up my spine, into the cerebellum, the oldest part of the human brain, transporting me into a timeless existence. All the pain I suffered is gone. All the hurt I've felt vanished. Everything. The feeling is acute, both pleasant and demanding, without being overwhelming. It spreads into my skull, and I have the impression of it flowing into my mouth and on into my nai, being released with each note into the valley. That strange flow becomes visible to my closed eyes, spreading like tendrils of white mist, surrounding Moira. Her body captures them, in a whirlpool of mist and, now, the mist is a light blue so pale it is almost white. It forms a shroud that clings to her, and she is dancing, hypnotic, feline. Like an afterthought, the mist follows her undulations. *She is trying to capture and amplify the blue-white mist,* I suddenly realize, and I start to doubt that my mind is functioning properly. *It hasn't functioned properly since I got here*. The tendrils grow stronger and stronger, flowing down from Moira, slow and serpentine, toward the people's torsos, moving left and right, in the same rhythm as the Shamane. The flow resembles a white river.

"Feel the people," Elna whispers and, as if a bandage is taken from my eyes, I see them differently: small red flames absorbing the faint blue tendrils from Moira. My eyes are still closed. In less than a minute, the lower part of the amphitheater looks like a net of almost white strings, each intersection centered round someone's head. I feel connected to them in a way that I can't understand. "The Mother's Web." Elna enlightens me.

Without a break, I start to play the Lonely Shepherd; my inner eye is eager to see if something changes in the strange world that was hidden from me until now. There are no changes and, when the time comes, I start to the Romanian Rhapsody.

"Breathe now," Elna whispers, just before I am ready to start El Condor Pasa and, for the first time, I see changes in the vision before me. Moira now looks like being made of light, though I am able to see even the smallest detail of her skin. She undresses, and starts to dance naked, without music, her body swaying left and right. The people, down in the amphitheater, imitate her, as if hypnotized by a female version of Ka, the python from Kipling's The Jungle's Book. "Play for the River Dance," Elna whispers and, note by note, the condor takes life from my nai and flies majestically over the valley. There is such force in the music, and I finally understand Moira's choice. "Be ready," Elna says.

Before I know what to be ready for, a shock moves through my brain.

"You are now inside the Second River of Thought," Elna whispers, I and hear her not in my ear, but directly in my

brain, and I feel her like a physical presence inside me. Strangely, I don't feel afraid of that trespassing. *"Few people can reach the Second River. Learn to fly."*

Instinctively, some part of me rises a few feet above my head, and I gather everything: the girls, Elna, even though she is behind me, Moira, Rune and the people in front of me. My song continues, as if there are two versions of me, acting in a separate, yet interlinked way. It's fully dark now, but I see everything with disconcerting clarity.

With the last note, silence falls around us, and no one moves. The light recedes from the people, flowing back to Moira, and then it vanishes. I see Moira breathing heavily and collapsing in Rune's arms. She looks exhausted, but neither Rune nor Elna seems to be worried. The part of me levitating three feet above my head still sees everything with a strange clarity, through the darkness.

"Come back," Elna whispers, and I feel her mind intermingling with mine, teaching me how to control that second me. "Now fly again," she says when I am whole again. I obey, and the second me flies above my head again. "Come back." This time she is doesn't help me, and I struggle to return the part that now seems to like acting independently from me. "Be gentle. That part is you." Guided by her whispers, it takes me a minute to accomplish the task. Alone. "Open your eyes."

Rune brings Moira to me. She is still breathing heavily, in the faint light of the torches. "Thank you," she says, and Rune moves down the hill, keeping her in his arms.

Thin light is passing through the clouds, hovering over a world that I have barely started to understand. The source is clearly a natural satellite, and I crave to see it. Its shape may clarify where I am now. My will is split in two. I would be less afraid if the invisible moon proves this is Earth, but it would be more exciting to see an unknown celestial body. Walking back, I try to understand what happened to me during the River Dance.

There may be something out there, something that is conscious and intelligent, listening to us, and Moira seems able to transport us into that hidden world. *Shamane*... the word starts to have a different meaning to me, and I feel like a storm is ready to break out in my mind. But it could be just a dream, one of the many strange dreams I have had in a brief period of time. *Even my presence here may just be a dream. A strange, long dream, the result of a traumatic coma.* Back in my room, I sit on the edge of the bed, head in hands.

"That was not a bad performance." Andrei's voice fills the room, seeming to come from the door, and it seems so real, as if there is a person or a loudspeaker there. I refuse to raise my head. It doesn't matter; the Head appears between my knees, staring up at me. He always finds a way to stare right into my eyes, and from that moment, I decided to name it the Head instead of Andrei's head; it was easier to keep some distance from my friend's horrible death. Sometimes, it doesn't work, and Andrei's head still fills my memory. "You could make good money, playing here."

"Money?"

"Just a generic term for civilized people like us. Here it's about food, skins and women. Whatever you want, in whatever order you want. Only alcohol is missing. Those two girls look good. What are you waiting for? We need some distraction. Play for them, and they will not refuse to please you in bed. Your sleeping bag is made for fun and for two."

This is strange. I never think like this. How can my unconscious mind be so different and so ... conscious of carnal pleasures...? It's trying to steer me in the wrong direction. Is this a test? "Are we so civilized? I see a floating head of a man who... Well, who died in a war started by civilized people, in another timeline, or on another planet, and even though he's dead he doesn't..."

"Beethoven, Mozart, Pink Floyd, Michelangelo, Shakespeare, Confucius. Wars and theft created them. The first astronomic observatory was made possible only by wars and theft. The shamans, wizards, priests or however you want to call them, needed food, clothes and shelter. This is how we started on the road to progress, by killing and robbing other people, so we could grow stronger, wiser and richer."

"And this is how you ended." I pointed at the severed head. "Quite a wise end."

"It happens, sometimes," he said and pouted like a child. "How do you feel?"

"Strange. I am talking to a floating head."

The Head rolls his eyes, but stays silent.

"I don't know if seeing you is different from leaving my own body with Elna's help. Was it a hallucination, what happened in the amphitheater? What is the River Dance?" Strangely, I am waiting for the Head to confirm that I really had an out of body experience, and that there is something there; I don't know where, I don't know what. Around or above. Everywhere. Something that Moira helped me to connect with.

"Does it matter?"

"I guess it does."

"Why?"

"It's the difference between Moira tricking their minds and mine into a collective hallucination and Moira helping them... Well helping them to see something I don't yet understand."

"Ah, the Rivers of Thought, connecting people with a higher intelligence. The Mother and her intelligent web. You need to sleep." The Head looks visibly bored by my ruminations and he vanishes. My strange thoughts are here to stay.

Why did he mention an intelligent field? My mind is moving hieratically from one piece of knowledge to another, and Penrose's theory of quantum consciousness comes to me.

That may fit, even though no one actually proved it. If I am to believe in coincidences, the simple fact that I remember that theory, after the River Dance, could make it the real thing. There is something out there. Or maybe not. I stand up abruptly and pace around the room, rubbing my chin. *I need to learn their language faster. It may take a while until I can talk philosophy with them.*

Chapter 8

Moira woke up late that morning, the humming of the previous night still vivid in her mind. *I've never had such a high level Communion*, she thought. *There is something strange about Vlad and his music. We already know that his mind is strange, neither Vlahin, nor Kalach.* She stood up, dressed and went out of the hut, to be greeted by a bright sun, its disc half visible over the mountains. *When was the last time I woke up after the sun*? She mused, smiling wanly. *I am hungry*. She turned and found Rune and Elna eating at the main table, outside the hut. "Who gave you the right to eat without me? I will curse you if there is nothing good left."

"Leftovers," Rune said, without stopping to chew. "Bear, rabbit. There is no more deer meat."

"Fish?" Moira asked, a trace of hope in her voice.

"That was the first thing we ran out of yesterday," Elna laughed.

"Bear then. It tastes better knowing that the animal tried to eat Malva. Where is she?"

"Sleeping, with Selma. They woke up some time ago; checked to see if Vlad was awake, and went to sleep again. I never knew anyone to sleep as late as Vlad." Elna's laughter filled the place. "He is a bad example for the girls."

"He is a late bird. Through the wall, I can hear him catching flies, late in the evening. Someone should teach him how to hunt. He makes way too much noise for a simple fly. I still wonder how he managed to kill that bear. He doesn't look like a hunter." Moira took a piece of meat, but she did not start to eat.

"His people may look different," Rune said. "But there is strength in him, or certainly determination. I've never sat on a life bear's back. You need a big heart to stick a knife into a bear's ribs, and then take a trip on his back. He did all that for a few strangers."

"Big heart, indeed, and there is kindness in him too. I have a feeling that he likes children," Moira said. "And he likes music too. His skills are a good addition to our clan."

"And the Communion?" Elna asked, amused.

"I may be wrong, but I felt six Amber Stones, yesterday evening, during the River Dance," Rune said, thoughtfully. He was not a shaman, but he had the Shaman Seed. With proper training, Rune could have reached three and a half Amber Stones, but there was no shaman left alive to initiate him and, anyway, he was too old now. If it was not done at the proper age, people could die during the initiation process. The brain was no longer flexible enough to accept the changes. The Vlahins knew that girls could become shamanes before the age of twenty. For men, the threshold was twenty-one.

"You are right," Moira said, still not eating. "This was the strongest Communion I've ever led, and our people are happier. There were too many minds for me to link with during the Communion, but I had the feeling that Vlad entered the Second River of Thought."

"Yes." Elna closed her eyes for a few moments, trying to recollect her interaction with Vlad during the Condor song. "His second self drifted away. He struggled a little to get back, but I helped him."

"He must have the Shaman Seed. But I can't feel it." Frustration filled Moira's voice; she still hadn't eaten anything.

"Eat," Rune said, gently. "Food helps you think."

"I don't feel Vlad's seed either. But," Elna raised her forefinger, "we've already agreed that his mind is different, so his Shaman Seed may be different too."

"But I can feel the Shaman Seed in the Kalachs, and they are different too. I know, I know," Moira raised the hand that was not occupied with the steak, "Vlad's mind is even more different than the Kalachs'. More different than everything we know, and more complex. I don't care that he is different; I am just frustrated that I can't understand him better. We need him, and we need the second man the Mother promised us too. That bearded man is the strongest one, and if Vlad is so ... strange..." Her voice trailed off; she was not yet able to grasp all the implications.

"I had an uncomfortable premonition," Elna said. "In that brief period of time, when I entered the Third River of Thought, I saw both of them. They were together, and they were dressed the same way, in those skins that are so soft and strange. And both had a backpack. We must talk about that when Vlad learns our language."

"He is advancing fast," Rune said, tentatively.

"Yet not fast enough," Elna shrugged. "We need to know."

"I may need to make a High Communion with Vlad," Moira said, and finally taking a bite of the chunk of meat impaled by her stone tool. "After he learns our language," she said after a while, impatience filling her voice. "That thing with storing words on ... paper," she struggled to remember the name, "looks ... important to me, though I am not yet sure why. It's just a feeling."

"If he can teach us how to make paper, we can store memories. It's made from a plant, if I understood him, not from skin. Who knows if that plant grows here? The girls told me that he stored words in both languages with the same signs. The sounds seems to be similar, so we may be able to learn the signs too," Elna said, and paused; something was bothering her. "Yesterday, I saw him looking at pottery. He tapped some of the pots, listened to the sound they made. He did not look surprised. Maybe he knows how the Kalach make it. It costs a lot of furs to buy pottery from them."

"He can probably do things for the Mother's House but, after he learns our language, he must join the hunters too. No one can hunt without understanding the commands. It's dangerous." There was some melancholy in Rune's voice; he could no longer hunt. He was once the Chief of the hunters, but the wound he suffered, in the last battle against the Kalachs, ended that. At least he was lucky enough to survive; Elna's mate was killed in the same fight. "If we take into account the music part, he may spend half of the time doing things for the House." He looked at Moira, who nodded. It was unusual for a man to spend so much time in the Mother's House, working with Moira and Elna for the spiritual good of the tribe, but they had never seen a more unusual man.

Vlad woke up late, to find there was no one in front of the hut. *I was expecting Selma*, he thought, and glanced up at the sky. *It's noon*. He still didn't understand why the girls took care of him by rotation, but that was not his worst worry. From the moment he woke, memories from the night before assailed him, and he chose to ignore them. Too many strange things had happened during the night, and he wanted to distance his mind. There was time enough to think of them later. Leaving the room, he went on Moira's terrace, and found three bowls on the table, one of them covered, the other two empty: one large and one small one. *Steak*, he sniffed. *Would that be for me?* His stomach grumbled, reminding him that his last meal was almost a day ago, before he played for the dancers. *Better wait for someone, to tell me what I can eat.* Unconsciously, he tightened his belt, then sat at the table. The empty bowls attracted his attention, and he pulled the larger one closer. *Coiling and earthenware technique. They know to make kilns. The color is not uniform. It may be that they used pit firing or a kiln with only one chamber.* His finger followed the small grooves in the surface; they looked like a spiral. The walls of the bowl were hard. The small one was different. *Pinch and pit firing technique. Why use this technique when the other one produces pottery of better quality? Maybe because it's cheaper to create earthenware.* His stomach grumbled again. *Where is everybody?* He turned, looking for a familiar face, and saw Elna walking toward him. Her eyes were fixed on the small bowl in his hands. *What's wrong?* Carefully, he put the bowl back on the table.

Elna sat across the table from and smiled. That calmed him.

Beginnings are always difficult, especially when such different cultures are involved. "Flam." He smiled sheepishly, and rubbed his stomach.

Surprised, Elna pushed the covered bowl toward him. "For you."

"Not know," he said, in his rudimentary Vlahin, and took a piece of steak from the bowl. Bear. *I ate this yesterday too. It's not bad, but I wish I could have some potato puree, tomato salad and a bottle of Feteasca wine. But that won't happen.* He bit off a large chunk and forced himself to chew well before swallowing it.

"You can eat whatever food you find on this table." She smiled, seeing his hunger, then realized that he could not understand. "Food here." She tapped on the table. "Vlad eat. No ask."

"Thank you," he said, still chewing, and she remained silent until he had finished. Now in a much better mood, Vlad remembered her staring when he was analyzing the small bowl. "Bowl?" He pointed again at it.

Elna stretched out her hand, and pushed the empty bowls in front of him, and moved to his side of the table. They looked at each other, and laughed. Neither knew how to say what was needed so the other would understand.

Vlad tapped the large bowl. "Good." Then he did the same on the small one. "Bad." Elna nodded. "Who?" He pointed at both bowls.

"Kalach." She followed his lead and pointed at the large bowl. "Vlahin." She pointed to the other one, but she could not say that it was made by another Vlahin clan, dwelling in the north western plain. Here, they were specialized in tanning and wood carving.

I should have keep my mouth shut and not said that the small bowl is bad. How could I know that it was made here? It seems the Kalachs are more advanced. They were the ones who killed Cosmin. But then, the Vlahins may be just as violent. I must be more careful. What should I say now?

With her shamane's senses, Elna felt his fear. *Why is he afraid? How can I tell that we were waiting for him? That the Mother sent him to help us? That we are in debt because he saved three of our children?* She placed her hand over his. "Vlad, friend," she said and smiled at him and, relieved, he smiled back, without really understanding why she had reacted that way. Elna touched the large bowl, looking at him again. *How should I ask if he knows how to make it? Maybe is too early for such talk.* Yet curiosity and need pushed her to try. She repeated the names, pointing at the respective bowls, then she pointed at him. "Vlad?"

Me what? Is she asking what kind of pottery my people have? "Vlad," he said, and pointed at both bowls. *Of course we can make them, though only academics would try to produce such relics.*

Elna's eyes enlarged for a moment. "Elna is Vlahin. Vlad?"

"Romanian."

"Vlad or Romanian?" she asked, pointing at the bowls.

She wants to know if I can produce them. The coiling technique is easy to master. To build a kiln may be more difficult. "Vlad."

"Would you make them for us?" she asked immediately, forgetting that he could not understand, but he deduced her wish from her expression.

"Yes."

She jumped up and ran inside Moira's hut, and for the next hour they had a dialog that was half speech and half mime, but it was somehow understood that he would produce pottery, sometime in the future.

In the evening, a weak wind from the south chased the clouds away, and Vlad saw the moon. This time, he felt more certain. *It resembles our Moon. I may be on Earth*, he thought, *nine or ten thousand years in the past. Or a parallel Earth. The latter would be slightly more plausible than time travel, but, I need more proof to be sure.* He laughed to himself. *How can I determine if a multiverse containing another Earth is more plausible than time travel? I may still be in a coma dream That's more plausible.*

Chapter 9

"Vlad isn't honoring the bond of the Mother," Selma said, her voice sad. One month had passed since his arrival in their village, and despite her hints, he had never taken the next step.

"Is this just with you or with both of you?" Elna asked.

"With both of us. Malva is upset too."

"Maybe their rituals are different. Are you in such a hurry?"

"It's not that I'm in a hurry, it's more that I feel rejected, even though the bond was not established in the proper way. It's almost one month since the Mother made the bond between us and Vlad."

"Selma," Elna said gently, "you can't reject what you don't know. Let me speak with him. He is fluent enough now in our language."

She caressed her daughter's hair, and went to find Vlad. He was with Malva, who was no less frustrated than

Selma, but it was her bond day, and she had to stay with Vlad. Elna observed the same disappointment boiling in Malva; she had seen evidence of it in recent days, but now it felt different. Her daughter was a patient girl, more so than Malva, and Elna could no longer ignore their distress. It would affect the young shamane apprentices, perhaps even hinder them from evolving to their real potential. And that was exactly what the shamanes feared. Year by year, the potential of the apprentices had decreased. Less than fifty years ago, there were plenty of shamanes with eight and nine Amber Stones. Now, there was only one, the Grand Shamane, the chief of the Amber Stone Ring. The loss of even half a stone was something that Elna could not bear to think about, for both her daughter and her niece; a young shamane's mind could easily be influenced by a bad bond.

"I need to kidnap this young man," Elna said, smiling at Malva, subtly raising the forefinger of her left hand. From Elna's silent gesture, and her tone and posture, Malva understood that something important was to be discussed, and she left without complaint.

Maybe they will discuss the Mother's bond, Malva thought, a sudden intuition coming to her.

"Do you know what a bond is?" Elna asked, when she and Vlad were alone.

"A link?" Vlad said, tentatively.

"A link, yes; but I am talking about the Mother's bond between a woman and a man."

"One woman and one man come together," Vlad said, without understanding what Elna wanted. "It's the way of life." *What's the Mother's bond?*

"What did you feel when you first met Malva?"

Does she feel that I acted strangely? I'm still acting strangely. No wonder, after what happened to me. He had hoped that, after a while, the strange feelings he had for Malva and Selma would vanish, but that had not happened. *She may think I'm crazy*.

"Vlad?"

"Fine," he said, avoiding to look at Elna. "I felt something strange for her. As if... As if I liked her. A lot. You have to remember that I had just got here, and I had been hunted by savag... by the Kalachs. I was not myself that day. In time, it will pass, and my mind will recover." *But who know when? I've been waiting for almost a month.*

"You were yourself. This is the bond I asked you about. And you also have a one with Selma."

"What does that mean?" Vlad asked, starting to think that maybe he was not mad, yet afraid of what complications the bond could bring.

"It's about amo."

"What is amo?"

"Mama amo bebe," Elna said the words for 'mother loves her child' and gestured like a mother cuddling her baby. She laced her arms around Vlad's neck, leaning her head against his shoulder. "Amo," she said again, her hand patting the left side of his chest. "Amo." This time she pated her chest. She stepped back and looked at him, a question in her eyes.

Vlad seemed to finally understand. "Elna amo Selma."

"Yes," Elna said, a smile spreading on her lips. "Amo. Now." She raised her forefinger. "Vlad amo Selma and Vlad amo Malva."

"No." He shook his head vehemently, and then realization came to him. "Yes," he said, sheepishly.

"Selma amo Vlad. Malva amo Vlad. These are the bonds."

"Vlad must mate with both Selma and Malva?" he asked, trying to figure out how he had come to this situation.

"No," Elna laughed. "Vlad mates only one of them."

"How do I choose?" Vlad asked, a sudden sadness filling his voice. Whatever he did, one of the girls would be affected by his choice.

"Mother helps her children choose. The girl is the one who chooses. That is the meaning of the bond." Elna wanted to tell him more, but she realized that it was difficult to make him understand when he lacked the cultural knowledge that a Vlahin starts to acquire soon after being born. And there were things for which she had no words to explain. Their language had no words to explain. Things that she knew at a subliminal level from her experience and training.

In modern people, things are similar, just at an unconscious level. A man sees a woman, and starts to flirt with her before he knows he's doing it. The woman encourages him too, without knowing it. Later, they act by volition. For the Vlahins, the bond appeared only in young people. The Kalach had it too, but at an inferior level, and their shamans were only able to access the First River of Thought consciously.

"I don't understand," Vlad said, shaking his head.

"You will. Let's have a first lesson about the Mother." Elna's palms touched his forehead gently, trying to soothe him, her thumbs moving in small circles. Then she pressed her brow to his.

Nothing came to Vlad for a full minute, and he began to feel impatient, but he did not dare move. The sudden spark took him by surprise, and he started, but Elna's hands kept him still and linked to her. The spark seemed to move freely through his brain, passing from one layer to another, starting from the oldest ones, the reptile parts, advancing slowly to each new layer evolution had added to the human brain. Then it vanished, and Elna released him. Unable to understand what had happened, he did not try to speak. There was a part of him which was curious to learn more, which wanted the spark to return, and there was a cautious part too, which felt relieved that the spark had vanished. His mind leaned toward caution, and he sighed, relieved it was over. But the force he had felt during the River Dance had acquired a new strength, and it now tumbled like a snowball rolling down a slope, growing. Deep inside him, in his primal unconscious mind, a small ripple began to move back and forth, releasing things that had remained dormant for a more than a hundred generations. Silent and slow, his primal mind was revolting against his neglect, against his previous life far from nature, sandwiched between steel and concrete. The storm was ready to rage inside Vlad, and none of them was aware of it, not even Elna.

"You have to acknowledge the bond. That's the man's task."

"How?"

"Like I just did. Lean your forehead on the girl's and let the sparks fly between you. There will be different sparks. More ... pleasant." Elna smiled, and without knowing, she sighed, relieved. Vlad was too caught in his inner world to see it.

I am not mad, Vlad thought, as relieved as Elna; he wanted to shout his joy to the world. *I am not mad.* His first impulse was to run after Malva and make the bond. He finally understood the uneasiness in both girls, and their subtle hints. But the spark Elna had ignited in his mind would not leave him alone, and it was late, anyway.

Back in his room, Vlad thought about what Elna called the River of Thought. He was less able than the Vlahins to feel the link with the Mother, through the Rivers, but he had other tools of comprehension: his knowledge, the result of many thousand years of evolution. Where the Vlahins could use their superior intuition, he could use the analytical tools of a technological civilization. *I need to review everything I know about shamans.* "Oh, uncle," he sighed, "I wish you were here. It would be easier for me to understand them, and you would be the happiest man in the world."

With an amused grin, he got up from his perch on the edge of his bed, raising his left hand. "Uncle, what do you think about the shamans?" He asked his hand with the same amused grin.

"They existed in some ancient cultures. Eliade wrote a lot about them. Some may exist even today, but I will not put my hand in the fire on that one. Most of them are charlatans."

"And the Mother?"

"This is all you can ask, after so many years of my teaching you? What is so important about that name?"

"Do you think that such an ... entity, whatever its name, may exist?"

"That's a good question, but I don't have a good answer. Yes, it *may* exist, but no one can prove it. Not even you, after ingesting those Siberian psychedelic mushrooms like they were candies. Don't do that again."

"Why? The shamans you are talking about must have some potions too. Wouldn't it be an interesting scientific experiment to use them?"

"Interesting for whom? Do you have any scientific tools to measure their effect on you? They must have developed some resistance to those substances. You might die from a dose that is benign for them."

"Fine, uncle," Vlad raised his arms. "I will not try it." *Or maybe just a little.*

That was worse than talking to me." The Head appeared in front of Vlad, in a strange position, like he was impaled by Vlad's left hand, the one which had impersonated his uncle. He looked like a puppet. Vlad shook his hand reflexively. "Stop. Doing. That," the Head said. "It hurts."

"I wish that were true. What do you want?"

"Mushrooms."

"If I die, you die."

"Are you sure?" The Head grinned. "So, you've learned about the bonds," he added before Vlad could answer. "And you think that you are sane. You feel better. It doesn't matter. What do you think about the bonds?"

"Strange but real."

"That's all?"

"Maybe they act like a handshake between two computers, the link made by modems, transferring the data before two people can start a conversation over the Internet."

"Who are the computers? What are the modems? What data is transferred? Think, man."

"Maybe the Rivers of Thought transfer ... thoughts. That would be the handshake. Still unconscious. The shamanes must be capable of conscious access. Elna seemed to be inside my mind during the River Dance. And the Mother's Web. What's that?"

"You think you are an intelligent, modern man, so you will call it an intelligent field."

"If this is Earth, why are ... weren't we able to feel ... what they feel?"

"Agriculture. Bad diet. Inflammation. Disengagement from nature. In that order. Only a few vestiges of your primal mind are still present in you. They may awaken soon. Think of that," the Head said and vanished.

Should I ask Elna if she can kill that annoying head? Maybe not. It's harmless. Sometimes, it's interesting. My unconscious mind seems to remember things that I thought I had forgotten. Bread is still difficult for us to assimilate. Today was a strange day.

The next day, after Vlad had honored his bond with the two girls, it was Selma's day, and Vlad was walking hand in hand with her. As on many other days, Malva and Rand joined them. Vlad did not much enjoy Rand's presence; he could feel something wicked in the young man, but he had no choice. If Selma and Malva found it normal, who was he to object? There was still a wellspring of guilt in his mind for taking so long to honor the 'bond of the Mother'. *Cultural obligations are the hardest to learn*, he thought. *Especially when they are so different from your own*. He knew more now, for sure, but he knew he had a lot more to learn. The Vlahins, he was slowly coming to realize, were deeply sophisticated people.

"Challenge!" Vlad heard Rand shouting, just beside him, and a little behind.

Vlad was still wondering what Rand meant when he felt a heavy punch to his stomach. He bent in pain, and a moment later, his knees buckled under a kick. He fell, face down, and Rand climbed on his back, his knee pinning Vlad to the ground. At the last moment, Vlad was able to twist his body, so Rand's knee would not press directly on his spine. The pain would have been sharper, and the situation dangerous. Vlad realized the young man wanted to inflict damage, and the spine was a weak point. His left hand immobilized behind his back, Vlad tried to turn his body more, but his long experience of combat told him that there was no way to escape. Like most of the Vlahin of his age, Rand was stronger and faster than him. His training in martial arts would make a difference, but they were useless right now. Vlad stopped struggling and lay still, waiting for Rand's next move.

"Do you yield?" Rand asked, louder than was necessary for Vlad to hear. People were already gathering around, attracted by the challenge. Unfortunately for both Vlad and them, it was already over.

"Yes," Vlad said, calmly. *What does this mean?* He asked himself. He knew nothing about challenges or the consequences of being defeated and yielding. *I hope he doesn't ask for my bayonet.*

"I won the first challenge," Rand bragged, still holding Vlad down.

"Does that mean that I have to stay like this until nightfall?" Vlad asked. Actually, the loser was supposed be freed after yielding, but Rand planned some more humiliation.

"You won, let him go," Selma said.

"I will let him go when I am ready."

"That's not the rule."

"You are just a woman," Rand said, "and you have no say in a challenge. It's for men."

"All the Vlahins, men or women, have something to say in everything. Do you feel more of a man by keeping your opponent immobilized after he has yielded?"

"I feel like a winner," Rand grinned.

"And you talk like a Kalach," Selma retorted, her voice losing some of its calm.

"Respect the rules," one man said, and stepped forward, toward Rand. This time Rand obeyed, releasing Vlad, but he did it as slowly as he could.

"I don't know what this challenge is," Vlad said, rubbing his left wrist, "but you attacked me without warning."

"That was his right," the man said. "You are a hunter, and you must be always aware."

"I am not a hunter, and in my world a challenge must be acknowledged by your opponent."

"You are in our world," the man said.

"You are right, but that doesn't make Rand less of a coward. He only dared to attack me from behind. Let's have another challenge."

"Selma," the man said, sternly, "you must teach Vlad our way. He doesn't seem to know that only one challenge may happen in one day, and calling Rand a coward is as bad as Rand not releasing him after the yield."

"Come, Vlad," Selma said, nodding, ashamed, at the man, and pulled him by the hand.

"Why is Rand acting like this?" Vlad asked, when they were alone.

"I don't know, Vlad. There is animosity between you two, but that is not an excuse for Rand's behavior. Don't tell me you like Rand," Selma said, before he could protest. "And Selo was right; you need to learn the rules. It's my fault that you did not know about challenges."

"And mine." Malva had joined them. It was already late in the evening, and she had had enough of Rand's company.

They had arrived in front of Vlad's room, and both girls were wondering how to tell him more without causing even more bad feelings, though he was less affected than they thought. The girls were not aware of his real mood; they saw things as Vlahins, and knew that Rand's conduct was close to how the Kalachs behaved. He had been completely dismissive of women, and that disconcerted Malva. Reading on their faces that something bad had happened, Rune stood up from his table and came to them.

"Rand challenged Vlad," Selma said, answering Rune's mute question.

"That's not enough to make both of you look so angry." Rune gestured gently at the girls.

"Vlad didn't know about challenges. We forgot to teach him," Selma sighed, guiltily.

"It's not your fault," Vlad said, and gently squeezed her hand. "He attacked me without warning. I don't mind that I lost. If it was a fair challenge, or a real fight, he would lose."

"He has the right to surprise you," Rune said. "It helps to make you a better hunter. He was not breaking the rules."

"I am not a hunter," Vlad said. "And I don't want to be. If there is a war against the Kalachs, I will fight with you," he added quickly, seeing the worried expression on Rune's face.

"Rand did not release Vlad after he yielded." Selma thought for a moment, if she needed to say more. She decided to talk with her mother first. Independently, Malva made the same decision. There was more than a simple challenge in what had happened, and the implications could be more complicated than they thought.

"That's not our way." Rune rubbed his chin. "I will address this with Darin."

"I don't want this to..." Vlad tried to stop him.

"Rand will challenge you again," Rune cut in. "Everybody must respect the rules, and everybody must know the rules. Make sure that Vlad understands." He looked at the girls, then left them alone, returning at his table.

Rune was right. Over the next two days, Rand found ways to challenge Vlad again. Each time, the young Vlahin displayed the qualities of a hunter. He waited for Vlad patiently, hidden behind the huts. The whole village was already aware of the game, and people pretended not to see what was happening. They were enjoying the game, but each time they were disappointed at how fast Vlad morphed into easy prey. Rand sneaked up behind him, crying, "Challenge!" and kicking him down from behind.

He is not a hunter, people thought, and most of the aura Vlad had gained by killing a bear with only a knife, vanished as if it had never been. The thrill of the game faded, and most of them did not care what would happen next. They had already decided that Rand would win two more challenges and the bond between Malva and Vlad would shatter. The only one still not aware of that was Vlad.

The next day belonged to Malva, and they walked together. There was something in her that disconcerted Vlad. She stayed mostly silent, and though she did not voice her worries, Vlad guessed that something was wrong. He tried to make her laugh, but most of his jokes were not funny to a Vlahin. His rough knowledge of the language did not help either. They were now on top of a rock overlooking the valley; Vlad was relaxed, knowing that Rand was hunting that day – his one month punishment had expired. Not knowing what to do, he relied on physical arguments, and embraced her from behind, letting warmth spread between them.

"I should have brought the nai and played for you," he whispered. "Would you tell me why there are clouds behind your eyes?" He turned her slowly, and their eyes locked.

"It's nothing," Malva said.

"Why do I get the impression that this nothing is related to Rand and his stupid challenges? I don't care about them."

"They are not stupid." *If Rand wins two more times, our bond will shatter*, she wanted to tell him, but she couldn't. It was like the problem with 'honoring the bond of the Mother' all over again. Malva was not allowed to tell him what five wins in a row for Rand would mean.

Vlad finally sensed that there might be something serious under Malva's sadness, and had the vague intuition that it was related to the challenges. *I will ask Elna*, he thought. His hand moved slowly behind Malva's neck, and he pulled her closer. His lips searched for hers. She did not understand what was happening, but she did not reject him, and his mouth became more demanding, pressing. With her shamane's senses she came to understand what she wanted and, eventually, she started to like it. Slowly, Malva answered him and an undercurrent passed between them, puzzling her. It felt like a Communion, a low level one, but a Communion nevertheless, and she gasped, pulling back from him.

"I am sorry if that upset you," Vlad said, trying to hide his disappointment. *And I thought it would make her feel better. What was so wrong?*

"I am not upset." She laced her arms around his neck, and their lips touched again, in a longer kiss. "What is this?" Malva asked, when their lips finally parted.

"A way to feel you better." Vlad smiled, and his hand tugged at her hair.

"Is this how you make a Communion?"

"What's a Communion?"

"Two people share their mind in the Mother's Web. It's done through the five Rivers of Thought. Did you feel my mind?"

I felt your warm lips. "No. Was it unpleasant?"

"No." Malva smiled, a hint of a blush on her face, and her lips touched him briefly.

"We do this with the girl ... with the girl with whom we have a bond. One like you."

"Do it again," Malva whispered and closed her eyes. Feeling that her sadness had finally vanished, Vlad's lips curved into a smile, and he pressed them once more against hers, his hands running up and down her spine. He taught her all the delights of a hidden pleasure that would come to life some millennia later. Without him knowing, Malva tried to feel his mind again, but she was not Elna. Untrained, all she could get from Vlad's mind were a few sparks. Even less trained, Vlad felt nothing. After a while, she stopped trying, and abandoned herself to this unknown pleasure.

In the evening, Vlad looked for Elna, wanting to ask her if there were some links between his lost challenges and Malva's low mood. The way he had upset both girls, by not knowing that the man had to acknowledge the bond of the Mother, was still fresh in his mind. He did not think it was solely his fault, as someone else should have initiated him, but he had ignored the obvious signals of their distress. He had his own worries, but they were hidden in his own mind. Those belonging to the girls were on display each day he had met them, and that meant every day.

"So, you have your own way of making a Communion," Elna said, before he could ask anything.

"Was what happened between us in the River Dance a Communion?"

"Yes, there are several methods; it depends on what is needed at a certain time."

"Then," Vlad rubbed his chin. "It's not really a Communion, what we do in our ... clan. It's just a way that a woman and a man feel pleasure together."

"Some Communions are like this. The Higher Communion happens after a woman and a man make love. It opens many hidden channels between them," Moira said, and joined them.

"So the whole village knows about the new ... Communion," Vlad laughed.

"Not yet, but it will spread. From what I understand is a pleasant thing." Moira smiled, and didn't tell him that Malva would be the one to spread it. She had already taught Moira and Elna and, tomorrow, she would use her knowledge on Rand, and a day later, he would use it on his second bond, and his second bond would spread it further. Moira gave it less than a month until the whole village was indulging in the new way of relating to a partner, be it bond or mate. Malva had made very clear to her how pleasant it was, and she was waiting to test that with Rune during the night.

He left the shamanes forgetting to ask about the challenge, and two days later, Rand caught him by surprise again, and Vlad yielded again. Standing up, he saw Malva fighting against her tears. Grinning wickedly, Rand raised four fingers and turned away. Malva refused even to speak to Vlad and, for the first time, she left him alone on what was their bond day. He walked after her, but she ran away from him, hiding herself in Moira's house, and even Selma ignored him.

I forgot to ask Elna about the challenge. I hope I haven't caused some irreversible damage. I never saw Malva so upset. He could not find Elna, so he sat on the bench on her terrace, trying to understand what had happened. He saw Selma, but she ignored him and went to Moira's house too. It was only later, in the afternoon, that Elna came home.

She saw him wringing his hands and sat next to him on the bench. She remained quiet, waiting for him to speak first.

"What a challenge really is?" Vlad asked, his voice edgy.

"It may mean many things."

"That idiot, Rand, shouts 'challenge' behind me and attacks me a moment later. If he wants to fight..."

"That's a Bond Challenge."

"And? Why can't he be fair?"

"He is being fair. A hunter must be alert and know what's happening around him."

"I am not a hunter."

"But you killed a bear," Elna said in a low voice, raising an eyebrow.

"That doesn't make me a hunter. That was the first animal I ever killed. You don't become a hunter because of that. You need years of training."

"Well," Elna said. "It's my fault. I should have asked you more about this. How many challenges have there been?"

"Four, and I've lost all of them."

"Rand wants to shatter your bond. It's not nice, but it's his right."

"That's why Malva is upset at me," Vlad said, morose.

"It's not pleasant to lose a bond this way. The bond should last until the girl has time to make her choice. If Rand is her only bond..."

"I will go after him." Vlad stood up.

"When was your last challenge?"

"This afternoon."

"Then you have to wait until tomorrow."

"That man, Selo, said the same. I did not think it was important. Elna," Vlad said, searching his words with care, "There will be always trouble if I don't know the rules."

"You have learned many things, but it will take a while to learn what a Vlahin learns in a lifetime. And the most difficult thing is that we don't know what you know. What things are different in your clan. I will spend more time with you each day, and if you see the girls upset again, don't wait to tell me, even if sometimes it may be a thing of no importance."

"Malva didn't tell me that our bond would be shattered."

"She couldn't. It's a bit complicated. Courting may be complicated sometimes." She smiled and took his hand between hers. "Just tell me when you feel that something is wrong. You must be careful with Rand. He is strong and fast. Even though he is young, only three of our people can win a fight against him."

"I will manage it."

"Rune might teach you some things. Before being wounded, he was our best hunter."

"I will talk with him, but there is no time for training. Rand will not wait for it. And..." He stopped for a while, not knowing if it was a good idea. "Elna, I am not a hunter. I am a warrior. My training is different. It's more like the Kalachs. I hope that you will not see this in a bad way."

"Training doesn't kill, Vlad. People kill." She squeezed his hand. "Good luck tomorrow."

The next morning, it was Rand's day with Malva, and he whistled for her to come out. From time to time, he glanced at Vlad's door. When Malva came out, Vlad did the same, and carelessly walked toward Elna's hut; he was supposed to pick Selma up. Behind him, Malva gaped, and her eyes begged Vlad to turn. She even tried to reach the first River of Thought and warn him. She failed. Rand saw the opening, and walked after Vlad, agile and noiseless, like a well-trained predator. Malva covered her eyes with her hand, and tears ran down her face. People around just turned their heads away; it was unpleasant to see such a unbalanced game.

"Challenge!" Rand shouted, and jumped onto Vlad's back to put him down. His arms went to surround Vlad's waist. They found only air. Vlad had ducked and, caught by his own inertia, Rand went forward, landing on his belly on the ground. Before he realized what had happened, he found himself pinned to the ground, his left arm immobilized. It was a carbon copy of the first defeat he had inflicted on Vlad. Neither of them said anything, and Rand tried to escape, but Vlad's hold was something he had not encountered before. It was an Aikido technique, and the young Vlahin felt a sharp pain in his wrist and shoulder. The pressure on his wrist grew steadily, the pain became sharper, and Rand moaned.

"Do you yield?" Vlad asked.

Stubbornly, Rand kept fighting. This was his last chance to shatter Vlad's bond. He swung his leg back, trying to hit Vlad in the head. It failed, and this time, Vlad increased the pressure abruptly, almost dislocating his shoulder.

"I yield!" Rand shouted; Vlad released his arm, and stood up.

Ignoring the few people around them, Vlad nodded at Malva, who smiled faintly, and then he walked toward Elna's hut, where Selma was waiting for him. None of the people who saw the fight believed that Vlad won because of his skills. They thought that it was just bad luck for Rand. They shrugged and walked away.

The only one who paid close attention to what had happened was Darin. He was more involved in the charade, and watched everything closely. *Is that man stronger than I thought? It doesn't matter, he will be dead soon. I have already agreed with Rune that Vlad must join my hunters. Soon, he will become food for the wolves.*

Chapter 10

"The Great Bull gave us a great day, today." Tohar, the Shaman of the Kala clan, pointed at the shining sun, but it was not the sun which pleased him. He was a small man for a Kala, but one of great importance. "Yesterday, I talked with Darin again, behind Moira's back. He is more and more willing to embrace the Bull."

"We must be cautious," Maduk said.

"You are always cautious, brother," Ragun, the Chief of the clan said. "We should pair you with someone bolder." He laughed, and his amusement was genuine.

"We need to be both bold and cautious," said Alma.

It was unusual for a woman to take part in a Kala council, but Alma was an unusual woman. She was a Vlahin, kidnapped by her mate, the Chief of the clan, when she was only fourteen years old. She was also a shamane. An untrained one, and not very powerful, but a shamane nonetheless. In Vlahin terms she had only three and a half Amber Stones, but that was enough to make her a power broker in the Kala world, as they did not know about her hidden powers. With Alma's help, her mate had become the Chieftain of the eight Kala clans in the area; a title that Ragun wanted for himself, but Alma had advised him to let Burgo become the Chieftain at her mate's death. "He is old, and you will only have to wait a few years," Alma had told him, four years ago, and he had to agree. Burgo was his father's right hand, and he was more powerful than the twenty-one-year-old Ragun. "Your power will grow, and Burgo will name you his successor."

"And I think that Maduk has something in mind," Alma continued. She glanced at her youngest son.

"I want to visit the Vlahin clan."

"A good idea," Tohar agreed quickly. "You must make them feel the power of the Great Bull."

"And how do you plan to accomplish that?" Maduk asked, his voice slightly derisory.

"By force. The bull is strong, so are his sons." Caught up in his words, Tohar did not notice Maduk's taunt or so Maduk thought.

Son, Alma thought, you should not confront the Shaman directly. *I agree that he looks stupid sometimes, because of his strong beliefs, but there are other ways to counter him. And he is more clever than most people think.*

"A show of force is exactly what I have in mind." Maduk stared at the Shaman, who took his time savoring his little triumph.

"The Great Bull will help you. Bring him Vlahin blood."

"What do you have in mind?" Alma asked.

"Blood may be not necessary," Maduk said, thoughtfully, ignoring his mother. "The Vlahins resent the power of their Shamane. Some of them want to be like us." In deference to his mother, he didn't come out and say that men should lead the clans, not women. "I want to embarrass Moira, so more men from her clan will look to us for guidance. Her mate was a powerful warrior, but he is crippled now. One of us will provoke a fight, but unarmed. We will advise Darin not to interfere and to leave Moira alone."

"There are not many of us who can win in unarmed combat against the Vlahins," Alma said, cautiously.

"The Great Bull will bring us victory." Tohar reassured Maduk; this was the first time the young man had agreed that violence was necessary to subdue the Vlahins. *But if you fail, Maduk, it will be your failure.*

Then why did we lose all the wars? "Darin is their stronger fighter now," Maduk said, evasively.

"Do you plan to fight?" Alma asked. "Darin will not interfere."

"No, I may be needed to stop the fight spreading."

"Use Turgil," Tohar said.

"That is a good idea. I will take him with me. It's easy for him to start a fight, and he will win, for sure. Only Darin is stronger than him." *It may more difficult to stop the fight. Turgil is as stupid as he is strong.*

"And after the fight?" Alma pressed further.

"I am the brother of the Kala Chief. Moira is obliged to invite me and my men to eat at her table. The fight must happen just before we start to eat. It will not be pleasant. For her. The Vlahin men will not be happy that she could not handle the situation, and they will think again about the Shamane's weakness. May the Great Bull guide them."

"So, you think that by small fights like this we can achieve what war could not," Ragun said, rubbing his chin.

"United, the Vlahins are too strong for us. They are better fighters, even though we train for war. We must divide them. We've already started to do that; now we need to go one step further to convince Darin. Once Darin and some of the hunters split from Moira, the Vlahin clan is ours." Maduk raised his hands to underline his plan.

"When do you plan to go?"

"In two days. I will take Turgil and four more men with me."

"What if things go wrong?" Alma asked.

"Then my plan will fail," Maduk laughed. "Let's hope that's not the case. I am too young to die." *I hope to see Selma again. She likes me. No one knows it yet, but she will be my mate. Not even Selma knows it.* Maduk laughed quietly, inside, and his hand touched the pocket with the expensive gift he had bought for her.

The Vlahin sentry had already alerted the village that a Kalach band was coming to visit and, as usual, Moira, Rune, Darin and the other shamanes were the ones to greet them. Malva was away with Vlad, so Selma was the only apprentice present. She always felt strange when she met Maduk. The story between them had started four years ago, a few days after her father was killed in the battle in which the invading Kalachs were defeated. She was wandering aimlessly, when the Kalachs came to negotiate peace. Two Kalachs captured her, undressed her and pinned her to the ground. It was Maduk who had saved Selma, and she would always be in his debt for that.

"You have grown, Selma." Maduk broke the custom and addressed her first, making her frown, yet she was not displeased. "You are a wonderful woman now. Moira, Rune," he bowed lightly, before the Vlahins could react. Selma was pleased, and her face reddened, but she said nothing.

"You want to talk with us," Moira said.

"Wouldn't it be better if we talked from time to time instead of fighting?"

"It was not us who started the fight."

"Let's not live in the past. We may have a better future together." Maduk's eyes rested briefly on Darin, as if his words had a special meaning for him.

"Come with us." Moira gestured toward the table in front of her hut.

At that moment, Malva arrived too, followed by Vlad. As news of the Kalachs' visit had spread, Vlad felt increasingly nervous. He had guessed already that the Kalachs were the savages who had killed Cosmin, and he struggled to calm himself. Absorbed, his mind wandered in the past, and he did not pay much attention to what was happening around him. Maduk saw the opportunity, and touched Turgil's arm. That strange man was crossing their path, and he did not look dangerous. Turgil grinned, and stepped away from the group, going closer to Vlad, who was still lost in his thoughts. Moira saw what was happening, and tried to intervene, but it was already too late. Vlad almost bumped into the Kalach man but, with a swift turn, he avoided the collision at the last moment.

"Get out of my way!" Turgil shouted in fake rage. He punched Vlad's chest, pushing him to the ground.

That moment, when Vlad's back hit the ground, the eyes of the many people gathered in front of the Shamane's house played a strange dance, and it was not Vlad they were looking at. Maduk's stare bored into Darin, the Chief of the Hunters. Moira's eyes begged Darin to interfere and help Vlad and the clan's pride, at the same time. Darin acknowledged her plea, yet feigned ignorance, his eyes moving away, catching Maduk's meaningful stare. There was nothing cold in Darin's reactions, just nervous strain and a spark of hate for Moira. Maduk chose that moment to show a thin smile, and he nodded at Darin. The whole ballet of glances took no more than a few seconds. Moira stepped forward, trying to reach the fighting men, before it was too late, her face already composed.

Ignored by almost everybody, Turgil jumped on Vlad, shouting a fighting cry, trying to pin him to the ground and savor an easy victory. His chest met a pair of hard military boots, and he flew over the fallen man's body, turning in the air like an involuntary gymnast before hitting the ground with his head and back, unable to understand what had happened to him. He grunted, almost paralyzed by the shock. A worried groan escaped Maduk, his mind unable to grasp the sudden misfortune and pain of his fellow Kalach. That was when all eyes moved back to the combatants, trying to understand what had happened. Their next blink brought another puzzle: with a speed that left them bewildered, Vlad was already standing. He did not really stood up; he jumped suddenly onto his feet. His right foot exploded into

Turgil's ribs, compressing his chest, turning him face down on the grass. Another blink, and the steel of his bayonet touched the Kalach's neck. The defeated man was almost unconscious, and he could barely breathe.

"Let him go, Vlad." Moira spoke calmly, a hint of pleasure enveloping her voice.

"He tried to kill me," Vlad panted, pressing the knife harder, keeping an eye on the Kalachs, who reluctantly stepped toward him. "If they come any closer, they will die." He pointed at the Kalachs, who seemed ready to attack.

"No, no, everything is well; it was just a game Turgil likes to play, sometimes with unintended consequences." She turned her head, and flashed a genuine smile at Maduk, the Kalach deputy Chief. "Let him go, Vlad," she repeated.

Maduk's right hand gestured brusquely, stopping his men from advancing. *Can Vlad take fight all of us? Turgil looked like an untrained child against him.* "The game was worth playing," he said in a bland voice. "It was a pleasure to the mind to watch such skills in action. This man is a worthy warrior." He pointed at Vlad.

"Yes, we all enjoyed it," Moira answered in the same neutral tone, her eyes deliberately fixed on Maduk, just to be sure that he had caught her amused expression. "Now let's enjoy our lunch together."

Keeping calm, Maduk nodded, and followed her. Two of his warriors lifted the fallen man; they joined the table later, when they were sure that Turgil's rage had subsided, and he could behave. Maduk had made that plain to them. At the table, Maduk broke protocol again, and instead of sitting opposite Rune, he took the seat opposite Selma. Moira frowned, but said nothing.

He wants to study Vlad, she thought, as he was sitting next to Selma. *No, he is studying Selma*, she suddenly realized, and glanced at Elna, who nodded, already aware of the situation. *I hope he is not going to ask to mate with her.* The high ranking Kalachs liked to take Vlahin mates, but they usually stole them.

The food was served and, for a while, everybody stayed silent. Moira wanted to let the Kalachs boil a little more; Maduk needed to rethink his strategy.

Maduk took a swallow of water from his beaker made from an aurochs horn and set it down on the table with a sigh. *There is nothing in that man that speaks of danger.* Maduk looked at Vlad from the corner of his eye. *Yet, he defeated Turgil so easily. I would have no chance against him either.* Maduk was the strongest warrior in his clan. *What kind of Vlahin is he? A warrior from the north?* He had heard rumors in the past that the further one travelled north, the stronger the Vlahins were. "Soon, we will come to exchange goods," he said finally, almost absently. "My mother desires some good furs."

"Everything will be ready," Rune said, in the same absent way.

"We have many things to trade." Maduk's hand slid over the table, his fingers drumming the wood. Briefly, he glanced at Darin.

Knowing that the Vlahins had fewer things to trade than the Kalachs, Rune just nodded.

"I heard that you have new weapons," Darin said.

"Yes," Maduk replied. "They are made of copper and better than everything else." He took the axe from the belt at his waist and placed it on the table. Slowly, he pushed it toward the middle, letting the Vlahins decide who would look at it first.

"It looks different," Rune said, indifferently, without reaching for the weapon.

Darin reacted as planned, and took the axe from the table. His thumb slid over the edge. "It's sharp."

"There is nothing stronger than copper," Maduk bragged. "Our people are able to make many things."

"Steel," Vlad said, sensing that Maduk wanted to embarrass Moira. *If I am on Earth, and near the Danube, we may be just before the start of the Cris-Starcevo culture. They just learned how to smelt copper. Agriculture is coming into Europe from Middle East. The Kalachs will move north and west, assimilating the hunter-gatherer indigenous people.*

"What's steel?" Maduk asked. *Is his knife made of steel?*

"Something stronger than copper."

"Can we see some steel?"

"Maybe," Vlad said.

"Copper is good for many things, not only for weapons." Maduk settled his left hand on the table, and placed a small figurine, tied on a rope necklace, onto the wood. He pushed it slowly toward Selma. "Have a look."

Selma found herself in the center of the discussion, in a way that she both liked and disliked. She did not want to react in front of Moira, and she did not want to upset Maduk. She looked at the little copper bird and nodded.

"Isn't it beautiful?" Maduk insisted. *I brought it from the far south for you.*

"Yes, it is." Cornered, Selma finally spoke, strangely pleased by Maduk's attention.

"It's yours."

"Is any meaning in your gift?" Moira asked.

"No, it was spontaneous. I apologize, if you feel offended by my gesture, and I hope that Selma will enjoy wearing it." *She can't know that this is a mating offer, but she will learning it soon;* he fought against the urge to smile at his chosen woman.

"Elna will give you a fur for your mother." *That piece is too expensive...*

"From mother to mother." Maduk laughed, pleased by the double meaning of his words, and for a while no one spoke.

Selma's fingers were burning to pick up the bird – it was a great gift – but she had to wait until Elna nodded to her. The approval came faster than she expected, but her mother had guessed that the more she made her wait, the more impatient she would be. Selma's hand closed around the bird and her eyes locked with Maduk's. She smiled timidly, and he returned her smile.

When lunch ended, several people stood up and left the table. Of the Kalachs, only Maduk remained seated.

"You must leave too," Selma whispered to Vlad, who was not aware that only the leaders would stay for the next part of the conversation.

"Fine, let's go."

"I have to stay."

He frowned and glanced briefly at Maduk, then left the table, throwing an unhappy stare at Selma.

"Quite a strong man," Maduk said, his eyes following Vlad. "He seemed afraid to leave you alone with me." He stared at Selma this time. "Am I such a scary man?" His eyes bored into hers, and the memory of when he saved her from rape came back to her.

"No, you were kind to me," Selma said, her voice pleasant.

"You should have chosen somebody else for your little game," Rune said. "Turgil was too obviously looking for a fight."

"Turgil is always looking for a fight. He has more muscles than brain. Isn't that so, Selma?" he asked, knowing well that Turgil was one of the two Kalachs who had tried to rape her.

"You should know better," she said, an involuntary smile on her lips.

"Of, yes, I know it. We came in peace, nobody wanted to play any games. I am glad that blood was not spilled." *Soon, I will come after Selma. She likes me too, and in a month she will be my mate.*

"We don't like to spill blood," Rune said. "The Mother cares for all her children. You are a bit different."

"The Great Bull has strength. Now and then, he likes a bit of blood."

"The Mother has both strength and compassion," Moira retorted.

"Let the Gods talk to each other," Maduk replied. *I need to end this conversation, it's not going in the right direction. Who could have guessed that Turgil would lose the fight?* "They will find their way to tell us what to do next. It was a pleasant meal. Thank you. Moira, Rune." He stood up and bowed toward them. "I hope to see you again," Maduk said to Selma, who blushed, and he turned away, before Moira would cut in. Seeing him walking away, Moira decided to remain silent, yet she took note of Selma's reaction. So did Elna.

"Next time he comes, I want Selma out of the way," Elna whispered to Moira. *We may have a problem because he saved her four years ago.*

Yes, Moira nodded, yet somehow the thought of a peaceful mating between a Vlahin and a Kalach passed through her mind. *Maybe this is the way to a longer peace. But there is no bond between them. I can't force this on Selma.*

Without consciously knowing why, Vlad was thoughtful and in bad mood that evening, and wanted to be alone. Sensing his irritation, from the moment he had to leave the table and leave Selma alone, Elna decided differently, and followed him through the small forest behind the village.

"Walking?" she asked with a smile.

"Walking."

"Are they the same people who chased you when you arrived here?"

"I suppose so, but they were too far away, and I was too scared to be sure."

"What would change if you knew for sure?"

"I don't know," Vlad shrugged. "Wisdom may come to me at some point, but I will not go and attack them, and there is no need to know more to see that the Kalachs are violent people. We have a saying: That's a wonderful place, too bad it's inhabited. It's bad that the southern shore of the river is inhabited by the Kalachs."

"We did not choose them as neighbors," Elna said, edgily. "That was once Vlahin land. The Kalachs invaded it a long time ago, killing many people, but at least we know now. We've defeated them five times, when they tried to take our village too. Is there anything else that bothers you?"

"Is there a bond between Selma and Maduk?"

"Do you feel the bond between Malva and Rand?"

"Yes."

"Then you will know if there is such thing between her and somebody else. Selma has another bond, with a young man from another clan, and there can't be more than two bonds." *It may happen, rarely, but you will learn this later. There is no need to upset you now.* "Twice a year, he comes to see her, in spring and in autumn. You will feel their bond. Vlad," Elna said gently, "there are no bonds between Vlahins and Kalachs. Some time ago, Maduk saved Selma from the hands of that hothead, Turgil, and she is grateful to him. That's all."

"And if Maduk asks for her as his mate? That copper bird..."

"We never give our daughters to them," Elna said abruptly, not willing to talk about that gift. With her shamane senses, she felt that it was not a spontaneous gesture, as Maduk had claimed. There was a hidden meaning that only a Kalach could know. "There are no bonds, and the girls would suffer."

"They may kidnap her..."

"That's true, they often try to kidnap Vlahin women. From what we saw today, Selma has a bond with someone who can defend her well."

"Have you visited their village?" There still was some tension in Vlad's voice, and he did not look at Elna.

"Yes, I was there once."

"Are their houses trapezoidal?" He remembered from a long time ago visit to the Lepenski Vir museum storing an archaeological site – relocated after the construction of the Iron Gate Dam – that the houses south of Danube had a distinct shape, built according to a geometric pattern. The base of each house was a circle segment of 60 degrees, creating an equilateral triangle, which morphed into a trapezoid after the tip was cut. The tip of the trapezoid base, a shape previously unknown in other human settlements, pointed into the direction of the wind. Those houses had an aerodynamic form, long before the term was coined by the human civilization. *If this is true*...

"What does *trapezoidal* mean?"

"I am sorry. I am ignorant and had to use a word from my language." Vlad looked around, searching for a spot without leaves. "Let's go over there." He pointed at a spot under a small ridge, where a sandy patch could be seen. Walking, he picked a stick up from the ground and, when they got to the bare patch, he draw a trapezoid and a rectangle on the ground. "Do you know this form?" He tapped the rectangle with the stick.

"Rectangle," Elna said in Vlahin.

"Your houses have a rectangle at their base." He looked at Elna, who nodded. "This is a trapezoid." He tapped again, this time on his second drawing. "Do the Kalach huts have this form at their base?"

"Trapezoid," she repeated, and enriched the Vlahin language with a new word. "Some of them, yes, but how did you know that?" Selma looked at him, trying to understand if he had already entered the Mother's Web. Both she and Moira had guessed, after the River Dance, that Vlad had a strong Shaman Seed, though they were not able to feel it, because of his strange mind.

"I can't explain now." *This is Earth*, he thought, *and we are at the Danube's Iron Gate. My Earth, or an alternate version of it. And across the Danube is Lepenski Vir. It will become the largest village on Earth for more than a thousand years. A melting pot of people from Asia Minor, who discovered agriculture and animal husbandry, and hunter-gatherer locals. I wish I knew what year we are in now.* He tried to remember more from disparate fragments of memory, just to find an anchor to a specific period, but nothing more came to him. *I am not able to sort it. Sorry, uncle*; he almost smiled.

Silence fell between them, each bothered by their own inner thoughts; there were important matters at stake.

He entered the Mother's Web without knowing, and saw the Kalach village, across the river, Elna decided*. But to see places, you must go into the second River of Thought. I need the sacred mushrooms to enter that River. How could he do it without using them? Is he stronger than we thought? He may become a strong shaman, but there is no one to initiate him. The shamanes can only make his second initiation, which is much weaker, and it's driven by the newly initiated shaman, not by us. Our last shaman died more than fifty years ago. It would be a pity, if Vlad can't evolve to what was meant for him by the Mother. I need to talk with Moira.*

Chapter 11 – Vlad

"Vlad you are here for some time already, and we need to understand each other better. You have shaman powers that maybe dormant. We need to make a High Communion." Moira's eyes are fixed on me, like she wants to find a way into my brain. I know now from what happened with Elna during the Condor song that a shamane can do that, but at the moment I don't feel anything. "It's important for us, and it's important for you too. There is power in you, Vlad. We need to learn more about it."

"What is a High Communion?"

"Two people share their minds in the Mother's Web. It's done through a River of Thought. You are one of the few people able to enter the Second River of Thought. We know this from the River Dance. It may be that you have the Shaman Seed, but we are not able to feel it. You are ... different. The strongest Communion happens after the woman and the man make love." Moira's voice is bland, as if she was speaking about shaking hands.

"No," I say firmly, yet I feel pressure mounting in me, from her eyes, from her mind. Moira's naked body resurfaces in my mind. So does my fear. I fear what Rune will do if he learns about the 'Communion'. "Stop doing this," I snap, feeling the pressure mounting even more. I want the 'Communion'; I can see Moira, naked in my arms, and I already know from the River Dance that she has a wonderful body, younger than her thirty-four years.

"I am not doing anything. There is no value in an unwanted Communion. Your desire is natural. Every soul wants to reach the Mother's Web. It's the highest spiritual bond that we can achieve." Moira frowns at me, seemingly unable to understand my reticence.

"I won't," I say flatly and stand up, ready to leave.

"Vlad," Elna says, gently. "I suppose that your ways are different, but for us this is something normal. It happens rarely, and only when we need guidance."

"What does rarely mean for you?" I ask, a touch of cynicism in my voice.

"I have twice had a High Communion with a man," Moira says. "Once, when I was initiated as a shamane. That was with a Vlahin man. The second time, it was a Kalach. I needed to understand them. That's it."

"Is Rune aware of this?"

"Of course he knows about them. I would not hide such things from him. He is part of my life. Even when it is done with a Kalach, a Communion is sacred."

"You can talk with Rune." Elna seems to understand better my reluctance yet, while she realizes that we are different, she doesn't realize how different we are, and that two months here have only scratched the surface of my old way of thinking. I am not a Vlahin. Not yet. It may take a few years to fully integrate in their society, and some things in me will still scream "man from the twenty-first century", with its good and bad habits.

"No way." I shake my head, vehemently. Talking to a man about making love with his wife is the last thing I want. It doesn't matter that they call it Communion, it's still the same thing: a man and a woman, naked in the same bed, pleasing each other.

"Vlad." Elna takes my hand, looking at me, and I avoid her stare, afraid she will enter my mind again. "It's not what you think. It's not like you make love with your mate; it's spiritual, and there is no shame in making a Communion. You join the Mother." She stares at me, but I only shake my head.

"Would you consider making the Communion with Elna?" Moira asks.

"No." I know they are upset, but I can't give a different answer, even though I feel pressure coming from both, through subtle actions that I can't understand, and another layer of pressure from my own hormones and mind. Silence engulfs us, and no one seems able to break it.

"The way you touch Malva and Selma with your lips," Elna says, reluctantly, after a while. "Would you accept at least that type of Communion with me?"

I feel the urge and plea in her voice, and while I don't understand why, I understand that they consider it important, and I am only a guest, trying to acclimatize into their society. Their eyes are fixed on me. "Yes." *When in Rome do as the Romans do. But I will never make a High Communion with any of them.*

"Tomorrow evening," Elna says, relieved, and I nod. "Thank you."

An hour before the Communion, Moira gives me a cup of some herbal tisane to drink. I taste it, and it's bitter. She tells me the names of the plants but, in their language, they all are unknown to me, and I assume that they are not used frequently. There are already some dozens of known plant names in my dictionary. I drink the potion in one shot, to get it over with, and she smiles at me. A little later, she makes me drink a second cup. It tastes different.

"Mushrooms?" I ask, and she nods, but this time doesn't give me the names. *They must be 'sacred' and known only to the shamanes. They may be dangerous too.* I remember from my uncle's lessons that most of the mushrooms used by the shamans for their spiritual journeys are poisonous, and I recall the strong headache I had after testing a Siberian Shaman's potion*. What if she makes a mistake with the dosage.*

"I know what you think, but there is not enough powder in the potion to be poisonous," Elna says and gives me her cup to taste it. After I sip a little, she drinks the cup, and points to mine. Her potion has the same taste, but it's much more bitter, and I can't escape drinking mine now.

"Undress," Moira says.

I was afraid that we would come to that, but somehow after two months with them, I was starting to be less embarrassed about being naked, even in front of their women. Before I even start, Elna pulls off her dress and stands, naked. It takes me longer to escape my shirt, trousers, shorts.

"You need to feel the ground," Moira says, pointing at my socks, and I conform, pulling them off.

While my mind is occupied with physical tasks, I don't really acknowledge Elna's beautiful body. Once I am done with the undressing, things change, and I crouch swiftly to hide my arousal.

"That's normal," Moira says, like she is speaking to a child. "Why are you shamed by your body? Stand in front of her. Any woman is pleased to see that she can stir a man."

Grudgingly, I obey, and she ties a band around my head, covering my eyes. The last thing I see is Malva and Selma entering the room. *I have seen them naked too.* The thought calms me. My hearing is amplified and, from the slight noise, I guess that the Shamane is doing the same to Elna, who takes my hands in hers, and places them on her shoulders. It seems that she can 'see' or feel me even when her eyes are covered. One of her hands presses against my chest, the other is on the back of around my waist. Moira's palm moves up along my spine, the way Elna did when I sang El Condor Pasa, and the same cupping glass sensation passes through my skin. Elna's hand slides up my chest and settles around my neck. The second drink seems to work better on me than the first one, and I feel slightly dizzy, as if I am floating pleasantly, like in the past, after a few glasses of good wine. Moira guides my left arm around Elna's waist. My right is caught by two hands. They are slightly smaller, and I recognize that they belong to Malva and Selma. I try to imagine how we look, and I almost laugh. *I am surrounded by four graces, and I am naked*. A gentle pressure from Moira's hand on my neck stops my reaction. It's like she has taken control over my body, for a brief time.

"Be silent," Moira orders, and she starts to hum a low tune. Malva and Selma join her, and we stand still for a few minutes. The drink settles deeper into my brain, and I feel like I'm floating. Elna's body is leaning against me, her breasts touching my chest but, curiously, I don't sense it as a sexual experience. It's a pleasant closeness, though, and I start to be caught up in their Communion game. I am feeling now more curios than afraid.

Elna presses her lips on mine, and I realized that she has probably rehearsed this with the girls. She knows what to do and, involuntarily, I answer to her pressure, parting her lips. I am trapped, and my lips are more and more demanding. My arms pull her closer, and she is not shy to answer me with the same passion. Suddenly, Elna's lips part from me and her hand moves around my head, forcing me to bow until our brows touch.

"Stay with me," she whispers, and I feel her mind filling mine again, like during the River Dance. The drink slows my reactions and, before I can panic, her control over my mind becomes complete, and she erases my nascent fear. *"We are now in the Second River of Thought. Open your mind,"* she says, inside my mind.

I see no river, and I have no idea what to do, so I just wait. An image forms in my mind, and I recognize Selma: a younger version of her.

"Why is she younger?" I ask inside my mind too, strangely driven by curiosity, not by fear.

"This is not a memory of yours, it's coming from me. I want you to be sure about that." Another image comes, and I guess that it's Selma again, soon after she was born. A frisson of fear passes through me, but Elna calms me, though I don't understand how. Moira is tying Selma's umbilical cord, and I see everything from Elna's perspective, even her spread legs painted with blood. *"I have made you part of the most important event of my life."*

"Thank you." I don't know what else to say.

"It's your turn now."

"What should I do?"

"Find an image inside your memory. Just think it, and I will see it."

I feel the need to show her something important, to match her gift. *"My mother,"* I say, and the image fills my mind. She is in front of our house. Unbidden, tears run down my face. I realize it only when delicate fingers collect them. *"I will never see her again."*

"Thank you. She is a beautiful woman, and I feel strength in her." Elna's voice flows inside my head, calming me. *"What's that behind her?"*

"Our house."

"It's large and ... different." There is a hint of surprise in her voice. My parents' house has two floors and just the living room is larger than Moira's hut.

"It's made of stones." Elna doesn't react at my words; maybe she has seen huts made of stones somewhere, and I change my perspective. I am now on a hill south of my city, aloft on a television tower, and everything lies at my feet, even the river Jiu. The city has more than three hundred thousand inhabitants, and it covers the vista up

to the horizon. *If this is not an alternative Earth, I am only a hundred miles from my hometown. From the site of my town.* I am thinking in my language, and Elna can't understand me but, patiently, she doesn't react, even when I feel her slight emotion, but she controls herself better than me. In that moment, I sense another presence in my mind. *"Moira?"*

"I see everything."

"What you see is my ... village." I have to use the word, as they don't have the concept of city. A helicopter is flying above me, and this time both women gasp, and the link between us is almost severed.

"What animal is that?" Elna asks, and I sense her struggling to control her anxiety.

"It's not an animal. We can build things that fly." None of them answer me, and I realize that the concept is too strange for them. *"Think of arrows."* There is no point in trying to provide more explanations.

"Yes, arrows can fly." Elna's voice feels calm, but something is telling me that she can't really acknowledge what she sees in my mind. It's a mirror situation, as I don't understand the Mother's Web or a River of Thought. *"Can you show us how you arrived here?"* she asks after a while.

"No."
"Is it difficult for you?"
"My friend died, when I came here."
"Did you arrive here alone?"
"No."
"How many..."
"One."

"Vlad," she says gently, *"it's very important for us to see that man."*

How does she know that it was another man? I feel my breath coming fast and irregular, even as both Elna and Moira seem to reach deeper inside me, trying to calm my mind. Cosmin's image surfaces, at the exact moment I saw the arrow piercing his neck. My mind slips away, and the image blurs.

"Vlad!" Elna shouts.

An explosion shatters my brain, and I feel a cold night falling over me. It's soothing.

Chapter 12

"Hurry," Elna said, her hand still on Vlad's chest – his body lay unconscious in Moira's arms. Malva and Selma grabbed his legs, and they moved in tandem to arrange his body in his bed. "I am still inside his mind, but I feel nothing."

"It's the shock." Moira took Vlad's pulse, and her hand touched his temple. "He is gone somewhere far from here."

"Mother!" Malva cried.

"Stay calm, Malva. We will do what we can."

"Take his hands, and try to connect with him," Elna urged the girls.

"His hands are cold," Selma said after reaching his palm, and then her left hand touched Vlad's shoulder. "He is losing his body's warmth. Why?"

"It's the shock. His heart is slowing down. Let's dress him." Moira went to the pile of Vlad's clothes and picked them up one by one. "This goes on first," she said, looking at his shorts. "Help me," she said to Malva, and it took them a few minutes to dress his lower body. Elna's hand was still on his chest, keeping the Communion alive – whatever was left of it with an unresponsive mind. Moira arranged the shirt over Vlad's shoulders and laid a piece of fur on his belly. "I am going to make a new potion."

For the tenth time, Elna probed Vlad's mind, but she found no spark of consciousness in him. At the same time, she felt something changing inside her. The subtle chain of changes resembled things that had happened during her initiation, and for a moment she was overwhelmed and almost lost the link. *It was the part of the initiation that happened with the man*, she remembered. *It's not possible to have a second initiation.* Yet changes were occurring inside her, stirred by some kind of catalyst that she could not understand. She stretched her mind and, for the first time, she caught a glimpse of Vlad's Shaman Seed. *No, that's not possible!* She cried inside.

Closed to the world outside, Vlad's mind was in a state of effervescent dreaming, at a level that Elna could not access. A part of a man's mind would always be out of the reach of the shamanes. The opposite was also true; a shamane's mind had a private place too. Images were coming to him and leaving him fast, most of them unfamiliar. There were people he had never met. *Savages*, he thought. They came in a strange way, as if they were Benjamin Buttons; born old, and growing younger with the passing of time, until they returned into their mothers' wombs. That inverse flow of blood and newborns made him nauseous, and he shook his inner head. For the first time, he realized that Moira and Elna were no longer with him. Fear mounted in him, and he lost even his inner consciousness, his mind floating inert inside the second River of Thought. He was not trained to swim in the Mother's Rivers. He was lost, afloat, a turbulent stream of water carrying him away, in a cold place of total silence.

"Bring Moira here." Elna's voice was sharp and urgent.

Malva sprang up, and left the room, running as fast as she could. Before she could speak, Moira sensed that something of importance had happened.

"Stir the potion," she ordered Malva, and walked quickly inside the other room.

"Feel him," Elna said, her voice tired.

Moira paced her hand on Vlad's forehead, and her mind stretched toward him. "It can't be," she whispered. "He is too old for this, and we are women. This may kill him."

"We can't lose him," Elna said, calmly. "Selma, lie beside Vlad, and take him in your arms. Lean your head against his. Try to reach him. Speak to him."

"I need to leave." Moira swept out of the room and ran to the place where she kept her herbs. She went from one pouch and jar to another. "This is not good," she whispered, her fingers touching some leaves. "Not good," she went to another jar. "Not good. Not good." Her voice grew more desperate with each rejected choice. "Maybe this." She picked up an old root and sniffed it, and then chewed it. "I wish it was fresher." She walked around the room several times, but only added a few leaves to the root. "Not enough," she muttered, but went out anyway and threw the leaves into the boiling potion that Malva was still stirring. "Bring me Vlad's knife." When Malva returned with the bayonet, Moira started to scrape small chunks from the hardened root in her hand and threw them into the boiling water.

"Will this be enough?" Malva asked, her voice querulous.

"I hope so." She saw the fear in her daughter's eyes, and embraced her. "Two shamanes and two apprentices should be able to save one man." *I wish I had witnessed another shaman's initiation*, she thought. "Stir the potion." Malva needed to work on something to calm her mind, and Moira needed to think. The Shamane went inside the main room again and placed her hand alongside Elna's, on Vlad's chest. Selma was still speaking to him, in a low voice. "I hate unexpected things." Moira shook her head.

"I hate only the bad ones. What happened today may change everything. Mother sent him to us for this purpose."

"Bring half of the potion!" Moira shouted, and Malva came, a minute later, a small bowl in her hands. The Shamane moistened her finger in the dark liquid, and tasted it. "It's strong," she said with a grimace.

Elna did the same, just to learn what plants her sister had used. "Maybe we should add a pinch of Long Night Mushroom powder."

"I should have thought of that." Moira left briefly and returned with her most precious jar, storing the powder which helped a shamane navigate through the Rivers of Thought. She pinched some powder between two fingers, and dropped it into the bowl, and then she frowned, undecided. Her fingers moved fast and added some more powder. *I hope it will not harm him.* Her finger stirred the liquid until the powder dissolved. "Malva, raise his head." *I need to be careful.* She picked up a spoon that was a copy of the one Vlad had on his army-knife, only hers was made of wood, and she carefully parted his lips. The bitter liquid filled Vlad's mouth, and she kept his head high until he swallowed every drop. "Now we have to wait," Moira said, staring at the empty bowl. "Take the other bowl from the fire," she said to her daughter.

Vlad stayed unconscious for three days, and at every moment, day and night, either Moira or Elna watched him, each helped by her daughter.

It happened that Selma caught Vlad's first sign of awareness; she sat with his head resting on her lap. It was midday. "Mother!" she cried.

"Easy, Vlad," Elna said, and placed her hand on his brow. "You have had a long journey, and you may still be traveling."

"What happened?" Vlad whispered, opening his eyes for the first time.

"Well," Elna said with a smile. "After more than fifty years, we have a shaman again." *He must have four Amber Stones.*

"What shaman? What does this have to do with me?"

"You are the new shaman." Elna bent and kissed his forehead. "You are quite precious to us right now," she laughed. "Selma, go and tell Moira." She waited until her daughter left the room and sighed almost imperceptibly. *You have shaman powers, but you are not yet a shaman, and I am not sure how well we can train you. At least you survived the unexpected initiation. We should have been more careful. But your Shaman Seed is so different.* She shook her head. *How could we know?* Unconsciously, she embraced him.

Surprised, Vlad did not protest. After a series of long nightmares that he could remember with unwanted clarity, he felt really well. His arms went around Elna's waist, and his head leaned on her chest.

Elna smiled, and her hand caressed his brow. *I feel like he is my son.* She tried to speak, but Vlad was now sleeping. She sensed that everything was different from the nothingness she had felt before in his mind. *Definitely four Amber Stones*; she measured his power with more accuracy – the Amber Stones were the same for both shamanes and shamans. *Possibly four stones. It will depend on how well he is stabilizing his new power. He needs training. We will know for sure in a few months.*

Late in the evening, she sat with Moira in front of the Shamane's hut. They were tired, but finally at peace. For three days, they had blamed themselves for their carelessness, though they knew nothing about a shaman's initiation. They knew that a late initiation could kill a woman or a man, and Vlad was twenty-two years old, two years older than was normal for a man's initiation.

"Feel my mind," Elna said, and with all her tiredness, Moira complied, stretching her mind.

Her eyes expanded. "You've gained half an Amber Stone," Moira breathed. "I've never heard of anything like this before. Your initiation was eighteen years ago. How could this happen? Is this because of Vlad's initiation?"

"We will know after you make Communion with him." Elna smiled.

"And who will convince him to do that, after everything that has happened? He did not want to make one with me, even before this. His traditions are so different from ours."

"He is one of us, now. I don't say that it will be easy, but give him some time, and he will understand that power comes with responsibilities. He will accept a Communion with you. I wish we could convince him to have a High Communion, but that will not be possible, now. Maybe in a few years..."

"You need to make your Amber Heart," Moira said, her voice low and mysterious. It was his third day fully awake, and Vlad felt better than at any time before in his new life. "That will be the mark of your power. Five years ago, I brought these from the shore of the Northern Sea, for Malva and Selma's initiation as shamanes." She spread five amber stones on the table, in a row, a palm's width distant from each other. They were different from anything Vlad had seen before – translucent and colorless. Without the tiny pieces of plants or insects, they would have look like ordinary glass. All the stones were shaped into an arrow point, two inches long, and carefully polished.

"They look like arrow points, not a heart," Vlad said, confused.

"True, but in the River of Thought, the arrow points to your heart, and there is something more. You will learn it soon. Pick one to your liking."

Without really understanding what he was doing, Vlad extended his arm, indifferent to what stone he should pick. His movement seemed aimless yet, after a moment, his hand worked under its own will and took the first stone on his right. Moira and Elna exchanged a glance, and both smiled, relieved. Unknowing, Vlad had just passed his first test as a shaman. He stared at the stone, trying to see what was caught in the old resin. There were small things, but nothing recognizable.

"I have my Amber Heart," Vlad said, just to say something. From the shamanes' reactions, which he pretended to ignore, something of importance had happened when he picked the stone, but he could not feel anything.

"That's just a stone. You have to make your Heart." Moira took out her Heart Stone from its special pocket, and placed it on the table. It looked similar to the one Vlad was still rubbing between his fingers, only the color was different. Moira's amber stone was still translucent, but it had a pleasant yellow color. A yellow heart could be seen inside

"What's different, apart from yours being yellow?" Vlad asked. *It looks like glass engraved with a laser. It has a frosted effect, except that it's yellow.*

"Nothing," Moira smiled.

"Then?"

"You have to infuse color into your stone. Yours will be yellow too, though a bit paler. The first three levels have a green color as their marks. Of course, no one is a real shamane or shaman before the third level. The fourth, fifth and sixth levels have yellow as their marks. The more you go up, the more the colors get stronger."

How can I paint the stone on the inside? Vlad thought. *Maybe an infusion of color, by boiling it? What about the*

heart shape? Would the amber survive? "What kind of painting did you use?"

"Mind painting." There was a touch of amusement in Moira's eyes, as she spoke, and Elna smiled at him.

Vlad blinked, and bit his lip. *Are they joking?* "How can you paint with your mind?"

"You have to make Communion with the stone, and then it will become truly yours, but amber is a difficult thing. It has its own personality. The second River of Thought will provide you with the color."

They are not joking; Vlad looked, puzzled, at them. "Will you show me how?"

"No, this is between you and your stone, but first you have to learn how to enter the second River of Thought. It may take a while," Moira said, thoughtfully. "You had an incomplete initiation, and we don't know how much is missing. Elna's part as a shamane was done properly, but we don't know anything about the man's part."

I am scared, Vlad suddenly realized. "Can I have some time to think about it?"

"There is no more danger," Elna said, sensing his fear. "At least, there's no big danger."

How small is small? "I need to think," he said abruptly, and stood up. Without realizing it, he grabbed the stone from the table, before walking away.

"The first step is done," Moira said, when she was alone with her sister.

"There is too much fear in him, right now. It will subside, and curiosity will make him want his Heart Stone, and then I will show him how to enter the River of Thought."

"Yes, it will be easier to practice with you. I feel a kind of bond forming between you two."

"Sometimes, I have the sensation that he is my son. I know, it's strange," Elna shrugged. "But it may help with his final transformation." The memory of her own son came to her, and she felt tears filling her eyes. Little Rod was killed by the Kalachs, eleven years ago, together with her mother, father and grandmother. Her son was only three years old. They were in a temporary camp, gathering food for the winter. Elna, her mate and Selma, who was six years old, escaped just because they went fishing on a small river, a few miles from the camp. The Kalachs wanted the four young women in the camp, and killed everybody else, even the children and elders. That was their way, driven by the Great Bull, who liked to drink blood. It was that year when she became the Shamane of the clan, taking the position from her mother, who was a much stronger shamane. The first tough decision took by Elna and her mate, who was now the Chief of the clan, was to move the village from the shore of the Great River to its actual place. It was still not far from a river which provided a lot of food, but better secured, with only one path linking the village and the river. And the women could foray for food north of the village, far from the dangerous border between the Vlahins and the Kalachs. In the twelve years that followed, only one woman was kidnapped by the Kalachs.

"Without knowing what powers he lacks, it's hard to know how easy it will be for Vlad to create his stone," Moira said, pretending of not seeing Elna's reaction. She already knew what had caused it. Moira had also lost a child, a daughter, but it had happened at birth. The shamanes always had two children, while the other women were allowed to have three. The Vlahin women were able to control when they were fertile and, over millennia, they had learned to grow slowly in numbers, remaining in close communion with the world around them. That's what the Mother had taught them. It's what the Kalachs had forgotten a long time ago, when they chose the Bull as their god. They made many children, and their rapid increase created unnecessary pressure on nature, forcing them to migrate in search of new lands.

"I don't think it is much different from what we do. Most of the skills are shared by women and men."

"You should not rush him."

"We have plenty of time. I want him to enter the Mother's Web several times. The first River of Thought, at the beginning. Everyone is able to go there, unconsciously; he just needs to be consciously aware of it. That should not be hard. Or frightening." Elna smiled, remembering how she felt when she did the same for the first time. It was not the conscious movement into the River that had frightened her, it was the pressure from all the minds she felt there. Almost all the people in the village burst into her mind at the same time. *Maybe I should go somewhere with him, far from the village. Then, only a few minds would be close enough for him to feel them*. With distance, minds faded until they could no longer be accessed. That distance varied for every shamane or shaman. The weak ones could feel other minds only inside a hundred paces radius. The strong ones could reach other people's minds at a few miles' distance. Even for shamanes with the same number of

Amber Stones, the distance could vary. For the same level of power, the skills could still be different.

Chapter 13

The hut was full. The Chief of the Kala clan's hut was the largest structure in the village, and the only one to have more than one room. The main one was thirty feet long and nine feet wide. At the back, a door made by a curtain led toward the smaller back chamber where Ragun, the Chief of the clan, and his mate slept. The construction was very different from the Vlahin's huts. The Kalachs dug the floor down to just below the level of deepest frost, which is in this area was around forty inches, trying to exploit the natural, constant temperature of the ground. The walls of the dugout were plastered with mud. When everything was done, a huge fire hardened the clay, making it almost as resistant as sandstone.

Ragun was sitting in his large, ornate chair with an aurochs skull on top, listening to his brother's plan. An intricate plan that had taken them many months to put in place, yet Maduk did not speak for long; there was no need for the warriors to know all the details. When all was said, one by one, the warriors left the hut, leaving only four people inside.

"Three days from now, it will be a great day," Tohar, the Shaman of the clan said, his eyes filled with pride. "The Great Bull who created this world came to me last night. He will grant you a great victory. Everything was clear in my dream."

"We are not going there to fight," Maduk said, not looking at the Shaman. *This idiot always talks too much*, he thought. *He will talk to my warriors too, and I may have issues when we cross the Great River. It's so easy to stir a man to fight.* He glanced briefly at his mother, but she did not interfere. "We want to trade and steal some women, and mate them with our men." *One of them will be Selma, and she will become my mate.*

"Yet fight you must, if that means glory for the Great Bull." Tohar continued to pester Marduk. "Darin, the Chief Hunter of the Vlahin clan, has already seen the right path. Crush them and they will embrace the Bull who created everything. You will become the Chief of the Vlahin clan."

Why hasn't the Great Bull convinced the Vlahins already? "Darin will become the Chief of the Vlahin clan." Maduk fought to keep his voice calm. "He will play his part in our plan, and he will recognize Burgo as his Chieftain. If we want to succeed, we should not kill Vlahins tomorrow."

I need you there Maduk. You will interfere less with my plans, and don't think that I will let you mate with a shamane. Turgil will take Selma. For a while... That's why I need some blood to flow. "What's a victory without blood? The Great Bull requires it tomorrow. Blood is the real path to glory. The Vlahins must fear us."

"You can cut your thumb," Maduk said, annoyed. *It rhymes with dumb.*

"Maduk!" the Shaman snapped, standing up. "Do not take the will of the Great Bull for granted. You are too weak. Turgil will accompany you, tomorrow. He will do what must be done. You can stand aside and watch his path to glory. Those Vlahin hunters must learn that men are born to rule, not women. Look at how many things we can trade with them. And the Vlahins? They can trade only furs and wild meat. That's the difference between a clan led by men and a clan led by women." *I need a shamane as my mate, but it's too early to plan that. After we take the Vlahin village, I will rescue Selma from Turgil and make her my mate. A shamane will help me with the Bull Dance.*

"A bit of blood will help." Ragun's hand made an almost invisible pacifying gesture toward Maduk, his younger brother. "Just one fight. One Kala against one Vlahin. It should suffice to please the Great Bull. Then you steal women. Then you can trade. Blood and trade will help them understand whose god is more powerful."

"Fine," Maduk shrugged, annoyed, suddenly understanding that some negotiations had taken place behind his back.

"I am going to prepare Turgil." Tohar stood up, a sarcastic smile on his lips, and left the hut.

"The situation required that we accept Tohar's request," Ragun said, before Maduk could speak. "If not he would have pestered me all night and seeded bad thoughts in your warriors. Whatever you think, good morale always helps."

"We need a good Shaman." Maduk spoke casually, looking away, but from the corner of his eyes, he watched his brother carefully.

"You might be accused of blasphemy."

"I might be accused of many things, Ragun. Being blind is not one of them. Tohar's father was a great shaman and our best Shaman for several generations. Loher, Tohar's brother, was a good shaman too. He should have been our Shaman. Both brother and father died in a strange accident, just weeks before Loher would have been named successor to the Shaman. I don't feel any spark of the Great Bull in our ceremonies or in the Bull Dance. Don't tell me that you feel it. People have started to talk. Some of them have the Shaman Seed in them. They feel it. They feel that Tohar has no spark and no seed. We can pretend that everything is well, but it's not. What's a clan without proper spiritual guidance?"

"Sometimes, Tohar is not able to guide his own feet," Alma said, "but son, you should not fight him. Let him fight himself."

"He has interfered in my plans."

"To interfere in the name of the Great Bull, that is a Shaman's business. Let our people know that the Bull is on your side and on their side. It will help you, and one death will change nothing. And it's too early to talk about having a new Shaman. Ragun became Chief less than four years ago. We don't need unnecessary confrontation right now. Tohar is obstinate, and we can handle him until the right time."

"Do you still want to take Selma as your mate?" Ragun asked.

Tohar's father thought Tohar was stupid too, and he is dead now. Tohar lacks the subtleties needed to overcome the Vlahins, but he is shrewd enough to advance his own interests. Maduk decided to keep that to himself. At least for now. "Yes, taking her as my mate will suit us, and it will suit Darin too. We have already agreed on this. His son is mated to the only other young shamane in their clan. He wants to be sure that his son will succeed him, after we help him to become their Chief."

"Darin's mate is not a shamane."

"That will make him a weak Chief, who needs our help."

"Does he understand that what will happen in three days is just one step in our plans? He seems too eager..." Ragun's hand gestured loosely, his eyes fixed on his brother.

"We will meet again just before going into their village. Tohar will be there too. I will remind him of that. We need ... if not a peaceful, at least not a very bloody transition. In time, we may be able to convert the young shamanes to the Great Bull."

"A symbiosis." *You are aiming too high, Maduk. I may need to clip your wings.*

"Yes. That will help us take over the Vlahins. Their men are not happy with the tight grip of power the Shamanes hold over them. They see us leading our clans, not the women. They see that we are more advanced. We have better pottery and weapons. We have better objects for daily use. We grow plants and animals. They are backward and they want to be like us. The Bull will fulfill their dreams."

And your dreams too. "Turgil wants Selma as his mate, too," Ragun said, casually.

That's why you asked if I 'still want her'... "Strange, his new desire, but I am the second Chief of the clan."

You may be, but if Turgil is the first one to spread Selma's legs... "Yes, you are. Go and prepare your men. Do it your way, but give the Shaman the blood he desires. Make everybody happy." *Some of the warriors already know that Turgil wants Selma. Tohar has taken care of that. None knows about our plans for you, brother. It will stay like this until it is too late for you to change things. You can take another Vlahin woman, but not a shamane. Turgil is too stupid to understand what power Selma could bring to him. He will crush her until she forgets about her shamane powers.*

"Ragun," Alma said gently, when they were alone. "You should not work against tour brother."

"I did not give my approval to Turgil."

"You let Tohar give him hope. You pitted Turgil against Maduk. That was not wise; you are stronger with Maduk on your side. The news that Turgil wants Selma will spread. Both Tohar and Turgil have big mouths. I pray that Maduk will not hear them before ... that day. Let things take their course." *Son, you are a good Chief, intelligent and cautious, maybe too cautious, but you have no vision. Maduk has one that may bring us farther than we ever hoped. I think that you unconsciously feel that.*

"I would prefer if Maduk was mated to a Vlahin woman who is not shamane. There will be fewer contradictions. In two or three years, I want him to become the Chief of the Vlahin clan, over the river. Darin will be only a transitional Chief." He looked at his mother, but she remained silent. "I will not interfere," he said, finally.

You already interfered when you should not have. She nodded and stood up, then left the hut. *I may need to kill Turgil*, she sighed. *Selma is too important to be left to that idiot. It will not be easy. After Maduk, Turgil is our best warrior. And Tohar protects him. Few will dare to try to kill him, whatever the incentives I can give them. At thirty-eight, Alma was still desired by men, and her shamane skills made them feel better in bed than any other woman. Alma was a shrewd woman, and sometimes she used a night of pleasure to advance her or her sons' interests.*

She found Maduk, at the edge of the forest, training with his copper axe. It was still a rare thing; they had received them from a southern Kala clan only six months before. It had cost them a lot of precious furs, but they were at least able to trade pottery and other objects they produced for the furs that the Vlahins, who were better hunters, provided. There were only three such axes in the clan, the other two belonging to Ragun, who inherited his from his father, and Turgil, who had received his six months ago. Turgil was not only a strong warrior; he was her nephew too, part of the large family ruling the clan. And Tohar had a copper knife.

"That's a good weapon," she said, a brief smile on her lips. Watching him train, she leaned against the trunk of an old tree. *My son is strong.*

"Mother, you just want to make me forget what happened." Maduk stopped training and looked at her. He smiled without mirth.

"What exactly happened?"

"Ragun traded with Tohar behind my back. He worked against me."

"He is the Chief and trades what he needs, with whom he needs. One fight will not spoil your chances."

"One fight may bring another, and I heard my men speaking about Turgil wanting to mate with Selma."

"She is a desirable woman. It is no wonder that men want her."

Marduk ignored his mother, and prepared to fight another imaginary enemy with his axe. His movements were becoming more and more fluid and, after a while, he managed to erase Alma from his mind. His peace of mind stopped abruptly when he almost hit her after a sudden turn.

"Am I a good target for training?" she asked, staring at the axe, which was hanging motionless only a few inches from her eyes. It looked larger than she remembered. *And dangerous*; she sighed almost imperceptibly.

"Am I a good target for evil games?"

"Your brother may play a different game than you want him to, because the clan needs it, but he will not play evil games on you."

"Then why did he promise Selma to Turgil?"

"He did not."

"Turgil has bragged that Tohar and my brother gave him permission."

"Tohar may have promised him something, but not your brother."

"How can I be sure of that?"

"Because I told you."

"Tohar would not have made such a promise without Ragun's agreement. Mating is at the Chief's prerogative." He started to move again in half pirouettes, cutting more imaginary enemies with his axe. For a moment, Turgil's face appeared inside his mind, and he moved faster, cutting one head after another. All of them belonged to Turgil. It calmed him.

"Tohar likes to talk a lot; it doesn't mean that he made any agreement, but why are you so ... upset by the thought of Selma going to Turgil? There are many Vlahin girls ready to mate out there." Her hand gestured north, toward the Great River, its waters glittering in the sun, less than half a mile below. The village was in a good spot, profiting from both river and forest. Food was easier to get, even in winter, and the river brought many dead trees they could use to warm their homes during the long cold nights.

"It so happens that we already agreed on this subject. It so happens that we both know what importance a shamane can have for us. It so happens that I like her." *And I already gave her the mating gift.*

"Oh, I did not know about that last thing. Would that be more important than the clan's need?"

"Aren't the first two things important enough for the clan?"

"They are, but don't let the last one blind you."

"My impression is that you want me to turn a blind eye to what happened."

"Nothing of real importance has happened. Go there and fulfill our plan, Selma included."

"We will go in two teams. Because of the latest arrangement between my brother and Tohar, I have to let

Turgil lead one of them: he is the second warrior of the clan. What do you think will happen if he finds Selma first?"

"He will be the lucky one. You and the clan will still gain from fulfilling the plan."

"Yes, Mother," Maduk said, dryly, and walked away.

"Maduk." Alma put all the gentleness a mother could offer in her voice, but he did not return. *The news about Turgil wanting Selma spread too fast*, she thought, staring at him walking away. *It did not happen by chance. I hope that Ragun did not lie to me. It makes no sense to try and persuade Maduk now, but I still have two days left. He must cross the Great River with a clear mind.*

Chapter 14

Five dug-out canoes were aligned tightly to the sandy bank, kept in place by long ropes. They were raw things; boats carved from one long trunk of an old oak, but good enough to carry both men and their merchandise across the wide river. Spread between the trees along the shore, forty men were ready to board them. The morning was cold and without wind. On the opposite shore, thin stretches of fog masked the land. That made the men more nervous than usual. They were going to trade with the Vlahins, but this time there was more than trading in their plans.

"Let's go." Maduk finally gave the signal, and people started to load the boats with pottery and other things they knew would appeal to the Vlahins. They were proud of what their people could produce, and considered the Vlahins backward. It did not count to them that most of the objects were made by slaves. Slavery was a common thing for Kala people.

When the last thing was loaded, the men moved, nervously, to board their designated boats. Three boats would go with Maduk, carrying all the merchandise. The other two boats went with Turgil, and they were the first to leave the bank. When the last man took his place, long oars started to move in long rhythmic sweeps. Half an hour later, the other three boats left the shore too. Heavier, they were slower to traverse the water, but Maduk was in no hurry. He knew that good timing was needed, and Turgil's team had a much longer journey in front of them. They would land on the opposite shore, several miles to the north, and take a hidden path that would lead them toward the northern road going into the Vlahin village. More mist came down from the mountains, almost covering the river. The oarsmen moved faster, afraid to lose direction. Around them, the Great River was calm and there was no sign of whirlpools or large rocks. Just half a mile downstream, the river boiled, and no boat could survive. With some sort of hidden irony, that place was named The Living Water. It was true that the water was like a living thing, crashing furiously through the rocks, but any man falling in there was a dead man.

"Men on the right, row harder," Maduk said, his hand trailing in the water, trying to feel the slightest change in the current. *It would be no harm if we landed a bit further upstream.* His mind went ahead, imaging his road toward the Vlahin village. He had walked that road many times in the past, and he still remembered the bitterness of his first visit. It was only a few days after they were defeated in the last attempt to conquer the opposite bank of the

Great River. His father, and Chieftain of the northern Kala clans, was dead, and he had to retrieve the body. His uncle was dead too, and he had to accept his cousin Turgil in his team. The young man was as unpredictable and stupid as he was strong yet, that time at least, it was Turgil who delivered the key to a fruitful negotiation. For whatever reason, Turgil's men splintered and went a few hundred paces to the left. They crossed paths with Selma, and Turgil thought of nothing better than trying to rape her and make her his mate. Maduk intervened and hit Turgil hard, in front of the men, a thing that the irascible thug had never forgotten. He carried the almost unconscious Selma in his arms to the village. That earned him better conditions from the Vlahins. It came in a package with Turgil's hate, though. *He is twenty now, and no longer a child, but his mind...* Maduk shook his head, staring through the thick fog.

"Slow now," Maduk ordered, feeling that the riverbank was close; there was no way to see his own fingers with his arm outstretched. In a few moments, his palm in the water felt the boat slowing. *I hope that I am right.*

The boat hit the bank harder than expected, and two men fell into the water. They had at least the luck that the water was not deep. One of them lost contact with the boat, and vanished from sight. "We are on the shore!" Maduk shouted. With his copper axe, he struck the wood of the boat rhythmically. "Men in the water, follow the sound of my axe!" When all his twenty men were out, they grabbed the boat, ready to pull it onto the bank. The next boat reached the bank a moment later, and the cafan, a Kalach leader of ten men, shouted the command to pull the boat out of the water. *It went well, with all that fog*, Maduk thought. A moment later, his boat shook like an infuriated bull, and he fell into the water. *Almost well.* His feet found the bottom, and he climbed out of the water. "Third boat, you hit us. Don't go downstream, the water is still deep at your southern end. Let's pull this one up," he said to his men. "One, two, now." The men grunted and pulled. "One, two, now." It took them five goes to pull it almost completely onto the bank. The fog was thinner now, and they were able to see six or seven paces in front of them. *I still don't know where we are.* "Don't unload the merchandise yet," he ordered when the last boat arrived.

"Twenty aurochs were spotted in the north-west mountains, a quarter of a day from here," Darin informed the hunters. "A good hunt will fill our village with meat for half a month. We should take as many hunters as possible."

"The Kalachs are coming today to trade. Maduk will have twenty men with him, as usual." Rune was split between the opportunity to replenish the clan's provisions and the need to protect his people.

"Ten hunters and the elders should be enough to protect the village."

"Ten hunters," Rune reluctantly agreed. *And Vlad*, he thought.

"I have a bad feeling about this," Moira said, her eyes thin.

"I second the bad feeling," Elna added.

"Feelings will not feed us," Darin said, trying to keep his voice calm.

"Take thirty-five hunters with you and leave fifteen in the village," Rune said. "Leave behind the slowest ones, so you can get back faster."

"Fifteen," Darin agreed. *Maduk will have forty warriors. I did what I could without opposing the decision of the Chief. It will not be my fault when... Those bitches are always meddling. Their end will come soon, and they will meddle no more.* "Announce to the village that only the north-west path should be used by women for harvesting. We should leave now." As Chief Hunter, Darin was also in charge of security. He stood up and, without waiting for an agreement from Rune, left the hut.

Walking out of the village, Darin came across the young women going to gather berries and tubers. "Follow us," he said, "the Kalachs will come from the south, and we have seen two bears in the northern area." Two miles later, at the point where they were to split up, he gathered the women and the old men who were in charge of their defense, and split them into two groups. "Malva, you are in charge of this group. "You take this area." He pointed north of the path. "Selma, you will lead this group. We will walk together for a while, as we will go closer to the river. Yesterday, I saw a good place with ripe berries."

They walked in silence for a while, until they arrived at a place where they had to enter the forest again. "There," Darin pointed to a small hillock south of them. "You will fill your baskets easily."

"Thank you, Darin," Selma said, and signaled the women to follow her. Two old men came with them too.

In the middle of the forest, Darin parted from his men. "I want to look at the riverbank." He pointed south, some hesitancy in his gesture. "You will go straight ahead and wait for me at the edge of the forest. Heno, you come with me," he said to his brother.

"Are you sure that this will work?" Heno asked, when they were alone on the path toward the river.

"It has to work. I am fed up with that stupid woman telling me what to do. I am the Chief Hunter. I feed the clan. You feed the clan. We protect the clan. We must decide for them."

Heno was not convinced, but kept his mouth shut; he was not a bold man and would have preferred a less dangerous path. They descended toward the river, and some patches of mist swirled around them. Heno touched his forehead, murmuring some words against the bad spirits inhabiting the mist. It was a Kalach custom.

When the last patch of fog vanished under the strong sun, and they could see the whole bank, Maduk saw that they were at the wrong place. There was no way to climb the steep slope with their heavy loads. *We are three hundred paces south of the landing place. Four hundred paces more and we would have entered the Living Waters.* He kept the thought to himself, but the most experienced men knew it too. Maduk shook his head when one of them tried to warn the others. The man's mouth clamped shut. *We can't row the boats;* Maduk looked at the stream of water, which was already faster than where they had started the crossing. His eyes followed the bank: for two hundred paces, they could walk along the bank. It was sand, and treacherous in some parts, but less dangerous than the water. A dead willow marked the end of the bank.

"We will walk and pull the boats to that willow," he said, pointing at it. "We take them one by one. Cafans, tie the ropes to the first boat." In a few moments, he picked the strongest ten men, and told them to pull the ropes. The caftans stayed in the boat, helping with their oars. Maduk walked in front of the men pulling the ropes, testing the sand with a sturdy pole. The path was easier than he thought and, soon, the boats were all lined up by the bank. *We still can't climb with the merchandise*; he measured the slope, then went into the water, up to his waist, and found that the current was almost normal. "We row from here," he ordered, and in ten minutes the boats arrived at the right landing place. "The Mother sent that fog to delay or kill us, but the Great Bull is stronger," he shouted as he climbed onto the bank. "Unload the boats."

The five Vlahin sentries were at the designated place, and the long row of people carrying heavy loads gathered in one place.

"We have come to trade," Maduk said.

"You are welcome to trade," one Vlahin answered. "Follow me."

It took them another half of an hour to reach the village. The loads were heavy and, while he was worried about arriving after Turgil's team, Maduk knew that he could not push them harder. The men were tired, and trying to force them would have alerted the Vlahins. He needed an unwary village for his plans. Moira, Rune and Elna were waiting at the entrance to the village, and Maduk sighed with relief. He was the first to arrive. He looked for Selma, but she was not there. *She must be in the village*; he thought. "We have come to trade," he repeated the words.

"You are welcome to trade," Rune said, and gestured toward the area in front of his hut. The Vlahins' furs and skins were already there, arranged by what they could be used for. Otter furs for shoes and boots, bear furs for beds or caps. There were five piles on the left, and immediately, Maduk saw that they had gathered things of good quality. The Vlahins would never arrange good quality furs over bad quality ones. The sixth pile was furs and skins of lower quality. "Pottery here." His boot scratched the ground. "Food here." He made another mark. "Everything else here." Waiting for his men to arrange the goods, he searched the village, looking for Selma, yet apart from the three leaders and fifteen hunters, there was no one else in sight. *The girls may stay hidden, but where is Vlad? Last time, Selma and Malva took part in the trade too. Why are they more careful now? Where is Vlad?* He was unwilling to ask Rune.

As Darin had told him, Turgil found Selma and the other four young women at the right place. They were harvesting berries, guarded by two old men. He had hoped to get closer and snap up the women before the men could spot them, but the Vlahins were better hunters. There was no way to steal the women without spilling blood, but Turgil did not care. The two old men were good archers, but once the Kalachs got closer, they had no way to escape; yet four of his twenty men were lying in the grass too, the shafts of the arrows rising from their chests. Though they had fled, covered by the old men, the women were easy enough to catch, and Turgil jumped on Selma, forcing her down.

"You will not escape now," he growled, and hit her hard. Almost unconscious, she offered little resistance when he undressed her. With a broad grin, he spread her legs. "I will make you a woman now." Selma tried to fight, but he hit her again.

"Leave her," Grod, who was Tohar acolyte, stopped him. "You must take her in front of her clan."

"I want her now," Turgil growled.

"The Bull forbids you. Don't upset Tohar. And you want to fight a Vlahin. You can't mate before a fight, it will drain your essence. You mate after the fight." *He is strong, but so stupid.*

Turgil stood up, and pulled Selma by her hair. "You are good looking," he said, his eyes moving up and down over her naked body. "I will enjoy you as my mate. Now walk." She tried to reach for her clothes, but Turgil stopped her. "You will walk naked. I want to see you."

With a sigh, Grod picked up the girl's clothes and carried them. He let the stupid man have his way with her nakedness.

From time to time, Turgil stopped to grope Selma, who forced herself not to cry. She did not want to give him the satisfaction. "You like it," he grinned. "The Kala are better at pleasing a woman than the Vlahins. You will learn that soon. I will mate with you in front of your people."

From his observation point, Vlad saw Turgil's men the moment they left the forest, taking the shortest path toward the village. The binoculars gave him an overview of both Kalach groups advancing toward the village.

"Warn the clan that a second Kalach troop is coming by the northern way," he ordered the apprentice hunter behind him. Then he saw Turgil taking Selma on his shoulder. *She is naked; I will kill that man.* For the first time since his arrival, the soldier's instinct to kill rose inside him. He was aching to fight.

Maduk was already worried, when Turgil finally arrived in the village. He frowned, seeing Selma carried on the man's shoulder, then he stared at Grod, who nodded, and Maduk felt relieved.

"She will be my mate, not yours," Turgil bragged to Maduk, putting Selma down in the middle of his men, then he raised the precious copper bird that Maduk offered to Selma. The girl carried it at her neck. "This is mine now," he winked at Maduk. "I see that you took the village."

She liked my gift. Maduk breathed deeply to calm himself. *I may lose her.* "Not yet, but they have only fifteen men to defend themselves."

"Free our women," Rune said, coming closer.

"We just want to make a mating agreement," Maduk said. "We are ready to pay a good price for them."

"We don't sell our women."

"I apologize for using a bad word. Let's say that we want to make an agreement with you. Mating Kalachs and Vlahins will bring our clans closer."

"You took our women by force."

"Our ways of mating may be different, but we care about our mates too. No harm was done to them. Why would anyone harm their future mate?"

"That's why you took Selma's clothes off? Send our women over here, so we can learn this from them."

Turgil always finds a way to surprise me with his stupidity. Without Grod... "They should stay with their mates," Maduk said flatly, knowing that he had the upper hand; there were thirty-eight Kalach warriors against fifteen Vlahin hunters. "And we want to celebrate our understanding with a fight which will please the Great Bull and the Mother." *Where is Vlad?* His eyes searched the village again. Only he could kill Turgil.

"The Mother doesn't like blood," Moira said.

"But the Bull likes it. Turgil will fight for us. Who will fight for you?" *The Vlahins don't look worried. Am I missing something?*

"I will fight for the village," Vlad said, appearing from behind the closest hut, and he saw Turgil grinning at him. He ignored the man, fighting hard to calm his breath. He had run the whole way to the village.

"Take care of my mate." Turgil pushed Selma toward Grod, but Maduk intervened and placed an arm around her shoulders, pulling her away. He took off his long leather vest, and covered her.

"Thank you," Selma whispered, without realizing that as he placed the vest around her, Maduk had taken her in his arms. As had happened before, four years ago, she found herself protected by him, and the warmth of his body spread into her. She stopped shivering.

Silently, Rune advanced, and took Selma by the arm. Smiling, Maduk embraced her tighter for a moment, and then set her free. She did not react, following Rune without speaking. *She liked to stay in my arms*; Maduk thought, rubbing his palms together, as if trying to keep the memory of Selma's body in his hands. *Once Vlad kills Maduk, she will be mine.*

In the middle of the field that lay between the two groups, Turgil raised his copper axe. "The Bull will have your blood," he said to Vlad, who unsheathed his bayonet.

Without waiting for an answer, the Kalach sprang, his axe falling at full speed toward Vlad's head. Selma gasped, turning her head away, and most of the Vlahins blinked; some closed their eyes. Maduk bit his lip. The Kalachs cheered. Only Elna had no fear; she understood some of Vlad's combat skills. His moves were deceptively slow, when he was not threatened, and he looked unwary most of the time. But there was something in him, which took over his body when he needed it. With her fine senses, she understood that they were reflexes induced by long training, at a level that neither the Vlahins nor the Kalach could reach. Almost before they knew it, the Vlahins saw Turgil crumpling to his knees, a red spot flowering on his chest. The great fight had taken only a few seconds.

Vlad took the copper axe from the dead man's hand, and hefted it in his left hand. "Winner's right!" he shouted and raised the trophy above his head. "Release the women," he ordered, pointing at the four women still in the Kalachs' hands. He advanced, balancing the axe, until he stood in front of the men holding them prisoner. There was a stare in his eyes that made the ten men in front of him step aside, and the women sprang up, running toward the village. "What happened to the two men who were guarding you?" he asked the last woman.

"They were killed."

"There must be a misunderstanding," Maduk said quickly. "We came here only to trade and find mates."

Vlad raised his left arm, and from behind the huts, the elders of the clan and some women came into sight, their bows nocked.

"Let's talk," Maduk insisted. "Let's find a peaceful solution."

Before the Kalachs could react, Vlad dropped his arm, and more than forty arrows flew, hitting the group who had killed the watchers and taken the women. The Kalachs in the remaining group huddled together, behind Maduk.

"Put your weapons down," Maduk growled. "There is no way to win this fight. That idiot almost killed us. It's better if we talk," he repeated, and raised his empty hands.

"Why should we talk with you?" Vlad asked.

"We made a mistake and have been harshly punished. The Kalachs will not seek revenge for their dead."

"Why should I believe you?"

"I am the second Chief of the Kala, and I always keep my word."

"Can you guarantee that no other Vlahin women will be kidnapped by your people?"

"I can."

"And Selma is mine. I want your word on that too."

"Selma is yours, and I will never try to take her from you."

Their eyes locked, and Vlad thought that Maduk was a man that could keep his word. *There will be no more hunting our women. Selma and Malva will be safe.* "Now, let's trade. You can take the bodies in exchange for the merchandise. The choice is yours." Vlad pointed at the seventeen fallen Kalachs.

Maduk nodded bitterly, and turned, signaling the remaining Kalachs to retrieve the bodies and follow him. Before leaving, he gave Selma back her copper medallion. Vlad frowned , but let her have it. *As Tohar said, the Great Bull would grant us a great victory. I need to know more about Vlad. He is more dangerous than I thought. Selma will be his mate.* Maduk sighed and kicked a pebble along the path. *At least she is safe from Turgil, now. Everybody is safe from Turgil now.*

"This belongs to the Chief of the clan." Vlad gave the cooper axe to Rune, who bowed curtly, unable to speak – it was a rare and powerful gift.

Vlad turned, and found Selma in her mother's arms. He embraced both women, and they stayed like that for a while, his hands stroking their hair gently. *I was so close to losing you*; he thought, and then his lips searched for Selma's. Slowly, Elna moved away from them, and the girl's arms laced around his neck, her lips answering his.

Chapter 15

The dug-outs crossed the Great River early in the morning. Eight men rowed in a cadence that betrayed their high skill. In front of the boat, a man stood, covered by a hood, his dark eyes seeming to see nothing. *I will have my revenge*, the man thought, and his palm clutched the hilt of his copper knife. *I always pay my debt.* He cocked his head, trailing his other hand in the water and watching the ripples flow past, as boat was steering silently toward the shore.

On the shore, two men were waiting for the boat to arrive, but they did not move to help the rowers pull the boat onto the sand. Once he felt safe, the hooded man came ashore. Finally, one of the two waiting men advanced.

Tohar looks troubled. It took Darin just a moment to feel the anger boiling in the Kalach shaman. *It's not my fault that Turgil was so weak. And he acted like an idiot, killing the old men guarding the women. There is even more hate between us now, and this is only delaying my plans to kill Moira and her cripple.*

"Who is that man?" Tohar snapped. There was no need to use his name, both of them knew who 'that man' was.

"A wanderer. He came from a place so far away that its name is not known to us."

"What kind of man is he?"

"He calls himself a warrior trained to fight in wars much larger than everything we know. We did not believe him at first, but he spoke the truth."

"Why was so hard to believe him?"

"He looks weak and slow, and we thought that he only tried to impress us to give him shelter. But he is deceptive."

"Why would he try to deceive you, by looking weak?" *Is Darin as stupid as Turgil was? I hope not.* The shaman threw a hard stare at Darin, but said nothing more.

"I don't know yet, many times he acted like a weak man. He still acts, but we are watching him closer."

"We lost twenty men and a copper axe. Have you any idea how much we had to pay for it?"

An axe is more important than a man's life. "It is rare, indeed. Good men are even rarer."

"Who is his god?" *Maduk had warned me that Vlad is strong, but I did not believe him that strong. Sometimes, Maduk gets the things right. He is a clever man, though. Just that he doesn't believe too much in the power of the Bull. He knows that I am not a real shaman. And I have to play this stupid game only because of that.*

"Vlad has never told us."

"He is strong and clever; he must understand that the Mother is for the weak. The Great Bull is strong. Would he join the power of the Bull?"

"I don't think so. He is Moira's pawn. She has entered his head." Darin's finger tapped on his temple. *You want Vlad to replace me, and take over the clan. It will not happen.*

Tohar thought for a few moments. "Then kill him." The resignation in his voice did not escape Darin's tight attention.

That's already planned, but let's see how much you want him dead. "It will not be easy."

"You think of yourself as a strong man between the Vlahins. Are you afraid?"

"Turgil was strong and unafraid. It did not help him much."

"I am the shaman of the Great Bull, and I did not come here to play at riddles with you."

"What plans do you have, if I kill Vlad?"

"That weakling Maduk wants us to stay away from your people for a while. I see things differently, and my will prevails among the Kala. I want Moira dead too, and you to be the Vlahin Chief. Would that satisfy you?"

"Yes."

"And you still need to send Selma away. I will make her my mate. It should be easier after Vlad is gone. Bring me some good news in..."

"It will be done in a month. It's too soon now, after what happened." *The hunt is already prepared, and Rune has agreed I can take Vlad with me. During the Great Hunt in autumn, we will hunt mouflons on the steep slopes. Accidents happen sometimes.*

"Bring me his head, and you will receive a copper knife."

If Vlad dies, I no longer care about Selma's fate. She will go into the other village, with her second bond. But if Tohar give me another cooper knife for Rand... "One month and a half, and everything will be settled. Make sure you have the copper knife by then," Darin said and turned abruptly.

When the Vlahins could no longer see him, Tohar spat toward them. *You can't trust a traitor. Once Moira is dead, Darin will be their chief until we move enough people on their shore, then Maduk will take over. For a while, until I find a stronger man to replace him. At least Maduk will no longer make trouble in our village.* Lost in his own thoughts, Tohar climbed into the boat, forgetting to give order for their leave. "What are you waiting for?" he barked, and three men pushed the boat into the water.

※

It was early morning when Elna asked Vlad to come with her. It was Selma's day, so all three walked together. Elna took a path that crossed the sparse forest between the village and the mountain behind it, until they arrived at a place from where the whole village could be seen. Half a mile further on, the Great River glittered in the sunlight.

This should be far enough; she thought. "Afraid?" She smiled at Vlad, who raised a brow, as he realized what was in the shamane's mind. Selma laughed quietly, squeezing his hand; she knew already, and she felt Vlad's fear. "It's a good place and a good time. Minds are in a better mood when it's sunny."

"You never give up," Vlad said. This was Elna's third attempt to teach him how to be a shaman. Until today he refused her.

"It's for a good cause. Why are you scared? You entered the second River of Thought during the River Dance. At the beginning, you must learn how to enter the first one. All people enter there, just that they are not aware. As a shaman, you must learn do it by will."

"Last time, I was almost trapped there."

"Last time was an unforeseen initiation. Things will be much easier now, and we will not do a Communion."

"You are talking as if this shaman thing makes sense for me too. I am not a Vlahin. In my world there are no shamans." *Apart from some charlatans.* "I don't understand any of this."

"Did you see nothing during the River Dance? Did you see nothing during our Communion?"

"How do I know if those things were real?"

"Your mother was dressed in white and red. I really envied her clothes. They looked as soft as your shirts. Made of cotton, you said," Elna laughed. "She is blonde with dark eyes. Your house is huge. I never saw anything like it. There was a flying thing in your visions, too. Did I dream that?"

"No," Vlad sighed. "What do you want me to do?"

"Let's sit there." Elna pointed at a small ridge, half shaded by the crown of a large tree. She sat, leaning her back on the warm stones, and Vlad sat too, sandwiched between the two women. "You must desire to enter the first River, consciously, but you must not want it too much. Just give your mind an impulse, open your third eye, and let them do it for you. Your unconscious mind is already there, in the River. You must close the gap between the two parts of your mind. Don't speak, just give your mind an impulse, and let it wander."

After five minutes of silence, Elna laughed. "You almost fell asleep. Let's try to open your third eye, without going into the River. Use mine first," Elna said, placing her palm on the back of his neck.

Looking into Elna's third eye, Vlad was plunged into the Mother's Web, through the first River, a world of strange colors, but the misty interlaced threads refused to morph into something recognizable.

"Look around you with your third eye," Elna said directly in his mind, *"and tell me what you see."*

"Threads," he said, belatedly realizing that he was speaking directly into her mind too. *"This whole inner world is a tapestry."* He remembered the threads Moira had sent toward the people in the amphitheater. *"Like during the River Dance."* Elna's touch tingled as she probed his body and mind with her inner sight.

"This is not your inner world, it's how your third eye sees the hidden world of the Mother's Web. Once you will become more experienced, you will be able to pass from one River into another, seeing more of the Web. A four Amber Stones shaman can enter into the second River too. We are together, and your third eye is open," she said, sensing some questions in his mind. *"I will go away, now. The River is yours."* Once she retreated, the bright web of colors started to fade in Vlad's mind until only a few faint threads remained. *"Focus on them,"* Elna whispered.

Vlad tried and some of the threads sparked.

"That's interesting; the sparks must be a shaman's trick. Some things work differently for women and men. Don't be lazy," she said when the sparks diminished, and the sparks intensified again. *"Try to find Selma. No, you don't need to turn your head."* She pressed her hand more firmly on the back of his neck, to stop his head from turning.

"What should I look for?" Vlad asked, still unable to understand what Elna wanted from him.

"Something different."

"The sparks are different."

"The sparks are part of the web, they are not people."

"I can't."

"You have not even tried. To be a shaman is to be tied to the world around you and see it through the Rivers of Thought. The strands of the Web are linked to you. Some of them feed your shamanic power; others link you to the five elements and the Mother's mysteries that lie beyond them. Any shaman must learn how to navigate the Rivers."

"Is this some form of quantum consciousness?" Vlad asked, mechanically.

"What means quantum?"

"I am sorry. It's how some of us name the web which links us to the Rivers." His conscious mind, half focused, finally made the link to his unconscious one, and two small flames appeared around him. Puzzled, he opened his eyes, and everything disappeared.

"Well, you just consciously entered the first River of Thought."

"You were those flames?" Vlad asked, turning left and right, to see both women.

"Yes. I think that's enough for today."

They are not lying to me; these things really exist. I am more and more convinced that Penrose is right and consciousness is a quantum process, Vlad thought. *And the Mother's Web must be something similar, a kind of quantum field, albeit at a larger scale.* After Elna left them, he found more pleasant things to do with Selma than dissecting some quantum processes that may or may not exist.

Back in the village, they found Darin talking with Rune and the shamanes in front of main hut.

"We were talking about you," Rune said, smiling, and gestured for him to take a seat. "I am sure that Selma will forgive us for the kidnapping. In ten days, Darin is leaving to hunt mouflons, and you wanted to see the mountains. You will join the hunters."

"Yes, I would like to see the mountains, but I am no hunter. I may be a burden for the hunters."

"You are good with the bow." Darin said. "It should not be hard to kill a mouflon, if it comes your way, and we don't need only archers. Some of us have to channel the mouflons toward the places where the archers are hidden."

Vlad's eyes swept the place, and found that everybody was expecting him to join the hunters. *Well, I have to become a Vlahin...* "Fine, I will come with you."

A few days later, Elna went with him and Selma again, and they went to the same place as before.

"Let's try once more to enter the Mother's Web. Use my third eye first," Elna said, placing her hand on the back of his neck.

The threads came back to Vlad, and this time his mind became more curious than scared. Slowly, Elna retreated, without telling him, leaving his third eye to display the threads for both of them.

"Find Selma," Elna said inside his mind, her inner sense probing him.

Vlad stretched his mind, and the same two small red flames appeared. He did not fear them this time, and let his mind wander around the flames. Suddenly, more than a hundred flames filled his inner vision. He gasped, opening his eyes, and his conscious mind retreated from the first River of Thought. "What was that?" he asked, his pulse racing.

"What do you think? And why are you scared?"

"People?" Vlad asked, irritated, his breath uneven. *Why doesn't she understand that such strange experiences need to happen a step at a time?*

Even without training, his mind had stretched into the village, nine hundred paces away. His Shaman Seed must be stronger than the four Amber Stones he has now. Maybe even stronger than mine. Why can't I see his Seed?
"Yes. Why are you afraid of people?"

"Because..." he started, and paused, and fought to calm his restless mind, using a breathing technique for almost two minutes. "I don't know what effect they might have on my mind. I don't want to become unconscious for days, again."

"You won't," Elna said gently, stroking his hair. "This is not an initiation. Let's try again. Please," she added with a charming smile.

"Give me a moment," Vlad said, standing up abruptly. He walked a few steps and his restless eyes swept over the valley.

"The Great River looks so beautiful from here," Selma whispered behind him, her arms around his waist. With a sigh, Vlad turned and embraced her too. He leaned his head on hers, both of them silent.

"Let's try again," Vlad said after a while, and they returned to the edge.

"The people in the village can't sense you." Elna placed her hand on the back of his neck again. "Moira can see you only if she is day dreaming or consciously connected to the Mother's Web. I am sure that she will not harm you," she said, smiling.

This time, Vlad was able to overcome his fear. He felt a touch of pride, seeing all those little flames, representing the people in the village. *"Can I see the village too?"* he asked Elna, using his mind.

"For that, you must enter the second River of Thought."

"Should I try now?"

"You seem very eager to try new things now, but for that you must ingest sacred mushrooms." Vlad felt her amusement, but said nothing. *"When the time comes, we will teach you which mushrooms can be used, how to harvest them and how to make the potion."*

"Is there something else I can try now?"

"Just practice how to enter the Mother's Web. Later, we will teach you the benefits."

Vlad severed the link with the first River of Thought, entered again and left it again. "It works." He looked at

Elna, smiling. She returned the smile. "Thank you. If I enter the second River, how far I can see?"

"Usually, twice as far as you can see people when you are in the first River."

"And if I want to see farther?"

"You need the third River of Thought. But only shamans with six Amber Stones can go there. And they can see everywhere on Earth. I entered the Third River of Thought once. It should not be possible for a shaman with five Amber Stones." *And?* Vlad gestured. "It may be that my real Shaman Seed is six stones. Something stopped me reaching it." *Can it be that not having an initiation with a shaman was the cause? That will not please the Grand Shamane. She despises the shamans. But if it's true...*

"You have five and a half stones now. Have you tried again?"

"I will try, after my new power stabilizes, but I need to take a stronger potion. That is not ... healthy."

"Our shaman entered the first River," Moira's voice interrupted them.

"Day dreaming?" Elna asked with a smile.

"The pleasure of being the Shamane. Vlad," she turned toward him, "be careful tomorrow, when you go to hunt. Avoid places with rocks that seem unstable."

There are plenty of such rocks in the mountains. "Is this something that appeared in your daydreams?" he asked, curious.

"I saw a falling rock when you entered the first River. Daydreaming allows you to see the future, but it is never clear. Everything is a matter of interpretation."

"Can you sense everyone in the first River?"

"The ones who are consciously connected, yes. With some effort, I may be able to distinguish others too."

"And it happens instantly. Like this." Vlad snapped his fingers.

"I don't know when you entered the River, but the link between us happens fast. The shamans with nine Amber Stones were able to talk at distance, from one village to the another. There is not much use in talk if there is a delay."

When they connect to another mind, they jump into a River of Thought and navigate it through the Web, like using a wormhole. The same when they see things at distance; Vlad thought. *It's not that they transfer thoughts at a distance; they are not long waves. And that would mean delay.* "No one can do this anymore."

"Eight-stone shamanes can talk in your mind at some distance. Up to a thousand paces, perhaps. Our power is diminished." Moira looked at Vlad, then looked away.

She wants to make a Communion with me. For her a half Amber Stone increase in power is important. And for the village too. "Can you guarantee that I will not have the same problems in a new Communion?"

"It shouldn't happen again, but I can't give you stone guarantees."

For a while, Vlad pondered, saying nothing; Moira's hopeful gaze stayed on him. "We can try today." *I may have an excuse to skip hunting tomorrow.*

"Thank you, Vlad." Gently, Moira's hand touched his face. "I should leave now," she said and turned away.

I connect to the Web, and the other person is connected too. We become are aware of each other's presence, instantly. It's not a real link; that would need a lot of energy. Our brain produces only tiny amounts of energy. It may be a kind of quantum entanglement.

Everything is a matter of energy consumption in the end. Vlad continued to ponder, watching her walk away. Lost in his inner thoughts, he did not realize that Elna had left too, until Selma leaned her head on his shoulder.

That evening, the Communion with Moira passed without incident. Apart from his initial fear, he felt nothing unusual. The shamanes realized that Moira's power had increased by a half stone – as happened to Elna – but they also felt that his power was becoming more stable, something they had expected to happen more slowly, over the next few months. Both women kept their discoveries to themselves; there was no need to alarm Vlad.

"Should we ask him to make a Communion with the girls?" Moira asked when the shamanes remained alone.

"I don't know how it will affect them." Elna was trying to remember something that her grandmother had told her just before her initiation. "We have no idea what happens when we merge our minds with a shaman. But I hope that they will do the initiation with him. He should be fully stabilized in half a year. Ah," she said, suddenly. "I just remembered. Grandmother told me once that the way of calculating the power of shamane apprentice's Seed has changed since the last shaman died. It was lowered, but I don't remember by how much. The girls may have more Amber Stones than we think now, and that would explain why Vlad was able to increase our power." She gestured between Moira and her. "We've got a half stone more. Maybe they will get a full stone."

Vlad woke up in the morning refreshed, and he felt ashamed to use the Communion as an excuse to avoid participating in the hunt; the shamanes would have felt guilty about his 'weakness'.

Chapter 16

At noon, Darin, his twenty hunters and five women followed the path up into the mountains to a wooden structure built at the edge of the forest, close to the foot of the cliff. Two hundred paces away, there was a waterfall. The sun above was spreading warm colors over the valley, which was surrounded by tall mountains.

"That looks like the Semenic Mountains," Vlad whispered to himself. *I was there a few times, but I came from the east. I was driving. I even skied there one winter. Now, we have come from the south through the gorges of a river that could be Nera, or I am just imaging that this is a known place, because I am missing...* He shook his head, then looked at the peaks; this had always been one of his favorite moments in the mountains, the moments that just preceded the sun's descent, when the sunset burst in its full glory, casting a rainbow of colors.

"We need to repair the hut first," Darin said. "It doesn't look too damaged. We may need branches." He glanced at Vlad.

"Just tell me how many," Vlad said. One edge of his bayonet was shaped like a saw. It cut thin timber much faster than a stone axe. He walked around the hut, just to see what kind of branches had been used. The hut was only nine feet wide, but it was thirty feet long. Here and there, small holes in the roof let him see inside: the hut was empty. *Oak and yew*, he touched the roof. *I need to cut yew branches, the oak seems to be fine.* The roof had a lattice of oak trunks a hand's width in size on top of which yew branches had been placed. Even though they were cut one or two years ago, most of the yew still had their foliage, keeping the interior of the hut dry. He went to find some yews with low branches, and cut twenty of them, as thick as a child's arm and five feet long. One hunter or another came to pick up the branches.

"We need thirty more branches." Darin told Vlad, who nodded.

It took them four hours to bring the hut to an acceptable condition, and then Vlad was free. He had his bow, but he had left his spear in the village. He was still uncomfortable with that weapon. While most of them gathered around the hut, Vlad found that he needed to be alone. He walked away and stood next to the waterfall, and looked at the outline of the mountain in front of him. The water's rushing sound was relaxing. *There was no waterfall in the Semenic Mountains*... He turned his head and glanced up at the tall cliff. It resembled a wall. *Moira warned me to stay away from falling rocks. There are plenty of those*. He moved twenty feet away from the cliff. That gave him a better view over the waterfall. It was not that big. *I want to see things from the top, but I don't know where it can be climbed, and it's late, anyway.*

Vlad closed his eyes and breathed the fresh mountain air deeply. The sight of Cosmin, bloody and still, came to him. *Why now?* The ghost had left him alone for almost two months. Some good or bad memories still disturbed him, from time to time, but not the body. He quieted his thoughts for a while, as he tried to ignore the dreadful memory. Shaking his head, he returned to the hut. Food was served, and he joined the hunters.

During the night, the roof rattled, and Vlad fastened his sleeping bag. Rain beat against the yew leaves, an early autumn storm that had been threatening the mountains from the end of the evening.

"The wind is howling like a mad wolf," Vlad murmured, then fell asleep again.

After they ate in the morning, Darin gathered all the people around him. "The rain will make our hunt more dangerous, but you are all experienced hunters, and today is for scouting. We will split into three groups. The women and two hunters will stay here. Nine hunters will come with me. Nine will go with Heno." He walked quickly among the men, and split them into three teams. "Vlad, you come with me," he said at the end. *Enjoy the hunt, today and tomorrow. Our little game will start later, and you will be the prey.* "Today, we will search this mountain," he pointed toward the waterfall. Heno, you know the eastern path around the cliff. We should return by noon."

They returned at noon, and Heno gave them the good news. "We saw two herds of mouflons. One of them had more than twenty animals. They are on the eastern slope, close to the peak. We can surround them easily."

"Twenty mouflons," Darin said, rubbing his chin. "We can kill ten of them, and ten will stay to preserve the herd. Mother's will." *In this case, the Mother is right. The Kalachs would kill the whole herd. They don't care about the next year. We can teach them, and they can teach us. They have more things to teach us. And we will no longer needs the shamanes.*

"Mother's will," the hunters repeated.

"The second herd was smaller, only fourteen animals," Heno continued his report.

"We can kill seven of them. Mother's will," Darin said. "After we finish here, we search the other mountain," he pointed to the western one.

The first two hunts were successful and, on the fourth day, they started again on the northern mountain. Here, Darin was lucky; he spotted two herds of mouflons, while Heno found only one. After the fourth hunt, they had already brought thirty-one animals for the women to prepare.

"Tomorrow is the last hunt," Darin said in the evening. They were gathered inside the hut, trying to shelter from the monotonous autumn rain."

The morning was sunny again, and the hearts of the hunters were lighter, after a night when most of them stayed wet. The stubborn rain eventually found a way down. Protected by his sleeping bag, Vlad was in a better mood. In fifteen minutes, they crossed the valley, and Darin split them up again, taking the same men with him, and leaving the same men with his brother, but they still walked together until they spotted the last herd. Silently, they split up, each team trying to get in a position from where they could drive the herd into a cul de sac. The men knew the mountains as well as the animals. They had hunted here for many years, and so had their fathers and their grandfathers.

Darin led them through a narrow path which wound under a wall of cliffs. Above them the hidden peak of the mountain towered up, invisible, from the path. A bitter, cold wind swirled among the rocks, howling from time to time, heralding the coming of the winter. They climbed the sharp slope until the path forked. The herd was on top of a small peak that was surrounded by the twin paths.

"We split up here," Darin said. "You, you, and you," he said, and the last one he pointed at was Vlad, "take the lower path. Vlad, you will take the rear. Spread out and be ready to drive the herd up, toward us. Heno will come from the other side. Once the herd gets to the top, there will be no way for them to escape. Wait for us to arrive at that tree," he pointed toward an old beech, half uprooted and half dead.

They split up in silence and Darin's team went up until they arrived at the half-dead tree. From there, Darin gestured at the team below, and the four men moved toward the lower path. Vlad did as he was told and stayed close to the mouth of the lower path. From their higher position, Darin's hunters were already able to see the herd.

"Rand and I will stay here for a while to see where the herd wants to move," Darin said. They waited until the other men vanished from sight, and climbed down until they arrived at a smaller path that appeared only here and there between the rocks. "We wait here," Darin said to his son.

Rand craned his neck to see the path below.

"Stay hidden," Darin ordered. "The ridge bordering the lower path gets smaller and smaller. From that rock that looks like a head, we will see Vlad. And from there," he pointed to a small juniper just below, "the ridge is no higher than a man's hip. This boulder," he pointed again toward an almost round rock, two feet in diameter, "will do the job. Look at its base and make sure that it will be easy to roll."

"I see Vlad," Rand whispered, as the top of his head appeared, above the lower path.

"Vlad will never be a hunter," Darin said. "Look at him, how carelessly he is walking. Not even a look up. And now, he is admiring the sun. He is useless."

"He is a good fighter," Rand said.

"Fighters don't feed the clan. Hunters do. And we are good enough fighters too."

Sunshine passed through a gap in the clouds. It fell just on the area around Vlad, and he raised his head, letting the sun play on his face. *It's so good*, he thought, eyes closed. *I may stay here for a while. In the last three hunts I did nothing. I don't even know why Darin bothered to take me with him.* Only in the first hunt had Vlad done anything that might with a little indulgence be called helpful. One mouflon came his way, and he shooed at it. The mouflon turned back toward the real hunters, but the hunt was already finished. The animal was lucky.

The clouds closed again and, disappointed, Vlad began to walk again on the narrow path, which was still slippery.

On his right there was a deep precipice. After half a minute, his shoulders became visible from Darin's place.

"Take position," he said to his son, and moved closer to the boulder. He pressed his hand on the cold surface, just to feel the stone. Rand did the same. "At my signal, you push. Just a few more steps, and he will arrive in the right position. "Now!"

Both men strained, and slowly, the boulder moved until it reached the point of balance. From there, and with a last push, it began to roll. There was no noise at first. Around them, the wind whistled, hiding the small noise the falling boulder was starting to make, a few seconds later.

Below, forty feet from them, Vlad stopped abruptly, as faint sounds arrived to him through the wind, but he was not yet able to recognize them or their origin. The boulder was now dislodging other stones, some larger than a man's head, and it was already halfway down. There were upward of a dozen falling rocks. Vlad finally saw them, and froze for a moment. There was a small crevice in front of him, which he could not jump over, and he turned abruptly, hoping to run back, but it was too late to run. From the corner of his eye, he had the impression of briefly seeing two men above him. They were moving quickly behind a ridge. He ignored them.

From their position, Darin and Rand heard a dull rumble as several boulders hit the path. The biggest one hit the ridge, breaking it just where Vlad was, and even more rocks started to fall. "That ridge is only three feet tall," Darin said. "We will find his body at the base of the precipice when we return. Let's go and hunt some mouflons. I feel in better shape now."

He moved up toward the main path, and picked up his spear and bow, leaning against the old beech. After one more look down, Rand did the same. Once all the falling rocks had vanished from sight, nothing moved on the path. Walking at a brisk pace, they joined the hunters a few minutes later. They were hidden behind rocks and juniper bushes. One of them was holding his spear upright. A signal for Heno's team. Resembling a dead tree, the spear did not attract the herd's attention.

"What wonderful animals we have here," Darin said. "They already have their winter coat, and they are full of fat. Today, we will feed our clan again."

If they were lucky, they could bring the number of killed mouflons to forty. That could provide more than two thousand pounds of meat, of the best quality for the winter. The ratio between meat and fat was perfect for the cold winter nights, when people needed more energy, not only protein. The only animals which provided a better ratio were bears and some fish. Another big hunt was planned to catch bears, and with the coming of the cold they would move to fish more than to hunt.

"Has Heno arrived?" Darin asked the closest man.

"Not yet. Garo will signal to us. He is the closest hunter to the herd, and can see the other side of the peak. He is behind that large rock that resembles a man lying down." He pointed north, toward the rock and the herd.

A hundred paces from them, Garo raised his spear, while his eyes swept the other edge of the meadow, from where Heno would arrive. Five minutes later, he saw a spear rising above a rock that was almost as large as a hut. Still holding the spear in his right hand, he gestured with his left to the closest man. The signal passed along until it arrived at Darin who, followed by Rand, started to crawl toward the herd. Seeing them move, the other men did the same, and soon all the hunters moved to encircle the unaware animals.

Seeing the rocks tumbling so close to his head, Vlad decided in a split second that he could not run back, and he could not jump over the small crevice in front. He lay down, on his left, leaning against the cold stone, and covered his head with his arms. A crack like thunder rang in his ears. It happened only two feet above his head. The largest boulder hit the edge of the ridge, splitting it, and a rain of stones, some as large as a fist, fell on him. The boulder jumped a little, then rolled further down. It crushed on the path on which Vlad was lying, just a hand's width from his left arm, which was covering his head. One splinter cut through his shirt, and he felt a sharp pain in the upper part of his arm. It was followed by a second pang of pain, and he felt blood running down his skin. Desperate, he leaned harder into the stone. More boulders rolled down, and some of them hit the path. With relief, Vlad noted that they were getting smaller and smaller. A few more came, and one of them had a curious trajectory. It did not hit the edge of the ridge. It touched a rock just a foot before the edge, and passed over the ridge, right into Vlad's arm. A protuberance knocked his skull with a dull bang. Vlad felt some pain, then he felt nothing.

The hunt was successful, and Darin counted eleven mouflons lying in the grass. There were only eighteen men to carry them down, and the men gathered to tie the animals onto the spears. Four animals were smaller, and they were tied together, in pairs.

"Where is Vlad?" the hunter who was supposed to carry a mouflon with him asked.

"He was with us on the lower path, but..." another one answered.

"Go and find him," Darin ordered. "Take the other two men who were with you on the lower path." *Vlad is a careless man. You will find him the precipice.*

The man cursed, but walked away, followed by the other two. At the end of the meadow, one by one they took the rocky path.

"Vlad is not a hunter," one of them said. "He should have been left at the hut to guard the women. He is better at guarding and fighting than either of the men we left there."

"Maybe Darin wants to train him."

"Train him for what? Soon Vlad will become a shaman and he will not be allowed to hunt."

"Is this really true?"

"Yes, Moira told me." The man was her cousin, and one of the hunters who did not like Darin too much.

"What's that there?" One man pointed to where the path seemed covered with boulders and fallen earth.

"Someone is lying on the ground. It must be Vlad. Hurry," Moira's cousin said and started to walk at a brisk pace.

They found Vlad unconscious, but still alive. There was blood in his hair, and more blood on his upper arm.

"I am afraid to move him."

"Let me check if his spine was affected," Moira's cousin said; he had some knowledge of wounds. He took Vlad's hand and pressed with the tip of his knife. Vlad's fingers moved. "The spine should be fine. Let's clean the dirt and pebbles off him." They finished without finding more wounds, and he checked Vlad's head: blood was no longer flowing. "It doesn't look like his skull is broken." He poured some water on Vlad's face, who moaned faintly. "That's good. Vlad," he said and slapped him gently. A second moan followed. "Vlad, wake up." He splashed some more water and, finally, Vlad opened his eyes.

"What happened?" Vlad asked, his voice barely audible.

"Some rocks fell on you. Drink some water." Moira's cousin pushed the flask into his mouth and squeezed.

Vlad gulped then coughed, and the pain grew inside his head. He moaned again, then touched his skull. "How badly am I wounded?" he asked, seeing his red fingers. *They tried to kill me*. The memory of the two men sneaking away, during the avalanche of stones, came back to him.

"One stone hit you on the skull, but it doesn't seem to be broken. And there are three cuts on your upper arm. Can you stand?"

Even when they look superficial, skull wounds may be dangerous, and I have enough issues with my head. "I don't know. Give me some more water." *Those two men... They could be Darin and his son. I don't have other enemies in the village. I can't accuse them now. I must wait until we are back in the village. I hope to make it.*

Two more men came to see what had happened and then Vlad was able to stand and walk. It was difficult to carry him on the narrow path. He had cut a band from his shirt and tied it around his head. For a proper bandage, he had to wait until they arrived at the hut. One man walked in front of him, and another one behind, one spear in their hands, making a kind of balustrade for Vlad to lean his arm on it. His steps were hieratic, and he had to stop many times and lean against the ridge. All three were tied together with a rope, and it took them a while to walk toward the end of the long path. There, they helped Vlad to lie in the grass.

A week later, back in the village, Elna and Moira had a look at his wounds.

"The ones on your arm have healed well and they will not bother you. The bone was not touched. Your skull was not actually broken, but there was a crack about a thumb's width. It's still not healed. We will make a poultice, and if things don't improve in three days, and you still see black spots, we will have a Healing Communion."

"You should have been more cautious," Moira said, careful not to remind him of her warning about the falling rocks. "One more accident like this and..."

"It was not an accident. Two men pushed a large boulder down onto me. It dislodged more small rocks. I was the last one on a narrow path. Darin sent me there, but I can't say that he was the one who tried to kill me."

"Are you sure?" Moira asked.

"I saw them, when they tried to hide, right above me, during the avalanche. I don't know anyone else apart from Darin and Rand who would try to kill me."

"A lost challenge doesn't mean that Rand tried to kill you."

"Then I don't know who they were. I don't know too many people in the clan, and I have no issues with the one I do know."

"Darin may be closer to the Kalachs than we thought," Elna said.

"Still..." Moira looked at her sister.

"Still," Elna shrugged. "What do you want to do?" she asked Vlad.

"Nothing, without proof, but don't send me hunting again."

Chapter 17

When they finished their work, Selma and Malva brought the bowl to Moira, who tasted it. "It's strong," she said, then poured a little more than half of the hot liquid into another bowl. "This should be enough for you to enter the second River of Thought." She offered the bowl to Vlad. "Two of our sacred mushrooms are inside. The Long Night and the Long Sight. After you make your Heart Stone, we will teach you how to make the potion."

Vlad sniffed, and thought the potion was similar to the one that Moira made him drink when he was unconscious during his unexpected initiation. His memory recorded it. He sniffed again, and hairs rose on his arms.

Elna come closer and touched his brow. "It will not harm you."

Vlad nodded and sipped a small quantity of the awful drink. He grimaced, then drank the rest in one shot, feeling as if a hot stone was falling into his stomach. Once he'd finished, he grimaced even more.

"We need to wait until the drink goes to your head."

When they left Moira's hut, it was full dark and cool, but the wind that had come up with nightfall had swept the mists away from the northern mountain behind the village. Only the shamanes came with him. The ceremony was not for the apprentices. Above them, the night sky blazed with myriad stars, and Vlad looked in awe again at the much denser Milky Way. Moira glanced eastward, through the scattered clouds, and noticed the sky growing luminous with the rising of the moon, though it was still invisible behind the smaller eastern mountain.

Once she reached the two poles in the double circle where she performed the Night Dance, Moira looked back, and she could see Vlad's dark shape against the nascent moonlight. Even in silhouette, there was a wrenching loneliness in the way he walked, his mind floating away. *He is afraid*, Moira thought. *Too much fear might kill the Heart Stone. I must talk to Elna. She knows him better*.

When he reached the circle, Vlad glanced eastward too, knowing that his final initiation would start at the full moon's rising. He resisted the impulse to hold on to one of the standing poles. *I am not so weak*, he thought. Gradually, his head ceased to spin, and he waited patiently for Moira's advice.

Moira felt no need to tell Vlad about the power of the circle. The place was sacred, not to be looked upon by uninitiated eyes, and only the shamanes could see it; the shamans could not. The shamans had their own sacred places, but there were common sacred places too. As she entered in the circle, the air within it seemed to become heavier, and utterly still. The wind was still singing softly, but stayed outside the circle.

"Don't be afraid, Vlad. Be still. If you are afraid, you won't be able to hear," Elna said, gently.

"Hear what?" Vlad asked, annoyed by his fear, but even more annoyed that Elna felt it .

"The wind. It's singing. The Mother is trying to get your attention. She is guiding you. The moon and the stars are speaking too."

They are too far away, Vlad thought, mostly to hide from himself.

"Take your clothes off," Moira said and she undressed, as did Elna.

"Are the Rivers dangerous? Do they bind to your mind?" Vlad asked as he took his shirt off, just to stop his incessant swirling thoughts.

"They might be dangerous, if you go there with an impure mind, but they don't bind you. They give you freedom. The ability to go wherever your mind desires. It's time," Elna said, seeing more light in the east. "Do you have the amber stone?"

"Yes." Vlad opened his left hand. The stone caught the reflection of a far away star and beamed faintly.

"We call the moon." Moira lifted her hands. Inside the circle, the air around her grew tense with anticipation, as she waited for the first bright edge to emerge above the mountain. "We call earth from which we were born and to where we return." She bent and touched the sand at her feet. "We call the five Rivers of Thought. We call the Mother to guide us. We bring Vlad, who died a man, and was reborn as a shaman. He requests passage into the second River of Thought. Receive him." She stretched out her hand, and pulled Vlad into the circle, her eyes fixed on the thin edge of the moon visible over the mountain.

As they had taught him, Vlad took up a pose close to what he would have called a Vitruvian Man. The wind was still singing around him, but he felt nothing on his skin. Moira had sealed the circle. At his sides, both shamanes put an arm around his waist. Elna's arm was in front of him, while Moira's was behind him. Elna placed her free hand on the back of his neck, and the cupping glass sensation came back to him.

"Open your third eye and enter the Mother's Web through the first River of Thought," Elna said in his mind.

Slowly, controlling his fear, Vlad opened his third eye and entered the Mother's Web, through the first River, finding the same world of strange colors and faint interlaced threads which refused to morph into something recognizable.

"Focus your third eye."

He breathed and focused his attention on the threads. Moment by moment, they gained light and the net was now clear in front of him. Two yellow flames, larger than those he had seen before, appeared just beside him, and hundred small, red ones in the village.

"We've joined you in the first River," Elna said. *"Ignore the people from the village."*

Vlad adjusted his mind and, slowly, the hundred red flames diminished until they became barely visible.

"Feel the net."

Vlad voided his mind of thoughts and let it drift without compass. The net became a mist of light blue so pale it was almost white. It surrounded him, and he felt his mind pulled inside until it was completely absorbed. The mist was now so dense that he could see nothing.

"You are in the second River of Thought. Play with the mist."

"How?" Vlad asked.

"You know how. Look inside you."

I see nothing. He cleared his mind again, waiting for something to resurface. *The wind is singing.* He imagined himself being the wind, and moved through the mist, clearing everything in his way. The same two yellow flames appeared in front of him.

"From now on, you are alone. Prepare your incantation to the Mother," Elna said, and both flames vanished.

From what they had told him, the incantation was a kind of spell made to open the way to the second River. *I want to know how to make a spell*, Vlad thought. *I want to know so many things. Focus.* He breathed deeply. *But I want to know,* his mind repeated, stubbornly. *Witches usually have a wand. I have nothing. Are the shamanes witches? What makes a witch, a witch? I want to know that too. Things are not going in the right direction.* He breathed deeply a few times, clearing his mind again. *Elna and Moira said that the spell would come to me. Maybe I am not a shaman, and everything was an accident. Like my arrival here. How should I know? Maybe my spell is related to knowledge. I want to know. Can be this an incantation? To tell the River what I want to know?* For a few moments, he pondered if it was worth exploring that path. *Knowledge has value. Maybe this is my key and my path.* He breathed once and started to recite:

"I want to know

Why the wind blows
Why the moon rises
Why were we born into this world.
I want to know
What the five Rivers are
And what is beyond them.
I want to know."

Each line came more easily, power coming from inside him, and power being absorbed from the two women still touching Vlad, though he was unaware of it. He no longer felt them. Inside the River, he was alone, and nothing from the outside came to him. As the energy increased, he found himself growing warmer and calmer. He finished his incantation and listened to the silence around him.

I have to carve the amber stone. He stretched out his left arm and opened his hand. The stone appeared in his inner vision, suspended in the second River. *There are no tools.* His third eye searched left and right, but it was only him and his stone. *What tools can be used to engrave the stone? I'm sure there are no lasers here.* His lack of knowledge irritated Vlad as much as the utter silence around him. *Elna did not tell me what tool she used.*

"Each shaman has his tools," she had told him a few days ago, her voice still fresh in his mind.

"Can I have a laser?" Vlad asked the River and waited a minute for an answer that did not come. *What else can I use? A beam? Moonlight? They can't engrave a heart in a stone. And the yellow color... Maybe inside the River they can.* "Can I have a yellow beam?" he asked and listened again. *Nothing. Maybe it's not that I have to ask; maybe I have to imagine a tool.* He forced his mind to create a

beam. He failed and stretched his virtual hand out to touch the stone. His finger simply passed through it. *Everything is virtual, here. I don't need a real tool. I need a virtual tool. An idea of a tool.* This time, he did not force his mind; he let it wander, and brief flashes of past things came to him. Malva. The bear. Selma. His notebook. Him writing Vlahin words. *A pencil...* His idea took shape, and a golden penholder appeared in front of him. *How can I use it?* He reached out and touched the penholder. It felt solid and, gently, he took the pen in his hand, and pressed the nib into the stone. It pierced the stone and, instantly, the stone became yellow. The moment he had drawn the heart, the penholder vanished.

"'I Want to Know' is your name in the Mother's Web and, in time, you will know." An unfamiliar voice spoke, and Vlad felt himself being expelled from the River.

His expulsion was so abrupt that he felt afraid again. Almost blind, he blinked at the moon. *Did I fail?* He did not try to ask the shamanes.

Elna came to him and placed her right hand on his chest, over his heart. "I Want to Know, meet Remember Always."

Elna moved away, and Moira performed the same ritual. "I Want to Know, meet River Dancer."

"So, did I...?" Vlad asked, feeling the need for a straight answer.

"Look at your Amber Heart," Elna said and, slowly, he opened his hand. The stone now glowed with a delicate yellow color, and there was a heart engraved into it.

He nodded with a smile and, feeling his legs going weak, he stumbled. Once the tension had left him, so did the adrenaline which had kept him standing. Expecting it, the shamanes caught him in their arms. After a while, they dressed in silence and walked down into the village, both women still helping him. In front of the hut, they embraced Vlad.

"This night is one of solitude and reflection," Elna said, and ushered him into his room.

Still not fully understanding what happened to him, Vlad stood, head in hands, on the edge of his bed. *I want to know... That's not a bad name.*

"So, you are a shaman, now." Andrei's head had a pensive look that took Vlad by surprise. It also seemed as if the details on his frowning face were sharper. "How do you feel?"

Such a perfect illusion, Vlad thought. *And so much for my night of solitude and reflection*. "Like I've been reborn. Everything looks different. Everything feels different. Is this what you want to hear?"

"Oh, you want to please me, your perfect illusion, on a night of reflection."

"Will this change in me affect you?" Vlad grinned, realizing, for the first time, that there was no fear in his mind; though there was nothing normal in his own head, Andrei's head no longer frightened him. Some pain still lurked in a corner of his mind – the memory of Andrei's death – but it was manageable. He could even think of Cosmin from time to time. At least, he was able to bring back the good memories. Like the one which had come to him in the morning, when he was not yet fully awake: their first trip alone, without their parents, to a seaside resort, close to the old Greek ruins of Histria. The only memories which still overwhelmed him, where those related to his parents. While Cosmin and Andrei were gone, and Vlad had fully accepted their loss, his parents were still alive, somewhere, or in some timeline and, even though he was not yet sure where this place was, he was sadly sure he would not see them again.

"Of course." The Head grinned back, and Vlad suddenly found himself sitting in an armchair, in a room that looked like it belonged in a medieval house. "I've always liked the Renaissance."

"How are you doing this?"

"Hmm; I was actually expecting a question about this marvelous place." The Head had somehow acquired hands; they were directly attached to his short neck. His right hand made an ample gesture around the large room. "I am quite disappointed. That's a fresco." He pointed at the ceiling, which was split in four compartments, each of them with its own story. "That's a fresco, that too, that too and that too." The forefinger of his right hand pointed at the four walls; the room was painted throughout. "But to answer your little question. After your ... transformation. I don't know if that is really the right expression to describe your actual condition." His hands parted, in an 'I don't know' gesture. "I found more ways to mess with your mind than I had ever imagined." His grin widened, and his mouth too, which seemed to surround the entire head.

"You resemble a hologram," Vlad said, thinking that he could still manage the situation, by abruptly changing the direction of their discussion, though now a sliver of doubt troubled him. "I will be able to see that grin even if I'm behind you."

"For a true connoisseur, I am an art form. Exquisite. Unique. Let's go back, now. The Renaissance."

"What about it?"

"I thought that becoming a shaman brought a spiritual evolution. I see nothing like that in you."

"Fine, what is this place?"

"The castle of Torrechiara." The Head stared at Vlad, expectation in his eyes.

"There are so many Italian castles," Vlad shrugged.

"This," the Head pointed again at the ceiling, "is one of the earliest geographic panoramas in the history of art. It depicts a spiritual pilgrimage, a love story, many things, everything laid out in four parts. It's one of the few among this type of painting to depict a woman's journey. It gives the watcher the impression that hers is an endless pilgrimage. Does that sound familiar to you?"

"Fifteenth century?" Vlad asked. He had the uncomfortable feeling that Head was asking him a riddle and, perhaps worse, the feeling that solving it might lead to something very unpleasant.

"The castle is older, but it was fully rebuilt in 1480. Remember that, for a viewer on the floor, the woman seems to be locked in a circular loop, and who knows from which of the four parts the woman will find her way out? There is a castle in each quarter. And a owner. You can't see it in the picture, but two castles are already blocked, and two are still free. There are only two possible ways out for her. An interesting riddle, isn't it? A spectator is nothing more than a bystander, and can't influence the woman's progress. All the paintings here were done by Benedetto Bembo. He is not especially well-known. There," the Head pointed at the southeast wall. "That's where the story starts. Cupid does what he does best: shoots arrows. The man has been shot in the breast, and clasps the arrow with both hands. Drawing his bow again, Cupid turns toward the woman, who has also been shot, but she does not appear to notice it. That is also an interesting riddle. Cupid fires his arrows without real discernment and, sometimes, his victims only feel the effect much later. You could link the woman's reaction to the part of the painting where the she finds her way out in the previous story. But let's go on." The Head flew to a second scene: the woman giving a sword to a knight, who is kneeling before her. "Do you know what this symbolizes?" The Head tapped on the proffered sword, producing a muffled sound.

"Chivalry. He has vowed to be her protector, and it seems that she has accepted him."

"Well, well," the Head clapped his hands. "It seems that something is finally working in your shaman head. In the previous scene, the woman does not know she has been touched by Cupid's arrow. Now, she accepts a protector. Who is her protector? Try to find the missing links. So many things depend on that." He winked and, the next moment, Vlad found himself flying, passing through the closed window, going higher and higher. The castle became smaller, until it vanished from sight, and he found himself alone in his room in the Vlahin village.

Did I dream that? Vlad asked himself, and his eyes moved around the room, searching for the Head.

"No."

He started, then looked at the place where the sound had come from: he saw nothing. *I've never heard of that castle. How could Andrei know...? No, the Head is not Andrei, it's just a figment of my imagination. A morbid figment. How could I know about...?*

He walked around the small room, feeling like he was in a cage, and went to the door. He paused, thinking that Moira might be outside – the Shamane had a habit of staring at the sky when she was thinking something through. He wanted to be alone, but his feeling of being caged was stronger, so he stepped outside to gaze up at the clear sky. Without the light pollution, to which he was so accustomed, there were far more stars to be seen; here, at least, the Milky Way deserved its name. The stars seemed almost close enough to touch, and the full moon shone so bright that he could make out details of the mountain peak behind the village. Caught up in the view, he forgot for a while what had happened. A shooting star crossed the sky, and Vlad shook his head, then looked around: he was alone.

"Torrechiara," he whispered. "I am sure I never saw that castle." He stretched, as if trying to push out a malefic presence, and tried to find a logical explanation. "I may have seen a movie." There was a nagging thought in a corner of his mind that, somehow, he had seen the castle from outside, but it was so elusive that he could not grab it consciously. *The Head was trying to tell me something. The fresco must be some kind of allegory similar to my situation here. A woman who doesn't know that Cupid shot her. It's too strange;* he shook his head.

After a brief glance at Moira's door, he walked away, and his path took him to Elna's hut. She was out front, sitting on the small bench along the wall of her hut. It was just a log, four foot long, one foot in diameter.

"Sit," Elna said, tapping on the wood of the bench. "What is bothering you?"

The Head. "The Mother."

"Ah, our new shaman is coming to life," she laughed quietly.

What should I ask? How should I ask? Undecided, Vlad rubbed his chin. *I don't believe they have the notion of blasphemy; I should be safe.* "How far does her power extend? Or how big is she? I don't really know what I want to ask." He smiled sheepishly, though she could not see him.

"Look there," Elna pointed at the Milky Way. "Everything you see is the Mother."

"That's a long way," Vlad said, tentatively.

"From there, our world looks the same, a tiny spot of light."

Vlad gaped; his mouth opened and closed, but no sound escaped him. "How do you know that?" he finally managed to ask.

"My grandmother was a powerful shamane, she had eight Amber Stones. She was part of the Amber Stone Ring. During my initiation, she transported me there." Elna's finger pointed at the Milky Way again. "The Rivers of Thought can go anywhere in the Mother's Web."

A Mayan Stela, from southern Mexico, came to Vlad; a depiction of a shamanic journey into the underworld with a number of unknown dimensions of time and space, marked by the undulating waves of the celestial planes. *Shamans, traditionally, go on a journey into the underworld, and this carving depicts such a journey. Or so we think. The Mayan shamans used a powerful hallucinogen: 5-DMT extracted from a toad. Were they really traveling through the celestial planes, or is that just our imagination?* Vlad asked himself, remembering his own failed experience with the Siberian hallucinogen. "Did you go to the Moon too?"

"Yes," Elna said, nostalgia in her voice. "My grandmother was able to go there. Once, I had the impression that I went too, but I am not sure if it was real, or just my imagination. I am not my mother and even less my grandmother. We are getting weaker. Our power is declining, and the Kalach may destroy us." *I hope that Vlad is able to reverse our decline*. The more she thought about what had happened to her during his initiation, the more she understood that the shamanes needed the shamans to realize their full potential, and that the opposite was also true. *The Mother's plan has place for both women and men. They complement each other, and they should not fight each other. That would only make us weaker.*

"Could you see the Earth?" Vlad asked, his voice edgy.

"It looks like the Moon seen from here, except that it has a blue color."

He breathed deeply. *Then it may be that the Head's knowledge about Torrechiara castle comes from the Mother's Web. A part of me did go there. I may be able to see my parents, if I learn how to do it.* "Yes, it has a blue color."

Both remained silent and, after a while, Vlad returned to his room. It was almost morning when he fell asleep.

Chapter 18

The beginning of autumn was the time when, Bron, Selma's other bond, would come to visit her. This time, instead of waiting for Vlad to learn the rules, Elna explained to him how the visit would interrupt the time he spent with Selma.

"You mean to say that for next ten days she will stay only with that man?" Vlad asked with a scowl.

"Everybody must respect the rules. You are not angry when Malva goes with Rand. Why are you upset now?"

"I don't like that either, but it was me who interfered between them."

"This is the same thing. Bron was Selma's first bond. We told you about their bonds"

"Until now it was just a story."

"Ten days pass fast." Elna took his hand and squeezed it gently.

"Maybe for you." He pulled his hand away and walked off briskly.

We may know soon who will mate with whom, Elna thought, watching him with a gentle smile. *I think Malva will go with Rand, and Born is a nice man, but he is not Vlad, and he is not here. Selma will go with Vlad.* Her shamane's sense of the future told her that the village would have two new matings in Spring. *Selma is older, so she will mate first. There will be two matings this autumn too. Who will initiate the boys in how to please a woman?* Each woman without a mate would take turns to initiate one boy for a month. As there were many single women after the wars with the Kalachs, Elna was still waiting for her turn. "No," she whispered after counting in her head. *I will be the first one in Spring. Vlad will cause problems. Why can't he take these things naturally? He made a fuss about just one kiss on the mouth. But it will be awkward for me too. He will mate with my daughter. Vlad is twenty-two. Maybe he is already initiated. Why initiate a man if he is not mating? Spring is still far off. I have to watch him carefully in the next days. He may react badly, and with his fighting skills...* She shook her head, and went to talk with Moira.

The visitors from the northern clan came the same day, late in the evening, and Elna sent Vlad to his room. He looked through the holes in the walls, trying in vain to guess which one was Bron. There were three bonds from that clan coming to the village, all men; girls never traveled to meet their bonds. Vlad recognized the man only when he took Selma in his arms, embracing her tightly. She laced her arms around his neck. "She will kiss him," Vlad whispered bitterly, and moved away from the hole. *I can't watch.*

The next morning, Bron came to take Selma away, and the first thing he did was to kiss her. The Vlahins seemed to appreciate Vlad's way of 'feeling' a girl. Warned by Elna, Selma glanced at Vlad's room, and saw that he was still inside. Feeling alone, she kissed Bron with the same passion in front of Vlad's angry eyes, and he saw everything through the hole in the wall. He just wanted to check if he could leave the room without meeting them. He kicked the wall, and bit his lip to stifle a cry. The noise was enough to alert Selma, and she linked arms with Bron, and pulled him away.

Elna saw her daughter walking away faster than a young couple would do normally, and she left her hut quickly. Seeing no one in front of Moira's hut, she breathed a sigh of relief. *Yet something has happened*, she thought, and walked toward Vlad's room. She knocked and entered without waiting for a reply and found him sitting, head in hands, on the edge of his bed. *He saw Selma kissing Bron*, she thought and suppressed a chuckle; sometimes his reactions to such normal things were hilarious. "What's your plan today?" She sat on the bed next to him, and played with his hair.

"I have no plans," he said, morosely.

"A shaman is not allowed to be lazy."

"I am not a shaman."

"Two shamane say that you are."

"I will work at the pottery kiln."

"Do you need help?"

"No, I want to be alone."

"Fine. I will come with you, to see how the kiln looks, and then I will leave you alone." *I hope Selma is not there.*

Vlad had chosen an isolated place for the kiln, just north of the village. It was a small plateau, almost round, some thirty feet in radius. Surrounded on three sides by the forest, it offered an impressive view over the village and the Great River. Some young couples protested – at first – it was a favorite spot for courting, but, with some minor complaints, they accepted that pottery was a more serious issue for the clan than their rendezvous. And Vlad was not working each day at his kiln.

He stood up and walked out of the room in silence, followed by Elna. "I have not worked much in the last few days," he said, trying to remember the last time Elna had visited his place.

Both shamanes and Rune came almost daily to see how his work was advancing, but he did not know that. It was a matter of great importance to the clan, but they did not try to hurry him. Though they did not know much about pottery, they watched him struggling to make the strange kiln. This was the second kiln Vlad had tried to make. The first one was easier to build, and gave him earthenware pottery and bricks for the new one but, for the moment, he had less than a tenth of the bricks he needed. It was a small kiln, firing at a temperature of around four hundred degrees Celsius, not hot enough to make good pottery or even good brick. The issue with these kilns was efficiency. In such small structures, the thermal loss was high.

"I still don't know how to make the second kiln," he said, sheepishly.

"At least we know now how the Kalachs are able to make their large pots. The coiling which you taught us works well."

"But if I am not able to heat the clay to a higher temperature, the large pots and bowls will be fragile. You will have to throw them away in less than half a year."

"They will still be cheaper than buying everything from the Kalachs."

"Perhaps," Vlad shrugged.

The difficulty of his task came from trying to make a double chambered kiln, so the pottery would be heated uniformly. The Kalachs's bowls that Vlad had studied had many patches of different colors, from light brown to almost black, because the heat was not uniform, and he supposed that they were using a firing pit. He needed to make sure that enough heat would get into the clay in a homogenous way, and for all his desperate search of his memory, there was nothing there to help him. He also wanted to regulate the firing atmosphere; oxidizing or reducing. He knew how to design modern ovens, and he was thinking in technological terms that could not be fulfilled with only bricks and sand mixed with clay as mortar. There was a large discrepancy between what his mind, still anchored in modern technology, wanted and his means. The structure would be both too fragile and hard to make. For some weeks, he thought of making quick lime, but he needed another kiln, and had more issues to solve. It was also hard to find fuel. It was not easy to cut logs with stone axes.

Nervously, he kicked a half-buried stone. "Bloody stone," he mumbled and walked on. His attention still inward, he saw the stone without really noticing it. After a few more steps, he turned quickly and knelt in front of the small pit left in the ground by the uprooted stone. Elna followed his hieratic moves, but chose to not interfere. "I am so stupid," Vlad whispered. "This is how I should make the kiln. Half-buried. See?" His finger dug a bit more, and Elna knelt beside him. "I will not need bricks to make the underground part. I will just put clay plaster on the walls and make a strong fire. This is our kiln." He smiled and Elna smiled back.

Relieved, Elna saw the spark in his eyes, and his determination. The clan would have pottery, and Vlad's mind would stay focused, away from Selma.

"I need two men to help me dig the pit. Tomorrow. I will need to find a good place, and make some calculations."

"What kind of place do you need?"

"A natural hole, some six feet long and three feet wide, in a place which is not too rocky."

"Let me think," Elna said, and closed her eyes, trying to remember if such a place existed close to the village. "Would a ravine be good?"

"No, not if water flows there when it rains. It should be at the edge of a flat surface."

"Would be that good enough?" Elna pointed behind him, at the edge of the meadow, a mischievous smile on her lips, and Vlad couldn't help but laugh.

"It was so difficult to find the right place." Caught in a fever of planning, he walked briskly, followed by Elna. "It's a bit small, but we may be able to enlarge it. Here," he pointed at the open part of the hole, "will be the mouth of the kiln. If I am able to find a way to build two chambers, there will be two mouths: one for the fire and one for the pottery." He took his bayonet and started to dig in one of the walls. He found pebbles, sand and clay. "Clay will help us."

Focused, Elna stood at the end of the hole, measuring it, and she finally understood what he wanted. "I will send you two men," she said and walked away.

It took them the rest of the day to fashion the hole the way Vlad wanted it, and four more to plaster the walls with clay, which had to be carried from half a mile away. From the edge of the pit, for half a foot, the walls arched smoothly inside, as if they were to be made into a Roman arch. There were three small transversal beams made of oak wood, to prop the half arches. They would burn through, but slowly enough, hopefully, to resist until the half arches were sufficiently hardened by the fire to stand by themselves. This was the point where Vlad finally let go of his modern technology; he decided to make a false firing chamber to store the pots. The usable surface was four feet long and two feet wide. From the long walls, he made two parallel shoulders, ten inches wide, and two feet tall. The kiln itself would be two feet higher, of which only one foot was above the ground. Leaning on the shoulders, there would be a grate made of clay, separating the lower combustion chamber from the upper firing chamber, with flues to transfer the heat from one chamber to another. He knew that after each firing he had to open the ceiling and extract the pottery, and that parts of the grate would need replacement. This way he could make a smaller mouth for the combustion chamber, and the heat retention would be higher.

When it was her day, Malva came to help him too. There was not much time for their usual fun, and with his mind absorbed by his tasks, Vlad did not sense that she was starting to be a bit more distant.

"The walls are ready. Now we need wood," Vlad told them just before they ate. As usual, he was eating at Moira's table. Rune and Elna were there, as was Malva. He frowned and turned to look for Selma. *She is still with that*... For the last seven days, he had only seen her in the morning, when Bron came for her.

"How much wood?" Elna asked, quickly.

"A lot," he said, morosely, his mind still drifting after Selma. "We need to pack the kiln tightly with hard wood like oak and ash, and make a three-foot-high mound of wood on top of it. The wood underground must be thick, something like a twelve-year-old child's thigh. Outside we can use smaller branches, and dried grass will be inserted between them. Then we have to cover it with earth. If we can spare some old skins, they will help us to pack earth on top. They will burn," he added.

Three days later, it was midday when they started the fire, and there was not much to see, as the wood burned underground, but there were more than fifty people around it, watching intensely.

"There will be nothing much to see," Vlad told them for the tenth time, but no one listened to him. He shrugged, and crossed his arms on his chest. *We will wait all day.* Still lost in his inner thoughts, he started when an arm snaked around his waist. He turned and found Selma. Bron was now on the way toward his village.

"Shh," she said, and pressed a finger to his lips. "Your kiln looks like a small house. Three people can sleep in it comfortably."

She came to see it. The thought pleased him. "Just be sure that you leave before the fire starts." Smiling, he pulled Selma round, leaning her back on his chest, and they stood there in silence.

The next morning, when the fire had died, and the heat had dissipated, Vlad was able to see and check the walls. He was worried about the half-arches, but they looked fine. One by one the upper parts of the arches and the parts of grate were taken out and inspected: they looked fine too, and one more week the kiln was ready for the first lot of pottery.

※

"I've decided about my mating," Malva said, and Moira came close and embraced her. It was almost night, and they were with Rune inside the hut.

"And who will be the lucky young man?" Rune asked.

"Rand, but you know that already. There are less than nine month of bond between Vlad and me. He can't be my choice now."

"Yes, he came here only six months ago. What else influenced your decision?" This time the question came from Moira.

"Several things. I know Rand better than I know Vlad, and I think that I like him more. We are more ... similar."

"Vlad is a stronger man. I have heard my daughter's heart speaking, now I want to hear the shamane."

"Yes, he is stronger, and Selma is a stronger shamane. They are better suited to lead the clan after you two. Rand's other bond is not a shamane, and he needs one as his mate to ... help him overcome some issues. He is restless, and I have the feeling that he thinks too much about the Kalachs, and that may spread divisions inside the clan."

"It's mostly Darin who sows division and, once his son mates with a shamane, Darin would like him to become the Chief of the village. We may have even more divisions."

"I thought of that too, but the choice for the next Shamane belongs to you, mother. I am not a strong shamane, I might only have four Amber Stones, but I think I will be able to make Rand respect the Vlahin laws."

"You might end up with four and a half stones, with Vlad's help. Or even five, if he initiates you."

"I don't think that Vlad would like to initiate me. He barely accepted a Lips Communion with you."

"As time passes, Vlad becomes more and more one of us. And he never had kissing issues with you," Moira smiled. "You received the first one."

"He told me that would not have been able to look into Father's eyes if he had a High Communion with you."

"Vlad said the same about the Lips Communion, and then we had it. He is adapting."

"We shall see," Malva said, only half convinced.

"Daughter, I am proud of you." Moira embraced her again. "You have acted with hearth and wisdom. You were both woman and shamane."

Rune came over, and Moira let her daughter go. Instead of embracing her, Rune raised Malva in his arms until she almost touched the roof of the hut. "Soon, I will no longer be able to do this." He smiled and put her down, and Malva laced her arms around his neck. "When do you want to have the mating?"

"In spring, I will be seventeen. That should be a good time."

"Spring, then."

"Have you told Rand?" Moira asked.

"I will tell him tomorrow, and then I have to wait for three days for him to make his decision about my choice. I think that Rand will accept. Then I have to tell Vlad. I don't know how he will react."

"He tried to shatter Vlad's bond, so I'm sure Rand will accept your choice, and Elna will deal with Vlad."

After a while, when Rand accepted the mating, Malva stopped going out with Vlad; that was the first step. Four days later, she went to his room, and sat on the edge of his bed, next to him.

"It's not easy to tell you this, but you already know it," she said and looked at Vlad, who nodded. This time, he knew all the rules and signs; Elna had made sure of that.

The bond came to me in a moment, Vlad thought. *And Elna said that it will vanish soon. Everything is still inside me now, and I feel the pain. I still love her.*

"I am sorry, Vlad."

"It happens sometimes."

"You still have the bond with Selma."

He closed his eyes and, recalling things, slowly realized that his feelings for Selma were deeper. He hadn't really looked before, as he did not really know how things would go being bonded to two girls. *It would have been harder, if I had to choose. I am still not accustomed to a dual bond. I am still not accustomed to bonds in general. A few months here have not made me a Vlahin.*

"We have a custom; we must offer a gift for the broken bond. I could not find anything better than the kiss which you have taught me."

"Malva, it's not needed," Vlad said, gently.

"I will feel bad, if I can't give you the gift." She stood up and, standing in front of him, took his hands, and pulled him to his feet.

Why doesn't she understand that this only make things worse? She is a shamane apprentice. Vlad thought. *It's like dying slowly by a thousand cuts.*

Malva laced her arms around his neck, tipped her head, and pressed her lips on his, plying and persuading, urging and unraveling. She had learned her lessons well, and her shamane skills were able to feel all his reactions and desires. And he capitulated, parting his lips, pressing stronger. They both drew back, breathless, eyes wide, lips parted.

For a moment they simply stared at one another, only inches apart, their bodies tensed and wanting. And then she widened the distance, releasing him.

To his surprise, Vlad found that the bond did become weaker and weaker, but he still thought that his feelings for Malva would stay longer than the bond itself. For him, the bond was still artificial. But it did not happen; a week later, he was able to see Malva just as a friend. The first effect of his broken bond was that he was able to spend every day with Selma, and looking back he realized again that he loved her more, and he could see her as his mate. He still did not like the word, but the Vlahin did not know about marriage. Thinking of Bron, he let one more month pass, and decided to ask Selma to be his mate.

"Oh, Vlad," Selma laughed when he proposed. "It's the girl who makes the proposal." She laced her arms around his neck and leaned her head on his shoulder. "But I have to say that I was touched."

"So you will propose," Vlad said, only to say something, yet his voice betrayed his concern. *They have so many strange rules*, he thought. *It takes a whole life to learn all of them*.

She felt the urge in his voice, and thought for a while what to say. "If I have to choose now, it will be Bron." She leaned her head back until their eyes locked.

Well, he thought. *One by one...*

"Our bond is less than nine months old. I can only choose you when we are together for more than nine months." *I will choose you, but I can't tell you now.*

"That sounds better than I thought at first," Vlad said, a smile on his lips.

She pulled his head down and kissed him over his wry smile, tugging his lips softly, urging him to follow, and he followed.

Chapter 19

The five Ring Shamanes arrived in the village in the middle of spring. Coincidentally, it was one day after Vlad's first anniversary in the Vlahin village. Nara, the Grand Shamane, and leader of the Ring, was with them. The news that there was a new shaman took her by surprise. She would have expected a sign from the Mother. That had not happened, and that made her resentful. There were also ten guards with the Ring Shamanes, meaning Moira and Elna had to work hard to accommodate them all.

The first encounter between Vlad and the Grand Shamane was cold. She did not like shamans in general; he felt her hostility, and could not understand what had caused it. Their meeting ended after a few minutes, when Nara stopped the conversation abruptly. He thought she was treating him like a servant, but said nothing.

"This man is dangerous." Nara, the Grand Shamane spat the words out, when only the Ring Shamanes remained in the room. Moira had given her hut to them, for the length of their stay.

"But he is a shaman." A seven Amber Stones shamane, Mina was the youngest woman in the Amber Stone Ring, or the Ring as it was known.

"Shamans are nothing but an abomination."

"They were also created by the Mother," Mina insisted.

"So are wolves and poisonous snakes. The Mother created the shamans to test our resolve. Gria was the Great Shamane, the only one who ever reached eleven Amber Stones. She foresaw that the shamans had to be eliminated, so the Vlahins would survive the attack of the Kalachs. She saw the Kalachs coming, almost two hundred years before they invaded our lands."

"What do you want to do?" Faro, another seven Amber Stone shaman, asked. She was older than Nara, older than the other Ring Shamanes, and had little chance of becoming Grand Shamane. Nara had eight Amber Stones and, at her death, the strongest shamane would take her place as the head of the Ring; there were two shamans with seven and a half Amber Stones waiting for Nara's death, but they were not that young either. At nineteen, Mina was the youngest, and it was supposed that, at some point in the future, she would become the Grand Shamane.

"What we always do. He must not be allowed to mate with that young girl, Selma. She is not strong enough to control him. He will mate with Mina, and give us strong shamane daughters."

"And the boys?" Mina asked, just to buy some more time; Nara had taken her by surprise, and there was no bond between Vlad and her. She did not want him, even though she was a special case. Her mate had died six months earlier, only a year after they came together. It was an accident, but deep in her mind, she thought of it as a crime. She could not understand why it had happened, and she kept everything to herself. *Was my mate killed to free me for Vlad? He died soon after we learned about the new shaman.* Older people, or those who had lost a mate, could not create new bonds. For them, things were the same as for other people who did not have a strong connection with the Mother. They had to find a mate by trial and error.

"A seven Amber Stone shamane is able to eliminate an unwanted baby. On the third day after procreation, you will know if you carry a boy or a girl and you know what to do. After he gives you two daughters, we will kill him. Don't worry," she glanced at Mina, "my guards will take on this task."

"Moira told us that he can rise a shamane's level through the Communion," Larn said. She had only six and a half Amber Stones and, together with ten others who had the same number of stones, she was the weakest shamane in the Ring.

"We will make sure that all twenty shamanes in the Ring make Communion with him. We have a few years in front of us to arrange everything."

"There is a purpose in having shamans too," Mina insisted. There were fewer and fewer strong shamanes, and a thought passed through her mind. *If a shaman can make a shamane stronger*... She shook her head, trying to avoid such dangerous thinking. "And he makes good pottery, better than the Kalachs."

"You are young, and one day you may take my place as Grand Shamane," Nara said, distaste filling her voice. "With age, you will learn wisdom and see that this is the only way. All shamans must be eliminated. Men who have the Shaman Seed will be gathered and used by the shamanes to make stronger daughters, but those men must not be initiated. Never. There is a destructive force in men, in some more than in others. They must be controlled, in case they harm the women or hurt the Mother's creatures. They can't be allowed to lead. You see what happened to the Kalach women; they are nothing more than slaves to their mates. Men need a wise woman to help them control their destructive force. I don't want to hear any more on this subject." Nara raised her hand to stop Mina speaking again. She breathed deeply to calm herself. "Mina," Nara said after a while, "Prepare your body to become fertile. You will mate with Vlad in two days from now."

"It takes a week to prepare my seed," Mina objected.

"I said that you are young, and I will repeat it until you understand. I will help you prepare your seed in two days."

"How will you convince Vlad to mate with Mina?" Faro asked.

"I have another bond in mind to mate with Selma, and I will make that bond stronger. Once his last bond is broken, Vlad can't form another one. Losing the bond will make him fall into Mina's arms. I will take care of that, but Mina should be ready to act too."

She doesn't care about me... Mina thought, but she did not dare to reply. *I will mate with a man I don't know, and to whom I have no bond. I must ask Moira to tell me more about him before the mating takes place. At least Selma will mate her other bond, the one she refused.* She realized that Nara was obstinate, and there was nothing she could do to escape the will of the Grand Shamane. Nara could force her to do her bidding. By accepting, she could at least exercise some control. It helped that she did not have a bond with another man.

A day later, Selma and Vlad were walking hand in hand when Mina found them. Moira had told her that he was alone, but now it was too late to ran away.

I pity them, Mina thought, knowing what Nara had in mind. *And I pity myself, if I have to mate with a man to whom I have no bond. The bond is strong in them. Maybe Nara will fail.* "I am Mina," she presented herself. "I know who you are, so we don't need any introductions," she laughed. *He is half Kalach... No, his mind is different, just as Moira said to the Ring.* "I am curious about where you came from. Well, I suppose that I am not the first person to ask that question."

"Far from here," Vlad said, evasively.

"So, it took you a long journey to arrive in the Vlahin lands."

"It took me a moment." A strange irritation, that he could not explain, was blooming in Vlad's mind, and he was struggling to suppress it.

"The Mother brought Vlad here. She has a purpose for him." Feeling his reaction, Selma gently squeezed his hand. "Moira has explained everything to Nara."

"Nara was quite busy yesterday," Mina said, disconcerted that she had not been told. "What was the Mother's purpose?"

"To help us. The Kalachs are getting stronger and stronger. There was a new migration from the south to the shore of the Great River. Soon, they will overwhelm us. Vlad is renewing the shaman line, and that will make the shamanes stronger too."

That struck Mina, and she had to breathe deeply to control herself. She was a seven Amber Stones shamane, but she was only nineteen years old. *What if Nara is wrong? I need to talk with her.*

"Selma," a voice spoke behind them, and Mina started, recognizing the Grand Shamane. "Would you like to walk with me? Vlad is in good company." Without waiting for an answer, she took the girl by her arm, and pulled her away. *"Take care of Vlad,"* she said without words to Mina. *"We are counting on you."* They walked for a few moments in silence, and then Nara looked at Selma. "Soon you will have your initiation. Of course, you have to mate first. Would you like to make a Communion with me?"

"Gladly," Selma said, a touch of elation filling her; it was rare for a Grand Shamane to look after such a young girl, and not a very strong shamane. After her initiation, Selma was supposed to become a five Amber Stone shamane.

"Tomorrow night would be good."

"Thank you," Selma breathed.

"Tell me more about your young man."

"He is gentle and strong at the same time. The Mother sent us a good helper."

"So, you really think that the Mother sent him here."

"Both Moira and Elna received a Trance Dream from the Mother. Vlad was in that dream."

"Yes, yes," Nara said, absently. *I don't like it that this is spreading. I bet they bragged about it in front of Mina too. She is still young and easy to influence. Why did Clira have to die so young?* A seven Amber Stone shamane, Clira was her right hand in the Ring, and they were of the same age. She was the only one who always understood Nara and her duty to guard the Vlahin realm. She hated the shamans as much as Nara, because she understood what a destructive force they were. Clira's parents were killed by the Kalachs, who were ruled by shamans. Her death promoted Mina into the Ring – one more thing for which Nara disliked the young shamane. "We are still evaluating that Trance Dream. It may be genuine," she added in haste, "but we want to be sure about it. I'm sure that you want the same. Sometimes, people take their own desires into a dream and make them into a message from the Mother."

"Vlad helped us to repel a Kalach invasion," Selma said, upset by Nara's words.

"It was not really an invasion. It was more that the Kalachs tried to steal some women. They wanted you, as I understand it."

"Yes, they captured me and four other girls. Vlad killed Turgil, the one who led the Kalach band, and then we defeated them. Turgil wanted me as his mate." Selma shook her head, the thought of Turgil making her feel sick.

"Turgil was a bad man even by Kalach standards, so you were lucky. It may be that not all the Kalachs are so bad."

"No, some of them are better," Selma said, tentatively. "There are good and bad Vlahins too, but the Kalachs are bad, in general."

"Even Maduk?"

"Maduk is better than the other Kalachs; he saved me once, when Turgil tried to rape me, but he is still a Kalach. How do you know about Maduk?"

"I met him once. He is the brother of their Chief, and they sent him to negotiate with us. His mother is a Vlahin. I wish that more Kalachs were like Maduk."

"It would be easier to work with them," Selma agreed.

"I think so too. You have a good political mind. I will ask Moira to invite him more often, and you can help her. Tomorrow evening," she reminded Selma, and left her alone.

Chapter 20

"Take off your clothes," Nara ordered, and Selma obeyed, even as she wished that her mother could join them as they had all agreed the day before; it was the usual way of a Communion. Nara sent for Selma earlier than they had discussed in the morning, but she understood that the Grand Shamane did not have much time for her. They were alone inside Moira's hut, which belonged to Nara during her stay in the village. "Lie on that bed, I will return soon." Nara went out, stared through the night, then returned, and sat at the edge of the bed, close to Selma. "Is it your first Communion?" she asked gently.

"No, I had one with my mother."

This will be different; I am much stronger than your mother. It may be that another person will participate in the Communion. Don't be afraid, I am able to commune with up to five persons."

"I am not afraid. You are the strongest shamane."

"We need to talk first. You will mate in a few weeks. Do you feel that you are ready?"

"I am eighteen," Selma said. "Most girls mate at seventeen."

"That's true, but you will mate with someone who is not a Vlahin. How do you feel about that?"

"Vlad is the same as us. I don't see any difference in how he behaves."

"Yet his mind is different."

"Yes, but that doesn't make him a bad person."

"I did not say that. I am only trying to understand how your mind will cope when mating with someone who is not a Vlahin."

"He is a good man, and we love each other. I will be fine. And he is a shaman."

"Is that important to you?"

"He is renewing the shaman line, so he is important for us in general. Our children will all benefit," Selma said and she blushed.

"How soon do you want to make a child?"

"Soon after my initiation."

"That's good planning. Your children will be stronger in the time soon after the initiation take place. The other person has not arrived yet, but we can start. Are you ready?" Nara asked, and Selma nodded. "I will tie this band over your eyes. The Communion works better if you can't see. You must focus on your other senses, and see only what comes directly into your mind from me. You know how it works, and I believe you also know about making the first step through our mouths."

"Yes, Vlad taught us that. We did not know that Ring Shamanes did it too."

"It was our little secret. Not our deepest secret, apparently." Her left hand touching Selma's neck, Nara pressed her lips gently on Selma's mouth. "*Relax,*" she spoke inside the girl's mind. *"Feel the pleasure coming to you."* Nara's right hand moved up Selma's thigh, and she started to caress her gently. Her mind worked to spread pleasure into the girl's body too, and Selma contorted slightly, as she lost control over her senses. *"Feel me,"* Nara whispered. *"Abandon yourself to me."* Her hand moved up, and started to fondle her breast. *"Someone else will join us now. Open yourself."*

Selma sensed another hand sliding up her thigh, and she gasped when it caressed her. She sensed the hand being more demanding and harsh, which complemented Nara's gentleness. A mouth found her breast and, from the beard scratching her skin, she realized that it belonged to a man.

"Let him feel you," Nara spoke again in her mind. *"You were meant for this."* She stopped kissing her, and pinned Selma's hands to the bed, above her head. *"Open yourself to him. Just open yourself."*

The pleasure became so strong that Selma began to writhe. Nara and the man were in control of her.

Now, my dear, you will get a surprise. Nara smiled, seeing the man pressing his knee between the girl's legs. She stretched her mind, this time inside the man's head, and opened a tiny channel that was blocked. A flood of feelings moved from him toward Selma, and she gasped, sensing the strong bond between her and the man. *"You have been bonded to him for a long time, but his mind was blocked. Now you know,"* Nara spoke again in Selma's mind. Gently, she took off the band covering the girl's eyes, and she found herself looking into the man's eyes.

"Maduk," Selma whispered, while the man rolled over her, ready for mating. The shock of the bond and the pleasant tension moving through her body took her will away, and she realized too late what was happening to her. She felt a brief pang, and then pleasure mounted again with the man's thrusts. *I am mating*, she thought, abandoning herself to him. Nara released her hands, and she laced them around the man's waist. Soon, she moved in the same rhythm with him.

"Yes, my dear, Maduk was meant to be your mate," Nara said in her mind. *"He was bonded to you from the day he saved you, but his mind was blocked. I have set things right. He made you a woman, and he will be a good mate for you."* Nara stood up, and vanished from the hut through a back door. *"Now,"* she sent a mental signal to Mina.

"Let's go inside," Mina said to Vlad. "We can talk there better."

She moved away the skin covering the door, and pushed him inside. He saw two people making passionate love. There was enough light to recognize Selma and Maduk. Vlad gasped, and fury mounted in him, then pain. He felt betrayed and bitter. Mina was no less surprised to see a Kalach mating with a Vlahin, but at least she was not emotionally involved. She kept her composure, though Vlad was in no position to sense her reactions.

The image of a fresco from Torrechiara castle came to him: Cupid shooting the woman. With the image, the

Head's words came too: The woman does not know she has been touched by Cupid's arrow.

The fresco vanished, replaced by Andrei's head, flowing slowly around him. "I warned you," the Head said, a wide grin spread on his lips. "You can't trust Cupid and you can't trust these savages. Vlahins, Kalachs, they are all the same."

Touching the back of his neck, Mina perceived the presence of the head too and heard them speaking, but she didn't understand what they were saying. *Is this a different Communion?* As their connection was weak, she was not yet able to speak inside Vlad's mind, as Nara could do, even at a distance, but she was strong enough to see what he was seeing; hear what he was hearing, and to control a man whose mind was in pain. She raised a mental wall between Vlad and the annoying head, which was constantly in motion. The Head just passed through the wall and smiled at her, and then it vanished. That was disconcerting; then she understood. *This is not a Communion. That head is Vlad too. He is speaking to himself. Why is he speaking to a severed head? Is this easier for him? I wish I knew the language and understood what he wants.*

"You are wrong," the Head said to her in Vlahin, appearing again. *"Look deeper inside you."*

Before she could react, the Head vanished again, and she rubbed Vlad's neck, her mind focused and alert, and the Head vanished from his memory. A moment of relative calm came to him and Mina used it to deepen her grip on his mind. His pain moved into her and, for the first time, she felt ashamed for what she was doing to him. *I have to do it...*

"They decided to mate today," Mina said, as if she'd known all along. *But I did not know about Maduk... Nara lied to me that she will push Selma's other bond to her.* "We should leave. It's not nice to disturb them during their first night together. It's a night of pleasure." Her voice wobbled for a moment, but she quickly recovered. She pulled him by the hand, her other hand still on his neck and, unable to speak, he followed like a tame animal.

Together, they entered the next hut, where Nara and Faro were waiting. Nara replaced Mina's hand on Vlad's neck, taking control, and guided him toward the bed.

"You are the only shaman we have," Nara said. "We appreciate your power, and we need you. You must forget Selma. She was not meant for you. You are meant for a greater cause, and Mina needs your help to evolve through a Communion. Are you ready?"

"Yes," Vlad whispered, totally subdued. A small part of him was still thinking that he was not himself, but he was not powerful enough to fight the Grand Shamane. He had no training as a shaman, and did not fully understand what was happening to him. The pain was still strong in him, but he wanted to forget that, to forget Selma, to forget everything. She had betrayed him for a Kalach. For a man who had promised not to touch Selma when Vlad spared his life.

Nara and Mina started to undress him, and Mina undressed too, and lay on the bed, naked. Nara pushed him onto the bed too.

"*You must make her feel good,*" Nara said directly into Vlad's mind, and desire started to mount in him. He had to please Mina. It was his duty. Nara guided his hand to

Mina's breast, and his lips searched for her mouth. *"Yes,"* Nara encouraged him, and the need to have the young woman grew stronger until there was nothing else in his mind.

Gently, he parted her legs, and Mina pulled him across her. His mouth found her breast and caressed it gently, while Mina's hands touched his back, arousing him. Soon, he moved up, his lips lingering on her skin, until he found her mouth again. He probed her briefly and, soon, both were moving in the same rhythm, pleasure mounting in their bodies. They were one, now.

"You are her mate," Nara spoke again in his mind. *"You are bonded for life. Do you understand?"*

"Yes," Vlad said between two grunts; he was moving faster and faster.

When it was all over, they lay on their backs, tired and satisfied. Mina rolled over him, leaning her head on his. Their brows touched, starting the Communion. She thought for a moment what image to send him. *I need to send something which doesn't hurt him, something to will tell him about a new start in life*. The memory of a sunrise came to her and, gently, she pushed the image into Vlad's mind. *"This is our beginning,"* she spoke inside him. *"It's warm and full of light, like sunshine. Open your mind to me, Vlad. Let me come to you. Come to me."*

"You are doing well," Nara said to her.

Selma's memory started to vanish from Vlad's mind, and the shaman power surged in him. It joined Mina's, and she gasped, feeling his strength. All her past Communions with men had been weak, and even her initiation was a pale shadow compared with what she was sensing now. Nara was taken by surprise too, and she felt herself being expelled from the Communion. She fought hard to keep her grip on his mind, but Vlad built a barrier that she could not pass. It was not a conscious reaction from him, more an act of self-defense; he perceived Nara's mind as being dangerous to him. He could not fight her, but at least he could keep her away. Mina felt his struggle, and discreetly helped him, careful not to be caught by the Grand Shamane. There was a silent struggle inside Vlad's mind and, for a few moments, Mina thought that everything was going well, but Nara had more tricks up her sleeve. She overcame the barrier Mina helped Vlad to raise, and she frowned, having the feeling that Mina was working against her.

"What are you doing?" Nara asked.

"Nothing," Mina said, trying to keep her calm.

At that moment, the Head appeared again, and Nara simply vanished. To Mina's surprise, the Head winked at her and vanished too.

That head acts like a shaman, Mina thought. *It may be just a form of self-defense in Vlad's mind*.

Once Nara was expelled, and he recalled what had happened to him during the last Communion, Vlad started to tremble. His mind descended into chaos. Feeling his fear, Mina remembered what Moira had told her, and how Vlad stayed unconscious for three days after his initiation.

"Stay with me, Vlad. I am strong enough to shield you. Nothing bad will happen to you." The tendrils of her mind moved around his and, slowly, she helped him overcome his fear.

The more she was connected to Vlad, the more she felt uneasy about what they were doing to this man, but she also started to feel for him – the power of the mating took over her. Their Shaman Seeds merged. Both of them felt enhanced, and while Vlad was inexperienced, Mina realized that they were exchanging Amber Stones. Her power grew, and she fought to keep it from spreading outside her. *I don't want Nara to know yet.* She waited patiently until her mind stabilized. *I am an eight Amber Stones shamane now. Nara will not be happy. And Vlad now has five Amber Stones. I need to help him.*

She lost some of her control over Vlad, and he started to panic again. He had the capabilities of a shaman, he could consciously or unconsciously use some of his powers, but he was not yet a strong shaman. Not until he could be properly trained.

"Vlad," Mina spoke into his mind. *"Let things come to you. Trust me to guide you. You need to absorb the Amber Stone. Like this."* She merged with his mind again, and slowly his fear of this new thing coming to him receded. *"Receive the Amber Stone. Bond it to you."* The Communion had reached its conclusion, but she kept it open, knowing that Nara could not join them, knowing that she was still too weak to fight the will of the Grand Shamane. She needed all her strength to face the more experienced woman. She needed to shield Vlad too. It was her duty to shield her mate.

Chapter 21

Awake, Selma let her mind float, the memory of the night still stirring her body, and slowly the realization of her situation came to her. In was past noon, and she smiled. Their night together had been longer and more pleasant than she had expected; she knew nothing about the potion Nara had fed Maduk to make him stronger. Maduk was still sleeping in their bed, snoring softly. *I am mated. Yesterday, I thought that Vlad would be my mate, now it is Maduk, and nothing can be changed anymore. Strange, the bond that existed between us.* If she had not relied so much on the way the bond was perceived by the Vlahins, she might have understand a long time ago that she was attracted to Maduk, as much he was attracted to her. *I need to talk with Vlad.* She was not looking forward to that moment. *He did not deserve all this, but there is nothing I can do for him. I am a woman now. I am mated;*

she repeated, still unable to fully understand how it had happened.

"What are you worrying about?" Maduk asked, finally awake.

"I need to tell Vlad," Selma said, her voice almost a whisper. "I don't know how he will react." *He may try to kill Maduk, and that would mean war with the Kalachs.*

"You already told him that you would mate with the other man that is bonded to you." Maduk was surprised by her statement, and he pulled her closer.

Feeling his worry, Selma leaned on him, her fingers playing on his face. "No, I chose Vlad, and I already told him, two months ago. We were supposed to mate in a week. What has happened is not our way of doing things." She blinked, trying to avoid thinking at Nara. It was making her mating feel soiled. "I am your mate," she added in haste.

"Nara told me that you..."

"She lied to you." Logically, Selma understood everything that had happened to her, and how the Grand Shamane had deceived her, but there was no way to change what had happened; their mating was complete and official, and her bond to Maduk was now strong. The mating was imprinted in her mind, and it would stay there for her whole life. She assumed that soon her bond to Vlad would start to fade. Maybe in a day or two. It was the usual way, yet she could not wait that long before speaking to Vlad. He deserved that at least.

"You are my mate now."

"Yes, and you may be in danger because of that. We must be careful."

"It's true that I broke my agreement with Vlad, but it's your Grand Shamane's fault, not mine. You are my mate now, and I will fight for you, but Vlad would not risk a war between our people."

"That's what I am thinking too." *Or at least what I'm hoping.*

She left the hut and went to speak to her mother first. She chose her words carefully, and told her that Maduk was her mate now. Elna was appalled. She did not want to lose her daughter to a Kalach.

"Mother," Selma insisted. "I am his mate, and nothing can change that."

"No," Elna shook her head. "This is not right. This is not our way. This must be reversed."

"You know perfectly well that it can't be reversed, Mother. My bond to Maduk is strong. You know that I was attracted to him, even before Nara revealed our bond. You warned me to stay away from him. The Grand Shamane made my mating official. The Kalachs know it too."

"Then Nara should mate with Maduk," Elna snapped.

"He is my mate. Please Mother, I have enough problems making Vlad understand." Selma's voice was filled with pain, and Elna started to realize how much her daughter had changed. For the first time, she probed the bond with Maduk in Selma's mind, and found it too strong for her daughter to fight against it; yet Elna still did not accept it. Not yet. She had to fight for her only child.

"Your bond to Vlad has not decreased."

"It's too early to say that."

"You know what would happen to you, if you are not initiated as a shamane."

"Maduk accepted it."

"He accepted it now; he will reject it, tomorrow. He is a Kalach."

"I trust him."

"Vlad trusted him too, and look what happened."

"Nara deceived him that I broke my bond with Vlad. Maduk acted in good faith."

"Both Nara and Maduk are deceiving you."

"You are wrong. Please, Mother, you know well that my mating can't be broken. I will have enough hard time to talk with Vlad. I am happy now, but he isn't. Please." Her voice was weak and, feeling her pain, Elna could not continue. Selma embraced her, and went to find Vlad.

It was evening again when she finally found him. Catching his eyes, she realized that he knew already.

"I am sorry, Vlad," she said. "Last night I mated with Maduk."

"Nara made sure to let me see you making love with him, and took over my mind too. I resisted her power, and I am still myself Vlad looked at her, and she bit her lip. "What a pity that I did not kill that treacherous swine, when I had the chance. Next time, he will not escape. I will free you, soon, Selma."

"I can't be freed, and I don't want you to interfere. Maduk is my mate now, Vlad. It can't be changed."

"This is not you speaking. Nara has taken over your mind and made you a slave to her will. When Maduk dies, you will return to normal."

"Vlad," Selma tried to remain calm, "you are still new to our ways. If you kill Maduk, I will only hate you, and I will never mate you. Ask my mother or Moira, if you don't believe me. The Mother separated us but, after the bond between us vanishes, we will remain friends. The same thing happened when Malva chose Rand as her mate. You know that. Even now, Malva is your friend. Please calm yourself. I am sorry for what has happened, but nothing can be changed."

"It will change," Vlad said bluntly, and turned away abruptly. He did not see her tears running down her face.

She return to Maduk, and told him that she had had failed. "I will try again, later."

"Maybe you should not try for a while."

"He may kill you, if I don't settle this."

"I am not that weak," Maduk protested, though he knew was unlikely to survive a fight against Vlad.

"Let me solve this, Maduk," Selma said, modulating her voice in the shamane's way. She was weak and not trained, but Maduk no longer protested. It was easier to turn someone's mind, when he knew that he had no chance. *I have to give Vlad the best separation gift*; Selma thought. *Maduk will not be happy that I stay away from him tonight. He may even guess what I am doing, but it's our way, and it's for me to make the decision.* She left the hut, and walked away, her mind still trying to find a way, and it was late when she entered the hut, where Vlad was alone.

"Vlad," she said, her voice weak. "We need to talk."

"Is the spell Nara placed on you fading?"

"There is no spell, and a mating bond never fades, you know that. I came to give you the separation gift. I will spend this night with you."

"Why should accept another man's leftovers?"

"Is that what you think? I thought you'd learned our ways and understood what such a gift meant."

"Yes, I remember now. You told me two months ago, when we decided to mate. You told me I had to wait until you informed the other bond about our decision. The girl makes the gift when she decides to mate with the other bond, then she mates. When will you mate, Selma? Next week?"

"You know..." she said meekly.

"You talked about the rules, and about respecting them, Selma. If the rules are not respected, there is no mating. You kept me waiting for almost two months, because of the rules. I am expecting you to respect the rules. Your mating is not valid."

"Vlad," she said gently, and came closer to him. "Please accept my gift. It's a unique gift, for a unique man." She tried to touch him, but he pushed her away, toward the door.

"Leave me." *Your subverted mind wants to trick me. If I accept your gift, I accept your mating too.*

Tears in her eyes, Selma left the hut.

Chapter 22

Aided by Selma and two of Nara's guards, Maduk tried to leave the village without being seen by Vlad, but he was being watched by the Vlahins, and he had no chance of escape. Nara's guards tried to interfere until Vlad unsheathed his bayonet. They stepped back, and several Vlahins from the clan pulled them away.

"Vlad; don't," Selma said, trying to get between the two men as they took the measure of each other.

Gently, Vlad pushed her away, ignoring her words.

"I know what you want to say," Maduk was the first one to talk. "I broke the agreement we made when you saved my life, but that was not my fault. Your Grand Shamane told me that Selma had rejected you."

"It's true," Selma interjected again, before Vlad could speak.

"You are lying," Vlad, said flatly to Maduk, ignoring her. "You arranged everything with Nara, just to deceive Selma."

"I am not lying." Maduk forced himself to stay calm; no one had challenged him like this before, and he knew that he was telling the truth.

"You are a Kalach. I've learned my lesson now. Never trust any of you. It would have been so simple to ask Selma or me about the bond. You did not even try."

"I trusted the Grand Shamane, and there was not much time."

"How convenient. But you know now that it was not true, and can make things right."

"Please understand, Vlad. I know that you are upset, and I am sorry for what happened to you, but nothing can be changed," Selma said, but Vlad ignored her again, staring at Maduk.

"What you want is no longer possible," Maduk said, unable to meet Vlad's eyes. "She is my mate, now. If it comes to that, I will fight you for her. You are stronger, and you will probably kill me, and then the war that everybody is trying to avoid will start."

"Nara has taught you well how to hide behind some lame excuses. You are safe in our village for now, but I will come after you, across the river."

"Vlad!" Selma cried, hoping to stop the madness. "This is not between you and him, it's between Maduk and me. He is my mate."

"Your mating was a trick. I need to save you from this new self that Nara has imposed on you, and I will do it," Vlad said and turned his back to them.

Selma tried to walk after him, but Maduk stopped her. "There is no way to convince him now. You said that the bond between you two will vanish soon. Wait for that day. As we agreed with Nara, I will hide outside the village until you are able to leave."

"I feel sorry for him," Selma whispered.

"I feel sorry for him too, as he is a man of honor, but life is like that sometimes. His loss is my gain, and I prefer things to stay like this." He embraced Selma and walked away, followed by Nara's guards.

For the next two days, the village was in commotion. Despite Nara's authority as a Grand Shamane, and Darin's discreet help, the fact that a Vlahin woman had been given to a Kalach infuriated people. They realized that Selma was now both bonded and mated to Maduk, but that did not make things right. A Kalach had sneaked into the village and mated with a Vlahin without consent from the Shamane and the Chief of the village.

Elna was furious, Vlad even more so and, after two days, Nara called a meeting to calm the Vlahins. She was experienced enough to know that things would eventually calm down, because nothing could be changed, and she just needed to show some compassion, and to tell them that the village would benefit by giving a shamane to the Kalach second Chief.

"You must help me," Nara sent a mental signal to Mina. It had taken her a while to get used to a second shamane having eight Amber Stones.

"I will," Mina said, but she chose to keep her help to the minimum. She did not say that to Nara.

"I understand that this is new to you, but times have changed. You have fought five wars against the Kalachs, and you won each time. But at what cost? How many good people have we lost in the fighting? We need to change course. We need to change the Kalachs' minds. We are not savages who want to attack them, but we can civilize them. Selma is a strong shamane, and her mate has agreed to allow her initiation. We will have a real shamane inside the Kala clan. She will make sure that they do not invade us again." Her mind stretched to soothe the people around her, to make them think that they were safer now. It took her a great deal of effort, and there were no obvious results. *It's a beginning*, she encouraged herself.

"It's not we who are changing them. They are changing us," Vlad said bitterly, and Nara stretched her mind, to subdue him, but she could not take over his mind. "The Grand Shamane did not act like a Vlahin. She acted like a Kalach. She treated us like we were her slaves. She forced us to do things that we did not want. Even the Kalachs would don't do this to their people. Their slaves are captured from other tribes. Nara is worse than a Kalach Shaman."

There was sudden silence, and Nara struggled to keep her composure. "Selma," she turned toward the young woman. "Do you feel like a slave? Are you not happy with your bond, with your mate?"

"I am happy. Maduk is my mate, and he is a kind man. I don't feel like a slave."

"Did you choose Maduk, or did Nara choose him for you?" Vlad asked.

"I know that you are upset, Vlad, and I am sorry for the pain I caused to you, but the bond with Maduk was older and stronger. He saved me once and, that day, the bond formed between us. It stayed hidden, because he is a Kalach and, two days ago, the bond came to life. Nara just set things on the right course. And you are mated too. I wish you the same happiness that is between Maduk and me."

"I am not a slave, and I reject a mate who was put into my mind by Nara's mischief. I am a free man. I want to choose my mate, like any Vlahin does. That is what makes us different to the Kalachs. I hope that you are a free woman too. The real Selma is the one who existed before you were subdued by Nara, two days ago. This new Selma is not the real you. Maduk is not your mate."

"I am real and free, Vlad, and Maduk is my mate. That can't be changed. Please understand that. Please, Vlad," she begged him, her voice suddenly weak. *Please don't kill Maduk. It will only make things worse.*

"Take him away." Nara thought this was an opportune moment to intervene, and two of her guards came and stood in front of Vlad.

One of them grabbed his arm, and tried to pull him toward the door. A second later, he was writhing on the floor, moaning in pain.

"The next one who touches me dies. I am not Nara's slave. I will leave the room when I want."

"Leave," Nara said into Selma's mind. *"Join Maduk at the edge of the village, and cross the Great River with him. Do it now, he has everything prepared. Keep in mind everything I taught you. We need you to be strong. Vlad will recover when the bond between you two vanishes."*

She looked at Vlad who, focused on keeping Nara's guards in check, did not see Selma sneaking away. "You are too violent, young man," she said to Vlad. "This is not our way."

"Is slavery your way?"

"Selma is not a slave, and neither are you. You have chosen to reject the mating. Selma accepted it. That was her right, and you have no say in that. We are peaceful people, and there is no need to push things further. By the authority of the Amber Stone Ring, I set a six-month probation period between Mina and you. I will ask you, at the end of that time, for your final decision. You may leave now."

"Don't you feel anything strange here, Nara?" Elna asked. "Three days have already passed from Selma's forced mating, and the bond between her and Vlad did not start to vanish. You acted against the will of the Mother."

"I am the one who knows best what the Mother wants. The bond will vanish. There is nothing more to talk about." Nara sent out her most powerful signal and, one by one, people started to leave the hut.

Elna suddenly realized that Selma was missing; everything was lost. She took Vlad's arm, and led him away.

Mina's eyes followed him, and there was a touch of sadness in them. *I need to talk with Vlad*, she thought as, watching them, the young woman perceived the closeness between Elna and Vlad. *She is like a mother to him. She may hate me, but it's better to speak to her first.*

She found Elna in the evening, sitting on the bench, leaning against the wall of her hut. Her cheeks still betrayed the traces of her tears. *My daughter was sold to a Kalach*, Elna repeated for the hundredth time. Sensing that she was no longer alone, Elna suppressed another flow of tears. Silent, Mina sat close to her, and leaned against the wall too.

"Have you come to enjoy my misery, Ring Shamane?" Elna asked, without looking at the young woman. "I have just lost my daughter. She was sold by the Ring to a savage."

"I knew nothing about Maduk," Mina said softly, "but I think that things are not as bad as you think."

"Go and replace Selma then. Take Maduk as your mate, if he is not so bad."

"You know that it is not possible." Mina waited for another reaction, which did not come. "You must give Selma some credit. Her bond with Maduk is strong."

"Selma didn't have a choice; the Grand Shamane twisted her mind."

"Nara is a powerful woman, but she can't create bonds. Only the Mother can create bonds."

"Was it the Mother who entered Selma's mind and gave her to the Kalach against her will?"

"The Grand Shamane is closer to the Mother than you or me."

"A shamane, who is close to the Mother, will never use her powers in this way. She will not act against a Trance Dream sent to us by the Mother. You know that Selma might die, if she can't have her initiation as shamane. Nara knew it too, and she did not care."

"Maduk agreed with Nara, and she will allow Selma to..."

"He agreed today. What will you do, if he will reject it tomorrow? Nothing. You will just lie to me again that Nara is close to the Mother. Both of you acted against the Mother. This is not our way, Ring Shamane."

"Elna, I did not know about Maduk. And it's not necessarily that Selma will…"

Elna slapped her hard, and Mina chose to ignore her outburst. "Don't tell me that my daughter won't die if she is not initiated, because you don't know it. Even if she survives, her mind will be broken. You are not a shamane; you are an evil woman."

"I am sorry, Elna," Mina said calmly. "I only tried to encourage you. I will stay here, in the village, and try to help Selma."

"Yes, you will raid the Kalach village and bring her back. Why does the Grand Shamane hate Vlad?" For the first time, Elna looked at Mina. "I may not be as strong as you are, but that doesn't mean that I am stupid. She wants you to control him. That's why you ruined both Selma and Vlad. For you everything is about power. The Kalach way."

"She doesn't hate him." *She hates all shamans.* "It's just that the emergence of a shaman took us by surprise."

"So, you hate him too, and have no shame to user your powers on him."

"He is my mate, and I helped him during the Communion. I don't want to control him."

"Should I pity you for mating with a man you hate? Or should I pity him that he is mated to a heartless woman, who enjoys other people misfortune and plans his destruction? I think the latter."

"I don't hate him. I came to you for help."

"Would you bring Selma back if I helped you? There's no need to say anything; we both know the answer. She is your victim as much as Vlad is. You worked with Nara. Two heartless women. Vlad was right, you are worse than the Kalach shamans. You may even enjoy spilling blood like their bull likes too."

"Selma is a woman at peace with herself."

"Which Selma are you talking about?"

"Elna, curse me if you want, but you know that nothing can be done. Selma is a happy woman now, but she will become unhappy if she sees your bitterness. I came to ask for your help, because I need to help Vlad, and you know him better than I do. He is the one most affected by all this. I don't hate him." She took Elna's hand, trying to create some closeness between them.

"Don't try to enter my mind," Elna growled, and pulled her hand back.

"I won't. You are the only one who can help me. Please, Elna. I have feelings for Vlad, and I want to keep him as my mate."

"If there is a bond..." Elna shrugged.

"We can't have new bonds; you know that. This is something different. I can't explain it. It's new and strange. Everything started to change during our Communion, and I don't know if it happened to him too. Vlad will come to you, and he needs to forget Selma. There is something strange about his bond to her. It may stay for longer than usual. We need to help him overcome that, and we have to prepare him to initiate your daughter."

"The Ring acted against the Mother. That's why we are losing our power. Because of your evil behavior." Elna's voice was cold; she stood up, and entered in the hut, the skin used as a door flapping behind her.

Mina breathed deeply, then she stood up too, and knocked on the frame of the door. "My mate is in your house," she said, calmly, when Elna's head appeared. "Am I allowed to join him?" Elna knew the rules as well as Mina, and she nodded, refraining from speaking, making space for the young woman to enter. "There is one more thing I need to tell you," said Mina. "Vlad is a strong man, but we have to protect him from the wrath of the Grand Shamane. I'm sure you understand that I have put myself in danger just by telling you that."

Two days later, Mina was sitting alone on small covered terrace in front of Elna's house, which was now her house too. Still avoiding her, Vlad was away, wandering far from the village, and Elna was helping Moira in her dealings with Nara. There was such animosity between the three women now. Leaning against the wall, she was thinking about how to get closer to Vlad. There were just two day before the other Ring Shamanes returned to their homes, leaving behind a whole village that had not yet healed. Faro came and sat next to her.

"It's getting colder," Faro said, and her shoulder touched Elna's. "I am bored by the catfight between Nara and the local shamanes."

"Maybe we should have been more careful in dealing with them."

"Oh, but Nara was very careful. Her plans worked out well. No mistakes were made; she got what she wanted, didn't she?"

"Yes, she got everything she wanted," Mina said, flatly.

"I am annoying you," Faro chuckled. "You know something? I am the oldest shamane in the Ring, and soon I will be seventy-three. Don't you think that I should be the one to make the first Communion with Vlad? I may not have another chance."

"Is that what you came to me for? To claim the Communion tonight?"

"Do you think it's possible? You are the best person to help me."

"You give me too much credit. I find it impossible to have a calm discussion with Vlad. He hates me for what we've done to him and Selma."

"So, you don't think that I have much chance. But I am a stubborn woman. Maybe I need to encourage the young man to want me. He is distressed and perhaps in need of an experienced woman to soothe him. We might try to change places this night." Her hand gestured loosely between Mina and herself. "What do you think?"

Mina turned her head away to hide her bitter amusement. Faro was a kind woman, and she did not want to upset her. "I don't know if Vlad wants to be soothed," she said, cautiously. "It's more likely that he wants to keep his hate within him. It consumes him, but also gives him a purpose in life. Nara was wrong and, now, six days after Selma mated Maduk, his bond is still there, and strong, which nobody expected. It has never happened before that a bond stayed so long. He wants Selma back. He wants revenge. So, I don't see what you can do. He hates us, the shamanes of the Ring. We are the source of his troubles."

"An experienced woman may win where a young one would fail."

You are obstinate. Are you so eager for such a troubled Communion? "I will not stop you."

"How do you think I would have a better chance to seduce the young man? Talking to him dressed or naked?" the old woman asked with a crooked smile.

This time, Mina could not hide her laughter. "Faro, you are teasing me. I must be in a dire state of mind to be so blind."

"That's what I thought. Your mind is ... drifting, searching for a path toward that young man."

"He is my mate."

"That will keep you under the same roof, but nothing more. Without a bond, things are not easy, but they may be also more ... interesting. It's a challenge. A fight in the good sense of the word. Winning such a fight is rewarding, or so I've heard from women and men who were able to win; it means a new life for them, together. It may take time, though."

"That's what I am thinking too. I am not yet accustomed to do it." Mina sighed.

"To seducing a man? All women are good at that, shamanes even more so. I tell you, behind his bitter-sweet dreams about the woman he has lost, that young man wants to be seduced and to start a new life. There is no way to get Selma back, and he doesn't look stupid to me. He is a good match for a woman like you." Faro smiled, and she stroked Mina's hair. "You are not Nara," she whispered.

The young woman leaned her head against Faro's shoulder. "It may be that he is also an important match," she said, without thinking. The worries about Nara's evil plans, which had troubled her for the last six days, had clouded her thinking. Realizing the slip of the tongue, Mina bit her lip and said no more.

"I don't think I ever told you. My initiation happened only a few months after the last shaman died. I was seventeen," Faro said, and took a deep breath. "It's like it was yesterday. I was a good prospect, and the Grand Shamane performed my initiation. Everybody expected me to get nine Amber Stones, after my second initiation had been performed with a man and, in time, I'd be a member of the Amber Stone Ring. The man initiated me, but I've got only seven stones, and I was mindless for a few months. Eventually, I recovered. They thought it was just bad luck, but for the next ten years, all the newly initiated shamane received two stones less that forecast. Some of them died because of that; they could not cope with the ... loss. The Ring had to change the way it predicted the power of a new shamane. The change gave young girls a different perspective, and they no longer died. Today, we still calculate the stones in the new way. That's not the end of the Ring's worries – there has been no new shamane with at least eight Amber Stones, which is considered the minimum for a leader. Who will take over as Grand Shamane after the last with eight or more Amber Stones died? At that time, there were six shamanes with nine stones, and all the shamanes in the Ring had at least eight." Faro remained silent for a while, her mind drifting in the past. Sensing that the old memories had a meaning, Mina stayed silent too. "Seven years after the rules were changed, Nara received eight Amber Stones, one more than forecast, and for a while, everybody was relieved. It did not last long, as no one else got eight stones until six days ago, when you had your

Communion with Vlad. Nara is now fifty-eight." Faro looked at Mina curiously, and stood up. "Long talks make me tired." She stretched her old body and yawned. "I will leave you to wait for your young man."

Was she trying to tell me the same thing that I am thinking about? That the shamanes lost some of their strength when the shamans vanished? That the Vlahins need both women and men to survive? Mina pondered, watching Faro walking slowly away. *Once, the Ring had both shamanes and shamans, but we always had a Grand Shamane, because the shamanes were stronger. They had more Amber Stones.*

Chapter 23 – Vlad

Each time I enter Elna's hut, Selma comes back to me. It's not that her memory has left me, it's just another reminder, another echo of what was mine and I lost. At the beginning, I contemplated leaving the place, to find another shelter. I did not. Selma has betrayed me. I will not do the same. My bond to her is still alive, and I don't want to lose it. It's a futile want, I know that; despite what everybody has told me, my bond will endure. The shaman in me knows it. Each thing inside the hut reminds me of her, and my mind lives suspended between past and present. I held her in my arms in that corner. I kissed her in this one. We talked there. We dreamt here. Her voice is everywhere and, sometimes, I even catch a trace of her scent. As any shamane, she always smelled of wild flowers. Selma likes violets. Some would say that this is not life, yet is the only one I have. In a corner of my mind, I still hope that she will be able to defeat Nara's conditioning and come back. That keeps my mind from crumbling, a mind which has never fully recovered after everything I lost when I arrived here. The only nuisance in this hut of lost memories is Mina. She still pretends to be my mate. She is not.

"Her place is not here," I tell Elna for the tenth time.

She looks at me, comes closer, her hand touching my face. "Mina belongs here, Vlad."

"Selma belongs here," I growl.

"However much I hate the fact, Selma now belongs to the other side of the river. You stay here; your mate stays here. This is the rule."

"What rules were we using when they did this to Selma and me?"

"They didn't respect our ways, but why should we do the same? Why should we behave like them?"

Each time I've asked the same thing, in the last seven days, Elna has always found a way to silence me. *I don't want to be like them*. The thought slows my mind for some moments. Yet, I do want to act like them and punish them. Defeated again, I chose to leave the hut and wander in the mountains behind the village. I find a place from where there is a fine view over the river. Under the bright sun, it gleams like a metallic band, and I remember that I have eaten nothing this morning. Each day I come here, I stay until it is almost dark; now I have to return earlier. I take my shirt off, and let the sun play on my skin.

My mind slips into the past, yet this time instead of Selma, it's Mina who disturbs my thoughts. I still remember the first night she came into Elna's hut. She wanted to join me inside my sleeping bag. I refused her, and she placed a fur alongside me, and lay there. During one moment of inattention from me, she placed her hand on my neck. Our minds linked, but I shook my head in anger and the link died. She did not disturb me again before I fell asleep but, in the morning, I woke up with her hand on my neck. I pushed it away, and ignored her when she asked me if I wanted to eat.

A few days later, she found how to open my sleeping bag, and I woke up with her naked boy leaning on me. For a few moments, I thought that she was Selma, and my hand moved to caress her. I was lucky that she did not wake. I don't think that I would have been able to reject her, if she would have started to stir me. It was not only my memory of making love with her during our Communion; it was that she was the only woman with whom I made love with in almost two years. There was no way to keep her away, but the next morning I was aware of who was lying next to me.

From the day that Selma left the village, each evening, Nara has come and pissed me off with a request for a Communion.

"We are stronger together, Vlad," she says, her eyes boring into mine. She is like a cobra, waiting for an opening to inject her venom into my mind, and I feel the tendrils of her mind searching for a weak spot. For whatever reason, I have so far escaped unscathed from her attempts, but today I feel that she is more desperate than before. She is leaving tomorrow.

"You, me and Selma?"

"All of us. Selma will help the Vlahins and Kalachs to come closer. She will deliver the peace we need. She is a strong woman."

Her voice is so genuine yet, deep inside me, I know that she has an ulterior motive, one that touches me. Once, Mina hinted to me that Nara has little love for me. I don't know why she warned me; maybe because she also has a motive that matches Nara's. They work together; it was clear from that night when they perverted Selma's mind during a Communion. A good cop, bad cop strategy. In fact, what Nara wants from me is a Communion that will give her even more power to pervert even more minds. I am precious to them only because I can help them gather more Amber Stones, but nothing will convince me to help this witch become even stronger. I already did a mistake an helped Mina became stronger but, at that time, I was both subdued and unaware of their evil minds.

"We need all the strength we can gather, and the shamans have an important role to play." She comes closer and takes my hands in hers. Before I can react, she speaks inside my mind. *"I can take you inside the Third River of Thought and show you the Moon and what you call the Milky Way. You are a strong shaman, Vlad but you need my help to evolve."* Her voice is so unctuous and gentle when she speaks my name, as if she wants to create invisible bond between us.

But it's not her inner voice or that insidious promise about evolution that paralyzes my mind; it's that mention of being able to see the Milky Way. The temptation is so strong that I feel, too late, the tendrils of her mind sneaking inside my mind.

"Stay we me, Vlad," she whispers. *"Together we can accomplish so many things. Like this:"* An image of Earth seen from space fills my mind. *"You have always wanted*

to fly. Your people use what you call machines to fly. We use our minds. It's easier. It's cleaner." Her arm moves around my neck, pulling me closer to her. *"See how beautiful our world is seen from above."* The image changes, and we move around the Earth. I see North America, and then East Asia. Logically, I know that we are not traveling through the Rivers, and those images are from her memory, but I feel subdued. I want to see more. Her lips touch mine. I try to move, but she keeps me in her grip. *"Let's make the Communion, Vlad, and then we can travel together as far as you want."* I can't move, but at least that keeps my lips sealed. With a last vestige of self-preservation, I keep them tightly shut. *" After that you can decide if a High Communion will help us even more."* She is restraining me inside a delicate net of filaments that stretches across my mind, and any hope of easy escape vanishes. *"You and I were born for a higher purpose, Vlad. The Mother gave us power to set things right in this world. That's why she sent you here. Moira and Elna saw you in their Trance Dreams, but they never understood your higher purpose. Join me, Vlad."* Her lips are trying to encourage me, as is her hand caressing my neck.

"What about Selma?" I am finally able to speak inside, and I am trying the same strategy I use to disconcert the Head: ask unexpected questions.

"Selma was hindering your evolution, and her purpose was to change the Kalachs. You need a stronger shamane. I will set the course of your evolution, and Mina will help you further. She will be a good mate for you. She is your mate, Vlad. You have to honor her. That's the Mother's

will." The pressure inside my mind is growing; Nara is able to insert more tendrils in my brain than I thought.

"How can we have a Communion without that potion Moira gave me?"

"I am stronger, Vlad. I don't need a potion to navigate the Rivers. Join me, and you will become stronger too. Any step in evolution is rewarding. Join me, Vlad." Her voice is not seductive now, she is speaking like a mother to her child.

"I still have a chance," I say in a language that she can't understand. That disconcerts her, for a moment, and the pressure from that net of tendrils enclosing my mind decreases. It takes her no more than a few seconds to tighten it again.

A tingle plays across the skin on my back; another hand is pressing on my spine. *"Stay calm,"* Mina whispers inside my mind too, and more tendrils sneak inside me. *"Don't oppose me. I am here to help you."* Her voice is as seductive as Nara's, and I am split between two shamans, each stronger than me.

"Mina has joined us," Nara says, and before I can react, pain shoots into my brain. Profiting from my weakness, Nara inserts herself even more inside my mind. *"I asked you to reason; now I ask you to obey."*

"No!" Mina says in a fierce voice. *"You must not give in to the pain."* I struggle to bring myself under control, and I hope that I can find some way to fight.*"You need to build a defensive wall. You built one when she entered your mind that night. You know how to do it."*

I don't know exactly what I am doing, but the pain seems to subside.

"As the Great Shamane, I have other ways to bring you to your senses. I'm going to open you up, Vlad, and learn all the secrets you possess," Nara says. *"Mina will help me and we'll see how resistant you are then. Communions can be done through pain too. I offered you cooperation and help, now you will learn pain and obedience. I will not leave until you obey me and accept the Communion."* Her face appears in my mind, and I am reminded of how the Head tortures me.

Nara smiles, her eyes sparkling as if she has detected my defenses and found them worthless. *"Such a weak wall will not help you much. Let's see what else you have to protect your mind."* The shamane whispers, and my body whirls around and then crashes to the floor. I know that I am not moving, and that everything is just a mind game, yet the impact leaves me breathless in the real world. And the pain feels very real. A circle of fire engulfs my waist, the flames black and noxious. They climb slowly toward my chest. The pain is unspeakable, but before the blackness can engulf me, the fire vanishes. *"Join me. Now!"* I have the feeling of entering, against my will, into the second River of Thought. *"See, Vlad. It's not so hard."*

"River send me back," I whisper without knowing why, and I feel two forces acting on me. One tries to expel me from the River, the second tries to keep me into it. I have the strange feeling that the River helps me too.

"I am behind you," Mina whispers, and I understand that she is the one pulling me out.

Nara roars with anger, and she sends a shock wave of fire through my brain. After that, there is nothing but pain and fear, and the desire to sleep forever.

"She is gone." Mina caresses my face. I am lying down, my head in her lap. "Few can resist the pressure of Nara's mind." I try to stand, but I feel too weak. "Don't try to move."

"Did we make the Communion?"

"No."

"Are the Ring Shamanes really so evil that they are happy to use torture?"

"Nara isn't the whole Ring," Mina says, evasively.

"Nara is the Grand Shamane and you two are the most powerful shamanes in the Vlahin world. You used your power to torture me for your personal advantage."

"I helped you as much as I could."

"You did not help me; you played me. You are so young, and yet you are even worse than Nara. I wonder how much evil will spread from you when you reach her age."

"I am sorry that I could not help more, but I stopped the Communion."

"You stopped nothing."

"She is right." The Head appears right in front of me, and our eyes lock. *"You are weak and ignorant and Nara would have broken your mind without Mina's help."*

"You just want Mina in my bed. It will not happen," I retort, remembering his past comments about Malva and Selma, when he pushed me to seduce them.

"That was a test not a push. One of the few you had passed." He eyes me speculatively, like a wolf scrutinizing a deer.

"And now?" I growl, and even to me looks strange that I can fill a soundless communication, happening inside my mind, with a characteristic of a real sound. Everything

feels discordant and wrong. *"Is this another test?"* I ask, my voice normal again.

"You need to grow up." His words stir a tightness between my eyes, as if my third eye tries to become awake. *"Ah, you remember it."* The Head grows arms, and his forefinger touches a place between his eyes, which look now larger. *"Are you afraid of your mate?"* The Head laughs, and his laughter looks warm to me, as if he did not really tried to mock.

"I love another woman, and Mina is not my mate."

"Vlad, who are you talking to?" Mina asks, and I realize that she is inside my mind.

"Get out of my mind."

"I am healing you. Who are you speaking to?" she repeats.

"Nobody."

"I see a floating head who is speaking to you."

"It's just an unwanted excrescence of my mind. A very boring one."

"No, it's something foreign, and it's not for the first time I've seen it."

"She helped you, and she still tries to help you, but it will be useless, if you don't want to help yourself," the Head says and vanishes before I can say anything.

"Mina, why did you help me?" I ask, involuntarily.

"You are my mate."

You did not want Nara to become stronger than you. As with the Head, I think in my mother tongue, so she can't understand, pretending to believe her. I am too tired and weak to resist, and before I can think more, and curse her, I am falling asleep.

Chapter 24 – Vlad

Two days later, I decide that I have had enough, and go to see Moira. *I don't want to be a pawn in anyone's game.* Mina is more powerful than me, and she may use her power like Nara did. The pain is still fresh in my mind, but it is not pain which frightens me the most, it is the feeling that I could become like Selma, an automaton guided by the wicked will of the shamanes. I still trust Elna and Moira, but there is no way I want to let a Ring Shamane sleep so close to me.

"Can I move into your house?" I ask.

"We are glad to host you, buy Mina will move here too." Moira guesses from the first moment what I really want.

"Is there no way to escape her?"

"Mina is a better person than I thought a few days ago, and she is your mate."

"She is not," I growl.

"Vlad," Moira says gently, "you are mated. I know how it happened, as well as you, but it changes nothing. A union made by the Grand Shamane can be annulled only by her. You have six months to decide. It's up to you to make them pleasant or not, or at least civilized."

Moira shuns me in the same subtle way Elna does each time I ask her to move Mina out of our hut. How can I ask again, after Moira has implied that I am an uncivilized man? Nervous, I do as I have done before, and find refuge in the mountains behind the village.

It is getting warmer, and under the sun's spell of somnolence, I'm almost falling asleep when I hear steps disturbing the dry leaves on the ground. My hand slips to the bayonet's hilt, but when I turn I see Mina, and I understand that my day is ruined.

She climbs the path and, silent, she sits next to me. "You did not eat this morning." She proffers a bag to me.

"I am not hungry."

"You ate nothing this morning," she repeats. "You need to eat."

"Why should you care?"

"I am your mate, Vlad," Mina insists.

"You are not, and each time I see you, I remember how I lost the woman I still love."

For the first time, I feel Mina losing her calm, and tears fill her eyes. That surprises me, as I know that she is not faking it. There are more things I want to shout at her, but they don't leave my mouth. I turn abruptly and leave her alone at the edge of the forest. Walking down the slope, I make the decision to leave the village. *I need food;* this is my first thought, and I decide to go hunting, the next day.

Mina follows me down the hill, but I ignore her, and I keep my decision to myself. She will not come with me.

In the morning, I take my bow and leave the hut with the pleasant feeling of a new beginning. "I want to walk a bit farther today," I say to Elna, trying to hide what I have in mind. To hide thing seven better, I take only my bow and a club with me. I don't take my spear – it will betray my decision to hunt. Mina is there too so, inadvertently, I speak to her too, yet I ignore her reaction.

The day is bright, and I walk until I meet the narrow river that flows out from the small lake. I follow it, hoping to find animals that come to drink water. After three hours, I arrive at the point where it flows into the Danube. I can see deer traces on the ground, but no living things. I climb back half of the distance, and hide in the forest, close to a place where it's evident that animals have come for water recently, maybe even this morning. Some hours pass, but no animal comes to disturb the silence of a landscape that seems stone-still; even the wind has died and I can remember the moment when it happened. *I am not very observant.* Knowing the wind is the first step to become a hunter, a thing I remember from Rune's stories. *And I am not really a hunter.* That may hinder my plans to leave the village, but I am too stubborn to renounce after only one day.

For almost two weeks, I wander through the forest to find places where I may be able to ambush an animal. Each day I find one that looks ideal, only to discard it, at the end of the day, as no animal comes close enough to get a good sight of it, even less to shoot or snare it. In the village, they still think that I am only wandering, and I don't feel the need to tell the truth. I would be ashamed if they knew that I was coming home empty handed, every day.

This morning, Mina has a bad dream and wakes me earlier than usual. In her dream, she clings to me, and her naked body stirs my instincts. I breathe deeply, and pull her hands from around my neck. She mumbles something in her sleep, but lets me go. This is another reason why I want to leave the village. Since she has worked out how to open and slip inside my sleeping bag, her wonderful body may arouse me too much, and I may lose my control. I am a man after all, and sleeping in the same sleeping bag as a naked woman makes it hard to resist the temptation. It doesn't help that the only time I have made love in this place was with her. Once I succumb to that strong temptation, there will no way to say that she is not my mate. It's so early that even Elna is not awake. *It may be my lucky day*, I think, to encourage myself.

Out of the village, I walk again toward the small tributary of the Danube. It is the fourth time I have used this path. As on the previous occasions, I set up my place for an ambush close to the small meadow, where there are hundreds of animal traces imprinted in the humid soil. I am still sleepy, and I have to fight to keep my eyes open. Despite my efforts, I flinch and wake up when a twig breaks in the forest, only a hundred paces from me. From my position, I can't see if it's prey or predator. At least I am on the top of a tall ridge that is not easy to climb. Even bears might have a hard time hunting me here. I moisten my finger and hold it in the wind: it's blowing from the right direction, hiding my scent from the incoming animal. There is another small noise, now only twenty paces in front of me, and I realize again that my observation skills are not the best. I have no idea what happened between the first and the second noise I heard. *Can I really survive alone if I leave the village? I must leave.* I shake my head and focus again on what I hope will be my first kill.

It's a giant deer. A male. The magnificent animal passes along the path along my ridge, but by the time I nock my bow, he is so close to the ridge that I can't see him anymore. *I can wait*, I tell myself, and I aim at the place where I expect him to come into view again. I see his large antlers first, and I tense my bowstring. When the whole body appears, I realize that the angle is so bad that, at best, I can hit his rear legs. That will not kill him, and it would be a pity to wound him for nothing. I stand up slowly, trying to find a better position, and I move very slowly, afraid of scaring him. Before I can find a new position, a loud noise pierces the silence, from the thick bush at the end of the ridge. A bear charges out at a speed that I would not have imagined for such a heavy animal. He crashes into the stag, and rolls to the ground with him. The fight ends in less than half a minute. I stare at the large male bear, then at the bush. The animal was probably there before I arrived. I am at least lucky that I arrived from the other direction; if not I would have been food for the bear by now. Watching the bear devouring his prey, I think again that neither hunting nor leaving the village count among my best ideas. I can't avoid observing that the bear starts his feasts with the soft parts, and his huge head is now fully inside the stag's belly. Just behind the bear, there is an old oak with twin trunks, each more than three feet thick. There is enough space between them for a man to pass. I climb down from the ridge, taking only my club with me. My spear is at home;

carrying it would tell everyone that am out hunting. I walk fast – the bear's head is still almost invisible – until I arrive at the old oak. I lean the club against the tree, and maneuver my body between the trunks. The back of the bear is only a foot away from me. I unsheathe my bayonet, and strike the bear on the left rear leg. The animal turns with surprising speed, and attacks me. His head passes through the space between the trunks, but his body can't. I am sure that under normal conditions the bear would have been intelligent enough to avoid the trap. I take my club and strike him hard on the nose. Once, twice. A bear's nose is a very sensitive point. If you look during the night with infrared goggles, you will see that the bear is almost invisible. The only red points are on the soles of its feet and its nose. Those are the places which stabilize its body temperature, and they are full of veins. My third strike finds his left eye. The bear rears back, and, in a moment, runs away. The stag is mine.

I am in a hurry, as I don't know how long the bear will stay away from his kill, but looking at the stag, I realize that I could not have killed it with one shot; the animal is too large, taller than me at its shoulders, and the span of his antlers is almost eight feet. First I cut off the head, and turn it so the antlers make a kind of frame. I cut two more branches, six feet long, and tie them tight to the antlers, making a raw stretcher. Apart from the head, whose antlers could provide material for tools, I decide to take only the legs, and tie them to the stretcher; the body I leave behind, bait for the bear or other predators.

I harness myself to the stretcher, and start to pull. After two minutes, I'm out of breath, and feel the need to rest. Looking back, I see four deep scratches in the ground, made by the poles and the antlers. The distance to the dead deer is only sixty feet. *At this rate, I will arrive at the village in two or three days.* In front of me, the slope is getting steeper. I measure again the stretcher, trying to calculate the weight of the load: it is probably more than a hundred and fifty kilos, maybe closer to two hundred kilos. I have no choice, and I discard one of the forelegs. Before pulling again, I glance at my watch, and decide to check again in five minutes, and see how far I have walked. I run out of breath again after four minutes, and lie on the ground. The distance to my previous resting place is no longer than two hundred paces, and the worst of the slope is still in front of me. Looking back, I see the bear approaching the dead deer. He stops a hundred paces from it, his eyes fixed on me, and a cold shiver passes through my spine. I look around for shelter, and go close to an oak with low branches. His head raised, the bear sniffs the wind, which blows from me toward him. Slowly, I stretch my arms to the lowest branch, ready to climb. *He is still a long way from me; I have enough time if...* The animal seems undecided, and so am I. *Maybe he is afraid of me*. There is no question that I fear him. After a while, he decides that the meal in front of him is easier than the one carrying a dangerous club, or maybe human flesh doesn't taste as good as deer. I breathe deeply and, going to the stretcher, I throw away the second foreleg. From now on it's easier, but the sun is past noon by the time I arrive at the end of the long slope.

Drained, and walking like a somnambulist, I arrive at the village when it's almost dark. Both Elna and Mina are worried, and Rune is preparing a team to go and search for me. When I arrive, all three of them, and Moira, are in front of our hut. They stare at me, and I breathe deeply, waiting for them to praise me.

"A giant deer," Rune said. "Malva was a toddler when last I saw one."

"I have never seen one." Mina comes closer and touches the antlers. "It's huge."

"Did you hunt it?" Moira asks.

"Yes," I say proudly; taking it from the bear is a form of hunting, more dangerous than killing a deer, even when is such a big one.

"No," all the women sigh, and I don't sense any praise in their reactions. What I feel is fear and tension.

They are just worried. They know that I am not a hunter. "It's a lot of meat." I point at the stretcher, smiling at them. No one is smiling back. In silence, they help me to carry the stretcher onto the terrace.

"We will deal with it tomorrow," Moira says, and then she stands in front of me. "Vlad, we need to talk." There is something in her voice that sounds upset, and I feel a touch of panic.

"Yes," I nod and, in that moment, I sense how tired I am. My legs are barely able to move.

"We will talk tomorrow." She feels my tiredness too.

I walk inside the hut, and sit on the edge of the bed to take my boots off. I wake up to find that someone is undressing me. With some effort, I open my eyes, and I see Mina taking off my clothes. It seems that I fell asleep after taking off my left boot.

"I can do it."

She doesn't answer, and continues to undress me, and helps me to lie down in the sleeping bag. "Oh, Vlad," she whispers, lacing her arms around my neck, "why did you hunt? The shamans are not allowed to hunt. The council may have to punish you, possibly with death."

Death? I fall asleep before I am able to answer her.

Chapter 25

"I am not a shaman," Darin said, "but it appears that I am more willing to apply the law than the Shamane of the clan. Vlad killed a giant deer. The shamans are not allowed to hunt. He must be punished."

There were twelve people gathered at the main table in front of Moira's hut. The two shamanes, Rune, three more women who had the Shaman Seed and five hunters. They formed the village council. Mina was there too but, being a Ring Shamane, she acted only as a supervisor.

"What he should be punished for?" Moira asked.

"For killing. Shamans are not allowed to kill animals. The Mother doesn't allow it." Darin's mouth flattened into a hard line.

"Are you sure that he killed that deer? Vlad is not a hunter. You know that; you rejected him from the hunters."

"He may have deceived us or he learned in the past months."

"It's quite a large animal," Rune said, absently. "I haven't seen one that big for a long time."

"That changes nothing." Darin was adamant.

"It's not easy to kill such an animal, Darin." Rune looked for the first time at the Chief Hunter. "How do you think Vlad killed the deer?"

"How should I know?"

"You are an experienced hunter. How would you kill a giant deer?"

"With a spear," Darin replied.

"Can you kill it alone?"

"Perhaps."

"You can't hunt a giant deer alone. You need a team to chase it and bring it in front of your spear." Rune looked at Darin, who remained silent. "Would you try to use a bow?"

"You would need to be very lucky to kill it with a bow. Maybe three or four archers, shooting at the same time, could do it."

"That's strange," Rune said, looking absent again.

"You could try to hunt one alone, if you want," Darin said dismissively. *A cripple can't hunt with a spear.*

"Why should I try? I agree with you that a lone archer can't kill a giant deer. What is strange is that Vlad left his spear at home. How did he kill the deer? What do you think, Darin?"

"Maybe he was lucky."

"We can't judge someone based on 'maybe'."

"Then wake him up." Darin threw a contemptuous glance at Mina.

"Hunter," Mina said coldly, and her mind stretched toward Darin, giving him cold shivers. "You don't give orders to a Ring Shamane."

"I apologize," Darin breathed, still feeling the shamane's pressure on his mind. *One day I will pay back these shrews; they should not be allowed to lead us.*

"But Rune and you are both right; we can't continue without Vlad." She stood up and walked toward Elna's hut. Vlad was still sleeping, and she had to shake him. "Wake up, Vlad," she said gently, touching his forehead.

"What happened?" Vlad asked, still not fully awake.

"Moira and the council are ready to hear you."

"What business do they have with me?"

"You hunted."

Hunted? He shook his head. *Ah, yes, the giant deer. The bear hunted it, but why should I tell them?* "And?"

"You are a shaman, Vlad. You are not allowed to hunt."

"Who cares? I want to leave the village, anyway."

"That will be not so easy."

"I don't care, Mina; I want to leave. My place is not here, between Ring Shamanes who torture people and subvert their mind. Some of the meat can stay here, to feed the clan; I don't need so much."

"Vlad!" Mina snapped, and slapped his head. "You are not listening. Shamans are not allowed to hunt, and you will be punished."

"Well, you kick me out of the village, and everybody will be happy."

"The punishment for such offense is death, Vlad. You forfeited a sacred pledge between the Mother and you."

"I never made such a pledge. I am not a Vlahin."

Entering the hut, Elna exchanged a brief look with Mina.

"Vlad," Elna said, sadly, and she sat on the edge of the bed, next to him. "If you plead like this in front of the council, there will be no escape."

"And what escape do you see?"

"I don't know. It depends on your story. Please be careful. Tell us everything before we go in front of the council."

"I don't trust Mina." *I don't need your approval to hunt, and you know how many bad rumors about my hunting skills Darin is spreading behind my back.*

"She is your mate, and a Ring Shamane. The final decision has to be approved by her." Elna sighed in frustration. "Very well, let's go in now."

"I want to make a statement," Vlad said when he arrived at the council, and sat on a bench that was placed there for him. "I don't recognize the right of this council to judge me. I am not a Vlahin."

"You are on our lands. You must respect our laws," Darin said. *He is quite stupid; it should not be hard to at least expel him, but I want him dead.*

"I have always respected your laws, bit this is a matter of faith, not common law. I don't worship the Mother."

"Please don't say that, Vlad," Moira said, a touch of sadness in her voice.

Vlad looked at her, and realized that he had probably said the wrong thing. "Please don't take me wrong; I respect the Mother, but I am a different type of shaman."

"It doesn't matter; you are on Vlahin lands. The Mother's rules apply here." Darin's voice was venomous and triumphant.

"It doesn't matter what you want, Darin," Vlad said coldly. "I've already told Mina that I am leaving the village. I have had enough, and it seems that you want me gone too. It will be a relief to everybody." He stood up and turned to leave.

Darin, his brother and another hunter close to him jumped up and walked menacingly toward Vlad. "You will not go without being judged," Darin growled.

"Do you want to fight me?" Vlad asked, unsheathing his bayonet. "It would be easier to kill you than to kill a giant deer. He crouched slightly, waiting for the three men to attack.

Vlad," Moira said, her voice gentle and sad. "Please come back and sit down. Darin, you sit down too. I did not permit you to use violence or to enforce a rule."

"He tried to leave."

"I will deal with that, Darin. Sit down." Moira's voice was now sharp and demanding and, breathing nervously, Darin returned to his place, followed by the two other hunters, who looked relieved. "Vlad." Moira nodded at his bench, and he returned too.

Mina came to Vlad and, crouching in front of him, took his right hand in hers. "Please Vlad, let the council judge on this matter," she whispered just for him.

"Why should I trust it?"

"Moira, Elna and Rune are your friends, and I am your mate. Please," she stopped his protest. "As a Ring Shamane, I oversee the council. What has happened is an important matter. Darin hates you, and has asked for the death penalty. It will not happen. We are not convinced that you killed the giant deer."

"I still don't recognize the council's right to judge me."

"Please, Vlad. Did you kill the stag?" Their eyes locked, and she sent some tendrils of her mind into his.

"You are messing with my mind," Vlad growled.

"Did you kill the stag?"

"No," he whispered, against his will.

"That's what I thought. Let us proceed then." She stood up and went back to her place, without asking for his answer. *He did not kill the stag.* Her words went directly in Moira, Elna and Rune's minds.

"Darin," Rune said, "you are the Chief Hunter. It's your right to question Vlad on how the giant deer was killed."

"Did you kill it by yourself?" Darin glared at Vlad.

"No."

"Who helped you?"

"An occasional friend."

"Was he Vlahin?"

"No."

"You hunted with a Kalach in our lands."

"I never said that he was a Kalach."

"Then who was he?" Darin asked, a little nervously, sensing that Vlad was mocking him.

"I was helped by a bear," Vlad said and, with the exception of Darin, all the people in the council started laughing. "Look," Vlad said, half annoyed, half amused. "It doesn't matter how much I wanted to prove myself as a hunter, I did not kill that stag. I snatched it from a bear. I was lucky that the bear attacked the stag and not me; I didn't see him, though it was quite a large male. Shaman or not, I am done with hunting. In two weeks, I was not able even to come close to an animal. Hunting is not for me. I am sure that you all realized that long before I did."

"Why should I believe you?" Darin asked, his composure recovered.

"You may challenge me, if that's what you want. I am ready."

"There will be no fight," Moira said. "Vlad is a man of honor, and ... I don't want to lose our Chief Hunter." Her last words struck Darin, and he swallowed hard, not knowing how to react. "As there is nothing for us to judge, the council is dismissed."

One by one, most of the people walked away. The shamanes and Rune stayed, and Moira gestured at Vlad to stay too.

"It's unlikely, but Darin may ask for a Truth Communion, to see who killed the stag," Elna said after a while.

"It should not be a problem, Nara is not here, and I've already made a Communion with all three of you," Vlad said, and then he realized that he had included Mina in the circle of trusted persons. He frowned. *Can I really trust her?*

"I am so glad that you did not kill the stag," Mina whispered, tears running down her face. She embraced him and, involuntarily, Vlad put his arms around her waist. Elna embraced them too, and they stayed like that, in complete silence. It felt strangely comforting to him.

That evening, for the first time, Mina joined Vlad inside his sleeping bag before he had fallen asleep. He pretended not to notice her body, leaning against his back.

"Vlad," she whispered as her left arm encircled him, "there is something important I need to tell you. I am pregnant. I carry your daughter."

Shocked, Vlad turned, lying now on his back and, before he could say anything, Mina rolled over his chest, leaning her head on his shoulder.

"We've made love only once..."

"Yes, but my seed was already started. I am sorry for not telling you earlier."

"You planned to have a child."

"Yes."

"Why?"

"Women always want children from their mates," she said, jokingly, and she caressed Vlad's face.

"Is there more that I should know?"

"Yes," Mina sighed. "I will not lie to you. Nara helped my body to prepare the seed in time for our mating."

"What interest has she in this?"

"You are a strong shaman."

"So she wanted a daughter who..."

"I don't care what she wanted. I care that we will have a child."

"Well," Vlad said, and put his arm around Mina, who nested in his arms, and fell easily asleep. Vlad could not.

His mind drifted into the past, recalling the most important things, starting with their High Communion and, this time, he felt Mina's subtle interference, both in the Communion and when Nara had tortured him. His unconscious mind had always known about it. *Mina helped me, but she also helped Nara subvert Selma. I am in such a strange position. I love one woman, and I am mated to another. How strange it sounds: mated. I would like to say married, but they don't have such a word. Three weeks ago, I hated Mina.* He listened to her even breathing; he did not want to wake her up. *I no longer hate her. I ... like her. Is this because she helped me, or because of the mating?* Elna had told him that mating was more than simply making love for the first time; it created an unbreakable bond between two people. *But I was not bonded to Mina.* Slowly, Vlad moved his left arm, which was still around Mina, and placed his hand on her shoulder. Pleasant warmth moved between them, but he felt more than that. *This is not only physical pleasure. I can't love two women. It's more that I like Mina. I wish I could kill Nara, but she is the Grand Shamane. There is nothing 'grand' in her. Apart from her powers.* The thought recalled all the pain she had inflicted on him. He shivered and, trying to escape the bad memories, his mind focused on Mina. That made him feel better. *I am mated with a woman who I hated, but I may like now*, he mused. *She carries my child. I am responsible for that child. I am responsible for the mother. Moira was right, it depends on me how these six months pass.*

"So, you are a responsible man now," the Head said, suddenly, and Vlad swept the room, searching for him. He found nothing.

"Are you ashamed to be seen?"

"Why should I materialize all the time in your poor mind?"

"I can handle a boring excrescence of my own mind," Vlad grinned. *"Why did you play that game with the Cupid frescoes in Torrechiara castle?"*

"I was trying to warn you about Selma."

"It was only a coincidence. You can't have better premonition than I have. I have none and you have none."

"Then?"

"That's what I am asking. Why did you play that game?"

"Did you like the castle?"

Vlad raised one eyebrow, and stayed silent for a while. *"Maybe. Show your bastard face."* The Head popped in front of him, arms crossed over a missing chest. *"I never saw that castle before. Is there any way to see my world again, through the Mother's Web?"* The lines of the Web appeared in front of him, linking him to the Head. There were only three lines, each of a different color: red, blue and amber. *Past, future and present*, Vlad suddenly knew. *My Shaman Heart is amber... This may not be the world and life I would have chosen, but it was not my call and, at some point, we all have to decide for ourselves what we do with what was given to us. It could have been worse.* A memory of Cosmin came to him like an afterthought.

"Old worlds die and new worlds are born. The chain of life is never ending." The Head flashed a gleaming smile, his teeth growing two inches long.

Their transformation reminded Vlad of cartoons from his previous life, and he saw too late that the Head had vanished. "Wait!" he shouted, and his angry voice woke Mina. "I am sorry."

"Forget the bad dream," she said gently, touching his arm. "Sleep."

It was not a dream, he thought, and fell asleep.

Chapter 26

Two months after Selma had mated with Maduk and left the village, Elna was both bitter and lonely for her daughter; she knew that nothing could be done; Selma and Vlad were mated in different families now. After some long negotiations, Darin brought her the news that she could visit the Kalach village; Maduk had invited her.

"Something is wrong," Moira said, the evening before Elna was set to leave.

"I have the same feeling, but also I have the feeling that Selma needs me there. I am her mother. At least I can negotiate her initiation as shamane. Maduk has promised to allow it."

"Yes," Moira said, reluctantly, "there is a link between your visit and Selma's initiation, but I am not able to discern it."

"Then I have to go. Even with Maduk's protection, I suppose that they will inflict some humiliation on me. I am a woman, and in the Kalach world women have a low station. I will survive. You have to prepare Vlad for Selma's initiation. He may try to avoid it, but Mina will help you."

"Are you hoping to bring her back with you?"

"It may happen. We must be prepared." Elna fell silent and, feeling her inner struggle, no one tried to speak. *Why do I have the feeling that I will not return soon? There is no violence in my path, yet something is wrong. I am a shamane, and I should not fear my future. What use is a premonition without the courage to confront it?*

On the southern bank of the Great River, Elna found Alma and Tohar waiting for her. She knew Alma from previous negotiations, but Tohar was new to her. The twenty-nine-year-old Shaman of the Kalachs had taken up his role only a few years ago. Elna had known his father, and while he was an enemy, he was a shaman too. *Tohar is not a shaman*, she thought. *He has only one Amber Stone. That's nothing. There is no man or woman without at least one stone.* A real shamane or shaman had at least three Amber Stones. There was no way to initiate them unless they had at least three stones.

"Maduk and Selma are with some southern Kala visitors," Alma said. "They sent us to meet you. You will meet them in the village."

Selma had no say in this. She would not have let a stranger come to meet me. That's the Kalach way. "You may go back, Darin," Elna said. "You should come to take me back in five days."

"Five days," Darin said and turned away. Elna's eyes followed him as he climbed into the boat, then she turned too, to face her hosts.

"Follow us," Tohar said.

"I know the road, Tohar, and I knew your father well."

The Shaman ignored her, and walked toward the village. Elna followed him. It was not a long distance from the Great River to the village, and Elna did not see many things different since her last visit. *Last time, my mate walked with me*, she thought. *I wish he could be here too.*

Tohar walked directly into his hut; Elna stopped, and then turned toward the hut which she knew belonged to Maduk.

"We go there, first," Alma said, pointing at the Shaman's hut. She took Elna by the arm, and thinking that Selma and Maduk were there too, Elna followed her.

"I will return soon," Tohar said, when both women entered the main room of his hut.

Alma walked toward the only table in the room. "Have a seat," she said, and sat on a bench. Elna seated herself on the other bench, across the table. "We need to talk before Selma and Maduk come here." Elna stared at her, but said nothing. "I will be brief. Tohar wants you as his mate."

"That won't happen."

"You don't have much to say in this. Any Kala can take you as his mate. It's our law."

"Are you still a Vlahin?"

"No. My mate was a Kala Chieftain, and my son is a Kala Chief."

And that's why you agreed to this?"

"I will agree to anything that helps my son consolidate his position."

"I have Maduk's word that I will be a guest here."

"And you are. Nobody will harm or kill you. Mating is a different issue. It's an honor."

"I did not ask for this honor," Elna said, acidly.

"And you will not be asked. Here, you must forget the Vlahin way. You must learn the Kala way."

"I won't be forced."

"There is nothing you can do, except agree. It will make things easier for both you and Selma."

"What has Selma to do with this?"

"She will not be initiated as shamane, if you don't mate Tohar willingly. Selma and Maduk must know that you agree."

"You are working against your own son."

"You are mistaken. Everything I do benefits my sons, though they are not fully aware of what happens here."

"Maduk and Nara have agreed to Selma's initiation."

"Yes, but there was no agreement about when that would happen. To make things clear, the initiation will happen after you mate with Tohar and give him a child. There is no need to wait until the child is born, you will show me that you are pregnant. As I know, you will be aware a few days after conception, but it may take a month until I am able to see the child inside you. The sooner you fulfill your part of the bargain, the sooner Selma will be initiated. Be aware that Maduk doesn't know what happens during the second part of the initiation, or that a man is involved. Let's keep it like that; he will never agree, if he finds out. One word to him, and Selma will remain like me, a woman who could have been a shamane. She has only one year left to be initiated. One year passes fast."

Elna closed her eyes for a few moments. *Both Moira and I were right, bad things are happening and they are related to Selma's initiation. At least Alma doesn't know that Selma may die if she doesn't have her initiation.* "Why is Tohar so eager to mate an older woman?" *I must be strong.*

"He wants his son to be a real shaman."

"There is no guarantee that my child…"

"I know, but there will be a second and a third. Once you make a new family, you will find it in your own interest to protect it. Because of your first child, you will even protect Tohar. You don't believe me, but I know better. I hated my mate, but once I gave birth to Ragun, I helped him to become a Kala Chieftain. And, after a few years, I saw him as a real mate, not the man who kidnapped and raped me at fourteen. You are an experienced woman, and you will adapt faster than a young, frightened girl."

"And if I refuse?"

"You can't refuse the mating, as no one will ask you. Of course, you can refuse to make children for Tohar, but you know the consequences for Selma, and you should also know that a Kala is allowed to kill his mate and take a new one, if children do not come in three years."

"You agreed that I would not be harmed or killed, if I came here. Maduk gave his word."

"Nobody will remember this in three years from now."

"Maduk's word doesn't have much value, these days."

"He is the mate of your daughter. Like me, you have no interest in harming him and his family. There is not much time left. Tohar is coming," Alma pointed at the door. "Selma and Maduk will come soon after. For the moment, they should not be aware of this little arrangement."

"Well?" Tohar asked, sitting on the only chair, at the end of the table. His black eyes bored into Elna's.

Elna was silent, waiting for Alma to speak, trying to gain more time. "I accept," she said finally, when the silence had gone on too long. *At least until Selma has her initiation, and then we will see.*

"Good," Tohar said. "I will make the announcement when Maduk and Selma arrive. I suppose that Alma told you what it means to mate with a Kala."

"You want a shaman child from me," Elna said. "You must learn what it means for the child if you don't learn some Vlahin ways with a woman."

"I am not a weak Vlahin," Tohar growled. "I am a shaman of the Great Bull. It seems that you've learned nothing from Alma. I will be your teacher, and you will learn what it means to be a woman here. I am not a patient man."

"Alma, I want to talk alone with … my future mate." Elna glared at the other woman, who frowned, but left the room. "You must learn patience, and you are not a shaman," Elna said to Tohar.

"I am the Shaman of this clan." Tohar hit the table and stood up, looking ready to jump on Elna.

She ignored the physical threat, and smiled coldly. "You are the Shaman of the village, but you are not a shaman. You can deceive the Kala, but not me. That's not my problem, but it may be a problem for our child. You father had three Amber Stones, and your brother too. You have nothing. That nothing may go into our children, if you don't play your part well. Alma is not aware of this. Outside, you are the Shaman, inside the family, I am the shamane. If not, you will never get a shaman son, and it doesn't matter how much you threaten me. It will not be possible. And I have ways to fight back, and make you the laughing stock of the clan."

"I can kill you."

"You may, but there is an agreement that I will not be harmed here. Maduk gave his word. And, let me show you something. Your father had three Amber Stones. I have five and a half Amber Stones." She stood up, walked behind Tohar, and settled her hand against the back of his neck. "Are you afraid?" she asked when he startled. Without waiting for an answer, she entered the first River of Thought. *I've never done this with someone who is not a shamane without using at least one of the three sacred mushrooms. With a Kalach it will be even harder. If I fail… I can't fail; Selma's life depends on it.* She connected to his mind, and pressed herself inside it as fast as she could. The faster the connection was done, the easier it was to enter in other's mind. The white filaments of the Mother's Web appeared in front of her, and she moved them around the red flame which was Tohar's presence in the Web. Slowly, the net surrounded him, and she tightened it until the flame was fully contained. Its link with the Web was now filtered through Elna's mind. *"Listen to me, Tohar. Like this, I can make people believe that you are a shaman or I can expose you as a liar*," she said inside his mind. *"Are you listening, Tohar?"* she asked, when no answer came from him.

"Yes," Tohar finally said.

It worked. She forced herself to stay calm, and broke the link with the first River and his mind. "This is a small part of what a shamane can do. In time, you will learn more. You are not able to lead a Bull Dance." That was the Kalach equivalent of the River Dance. "People feel it; they know what happened when your father led the dance. I can lead the dance through you, and no one will know." She looked at Tohar, who was too baffled to talk. Even his father, who was considered a strong shaman, could not speak inside his mind.

What else can she do? But if she can help me with the Bull Dance... "You are the shamane in our house," he said, tentatively. "I am the Shaman, and you will behave like a Kala woman when someone else is present."

At least he is not stupid. "Why should I make my mate look weak in front of the clan?"

She is not stupid, and if everything stays hidden... "How fast will you be able to make your seed? I need our child as soon as possible."

He knows that we are fertile only when we want to be. One day, Alma will pay for this. "In one month." *He can't know that I can do it in two weeks, and I need to know more about how well Selma and Maduk are getting on. Once I become pregnant, I will lose some leverage.* That moment, for the first time, she became conscious of her fate; that she would have a child with a Kalach man she hated. She felt nauseous and lost, but she steeled herself. *I have to do this for my daughter.*

During the day it didn't bother her too much, but in the evening, Elna felt more and more anxious about sleeping with Tohar. They were alone, in the second room of his hut. "We need some more time to get used to each other."

"The best accommodation passes through our bed."

"We should wait for that kind of accommodation," Elna said flatly. "And don't try to use violence."

"It may surprise you, but I am not a violent man. Outside, I must carry the mask of the Shaman, and I am tired of it. Inside, I want to be myself. I am ready to wait more for a warmer response, but there is only one bed here, and we will sleep in it."

"Thank you, Tohar." *I need to know him better*; she thought, as she undressed and lay in bed next to her new mate. Tohar kept his word, and fell asleep fast. Elna could not.

It was late when Alma met Ragun, who had been trying to avoid her. She went to his private room, reserved for the Chief and his mate. Ragun's mate knew better than to stay and left them to talk.

"We will have two shamanes in the clan," Ragun said, trying not to growl at his mother. *I may need to kill Selma... No, I have to kill Maduk. Maduk will be too dangerous if she dies. Then I will make her my mate.*

"Oh, Ragun." Alma touched his chin. "You've got everything wrong. Once we have Elna to help that useless Tohar, there is no need to initiate Selma."

"Maduk is an insistent man, and Selma will persuade him, the same way you persuaded father. I can postpone it for a year or two, but..."

"You know almost nothing about the Vlahin world." *That's the main difference between you and Maduk. He always tries to learn more about our enemies*. "Selma has to be initiated within a year. After that, the chance is gone. I am sure we can handle this."

"What changed your mind?"

"My mind changed because she is changing Maduk." *She is changing him too fast, and we can't afford trouble now. Maduk will challenge you at some point, but it's for me to decide when.*

"Under that woman's influence, Tohar may become dangerous."

"Elna will help Tohar to lead a decent Bull Dance. The clan needs that. But," she smiled at him, "I've already talked with Burgo about an eighteen-year-old shaman. In two years, he will be the right age to become our Shaman. Then Tohar and his mate will have an unfortunate accident. The same kind of accident that killed his brother and father." *Maduk still thinks that Tohar killed them. One day I will tell him the truth. We needed a weak Shaman to make peace with the Vlahins and subvert them.*

"You convinced Burgo to interfere in a matter of the Bull?" Ragun asked, incredulous.

Son, you have no idea how easy it is to convince a man when you are in bed with him. "Why not? In three months, I will mate with Burgo. He is lonely," Alma laughed. "That will help you become Chieftain when he dies." *He will die sooner than he thinks, and Maduk will be our Chieftain, not you.* She felt pain mounting inside her. *There is no other way*, Alma shook her head. *And the change must be orderly. I may be able to keep you alive, Ragun, and send you away, but there are no guarantees. You acted too much against Maduk, and he started to resent you. That ploy to give Selma to Turgil was even stupid, and Tohar encouraged you. The last game will be between Tohar and me. Some of the Kala laws are so stupid. Maduk may be able to change some of them.*

Ragun's eyes grew wider, but he said nothing.

Chapter 27

Five days later, Darin returned to the village without Elna, and he faced Moira and Rune. "She mated with Tohar, the Kalach Shaman, and chose to stay there." He forced himself to stay serious when he wanted to burst into laughter, seeing their faces. *One shrew less here;* he thought. *This will weaken Moira even more.*

Moira and Rune stared at each other, and neither of them could speak. "Are you sure?" Moira finally asked.

"That's what she told me," Darin said. *You can send your cripple across the river to check.*

"Thank you, Darin," Moira said, and he left them alone. "We both had a bad feeling, but this..." Moira leaned her head on her arms. "We didn't foresee anything like this. Elna was forced to..." She could not say the word mate. "It must be related to Selma's initiation as a shamane."

"Darin told me what happened," Vlad said, seating himself, Mina beside him. "He seemed pleased by the new situation. I will go there, to see what happened."

"You will be in danger, Vlad," Moira shook her head. "They have not forgotten you. They will never forget you."

"What exactly can't they forget?" Mina asked.

"They sent twenty men to steal women, and they took five of them, including Selma. Their leader challenged Vlad to combat. Vlad killed him. Then Vlad heard that two old men, guarding the women had been killed. All the Kalachs were killed."

"I should have killed Maduk too. How could I think that he could be trusted?"

"This may upset you, but my feeling is that Maduk can be trusted," Mina said, and she placed her hand over Vlad's.

"How much can we believe Darin that Elna accepted the mating?" Vlad asked, trying to ignore Mina's words.

"In this case, we can trust him. He is a duplicitous man, and too close to the Kalachs, but he is not stupid. He will not lie, when we can check." Moira knew that she could have a Truth Communion with Darin and get answers.

"Then I have to go. I will not leave Elna there," Vlad insisted.

"Things may get ugly," Rune said. "It's better if I go with a few elders. I don't think that they will attack us, but if they do," he shrugged, "we are old men."

"If they attack, I will kill Ragun and Maduk," Vlad said.

"What makes you sure that you will be able to meet them?" Rune asked.

Vlad could not answer, and in those moments of silence, he saw Mina. Eyes closed, she was searching for a hint of the future. Moira gestured for Vlad and Rune to remain silent. It took a while until Mina opened her eyes again.

"Let's not talk about fighting. I don't think that violence will solve anything. The Kalachs will not provoke us unnecessarily. Keep peace when you go there, and they will keep it too." Mina's voice was calm.

"Isn't what happened to Elna a provocation?" Vlad asked.

"We don't know yet what happened. My feeling is that she agreed to mate with Tohar. I know it sounds absurd, but there must be a reason behind her choice. Perhaps she was forced to accept, but violence was not used. It's related to Selma's initiation, but I don't know in what way. Vlad should go there. They will be even less inclined to provoke a fight with a man who can kill any of them." For the second time, Mina placed her hand over Vlad's while she spoke.

"Vlad can kill one of them, but if more Kalachs..." Moira said, tentatively.

"I can't foresee any violence," Mina repeated, "and I wouldn't ask Vlad to go otherwise."

"How ... certain are these premonitions? I will go anyway, but I am just curious. And maybe you can guide me on how to..." *Why can't have I premonitions too?* Vlad thought. *Are they only for the shamanes?*

Before answering, Mina took Vlad's hand between hers. "It's not like we look into the future to see what will happen. We can't do that. We have feelings about things that may happen and things that may not happen. There are no guarantees. If you ask the Mother for guidance, most of the time, you will receive a cryptic answer. It's just a feeling. You have to interpret it, and you have to decide from what you should do and what you shouldn't. Two shamanes may make two different decisions. It comes with experience, and you have to be careful, but you also must take risks, and sometimes you have to guess about other people's actions and risks. I am sorry if you feel disappointed because of my request to go there and see what happened to Elna."

"You did not disappoint me; I just wanted to know. I need three men who are not close to Darin," Vlad said. "Mina may be right, but they must be prepared to encounter violence. And you must be prepared if we do not come back."

"Preparations are always necessary." Mina squeezed Vlad's hand. "But you will return."

"I will get you the men. Two of them are Elna and Moira's cousins. One is my cousin. Come with me." Rune glanced at Vlad.

"Mina," Moira said tentatively, when the men had left. "There is something we need to talk about before Vlad leaves." She was not sure how to continue.

"You want Vlad to initiate Malva." Mina stood up, moved around the table, and seated herself next to Moira. "As Vlad said, it doesn't matter what my premonitions reveal, we must be prepared. We need three days to arrange everything for Malva's initiation."

"Thank you," Moira whispered. "It will not be so easy to convince Vlad."

"Why? He knows that Malva will become a stronger shamane if he makes the initiation. Her Shaman Seed has four Amber Stones. With his help, she will have five stones."

"Vlad is ... different. He may be a shaman, but he sees what happens during the Communion in a bad light."

"A High Communion is an honor. Why should he see it in a bad way?"

"Vlad's people are more like the Kalachs in this aspect. They can't accept their woman being with another man, not even in a Communion. What makes him different to the Kalachs is that he will never try to take another's man mate. We had a hard time convincing him even to have a Lips Communion."

"Let me speak with him."

"Mina," Moira said gently. "Please, don't push him. Let's speak with him together. I wish Elna were here. She knew him better. She was... She was like a mother to him."

During the High Communion with Malva, Vlad was fully awake and himself, and he found, to his own surprise, that the Communion itself brought a more interesting and pleasant experience than anything else he had encountered so far. It was mystic and enhancing, and he felt closer to the Mother. For him, the Mother's Web resembled an intelligent field, and his mind went back to a book Cosmin had given him some time ago. It was interesting but, at the time, Vlad took it to be a fantasy, and he decided that the Universe could not be intelligent. Now, he was no longer so sure. The Rivers connected human minds, and the Rivers connected him with something else, something that felt like another consciousness, at a different level. Something vast, omnipotent and benevolent.

There was also the intimacy with Malva. Something that Vlad could not deny that he had enjoyed, something that he had to forget. It was easier for the Vlahins; it was hard for him. Too many years of living in a different culture were not easy to erase. He knew that he would never talk about his night with Malva to anyone, but he wanted more. He wanted to be a disciplined shaman and forget everything that did not belong to the spiritual initiation.

For the first time, I felt like a shaman, he thought, when he woke up, the next morning. *Is this my reason for being here?* He opened his eyes, and found Mina sitting on the edge of his bed. "Where is Malva?"

"She is with Moira," Mina said, and kissed him.

Vlad embraced her, and made space in the bed so they could lie together. "You don't feel upset about ..." He could not finish.

"Why should I be upset? You pleased the Mother, and Malva is now a much stronger shamane than we anticipated. And you too."

"But I..."

"You pleased the Mother. I was right there during the Communion. And you have six Amber Stones now."

I am talking about what happened before the Communion, Vlad thought, but let it drop, and focused inward. *I have six Stones, indeed.* "How many Amber Stones does Malva have?"

"That's for her to tell you." Mina turned and leaned her head on his shoulder. "I am proud of you, Vlad."

Malva burst into the room, as if she was still the young, unmated girl he had met in that meadow between the mountains, a year ago. "Vlad!" she cried. "I am sorry," she said, seeing them together in bed.

"Come," Mina smiled, and made space for Malva to join them. "Tell Vlad."

"I have six Amber Stones," Malva said, her voice filled with joy, and she embraced Vlad, who did not know how to react.

Faro was right, Mina thought. *We get two more stones when our second initiation is done with a shaman. I will be more certain after Vlad initiates Selma. It will not be easy to convince him.*

☙❧

As his boat approached the bank, Vlad saw Selma and Maduk waiting, hand in hand, on the sandy bank. *That was done on purpose*, Vlad thought and shook his head in anger. *I have to be calm and ignore them. I am here for Elna. I can't deal with that traitor now. What I can do with Selma if I get her back?* he suddenly realized. *Nothing... I have to forget her. It won't be easy, I still have that stupid bond.*

Crossing of the river, he recalled all the advice Rune and Moira gave him. The Kalachs valued strength, and their interactions were full of posturing and display.

"They are like two stags displaying their antlers before the fight for females," Rune said to him. "The Kalachs rarely fight inside the village. The posturing allows them to establish a hierarchy. You must behave similarly, but you are a stranger. Too much posturing and they will fight you and, as they know your strength, they will fight you as a group, two or maybe even three of them against you. You must tread a fine line."

Two people will find two different lines, Vlad thought, and started when the boat hit the bank. He was in front, and jumped easily onto the dry sand. Three more Vlahins joined him, and they pulled the boat onto the bank.

"Vlad," Selma said with joy in her voice, when he faced them, "I am glad to see you again." She was glad, but she also felt that the bond between Vlad and her had not vanished. The bond meant different things to them. While they were apart, she still felt the bond, but it was only now that she could felt its strength. Her bond and mating with Maduk had eclipsed everything else. She learned about Mina, but she felt no other bond in him.

"I came to see Elna." Vlad's voice was cold, and he did not even look at her, staring at the village behind them.

"I know that you are surprised, as we were too, about Elna and Tohar," Maduk said, and pointed across the river. He stretched his free hand toward Vlad, as Selma had taught him.

Vlad glanced at his hand, and his eyes narrowed. *Instead of punching him, I have to shake hands with this snake.* He accepted Maduk's greeting, but his grim posture told a different story. "This is the second surprise of this kind. Where is she?"

"Mother is a strong shamane," Selma said, mildly upset, and she squeezed Maduk's hand. *And Tohar is not a shaman, able to coerce her.* Vlad's wolfish posture took her aback. He had always been gentle before, and she did not recognize this new stance. She did not know about martial arts, but she was sensitive enough to sense, though his face was cold and seemed unfeeling, that everything in him was calculated, cool and ready for a fight. And she could feel the clouds gathering behind his eyes too. From the corner of her eye, she looked at Maduk, but he did not know what was going on. Vlad's threatening stance differed too much from how the Kalachs or the Vlahins would present themselves in tense situations. Vlad did not look tense at all. He looked almost lazy, but Selma thought him lethal.

"Yes, she is," Vlad said flatly.

"And you... You have six Amber Stones now." For a few moments, wonder suppressed Selma's fear.

"It happened. Shall we go?"

"Six stones?" Maduk asked. He knew that Tohar's father had had three Amber Stones, and no one had heard of a six-stones Kalach shaman for so many generations that it was no longer thought possible. A shaman with six Amber Stones was almost a legend. Elna had five and a half stones, but she was a woman, and she did not count much in Kala world. They knew that the Vlahins had strong shamanes, but they were so different.

His two hosts hadn't moved, so Vlad stepped forward. He took care to walk slowly, and Selma and Maduk followed him. After a while, Maduk walked in front of Vlad, pulling Selma along with him. He had to lead the visitor. Vlad ignored them. The three Vlahins who came with Vlad followed them.

There were three people in Tohar's hut when Vlad entered. He recognized Elna, and supposed that the man was Tohar. He had no idea who Alma was.

"Elna," he nodded, then he did the same for the other too. All this time, his tense eyes, did not move from Elna.

She surprised him with her calm posture, as she was not affected at all by being a Kalachs' prisoner.

"My mate, Tohar," Elna gestured at the man. "And Alma, Maduk and Ragun's mother. Be welcome, Vlad." She made no gesture to embrace him, as she would have done in the past, and Vlad decided to follow her lead.

"I need to talk with you." Vlad kept his voice cold and distant.

"That's why we are here, to talk," Elna said, then smiled and gestured at the large table at the end of the room. "Let's sit there."

She walked, followed by Tohar. At the table, Tohar sat in the only chair, and Elna sat at his right. Alma sat next to her, so Vlad could not sit next to Elna.

"Vlahin man, you stay there," Tohar pointed at the middle of the bench across from Elna.

Being in the middle would put Vlad even farther from Elna. He ignored the Kalach Shaman and sat directly in front of Elna, his right hand almost touching Tohar's left.

"Move there," Tohar said, irritated.

"Be quiet, Tohar," Vlad bent his head and whispered only for him, "you don't tell a shaman what to do." From close up, he stared at the man, who seemed torn between his fury and his fear. While their relation was better than both had expected it, Tohar feared Elna too, because she could reveal his weakness, but she was a woman. Vlad was a shaman, and he was not a Vlahin. What's more, he had some Kala traits. That made him dangerous. The Kala would never accept Elna, but they could accept Vlad as their Shaman. "I came to see Elna," Vlad said, his voice pleasant. "We miss her, across the river. She is a strong shamane. Then we learned that she is now your mate. Both of you can come and visit us."

"We will think about it." Tohar's voice was now calm and even.

The man is not without qualities, Vlad thought. "It should not be a hard decision. We are expecting Selma for her initiation too."

"There is no hurry," Alma said, "and we will talk to you when the time for Selma's initiation comes."

"Are you a shamane?" Vlad asked, knowing well that she was not.

"I could be."

"Then let the shamans and the shamanes take care of this. You gave your agreement for Selma's initiation as shamane." Vlad looked at Maduk this time.

"This is a Kala village," Alma said, before Maduk could speak.

"Then let the man speak," Vlad retorted and pointed at Maduk. "This is between the shamans, Maduk and Selma."

Vlad." Elna intervened for the first time, "Selma's initiation will be in three weeks from now."

"Has her mate agreed?" Vlad looked again at Maduk.

"We need to know more about what happens during the second initiation, with a man," Alma said.

"If Maduk wants to know more, he can ask," Vlad said. "What you want is of no concern to me. You are not a shamane."

"Vlad," Elna said gently, "Alma is an important woman in this clan." *Please, Vlad, think more, and don't antagonize her for no reason.* "Give me your hand." She stretched her right hand across the table while her left touched Tohar's knee, to calm him. Their hands clasped, and Elna and Vlad entered the Mother's Web through the first River of Thought. *"Vlad, you should be more cautious. Alma wants to bring up the issue of what happens between the man and the woman during the initiation. Be aware that she already knows that they make love, but if he learns about it, Maduk will never accept the initiation,"* Elna spoke into Vlad's mind.

"Selma's initiation. This is how they coerced you to mate with Tohar?"

"Yes, but forget about me for now. This is about Selma. You must initiate her."

"Mina and another man will initiate her."

"Vlad, we don't have time to argue about this. Promise me that you will initiate Selma. Vlad!" she said, anger filling her inner voice, when he did not answer. *"Promise me."*

"I will do it."

"Good, now let me handle Alma."

"I want Maduk to state his agreement about the initiation in three weeks from now. And you must come too."

"It may be that I will not be able to come, but my presence is not so important."

"I've never heard that a mother's presence is unimportant at a daughter's initiation." A few month ago, before Maduk took Selma away, it was agreed that Elna would initiate her daughter. They had never discussed it again. Vlad was in no mood to talk about Selma.

"It's less important than the initiation. Mina is a much stronger shamane."

"Once Selma is initiated, you must return. Moira and the village need you."

"Selma needs me more. Moira has Mina to help her now."

"I won't accept that. Your place is not here."

"That's for me to decide. We must stop now. Tohar is already fretting." To Vlad's chagrin, Elna broke the connection.

"Did you talk inside your minds?" Maduk asked, curiously. He had learned from Selma that the shamanes could talk directly into other people's minds. Tohar knew it too, but he had good reason to say nothing.

"Yes," Elna said, and smiled at Maduk, her hand still gripping Tohar's knee.

"And what did you talk about?" Alma asked, looking at Vlad.

"Mostly about Elna and Tohar's mating."

"And what did you learn?" Alma's hand gestured loosely, betraying her nerves. She did not like this arrogant shaman, yet she knew that he was strong, and she also guessed that he was in mood for a kill. Living so long between the Kala sharpened her senses, and she could see what her son couldn't.

"That Elna feels well in her new family." Vlad avoided saying that Elna willingly agreed to her mating. With his new senses, which he was still not able to use at full capacity, he could feel that Alma was aware of the ploy that forced Elna to mate with Tohar. He also sensed that she was relieved at his statement, though nothing showed on her face. "So, Maduk," Vlad turned toward him. "You had an agreement with Nara about Selma's initiation."

"Yes, I agree that she will have it."

"The timing will be our decision," Alma said.

Yes, the timing," Vlad said. "Is three weeks acceptable for you, Maduk? There are windows of opportunity when the initiation is easier to make. Three weeks is the first one. Elna forecast it."

"We will think about it," Alma snapped.

"All the conditions we talked about will be fulfilled in three weeks," Elna said, locking eyes with Alma, her voice pleasant.

"Maduk?" Vlad asked the man, who was visibly caught between his mother, and the pressure raised in Selma's name around him.

Selma placed her hand over Maduk's, and that added more pressure on him. She loved her mate, but she also resented not being allowed make this decision that, normally, was hers to make. She breathed deeply, and forced herself to ignore her anger. *Say yes, Maduk.* She tried to push her own thoughts into his mind.

"Maduk will communicate his decision to you when he has made it," Alma said.

"Is it so hard to make such a simple decision?" Vlad asked. "It's only to keep the agreement you had with Nara. The one who brought Selma to you." *Make the decision, Maduk*. Vlad also used his powers, guessing that Elna was doing the same.

"He will..." Alma's voice was nervous now.

"Selma will have her initiation three weeks from now." Maduk overrode his mother, without really knowing why he was doing that in public for the first time. He avoided her livid stare.

"I think that is a good date," Tohar said, just when Alma wanted to voice her opposition again, and he did it on purpose. "The stars are well aligned for Selma. She carries the Great Bull's essence with her. Maduk has taken care of that."

Alma bit her lip, feeling the taste of blood. *They think that they have won*, she thought. *Let them enjoy the moment. In three or four days, I will tell Maduk what a man does to the woman during the initiation. Ragun and Tohar will be there, and his bitch too. And the most important men of the clan. Maduk will have no choice. He will forbid the initiation, or he will become a laughing stock. I had such big plans for him, but he is too weak.*

Vlad did not understand what Tohar meant, but he was pleased that the Shaman did not oppose them. Selma was blushing, and he realized what the impregnation really meant. "A union of essences from two gods may make her a stronger shamane."

"Will Selma get six Amber Stones?" Elna asked, knowing well what had happened to Mina, and Selma had five Amber Stones in her Shaman Seed. In the past, she had talked many times with Moira, as both feared that Vlad would refuse to do the initiation, but now she had his agreement, and she knew that, for all his sorrow, he would keep his word.

"The Bull's essence may bring one more stone," Vlad said cryptically, and Elna frowned, not knowing what was in his mind. "Thank you, Maduk." He turned toward Selma's mate. "You are a man who keeps your word." *Let's hope that this time it's true.* He stared at Alma as he spoke, his eyes cold.

"We should eat now," Tohar said, and Elna went out of the hut, to where two women were preparing the food, and in ten minutes, steak, bread, and grilled vegetables filled the table.

Sensing the sweet scents of fresh baked bread, Vlad forced himself to ignore it. After more than a year without tasting bread, he was already salivating.

"You have eaten bread before," Maduk said.

"It's a common food in my ... clan." For the first time, there was no coldness in Vlad's voice as he spoke to Maduk, but neither was there warmth.

"How are Malva and Moira?" Elna asked after a while.

"Moira has not changed much, since you left," Vlad said with a forced smile. "Malva now has six Amber Stones, and she is the newest shamane of the clan."

Startled, both Elna and Selma began to think that maybe Vlad had not mentioned one more stone just to please Tohar and his Bull. They continued to eat through sporadic strings of conversation, and Ragun joined them after a while. He ate in silence and left without saying a word. That convinced Vlad that he could not stay overnight, and strangely, Elna approved his decision, disappointing him; he thought she would want to talk more with him. She felt his frustration and persuaded him to stay after all the others, except Tohar, had left the hut.

"You should not eat bread," Vlad said. "It will affect your shamane powers. Yours too," he said to Tohar, just to please the man.

"You ate it though. Quite a lot," Tohar said. *I don't need to fear him. He will not try to take my place here.* Tohar was not a shaman, but he had an acute sense of observation. It was his survival strategy.

"Once in a while, it will not harm you much. You should also avoid milk products."

"The Vlahin women who ... have joined the Kalachs, have lost their power to decide when they are fertile," Elna said, after she assimilated the disparate threads of information.

"That's not for a woman to decide," Tohar said. "Or a man," he added. "It's the Great Bull's prerogative to decide when a child comes to life."

"Well it looks like the bread decided for us." Elna laughed, and Tohar smiled too. "I don't want to lose my shamane power. Neither do you." She looked at Tohar, who nodded.

"I have to leave," Vlad said and he embraced Elna, who responded heartily, then he shook Tohar's hand. There was no trace of hostility in the shaman's stare. *In private, they act differently. I will come again after Selma is initiated.* Outside, he found Alma, looking upset. "Join me, Alma," he said before she could speak. He took her by the arm, and they went together down the path toward the river. "I want to show you something."

"I know the river," she said flatly.

"Generally, there is nothing interesting on the riverbank, but we may able to see some unusual things." His mind sent some obedience signals, but he was not sure yet of his power, and kept a strong grip on her arm. Walking down, he saw Ragun climbing a rock, from where the whole valley could be seen.

Behind them, Maduk questioned Selma with his eyes, but she just shrugged.

At the riverbank, Vlad took Alma to a place from where Ragun could be seen like a small animal, on a rock four hundred paces distant. He took out his binoculars, and focused them until Ragun's face became visible. "Close your eyes, Alma," he said, and placed his hand on her neck. She shivered, but obeyed him. Entering the Mother's Web, he sent tendrils into her mind. He was not trained enough to fully take her over, but he didn't need to be. "Open your eyes." Seeing through her eyes, he placed the binoculars in front of her so she could see.

"Ragun," she gasped, unaware of the binoculars.

"*You see now through my eyes, Alma. I can watch your sons from far away, and they will be totally unaware of it. They won't ever know what killed them. Stop Selma's initiation and you will lose your sons.* He ended the link between them abruptly, and Alma breathed heavily to regain her composure. "Don't disappoint me, Alma."

"You just want Selma in your bed, shaman."

"You are mistaken. Her initiation will not be a pleasure for me, but I have no choice. Don't harm Selma and your sons will stay alive. I always keep my word."

"You still love Selma."

"I still have the bond. That's different from being in love."

"Give me your shaman word that you will not kill Maduk and take Selma."

"I don't like to kill, Alma. You have my word. I am mated, and I am expecting a child from my woman. You are still a Vlahin, in a corner of your mind, so you know what that means."

"You have to talk with Selma. Tell her to change Maduk slowly; if not blood will flow," Alma said and, turning abruptly, she left him alone. *It was a mistake to bring Selma here. It can't be overturned. I have to live with that.*

Chapter 28

The stone was cold and refreshing. Vlad often came to this place when he needed to think. There was a hidden power here, something that Elna and Moira were not able to feel. Not even Mina, who was the strongest shamane in the village, was able to feel it. None of them were aware that the shamanes felt the energy in some places and the shamans felt it in others. There were also places where the energy was apparent to all of them. The stone vaguely resembled a chair, and Vlad thought it was a trick of nature. He was wrong; some three thousand years earlier, men had carved the stone. Rain, wind and snow had erased the traces left behind by their stone tools. His legs were suspended over the precipice, as the whole 'chair', built on an overhanging rock, was suspended too.

"The Great Mother touches many places, though there are not so many now as they were in the past," Mina has told Vlad a few weeks ago. She was training him to become a real shaman. "These places are gates, at certain times, which exist always in several worlds, and of those, is close to the village, but it can't be seen by shamans. In the past more powerful shamanes were able to use them. I am not that powerful," she said, a trace of disappointment trailing in her voice.

Is this place a gate? Vlad's hand touched the cold stone, and he could feel the hidden power inside, but he was not train enough to know how that power could be used. *In a week, I will have to decide*, he returned to his own worries. After he initiated Selma – who became indeed a seven Amber Stones strong shamane – by a curious turn that no one understood, his bond with her almost vanished. He loved Mina, but he did not want to keep a mate who was chosen for him by Nara, ; however, Mina had told him that once their mating was broken, there was no way that they could mate again. The Vlahin laws were forbidding it. *Our daughter will be born in three months, but I feel like a slave because of Nara*. He rubbed his chin, and sighed. *I can't break the mating*, he finally decided. *Mina is everything to me now. I must find another way to pay Nara back. That woman is evil*. He found some consolation in the thought that at a certain point, Mina would become the Grand Shamane of the Vlahins. She had her flaws too, but she was not Nara. *All of us have some flaws*, he thought.

Caught in his inner thoughts, he missed the first tremor. The second one was stronger, and a long noise, resembling a deep growl coming from the Earth's belly, filled the air. Frightened, Vlad tried to climb out of the chair. The Earth shook harder, and his foot slipped, then his hand. Unable to find a handhold, he saw the stone sliding away in front of his eyes. *I will not stay with Mina after all.* His last finger lost its grip on the stone, and he fell, his thoughts flying with him. Andrei's head came back to him.

"We are flying again," the Head grinned. "Who knows where we will go this time?"

"To the grave." The shock came before Vlad could say more. It did not feel like a crash, but more like he was being stretched in all directions, by a strange force. He gasped and closed his eyes. *Farewell, Mina.*

The Vlahin village was shaken but, as all the huts were made of wood, there was almost no damage. People were scared, even those old enough to remember the last earthquake.

"Stay calm," Moira shouted, "it will pass soon."

Elna covered her mouth with her hand and shook her head in pain. "Vlad is no longer with us."

"What do you mean?" Mina asked.

"The Mother has taken him away."

"He is dead." Mina burst into tears.

"I did not say he was dead. He has left us the same way he came." *One man died when they arrived here. Who knows where he is going now? Who knows if he is still alive? I can't say this to Mina. Deep in her mind there will be a well of hope. It will help her.*

"Will he return?" Mina asked, her voice trembling, and her eyes filled with tears that did not fall.

"I don't know. I am sorry, Mina. You are a strong woman. You must be strong for your daughter." Elna came to her, and placed her arm around the young woman's shoulders. It was her first visit since she was mated to Tohar. "We are stronger because of Vlad, and we are stronger together."

The earthquake ended as suddenly as it had started, and people returned to their huts to check for damage. A few had light wounds, but no one had been killed. The only one who did not feel better was Mina. Elna helped her to sit, and stayed with her, holding the younger woman's hands in hers. *I lost my mate too.* Mina could no longer keep her tears, and leaned her head on Elna's shoulder.

The sun was so strong that it burned through his closed eyelids. Slowly, he opened them and looked around him. The place seemed familiar, somehow old and new at the same time. He blinked and, realizing that he was leaning against a small wall, he tried to move. Pain shot through him and he moaned. There was a fog in his head. *Because of the pain*, he thought, touching the back of his head. *Where have I seen this place before?* The more he looked, the more he had the sensation that he knew the place, yet something was different. Groaning, he tried to stand up and look out over the valley. He couldn't, but he did get a glimpse of the surroundings. *This is the hell-hill. I am back in my world. Back in the war. I had such a long dream. Where are the others?* Vlad stared around, and saw people climbing toward the top of the hill. *They are not soldiers,* he thought with relief. His eyes moved again, taking in his surroundings. *These columns were not here. I guess I've lost some memories, because of the shock. These columns could not have appeared overnight. How badly am I wounded?*

"Cosmin, Dan, Andrei!" he shouted. "I am here. I am wounded, but I feel fine. It's not a serious wound." *How badly am I wounded?* He repeated, but he was afraid to check. His body was aching, but there was no blood. "Hey! Don't joke with me. Where are you?" He moved a leg, then the other one. The pain raced up and down, but he could move his legs. *I may have been knocked around by the shock of the explosion, but my spine seems fine.* He felt his head, gingerly, from his brow to his back. *No lumps, it looks fine. So why is my head hurting so badly?* "Cosmin, Dan, Andrei!" he shouted again. "Where are you? I don't like this joke." For the second time, he tried to stand, but his legs were too weak. *Where the hell am I wounded? Spine? I just checked it.* Fear rose in him again and he turned his upper body left and right. The same sharp pain passed through him, but he had control over his body. *Did they leave me here? That's against the rules. Maybe they thought I was dead. I am not dead,* he shook his head, and that only increased his pain. *That was not a good idea.*

The people climbing the hill were closer now, and he saw them clearly, though his vision was a little blurred. *Women. What are they doing here? This is the front line.* He passed his hand in front of his eyes and counted his fingers. Then he touched his nose with the forefingers of both hands. *I feel normal. Maybe my comrades had to retreat and thought I was dead. Where is my rifle?* He looked around and found nothing. *I still have my bayonet. What can I do with a bayonet against a rifle?* The women had almost arrived; he could hear them breathing hard behind the wall, which was only three feet tall. *What are they doing here? We are at war. How long did I lose consciousness for? Could it be days? But I don't feel hungry.*

Four women burst into the open, and quickly walked toward him.

"What are you doing here?" one of them asked him in a language that he did not understand, her voice filled with anger.

"I don't understand you," Vlad said. *What language is this? This must be another bad dream.*

The woman gripped his shoulder and shook him. The pain made him moan, and he could not respond. Suddenly, her eyes widened, and she retreated as fast as she had come to him.

"Are you crazy?" Vlad asked, overcoming his pain. "I've lost my platoon. Did you see six men dressed like me?" *She doesn't understand me.* "I may be wounded," he spoke again, just to keep his mind busy. "I need a doctor. Do you understand me?"

"Shaman," the woman said; finally something intelligible for him.

"Oh, I am still dreaming," Vlad sighed and closed his eyes, trying to ignore the strange woman.

"Who are you?" the woman asked again, in a language that Vlad realized was close to the Vlahin language.

A never-ending dream. "I am Vlad," he said, with a deep sigh. *I feel like I'm in the movie* Looper. *A looper dream,* he thought, amused.

"You are a shaman."

"If you want me to be, I can play that role for you, but I would prefer another role. I am a soldier, even though I like to think of myself as an engineer, but no one asked my opinion when they drafted me and sent me to fight in a bloody war. And I did not like my last dream."

"What dream?" She understood only half of his words.

I am getting tired. "I dreamt about some savages. The Vlahins. Does that help?" *Maybe this dream is more cooperative.*

"Men are not allowed here. They are impure."

This is what I was missing, to be called impure. "I can bathe, if you really want me too. Just take me to a nice place with hot water and good food."

"Your mind is impure."

"I am sorry, but that I can't change that. I like my mind exactly as it is."

"But you are a shaman."

"Yes, I have six Amber Stones. Are you satisfied now?" *Andrei's head will start to fly around me. At least my friends are alive. I hope I meet Cosmin soon. When this new dream ends.*

"What should I do with you?"

"You can send me a better dream. Please."

"You must leave the hill."

"I would like that, but I'll need a little help. There are some issues with my body." He stretched his hand out and, reluctantly, the woman grabbed it and helped him stand. *Better.* "Thank you. You are?" he gestured at her.

"Moira."

Why couldn't she have another name? "I once met a woman named Moira, but you look different. She was a shamane too. Why are you dressed like this?" He realized the woman's dress was somewhere between late roman and early medieval. *This timeline must be somewhere in the eleventh century, so at least I am not dreaming about savages again. They look peaceful. Let's hope that the men are peaceful too. Why are they impure? Too violent?*

The woman started. "We all dress like this."

If you say so. "Where should we go?" *I am impure and must leave the place. Why can't I have better dreams?*

"I have to take you to the Shamane. She may want to punish you."

"Why?"

"Because you came here."

"The Mother sent me here," Vlad joked, but the woman covered her mouth with her hand, and looked serious.

"You are a shaman," she whispered.

Vlad ignored her, and finding that he could walk, he moved to look at the columns. Grouped three by three, they resembled Ionian architecture. *They look well maintained*. "Ionian?" he asked, but the woman only shrugged. "Greek?" *I have to give up*. He passed his left hand through his hair, and saw the scar on the back of his hand. *This is from when I chased that bear to take his prey. The giant deer. My dream was more than a year and half long. Where am I now? Not where, when? This woman should have made the sign of the cross seeing a pagan in front of her. The Balkans were Christianized some centuries ago.* He sensed movement behind him and, turning, saw another woman who was staring at him. "I am Vlad," he said politely.

"You are a shaman."

"Yes," he sighed. *Here we go again*. "You are a shamane." He blinked, and stared at the woman again. "Three and a half Amber Stones." *Moira is a shamane too, she has three Amber Stones.*

"I am Elna. Let's go down. Even if you are a shaman, you are still not allowed to visit this place. Moira, double the guards for the Mother's Sanctuary."

Moira and Elna... It's a new dream for sure, but without much imagination. It's boring to hear the same names again. "I understand that I am ... impure."

"Men usually are, but that really just means they can't be left in charge. They can't rule themselves. Left alone, they are too violent. That's why women take care of them. You may be an exception. How did you get here? None of our guards saw you climbing the hill."

"Teleportation," Vlad shrugged, slightly amused by her reaction. *Or something like that.*

"What does that mean?"

Vlad scratched his head, and then he remembered Cosmin's words about portals and going from one place to another. And now that he had started to think, he felt the energy surrounding him. "There is energy in this place. It can transport people from one place to another."

"That's why this place is sacred, because of the energy, but we did not know about ... teleport..."

"Teleportation. It has happened to me twice, but I have no control over it." *If I was on a parallel Earth before, then I must be in some kind a future that I have created. How many years have passed?* He had the feeling that he had returned in his own time, except that it was a different future, created by his actions in the past. *I left behind a modern world and returned to a medieval one. Is this ... evolution the result of my actions? They are right to punish me, if this is my work. They are not to know. At least there is no war.*

At the foot of the hill, two men, armed with knives, joined them, and Vlad automatically touched his bayonet.

"Our guards," Elna said. "They will escort us to the village."

"May I see your knife?" Vlad asked the closest guard, who hesitated, but unsheathed his knife and gave it to him. *Bronze*, Vlad thought, touching the blade. *They are still in the Bronze Age. Or maybe the guards don't need better weapons.* "Do you have other weapons?"

"We have spears and bows for hunting," the man said, taking his knife back.

"And if there is a war?"

"What does *war* mean?" the man asked, confused.

"Moduk," Elna said, gesturing with her forefinger, and the man moved forward, leaving her alone with Vlad. "Why did you ask about wars?"

Moduk, it sounds like Maduk... Vlad thought, annoyed, and for the first time realized how the road was constructed; it resembled Roman work. *Via Apia looked similar. It looks like they have a well-organized society, not a Bronze Age tribe.* "Just curious," he shrugged. "So, do you know what war is?"

"I am a custodian of the Mother, and I've read many old books. We have not had a war for more than three thousand years. And even those distant wars were not started by us. People from the east invaded our lands."

"Why did they invade your lands?"

"Their tribes were dominated by males. War was their way of life, and they tried to conquer us, but the Mother helped us to defeat them and, in time, they became like us, accepting women's leadership."

"Really?"

"A shamane never lies," Elna said, her voice controlled.

Quite a peaceful place, no wonder they don't need stronger weapons. Men are bad, so I am bad too. That may pose some issues for me... "I apologize. Please understand that I come from a different place." *Or from a different dream.*

"Shamans don't always tell the truth," she said, tentatively.

"Both shamans and shamanes may use different aspects of reality, when their interest requires." Vlad smiled, apologetically.

Elna raised her hand abruptly. "I have five fingers. Would you tell me I had a different number if your interests required it?"

"That's too simplistic a question, Elna. Reality must be more complex to allow different interpretations, but if my life depended on it, I could see three fingers on your hand." He looked innocently at her, and she laughed. *At least they have a sense of humor.*

"You don't resemble our shamans."

"Do you still have shamans?"

"Yes, they live in Sanctuaries."

Prisons? "Ah, you need them to initiate the young shamanes," Vlad said, looking away, and a large predatory bird came into his vision. *There was a flying bird in the start of my other adventure – or dream.* He realized that Elna had not replied. "Not a pleasant subject to talk about."

"Yes, they help us during the initiation," she said, sheepishly.

"How strong are your shamans?"

"Three or four stones."

"What happens to those who have higher potential?"

They are not initiated. "There are no stronger shamans."

I asked you something different. It may be too delicate a subject for a conversation with a stranger. We may have time for it later. It seems that my dreams are getting longer. "Why do they live in Sanctuaries?"

"It's better like that."

"Are they allowed to leave?"

"Satu, our village is there," Elna said abruptly, pointing toward a collection of houses.

"How many people are in the village?"

"Eight thousand and seven hundred," she said proudly. "It's the largest village in the region."

In my time, the largest city in the area has more than a million... "Who is the Shamane?"

"Mina. She has four Amber Stones."

Mina... he thought, more and more annoyed by those names." And how strong is your Grand Shamane?" *If this is not another coma induced dream, and this place is real, and so much time has passed since ... since I was here, how is that the names did not change at all? There should have been at least some small alterations.The language has changed somewhat, but I am still able to understand them. But I did not understand the first words of that first woman. Why do they have two languages? Can be that this one is liturgical? Like the Latin in the early medieval times?*

"Her name is Selma, and she has six Amber Stones. She is the strongest shaman in half a century." She looked at him. "You have six Amber Stones too."

They don't have much imagination with names. "Does it bother you?"

"No," she lied, forgetting that a shamane never does that.

They arrived after half an hour of pleasant walking, and he saw that the village was clean. There was even a sewage system that looked efficient to him – there was no foul smell in the village. *Compare this with our medieval cities*, Vlad thought. *They were just a source of infections.*

In the central, rectangular plaza, the size of a soccer stadium, Selma led him to the main building of the village. It was four stories, and none of other buildings had more than two floors. "This is the House of the Mother. The Shamane lives and works here. I live here too, close to the library. If you want to take a shower," she pointed toward a door with an unknown inscription on the frame. "That's the bathroom."

Phonetic writing, Vlad thought and pushed the door. *Strange how they resemble Latin letters.* There were some ten women and men taking showers in the same room, and three children ran among them. They stared briefly at him, finding his clothes strange.

At least they don't consider water and soap as an enemy. They are used to being naked so, for sure, they are some kind of distant grandchildren of the Vlahins. Having no choice, he undressed, placed his clothes on a bench and went under a free shower. There were two taps, resembling the taps on wine barrels, but these were made of bronze not wood. *Showers are everywhere the same.* There was a sign on each of them. *A variant of Latin letters, again, but it's a 'p' and a 'd', nothing in common with water, cold or hot in Vlahin. Which is for hot water?* He turned the one on the left, and cold water poured down his spine. "Ouch!" he cried, and stepped back. One of the children, a girl, chuckled, and Vlad smiled at her. She ran to a different shower, hiding behind her mother, who ignored her. The six-year-old girl still watched him, smiling too. He winked at her, then played with the second tap until the water was to his liking. *It's so good*, he sighed when the warm water played on his skin. *How much I missed showers in the other ... dream.*

The Shamane had already been informed about his arrival when Elna brought him in front of her. She was sitting in a chair, which was elegant, but did not look like a throne to him. For a while, they stared at each other.

"I am Vlad."

"Mina," the woman said, taking him in. "Take a seat. Why did you climb the hill?" she asked after Vlad seated himself on a chair at her left.

"You should ask the Mother." *I hope you will not accuse me of blasphemy.*

"Is this ... teleportation a true thing?"

"Look at me," Vlad pointed at his clothes. "When was the last time you saw someone dressed like me?"

"Never," the woman agreed. "You are neither from the Far East, not from the Far South."

"You mean that I am not like this." With his fingers, Vlad pulled at his eyelids, hoping that the geography and population of this place matched Earth. *I should look like a Chinese or Japanese...*

"No you don't look like them," Mina said, slightly amused. "Where are you from?"

"It's difficult to explain."

Mina's eyes narrowed, but she said nothing.

"I am from this place, but not from this time."

"You must be tired and hungry. Tomorrow morning, we will leave for the capital to meet the Grand Shamane." *He is powerful, and I can't handle him, but he is an interesting man. I never saw this man, that much I know, yet I have the feeling of knowing him.*

"May I ask a question?" Vlad asked and she nodded. "Your names, Mina, Elna, Selma and Moira. They are very old names."

"Yes, they were the shamanes who invented writing, and settled our civilization on a different path. There was another one, Malva. They were blessed by the Mother and their names are sacred, so only the shamanes can have them."

My Vlahin dictionary, Vlad thought. *that may explain the resemblance to Latin letters.* His mind became nebulous and, silent, he left the room, led by Elna.

"How do you find this new world?" an unknown voice asked inside Vlad's head.

He was lying in bed, his head resting on a pillow, in the small room that Elna brought him to. The softness of the bed was a blessing after sleeping for so long in a bag.

"Who are you?" Vlad asked, annoyed; he wanted to sleep. *It's not Andrei's voice.*

"Here, they call me the Mother."

"A mother with a man's voice." *The Head should appear soon. Strangely, how I miss him.*

"Does it bother you? I thought things would be easier for you."

The next moment, Vlad found himself in a room that he knew well: the library of his university. One which no longer existed. He was sitting in a chair, and in front of him, across the small table, sat his favorite teacher.

"I suppose you are the *Mother*," Vlad said. "And I suppose that you extracted this," he gestured around, as the man did not speak, "from my memory."

"Everything comes from my memory," the man said. "Even your memories."

"Am I in a dream?"

"You should already know the answer."

"Can I return to my world?"

"This is your world." The man snapped his fingers, and one of the walls vanished. Satu village came into sight.

"And this?" Vlad pointed at the library.

"It's just a memory now. One cubic mile of a black hole, compressed matter in the middle of the galaxy, stores your old timeline."

"Is the Torrechiara castle part of that timeline?" Vlad asked with a sudden intuition.

"Of course," the man smiled, and morphed into Andrei's head.

"So you are... You pissed me off all the time, there. Why?"

"It was easier for you to talk with an alter-ego than with the *Mother*. Now, you feel uncomfortable."

"It was so easy that I thought I was crazy. You just tricked me. I wouldn't expect such a thing from the *Mother*. Have I changed ...?" Vlad's voice wobbled and the Head nodded. *I've lost my parents.* "Why me? What was so special that you chose me for this task? I did not want it. I did not want to lose my..." His voice cracked, and he sat silently, tears running down his face.

"There is nothing special about you. Cosmin was my choice. He was well prepared to join the Vlahins. It just happened that you were trapped inside the vortex when I moved him back in time. Without that ... accidental event, you would have been dead by now."

And my parents still alive... Vlad closed his eyes, trying to calm his mind. "Is there any chance to get everything back?" *To get my parents back?*

"No."

"You enjoyed it, destroying my world." *Killing my parents.* Unable to control his tension, Vlad stood up, and walked around the room.

"That night, when you were on the hell-hill, cut off from the world, both Prometheus AI of the Western Alliance and Baidu AI from the Eastern Alliance made a series of errors. They tried to compensate, but they ended up making even more errors. Each error made way for the next one. By the time you woke up, more than two thousands nuclear bombs had reached their targets. Your world was destroyed, and three billion people were dead, but you did not know. You, and your immediate chain of command, were like a dinosaur's tail. It did not know that the head had already blown up."

"My city?" Vlad breathed.

"It was not hit, but the military base at Caracal was nuked. It did not matter much; the radioactive cloud would have reached Craiova anyway. "Tragedy makes for great stories, but there is not much to tell after a nuclear war. From my estimations, in ten years, Earth's population would have dropped to less than ten million, and there were no guarantees that the human race could survive. It's such a pity that everything you had built vanished; you were creative people, at least that I grant to you. Sometimes, I reconstruct the Sistine Chapel, sit under The Last Judgment, listen Beethoven and read Omar Khayyam. You liked Khayyam too." The Head looked at Vlad and started to recite The Shears of Fate:

> "Khayyam, who stitched the tents of science,
> Has fallen in grief's furnace and been suddenly burned,
> The shears of Fate have cut the tent ropes of his life,
> And the broker of Hope has sold him for nothing!"

It's gone... Everything I knew is gone. Fate... Vlad breathed deeply, and both his martial and shaman training worked to calm his mind. "At least, did I do any good there?" He gestured delicately, as if his past with the Vlahins was just a fragile porcelain object.

"You solved some issues. You created new ones."

"Was what happened to Selma the tipping point?"

"In the old timeline, Turgil kidnapped her, and made her his mate. She was never initiated as a shamane. The Vlahins were defeated and assimilated by a population with superior technology, but with a lesser understanding of their environment, and to eager to ... kill and make wars. Your history was an interminable procession of wars. In this timeline, it was assumed that you would be her mate. Well, initially it was supposed that Cosmin would be her mate, then you... Your failure moved everything to the other extreme: the shamanes subdued the Kalachs, and created a peaceful society growing in symbiosis with the planet, but using mind control with the results you have already seen. Now, there are around five hundred million people on Earth, instead of eight billions. In your old time line you would have been on the hell-hill now. Dead. You were supposed to create the middle ground timeline. Well, Cosmin was supposed to create it. We were tricked by fate, which is more powerful than any plan. The butterfly effect."

I am a bit bigger than a butterfly. "What happens now?" *I deserve some rest.*

"Endings. Beginnings. Old worlds die and new worlds are born," the Head said with deliberate vagueness. "Change. Maybe."

Vlad frowned, thinking for a moment. "Do you expect anything more from me?" he finally dared to ask.

"Yes."

"Can you send me back there?" *Mina and my unborn child are waiting for me.*

"We are faced with an interesting conundrum. Should I send you back, or should I keep you here? Both options may or may not achieve something," the Head said, before vanishing, together with the library.

The End

Other books by Florian Armas:

ERRANT ARDENT

Book One and Two of the
Chronicle of the Seer

Printed in Great Britain
by Amazon